SO-CWW-949

Books by William Lavender

FLIGHT OF THE SEABIRD
CHINABERRY

Flight

of the Seabird

A NOVEL BY

William Lavender

SIMON AND SCHUSTER
NEW YORK

Designed by Elizabeth Woll
Manufactured in the United States of America

1   2   3   4   5   6   7   8   9   10

Library of Congress Cataloging in Publication Data

Lavender, William.
  Flight of the seabird.

  I. Title.
PZ4.L394FL   [PS3562.A848]   813'.5'4   76-53793
ISBN 0-671-22662-2

TO PATIENCE,
my best friend

She was late, and driving fast. Meg was a fast driver anyway—she handled the battered old pickup truck with a light skillful touch backed up by firm control, just the way she handled her stallion. She felt comfortable behind the wheel. Capable and secure. Driving was one of the few things she did with solid self-confidence.

Bart was always growling at her about her driving. Bart was always growling at her about something, and driving was one of his favorite subjects. She was a better driver than he, and they both knew it. She tried to hide it, because she knew it galled him, but it was common knowledge nevertheless. She had learned very quickly that Bart was infuriated by any skill she displayed—other than cooking and sewing—that equaled or excelled his own. Yet he expected her to pull her own weight on the ranch and shoulder as much responsibility as he—which she did.

Meg loved her old pickup as much as Bart hated it. It was the single object of value she had inherited from the breakup of her parents' ranch, when her father had died and her mother had sold out and moved away, four years before, and it was the only significant material possession she had brought to her marriage to Bart Hannah, two years later. Bart had wanted to get rid of it immediately, trade it in for a sleek new model, but Meg had balked. Bart had insisted; Meg had grown defiant, her dark eyes blazing dangerously. It was one of the few times in her twenty-one years of life she had ever defied anybody about anything—she was amazed at herself, still, to think of it.

Bart refused to use the truck. He borrowed his cousin Herb Duggan's ton-and-a-half when he had hauling to do, making his tractor available to Herb in return, otherwise driving only his high-powered luxury car, a vehicle Meg detested. She thought it out of place on the ranch, she said. Secretly she regarded its plush elegance as a mockery of the hardship and privation that had been the dominant conditions of her childhood. The big car was alien to her nature; it intimidated her, made her feel even more timorous than usual.

In her rattly old pickup, though, Meg felt coolly efficient. On a Saturday she could usually leave the ranch after lunch and sail the twenty-five miles down to Caxton, load up with a week's supply of groceries and sundries, spend an hour or so—as long as she dared—socializing with a few people she knew there, then coax the little vehicle back up the long grade to the foot of Stag Mountain and be home in time to have supper on the table when Bart expected it, at six sharp.

Usually. Today she was late. The warm spring sunshine was already slanting low, the bright beige desert floor turning a tawny golden and the distant mountains deepening to violet, and she still had ten miles to go. She gripped the steering wheel harder and leaned forward, as if to force the tired old truck to higher performance as it climbed the taut white ribbon of State Highway 78, slanting up across the tilted desert plateau. Far up ahead to the left she could see the dark narrow line of County Highway 15 snaking up into Stag River Canyon and disappearing into its long somber late-afternoon shadows. Halfway between the mouth of the canyon and the state highway, a bright-green mass of mature cottonwoods, clearly visible miles off, marked the location of the Hannah ranch.

Meg's artist eye roved constantly over the spacious landscape, noting every detail. She saw the world in terms of color variations, light and shadow, perspective problems, canvas design, pigment mixtures, brush strokes. She was a painter—had thought of herself as nothing else since the day she had won a set of brushes and a big box of watercolors as first prize in a contest at school, when she was ten years old. Now a talented amateur, politely admired by a few friends and relatives whose artistic judgment, she well knew, meant little, she dreamed vaguely of someday bringing her work to the attention of acknowledged experts, who according to her imagined scenario would immediately see to it that she got the higher level of training she needed. She had no idea of how to go about transforming this fragile secret dream into reality, nor any expectation of ever doing so.

Meg braked slightly as she approached the turnoff onto County 15, took the turn with a screech of tires, and headed her truck toward the Hannah cottonwoods, now less than three miles away. She looked up at the craggy north face of Stag Mountain, looming in the distance like a giant stone monument, and thought how much she'd like to stop and watch the colors fade and the mountain grow dark as the sun sank. Instead she strained forward farther over the steering wheel, frowned with fretful impatience, and hurried on.

Bart had his head buried in the engine compartment of his tractor out back when Meg's pickup came around the low bungalow ranch house and creaked to a stop on the gravel driveway. When she shut off the chugging motor the sudden silence was startling. Bart did not look up. Meg sat still in the truck cab for a few seconds and gazed at him. She knew he had come in from the fields early in the afternoon, since it was Saturday. She knew he had been waiting for her to return from town for an hour now, his irritation growing constantly. She knew, too, that at this moment he was indulging in a characteristic bit of play-acting, pretending he was unaware of her arrival, was unaware that she had even been away, was unconcerned about her presence or absence one way or the other. Not too far wrong, anyway, she thought. What he's concerned about is having his supper on the table at six o'clock.

She got out of the truck, went around to the back and lifted out two large bags of groceries, and started for the house. The back door was closed. She glanced over her shoulder at Bart. He was still bent over the tractor, his fingers deeply entwined in its mechanical workings, his face contorted with concentrated effort. Meg maneuvered the door open with an elbow and two fingers. When she came out of the house again she saw that Bart was still not inclined to acknowledge her arrival.

She went toward him, forced a little smile—wasted, because he didn't see it—and said, "Hi."

"Sure are late," he mumbled, still not looking at her.

She leaned against the tractor, pushed her loose light-brown

11

hair back, and sighed inwardly. "Sorry. Time sort of slipped by today. Want to help me get the stuff in?"

He didn't answer.

"Don't worry, I'll have supper ready on time," she said.

He glanced at her now, then went on with what he was doing. "Got all dressed up today, I see."

"Oh . . . not really."

She was wearing a short skirt—trim and snug, showing off well-shaped hips and splendid legs—and a white sleeveless blouse that accented the warm tan of her arms and shoulders. Both skirt and blouse she had made herself; both were favorite things.

After a moment he said, "You usually just wear your blue jeans to town. Sump'm special today, or what?" He was trying to sound casual and chatty, but Meg clearly recognized the hard edge of belligerence underneath.

"No, no . . . nothing." Self-consciously she tugged at her skirt. She felt flustered, hoped it didn't show. "I just . . . get tired of wearing jeans all the time, that's all."

Abruptly she walked away from him, went to the truck, picked up two more bags of supplies and carried them into the house.

Bart worked a few seconds longer, then straightened up, rubbed his back, and scowled at the tractor engine. He was a large man in his mid-twenties, hard, square and athletically muscular, with thick arms and neck. His stiff dark hair was cut short, and flecked with the beginnings of premature gray. He wiped his hands on a greasy rag and started leisurely for the house.

She looked at him in mild surprise when he came into the kitchen empty-handed. "Bart, aren't you going to help me unload?"

"In a minute." He dropped into a kitchen chair and slouched. "First I want you to tell me why you got all dressed up today."

"No reason. I already told you." She began to empty her grocery bags. "Gosh, do I have to have a reason for every little thing?"

"People usually have reasons for things."

Meg shrugged. "Well, that's just silly," she said, and went on with her work.

Bart's face darkened as he watched her. Then he got up and went out to the truck, and took up the job of unloading. When he had finished he went out again and got into the pickup, to move it across the yard and into the garage.

Meg froze, and winced repeatedly as she heard the starter grind and stop, grind and stop, and grind again. In between grindings she could hear Bart cursing. Finally he got the truck started, jammed it viciously into gear, and roared off. Meg continued working, her lips pressed grimly together.

He came stomping back through the kitchen, on his way to the bathroom to wash up. "I hate that goddam crate," he muttered as he went by her.

"I know, Bart," she said quietly.

From the bathroom, with the water running, he yelled, "Damned if I know how you get down to Caxton and back in that fuckin' thing."

And very softly, so that he didn't hear, she said, "It's easy. I know how to drive it."

They sat down to dinner in silence, and ate in silence for several minutes. Meg watched her husband out of the corner of her eye.

"Like the stew?"

" 'S all right," he mumbled.

More silence.

Then Bart said, "Ol' lady Cutler called."

Meg blinked at him in surprise. "She did? When?"

"Little while ago."

Meg waited. "Well, what did she say?"

"Wanted to know if you were coming over to paint tomorrow. Told her I didn't know. Told her I never know *what* the hell you're gonna do."

"I can't imagine what you meant by *that*."

"I meant you're secretive, that's what I meant. You never tell me anything."

Meg dropped the subject. "Wonder why she called today. She knows Saturday's my day to go shopping."

Bart threw a peevish glance at her. "Guess she figured you'd be home at a reasonable hour. *I* did."

13

Meg sagged. A weariness came over her face. "Aw, come on, Bart. I wasn't all *that* late. Will you lay off, please?"

"I would if you'd just be honest and admit the reason."

"There *was* no reason. It just took me a little longer than usual to do my shopping, that's all."

"That's okay, kiddo." His manner was suddenly flippant. He reached across the table and speared a roll with his fork. "I *know* why you were late. *And* why you got all dressed up today." He opened his roll and buttered it, looking smug as a small boy with a dirty secret, waiting to be begged to tell.

Meg refused to beg.

He eyed her suspiciously. "Rick Jennings is in town, isn't he?"

Meg gazed at him blankly, without answering.

"Well, isn't he?"

"Yes, he is. What of it?"

"Well, I think you ought to tell me all about it. You went to see him, didn't you? Bet he was glad to see you, wasn't he? Did he ask about me? Didn't he even say, 'Give my regards to the second-string quarterback'?"

"Bart, you're—" Meg's voice was tight. She stopped and began again, more calmly. "Look, I went to the drugstore to get some toothpaste and things. Rick was there. He's got his degree in pharmacy now, and is working in his father's store for a while, just as a start. We said hello, and chatted a bit. Then I bought the things I needed, and left. I must have been in the store all of fifteen minutes. Is there anything wrong with that?"

"Hell, no. And since there's nothing wrong with it, why keep it a secret?"

"I wasn't, Bart. I just . . . I didn't think it would interest you. It was nothing."

"Hah! You're damn right it doesn't interest me. It didn't interest me all through high school, when every damn girl in the place was panting madly after Ricky-boy's body, just because he was the star quarterback. *I* was satisfied to be backup quarterback, because *I* had more important things to do than concentrate on football."

She closed her eyes. "Sure, Bart."

He ate for a while, chomping vigorously, then resumed his monologue. "I know exactly what you're thinkin', Meg. Every day you think it. 'If I could've made it with Rick Jennings I could be the wife of a big-shot druggist, living in a fancy house in town. Instead o' that I'm stuck out here in the boondocks, married to a goddam clodhopper.' "

"Oh, Bart, that's not true. I never—"

"But you still haven't given up, have you? You're still workin' on him."

She stared at him and shook her head slowly, as if trying to comprehend something incomprehensible. "I can't believe you, Bart. Are you trying to say that I'm . . . that I'm *seeing* Rick? That I'm carrying on with him, or something?"

"No, sweetheart, I'm not sayin' that. 'Cause it takes two to carry on, and the other party's not interested. Right?"

"I don't know anything about the other party. I know *I'm* not interested."

"Don't try to kid *me*, baby!" He scowled and pointed his fork at her. "You've had hot panties for pretty-boy Ricky ever since you were a sophomore at Caxton High, and you've still got 'em, hotter'n ever. Don't try to deny it."

She got up quietly, saying, "I'd better call Mrs. Cutler back," and went into the front hall, to the telephone alcove.

Bart's narrowed eyes followed the movements of her hips as she left the room. Then he turned back to his plate, his face dark and brooding.

Meg's hand was trembling as she sought out the numbers on the dial. As she listened to the buzz of the phone ringing at the other end she could see again Rick Jennings' handsome face, smiling at her in that easy superior way he had, making her feel insignificant, and could hear him saying, almost exactly as Bart had guessed, "How's my ol' second-string quarterback?"

When she came back from the phone Bart was standing in the kitchen, finishing his coffee. Meg went to work clearing the table, and Bart sipped his coffee and watched her.

"So you're goin' up to the Cutlers' again tomorrow."

Meg nodded. "If I can get in a good day's work, I can finish the painting."

Bart's well-used scowl got a little more use. "Always traipsin' up and down the countryside with that damn paint parapher-nalia! How come you don't stay home once in a while?"

"What for?" she said placidly. "So you can yell at me that much more?"

He continued to watch her as she scraped and stacked the dishes and started to fill the sink with hot water.

"There's one thing about you that just gripes the shit out o' me," he said. "When I feel like havin' a good fight, you won't fight back. You're such a goddam *mouse.*"

"Sorry about that. Maybe you should have married Rita."

"Maybe you're right. One thing for damn sure, she was a hell of a lot more fun to fight with. Full o' piss and vinegar, that gal. Never a dull moment."

"I've heard," Meg said dryly. "Many times."

Bart heaved a sigh. "Only trouble was, with Rita it was fight, fight, fight, all the time." He finished his coffee and set the cup on the counter with the other dishes, and stood close beside Meg, gazing at the long silky brown hair that flowed over her shoulders.

"In the long run, I'd rather have a mouse." His hand went around her waist and crept caressingly down over a buttock.

She plunged her hands into the hot suds. "Bart, could we get a dishwasher this year? You said we could, maybe."

He grinned. "You know exactly when to ask me for somethin', don't you? You know when I'm vulnerable." His lips nuzzled her ear.

"But, could we?"

"We'll see." His hand was exploring the curves of her body. "Right now I'd rather get us a baby." His voice was marshmallow.

"A baby?! I don't even feel grown up myself yet."

"Quit your kiddin', sweet stuff." He continued to nuzzle her.

"I'm not kidding. I'm not ready to be a mother."

"What d'ya mean, you're not ready? You're a big girl now, two years married. When you gonna be ready?"

"Bart, do we have to go through all that—"

He took hold of her with both hands, turned her toward him and pulled her up close. "Come on, sexy, warm up a little. Give us a kiss."

She let him kiss her once, then evaded his lips. "Let me finish the dishes, will you, Bart? I don't want to spend the entire evening in the kitchen."

Bart looked around quickly, struck with a sudden thought.

"Hey, you're right, let's get this place cleaned up. The Duggans'll be here pretty soon."

"Oh, no!" Meg wailed, and pulled away from him. "Why?!"

"I invited 'em over for drinks, that's why. You got some objections?"

"No, but . . ."

"So what's wrong? You're always complaining we don't have any social life. So I invite some people over, and you complain about *that*."

"I don't consider sitting around drinking with your cousin who's married to your old flame exactly social life."

"Who would you rather have?"

"I don't know. We don't know anybody."

"Maybe you'd like to invite Rick Jennings."

She pressed her lips together and turned back to the dishes. He glared at her for a moment, then put his arm around her waist again.

"Come on, Meg, don't be a drip. Herb and Rita haven't been over in weeks. It'll be fun."

"Sure. It's always fun watching you and Rita pawing at each other. *Breathing* at each other. Remembering secret moments of passion."

"Aw, cut it out, Meg!" He laughed, and poked her playfully in the ribs. "It doesn't mean anything. Rita's fun to flirt with, and she used to be fun to fight with. But when it came time to settle down, I married *you*, didn't I?"

The nuzzling began again, while his hand moved caressingly up and down her back. "And you want to know why? 'Cause Rita doesn't come close to being in the same class with you, that's why. You're my little mouse, the sweetest little mouse in the world."

Again she pulled away from him. "All you're interested in is making a mother out of me. Well, you can't, you know. I'm on the pill."

He growled at her with a sudden harshness. "Goddammit! One o' these days I'm gonna take those pills of yours and flush 'em down the toilet!"

"No you won't," she said coolly.

"Why the hell won't I?!"

" 'Cause I've got 'em hidden."

His chest heaved in fury. "Bitch!"

Abruptly he turned and strode out of the kitchen, went down the hall and into the bathroom, and slammed the door. Meg went on washing the dishes.

"Second-string quarterback," she muttered under her breath.

2

In the evening the Duggans' station wagon rolled to a noisy stop on the gravel driveway in front of the house, and Rita Duggan came flowing in, without knocking, all smiles and glitter, and calling out in a vibrant contralto, "Hel-lo-o-o-ooo! Anybody home?"

She was somewhat short and decidedly busty, with luxuriant auburn hair done up in a sculptured coiffure. She wore a silky floor-length dress that exposed vast areas of creamy flesh from the waist up, front and back. The dress was a dazzling combination of green and orange, the green of which was a perfect match for her luminous eyes. Her heavy exotic perfume filled the house immediately.

She found Meg in the living room and enveloped her in a sweeping embrace. "Meg, sweetie! How *are* you?"

Without waiting for an answer Rita glanced quickly around and said, "Where's that big beautiful hunk o' man?"

"Still in the shower, I think. He's been working on the tractor all afternoon, and was just covered with—"

Rita laughed, a deep throaty chortle. "Just like him, the big lug." She noticed that Meg had paintbrushes in her hand. "Don't tell me you're painting! On Saturday night?! Don't you ever quit?"

"Oh, no, I'm not, I'm . . . I was just putting things away—"

Herb bellowed from the front stoop. "Hey, somebody, open the sesame!"

"Herbie brought a keg," Rita said to Meg, and went to the front door and held it open.

Herb came in, making an elaborate comic routine out of staggering under a keg of beer on his shoulder. He stopped, swayed drunkenly, eyed Meg, and croaked, "Evenin', lady! I'm your friendly neighborhood bootlegger with a free sample for ya! Tell me where you want it."

Meg gestured vaguely. "In the kitchen, I guess, Herb."

Herb lumbered on through to the kitchen. With thinning hair and a slight frame that was puffed out by a soft flabbiness, he was no match for his cousin Bart Hannah in physique. At thirty he looked forty, by a good margin the senior member of the group.

He came back into the living room rubbing his shoulder. "Goddamn, they musta made that beer out o' heavy water!"

He glanced at Meg, did a double take, and looked her up and down with a leer. "Wow! Too bad I had dinner already—you look good enough to eat!"

Meg was wearing a simple black turtleneck pullover and a tweedy wool skirt, and felt, as she always did in Rita's presence, uncomfortably underdressed. She smiled weakly and fidgeted with embarrassment.

"Oh . . . these are just some old things . . ."

"I ain't talkin' about the clothes, gorgeous," Herb said, his leer growing broader. "I'm talkin' about the body inside 'em."

"Down, boy," Rita said, and patted her husband on the head. "Go chase Bartie out of the shower, so we can get this show on the road, as they say."

"Okay, sugar." Herb started obediently for the back of the house. "But I wish Bart was out here and I could go chase *Meg* out o' the shower." His snickering laughter rang down the hallway.

Rita chuckled gently, like an indulgent mother amused by her show-off child. Meg turned to her easel, which was standing by the front windows, and Rita followed her, squinting at the unfinished canvas there.

"Meggie, what in the world *is* that?"

"It's a landscape I'm doing for the Cutlers."

"Landscape? Looks more like the inside of somebody's head."

Meg blinked. "Excuse me," she said dryly. "I was just going to put it away."

Rita pointed at the center of the canvas. "What's this thing?"

"An oak tree. You know that big oak tree on the Cutlers' place, up by the river?"

Rita looked blank. "Not really."

"Well, they have this big beautiful old oak, and they sort of commissioned me to paint it."

Rita arched an eyebrow. "Ah-h-h! A *paying* job, eh?"

Meg grew flustered. "Well . . . they're going to buy it if they like it."

Amusement crinkled Rita's eyes. "That's nice." She turned away.

Meg hurriedly lifted the canvas off and folded the easel. "Let me get this stuff put away. Bart doesn't like me to leave it out when company's—"

"Hey, Rita-baby!" Bart stood in the doorway, magnificent as a Greek god, dressed in a bath towel wrapped around his waist. "I was waitin' for you to come scrub my back, like you used to do."

Meg stared at him.

"I sent Herbie!" Rita shrieked. "Isn't that good enough?"

"Herbie don't thrill me," Bart whined. "The touch just ain't the same!"

Rita threw back her head and howled with laughter. She flew across the room, lifted the back of Bart's towel-skirt, and administered a sharp slap on a bare buttock. Bart yelped and bounded away down the hall, and Rita went in pursuit. From the darkness at the far end of the hall came sounds of giggling, of light scuffling, then a squeal from Rita.

"Hey, cut that out! Fresh!" It sounded like an invitation to continue.

Herb was standing in the doorway to the living room, grinning at Meg. "Ain't they a couple o' clowns, Meg? I swear to God, I think we married ourselves a couple o' circus clowns." He ambled across the room and flopped down on the sofa.

Meg busied herself putting away her painting things, trying not to appear self-conscious and clumsy. Without looking at Herb she could feel his eyes taking in every movement of her body.

From down the hall Rita's voice sounded again, this time low and controlled, saying, "Go on, now. Get dressed." She came back into the living room walking slowly, smoothing her hair. She smiled, unperturbed, at Meg.

"Honestly, sweetie, I don't see how you keep up the pace, being married to that sex maniac."

Meg said nothing.

Herb gazed at his wife with a genial grin that had a faint hint of annoyance showing around the edges. "If you think he's all that great how come you didn't marry him yourself when you had the chance?"

Rita sank down on the sofa next to Herb. "I'll tell you, sweetie. After Bart and I spent a year together we both knew one thing. We were well on our way to burning each other out, mentally and physically." She laughed her throaty laugh, glanced up and saw Meg staring at her stony-faced. She went on. "No, the truth is, I'm a domineering woman, I admit it. I need a man I can boss around. That's why I married *you*, sweetie." Playfully she mussed her husband's thinning hair, leaned over and nuzzled him. "You're a cute lamb, yes you are."

Then she leaned back in the sofa, sighed, and looked at the ceiling. "Only trouble is, once in a while I get a taste for something stronger than lamb."

Herb got up. "I'm gonna tap that keg," he said. He went out to the kitchen.

Rita leaned forward toward Meg. "Do you ever feel that way, Meggie? Do you ever feel like you've just got to have a *change?*"

Meg frowned and tried to formulate a thoughtful answer. "I don't know, Rita. Sometimes I—"

Herb yelled from the kitchen. "Draw a pair for you two?"

"No, thanks," Rita yelled back. She looked quickly toward Meg. "You got some hard stuff in the house, sweetie? I don't propose to sit around guzzling beer with those two male animals all evening, do you?"

"Oh . . . yes, I think there's some bourbon in the cupboard." Meg got up and went to the kitchen, and fixed a large bourbon and soda for Rita and a small one for herself.

In a few minutes Bart appeared, dressed, and he and Herb went to work on the beer keg. After a while the men drifted out back briefly, discussing the work Bart was doing on the tractor, then returned and joined the women in the living room. Rita was still sitting on the sofa, and Bart settled beside her. Herb took a chair near Meg's.

Rita tapped Bart on the arm. "Guess you know we almost didn't make it tonight. Herbie's been babysitting a sick bull."

"That would've been a lame damn excuse," Bart said.

Herb protested. "Not *any* ol' bull, Bart. Black Jack, my prize stud. Worth his weight in gold."

"Oh, *that* bull." Bart swigged his beer. "Hell, that bull ain't sick. He's just tired from all that screwin'."

Herb and Rita and Bart all laughed loudly. Bart slapped Rita on the knee.

Meg smiled weakly, tried to think of something to say. "It would have been too bad to be stuck at home for that."

Bart shot his wife a sharp look. "*You* should talk. Remember when you wouldn't budge out o' the barn for a week, when Pal was sick?"

"That's different," Meg said stiffly.

Rita came to Meg's defense. "Sure it's different. Pal's a beautiful horse. If I was a mare I'd really swish my tail for him."

Bart cackled, and slapped Rita's knee again.

"How come women are so nuts about horses, anyway?" Herb asked.

" 'Cause most horses are smarter than most men," Rita said.

"No kiddin'," Herb said. "You go down to the County Fairgrounds and take a look at the young kids riding in competition. The girl riders outnumber the boys three to one."

"You're exaggerating," Rita said.

"He's right," Bart said. "If it wasn't for women, horses would be just about extinct by now, 'cept for work animals. And the reason for that is very simple." He took a draw on his beer and continued, with his eyes fixed on Meg. "The reason girls love to ride horses so much is, it's the ideal substitute for sex. A girl can spread her legs over a saddle and have herself a nice massage, anytime, for as long as she likes. No fuss, no bother, and no fear of pregnancy."

Herb produced an appreciative guffaw.

Rita was amused but scornful. "That's a bunch of crap, and you know it!" She poked Bart in the ribs with an elbow.

"A scientifically proven fact," Bart declared. "I read it someplace."

Meg gazed at her husband with a blank expression.

"Ah, me, the life of a rancher's wife!" sighed Rita. "It ain't easy, is it, Meggie?"

The men made repeated trips to the kitchen for beer, finally brought the keg into the living room and set it on the coffee table, over Meg's protests. Then they launched a rambling conversation that ranged over the subjects of the precarious health of cattle, current beef prices, ranch equipment, the mending of fences, and which teams looked good in the National League pennant race. Rita consumed several large bourbons and settled more and more toward a reclining position on the couch. Her eyelids drooped languidly. Meg nursed her watery drink for a long time, then began to nurse a second. Her eyes drifted from Bart to Herb to Rita, and back again. She stifled a yawn.

Without warning Rita sat up, opened her eyes wide, and snorted loudly. "God! What a boring evening! How come you creeps don't ever take us girls anyplace?"

"Like where?" Herb asked. "Caxton?"

"Hell no, not Caxton! Someplace where there's some action. Some *life*, for God's sake! How come we don't ever drive down to the coast? I hear there's a marvelous new nightspot at Diamond Bay."

"I'd love to go to Diamond Bay sometime," Meg said. "I'd love to paint the fishing boats—"

"Jesus H. Christ!" Bart growled. "Knock it off, you two! It's eighty goddam miles to Diamond Bay!"

Rita moaned softly. "Somebody please think of something to *do!* I'm going *mad!*"

"How about a party game?" Herb said. "How about charades, or somethin' like that?"

Rita snapped her fingers and froze, her eyes alight with an idea. "I got it. Spin-the-bottle. Swinger version."

"How do you play?" asked Herb, all eagerness.

"A girl spins the bottle, and whatever fellow the bottle points to, she has to go to bed with him. Only rule is, if the bottle points to her husband, she has to spin it again. No fair going to bed with your own husband."

There was a moment of silence while a subtle tension grew in the room.

Herb stared at his wife in wide-eyed astonishment. "Holy Moses, where'd you ever learn *that?*"

"Just made it up, sweetie. Came to me in a flash."

"Not a bad game," Bart said casually. "No losers. Everybody wins."

They all looked at Meg. She gripped her glass hard and gazed

24

at Bart. "I think you've all had too much to drink. You're being very silly."

Bart made a small noise that sounded like a snort. Herb snickered.

"Just trying to be helpful, sweetie," Rita said. "After all, you've got to admit, your party *is* dull."

"It's not my party," Meg said icily.

"Aw, come on, Meg!" Bart said. "Can't you try to act a little like a . . . a *hostess*, for Christ's sake?"

"Sorry," Meg said in a mumble. She fixed her eyes on her drink.

"Well, she's right, Bartie," Rita said. "It's not her party, it's yours. So entertain us. Make us laugh."

Bart looked at her thoughtfully. He winked. "Okay."

He dipped his fingertips in his glass of beer and flicked them at Rita. She shrieked and slapped at him, causing his beer to slosh into his lap. He swore and jumped to his feet, reaching for a handkerchief. Herb rocked in his chair, shaking with laughter.

"Aw-w-w! So sorry, lover." Rita's sympathy was mocking.

Bart dabbed at the front of his slacks with his handkerchief. "I swear you're not the woman you used to be, Rita. I can remember how on a hot day you'd lie naked and let me pour a cold beer all over you."

"You're a big fat liar," Rita said with a coy smile. "We did that once. You make it sound like a habit."

The sound of a door closing in another part of the house stopped them abruptly. Meg had left the room. Bart and Rita looked blankly at each other.

"All right, you guys, now you did it," Herb said in a sober voice. "You got Meg all mad."

Bart frowned. "Goddam!" he muttered.

Rita giggled. "Meggie's gonna pout awhile. That's okay, let her pout."

She drained her glass and held it up to Bart. "Fix us another one, will you, big fella?"

Bart took the glass and went out to the kitchen, looking morose.

Herb came across the room and sat down next to Rita, and gazed at her earnestly. "Look, honey, aren't you two, uh, playin' a little bit rough? You got Meg all upset."

25

"Kidding, sweetie, just kidding. Nothing else to do."

"Meg's kinda sensitive, y'know."

"Sensitive, my ass! She doesn't know what time it is. I swear to God I think she was a virgin when Bart married her."

"What's that got to do with anything?"

"Meg's never gotten used to the idea that Bart and I were lovers once. It never was a secret, so she needn't start acting huffy *now*. Hell, it doesn't bother you, why should it bother her?"

Herb looked pained. "Well, I think this is too bad, y'know? Why don't you go talk to her, tell her you didn't mean anything. Patch it up. Okay?"

Rita smiled and patted her husband's cheek. "Got news, sweetie. I *didn't* not mean anything."

Bart came back into the room, carrying two drinks. "I'm switchin' to bourbon. Sick o' that beer." He handed one of the glasses to Rita. "How about you, Herb? Want one?"

"No." Herb got up and went back to his chair and picked up his beer glass.

"It's no, *thank you*, sweetie," Rita said. "Say no, thank you, like a good boy."

"What'sa matter with him?" Bart asked.

"He's got the hots for another man's wife," Rita said, and sipped her drink. "But he wants to pretend it was horrid of me to try to fix him up."

"That's a crock," Herb muttered.

Bart gave Herb an understanding look. "You sure don't have to pretend with *me*, pal. I know exactly how you feel, and believe me, I sympathize."

Herb ignored this, kept his eyes on Rita. "I still think you ought to go and apologize," he said.

Rita stared at him. "You really *do* go for little Meg, don't you, Herbie?"

Herb squirmed. "Well, I mean . . . what the hell?"

"Don't try to hide it, sweetie, Mama knows all your thoughts. I wasn't just thinking of my own pleasure when I suggested spin-the-bottle."

Bart had sat down next to Rita. He leaned forward, studying the other man. Herb sipped his beer and looked uncomfortable.

"Tell you what, Herb," Bart said. "*You* go and talk to Meg.

Tell her we spun the bottle on her behalf, and what d'ya know?—it pointed to you."

Herb permitted himself a sheepish grin.

"I'm not kidding, Herb. Go to it." Bart's eyes bore into Herb, and his voice went low and hard. "I'm not kidding, Herb," he said again.

Herb's grin went from sheepish to sickly. "Shee-it," he mumbled.

"Go ahead, sweetie," Rita smiled at him across the rim of her glass. "Give it a try. What can you lose?"

Herb snickered. "My life. Meg'd knock me right on my ass, and you know it."

"Not if you're sincere." Rita leaned forward, gazing intently at Herb. "Let me tell you about Meg—she's one of those old-fashioned girls who think that love and sex and respect and affection are all the same thing. A girl like that, you got to smother with sincerity. You go tell her how much you've always secretly admired her. Tell her how beautiful, how adorable, how desirable you think she is. How sensitive, and all that. Tell her how terrible you think it is that Bart doesn't appreciate all her good qualities."

Bart emitted a soft chuckle. "What the hell you tryin' to do, break up my marriage?"

Rita's eyes remained fixed on Herb. "And above all, be very, very sincere."

Herb looked from Rita to Bart and back to Rita. The grin had disappeared from his face and was replaced by a high pink flush. "You two really mean it, don't you?"

Rita glanced at Bart. Bart twirled the ice cubes in his glass around with his finger.

"You got the message, pal."

Herb drained his beer glass and got to his feet. "Well, I tell you what. I'm goin' to the john."

Rita smiled up at him. "That's a good idea, sweetie. You can't hope to be a great lover with a bladder full of warm beer."

"Then I'm gonna knock on Meg's door and ask her if she'd like to go for a drive. I think she and I both need a little fresh air." Herb went off down the hall.

Rita set her drink down and leaned back on the couch. She sighed. "Poor dear Herbie. Poor Meg. They just don't know how to get any fun out of life, do they?" She leaned her arm on Bart's back and let a finger play lightly through the hair at the nape of his neck.

Bart turned and looked at her, his eyes narrowed quizzically. She turned her head toward him so that their eyes met directly. "No," she whispered. "I'm not trying to break up your marriage. But I just can't stand the idea of her having you *all* the time."

He put his drink down and leaned over her and gazed hungrily at her lips. Her eyes invited him on.

Through the thin plaster walls of the house came the sound of rushing water; Herb had flushed the toilet.

Bart moved down and covered Rita's mouth with his own. His hand moved along the curve of her throat, slipped under the strap of her dress and pushed it off her shoulder, found a breast and closed over it. Rita inhaled deeply and arched her back, thrusting herself obligingly toward him.

Then Herb was back, standing in the doorway and coughing softly.

Bart sat upright and spat out his opinion of the interruption: "Shit!"

Rita hastily pulled herself back together.

"Sorry to spoil the game, folks." Herb was earnestly apologetic. "Meg wouldn't talk to me. She's not havin' any part of it."

"One hell of a big effort you made!" Rita snapped at him.

Bart picked up his drink and finished it off. "Only one thing left to do," he muttered. "Get fuckin', stinkin' drunk." He got up and lumbered off to the kitchen, taking his glass with him.

Herb gazed down at his wife. "I think we ought to go, Rita."

She gave him a thin smile. "You just never were much of a lady killer, were you, Herbie?" She rose unsteadily and followed Bart into the kitchen.

Bart poured himself a jigger of whiskey and belted it, and poured another. Rita laid a hand on his arm.

"Take it easy, big fella."

"No way. No way I can take it easy." He gulped his drink again and glanced at Rita's glass. "Refill?"

"No, thanks." She set her glass on the counter. "I guess we'll be toddling along now."

Bart glared at her. "Not yet you don't, sweetheart. There's

one more item on the entertainment program tonight. Meg's gonna come out here and apologize for her lousy behavior."

He slammed his glass down and headed for the door to the hall. Rita pulled at his arm.

"Ah, no, Bart. Leave her alone."

"She can't insult my friends and get away with it. She's gonna apologize or I'll damn well know the reason why."

He pulled himself out of Rita's grasp and moved toward the hallway, but she was in front of him again instantly, blocking his path.

"You haven't changed a bit, have you?" The steely-hard edge to her husky voice startled him. "You still think you can get your own way just by bullying people, don't you?"

"I'm not bullying anybody, goddammit! All I want is for my wife to show a little respect for my friends."

"Crap. I don't need respect from Meg. I couldn't care less—"

"Well you're gonna get it, whether you want it or not." He made a move to brush her aside.

She held her ground. "I should've warned her about you. The only reason I didn't is because I knew she'd never believe anything *I* said—"

"Aw, shut up, Rita. You're runnin' off at the mouth about something you don't know a damn thing about."

"The hell I don't! I took an advanced course in survival training from you, buster, and I've got the scars to prove it."

Bart's eyes were throwing sparks of fury, but his voice remained calm. "Will you please get out of my way?"

"You lay a hand on her, you bastard, and I'll never speak to you again."

"What the hell are you talkin' about?! I have *never* laid a hand on Meg. That's her damn trouble—I treat her so nice she's spoiled. But this time she's gone too far, by God. She's gonna apologize—"

Herb pushed his way timidly between them. "Aw, cut it out, ol' buddy," he said to Bart. "Calm down, everything's all right. We gotta be goin' now, anyway."

Bart pushed the other man aside with a quick sweep of his hand. "You stay out o' this, Herb. It's none o' your goddam business."

Herb appealed to Rita. "Come on, hon. It's gettin' late—"

"Wait a minute, please."

All eyes turned to Meg. She was standing in the doorway, and her soft voice reduced the turbulence to stillness instantly. She spoke haltingly, searching for words.

"I *do* want to apologize. I'm sorry I was such a . . . I threw such a wet blanket on the party. I'm not very much fun, I guess."

"Forget it, sweetie." Rita reached out and squeezed Meg's hand. "It was mostly my fault. I get to feeling disreputable now and then, I must admit. Forget it."

"It's just that . . . I just don't like that kind of game."

"Just kidding around, sweetie, no big thing at all," Rita said casually. "I just keep forgetting what a really old-fashioned girl you are. Don't get me wrong, that's not a criticism—that sweet old-fashioned quality is part of your charm. But, seriously, I can't help thinking you'd be better off, and a lot happier, if you could just . . . well, loosen up a bit, you know what I mean? Living *is* just a game, after all, so why not get all the fun you can out of it?"

"Yes." Meg twisted her fingers together nervously, looking like a child being lectured by the teacher. "Yes, I'm sure you're right."

Rita smiled sweetly and continued. "And especially I wish you wouldn't get so uptight when I flirt with Bart. I get these periodic seizures of boredom, y'know, and start looking around for diversion—but it doesn't mean a thing, really. Bart and I *had* our little fling, and then we made a mutual decision to go our separate ways. Now I'm a happily married woman, and I plan to stay that way. Hope you can do the same."

She patted Meg on the cheek, took Herb by the arm and turned her smile on him. "Come on, lamb. Take me home and fix me a nice cup of hot milk, and maybe I'll let you make a little love to me." She smiled once more at Meg, threw a quick glance at Bart, and led her lamb away.

"G'night, folks," Herb called awkwardly over his shoulder. "Talk to you in a few days, Bart."

As they were going out the front door Bart came to life. He hurried after them, calling, "Hey, Herb, don't you want to take the keg with you? It's still got a lot of juice in it."

He went into the living room and grabbed the beer keg, and followed the departing guests out to their car.

$$3$$

The Duggans' car sat in the driveway with the motor idling for almost ten minutes before it drove away and Bart came back inside. Then he spent another ten minutes having a last solitary drink, closing up the house, and putting out the lights. When he went into the bedroom he found that Meg was already in bed. She lay quite still, with the covers tucked around her ears, as if asleep. Bart stood for a long moment gazing down at her before going into the adjoining bathroom. In a few minutes he came out, undressed quickly and completely, turned off the last light, and slid naked into bed beside Meg. She continued to lie silent and motionless, with her back toward him.

"Hey. Wake up." His voice boomed in the stillness.

She stirred and turned partially toward him. "Yes, Bart. I'm awake."

He reached out and pulled the covers down away from her face, and saw her eyes gleaming wetly in the darkness.

"You made some sarcastic remark tonight about how you guessed I should have married Rita," he said. "And you know something? Maybe you were right. I mean, no kidding. Maybe I should have, and maybe you should've never got married at all. Maybe you'd be happier just bein' an old maid, foolin' around with your paint junk."

"Maybe so," she said placidly. "What do you want to do, Bart? Do you want a divorce?"

He snorted. "Hell, no. That's just the trouble."

"Herb wouldn't be any obstacle. I'm sure Rita would dispose of him without batting an eye."

"That's not it. I wouldn't be married to Rita on a bet. She's a great gal in many ways, but she's a bitch, a natural-born bitch."

"You call *me* that a lot, too."

31

"Aw, you know what I mean. She really *is* a bitch. There's something about Rita—she brings out the beast in a man."

"I don't see Herb acting like a beast."

"Do you have to contradict everything I say?"

"I'm sorry. I just thought . . . you know, Herb's a nice guy."

"I don't give a damn about Herb, I'm tellin' you what she does to *me*. Hell's bells, if I ever lived with Rita again I'd wring her neck inside o' six months, for sure. No, thanks, I don't need that."

"Well . . . maybe we ought to examine the other side of the coin. What *I* need."

"Yeah?" He chuckled at this. "What do *you* need?"

She was a long time answering. "I don't . . . I don't really know."

He laughed again and rolled toward her. "You just leave it to me to decide what we *both* need, baby." His hand was under the covers and snaking up along her thigh beneath her nightgown. "I need a well-behaved little mouse who takes care of her household responsibilities, who has a great body and knows exactly what it's for. And I need for her to give me sons. Be fruitful and multiply, like it says in the good book, y'know?" His hands roamed over the smooth curvature of her waist and hip. "Now, what *you* need is a good strong man providing you with comfort and security, and three square meals a day. A man who takes care of any problems that come up and keeps your pretty little head free of worry, so you can fool around with your paints and canvas and all that stuff as much as you want."

He was up on an elbow, leaning over her. His lips wandered over her face and along her neck, planting quick kisses.

"In other words, baby, what you need is exactly what you've got, so why don't you just relax and enjoy it?" His hands were moving quietly and expertly, working her nightgown up.

Meg murmured fretfully, "Not now, Bart, please? I got terribly upset tonight, and I don't feel—"

"Aw, no, baby, just forget about all that, it's not important. Anyway, I was blaming you for something that wasn't your fault at all. It was Rita's fault. I'm tellin' you, she's a bitch, that woman. But you, baby, you're an angel."

He had her nightgown off and was exploring her body eagerly with his hands and his lips.

32

"I thought you were mad at me," she said.

"Ah, Meg, honey, you know how it is with me. Sometimes you make me so mad I could bust, but I can't *stay* mad. You're just so sweet and beautiful, and so . . . You're my own little mouse, yes you are."

No more words were spoken as his concentration increased. In a few minutes he came over her, nudging her legs apart.

Meg twisted her head far to one side and took his burning breath on her neck and shoulder, and listened to his furious blowing and deep rumbling grunts with a curious detachment. In a little while she closed her eyes and tried to imagine it was someone else.

But who? Her mind ran through a meager selection of candidates.

First, the image of Rick Jennings and his bright charismatic smile. Rick Jennings, star quarterback. Dr. Jennings, brilliant young pharmacist. His face swam before her enticingly, winked at her, but then drifted away, would not come back into focus.

Herb Duggan? Sweet, gentle, good-natured Herb? Impossible.

Mr. Powell, her art instructor in junior college, for whom she had nursed a wild, short-lived passion? Mr. Powell smiled at her with kindliness and a wistful yearning hunger—but his eyes were rheumic, and his teeth were stained an unappetizing yellow.

She sighed, and gave it up.

4

In the morning a gray mist lay like a blanket on the quiet earth, and drifted in stealth up the long slant of land toward the mouth of Stag River Canyon and the dark brooding bulk of the mountain beyond. The vernal-equinox sun would be a long time showing; at that time of year—late March—the tremendous shadow of the mountain massif covered the Hannah ranch until almost nine o'clock and steeped it in a lingering chill.

In that shadow Meg came out of the back of the house, carrying her canvas and easel and taking extreme care not to make noise, and walked rapidly across the yard to the garage. She was dressed in jeans and an ancient sweat shirt that was splattered with colorful testimonials of a hundred previous artistic endeavors. She quietly loaded her things into the pickup truck, made two more quick trips to the house for additional supplies, then climbed into the vehicle and cranked it into coughing life. After a short wait for warmup she backed the truck out and drove off. At the junction of the Hannah ranch road with County 15, two hundred yards from the house, she turned right and headed toward the canyon.

She drove slowly—for her, unaccustomedly so. There was no need to hurry; the morning light, blocked by the mountain wall to the southeast, would not be right for painting for a while yet. She would have a little time to kill. Her artist eye moved constantly as she guided her little vehicle up the narrow blacktop strip. She watched the infinitesimal shifts of light and shadow, the fading of dark bluish hues and the slow growth of warm tones as the day matured, and gauged the subtle changes of angle and perspective in distant vistas as her position of view was altered. She breathed deeply of the sharp morning air, and felt good.

34

She had thought to turn off at the Cutler ranch road when she reached it, drive the two miles up to the house and visit briefly with the Cutlers—genial elderly people who were always happy to see her—then return to the county road and continue on the mile or so to the site of the ancient oak, not far from the river, where she would set up her easel for the day's work. Over a little ridge and around a curve, and the tall wooden signpost marking the entrance to the Cutler ranch was visible, a quarter of a mile ahead.

Meg slowed slightly on the approach to the Cutler road and prepared to make the turn, but impulsively braked to a stop instead, and sat for a moment in an unexpected seizure of indecision, with her vehicle idling impatiently in the road. It was such a crisp and sparkling morning, she thought—Stag River would be leaping like a wild thing, and maybe, at this hour, the silver glint of feeding trout might be seen. Suddenly the thought of sitting in the Cutlers' stuffy parlor and chatting about trivialities seemed distasteful to her. They'll want to see the canvas, which won't do—it isn't yet finished. In the afternoon it would be done, and she would take it to them then. At that moment the thing she wanted to do most in the world was sit on a rock by the river and watch its ceaseless thrashing surge, and fall under the tranquil spell of solitude. She put the truck in gear and drove on.

Another turn, past rugged granitic outcroppings, and the road dipped downward briefly to lead past a long dense stand of willows and tall young cottonwoods on the right-hand side, marking the line of the river's edge. Then a break in the trees, and a small semicircular clearing, and just beyond it the glittering river, in full view. On the other side of the road a footpath wandered up a gentle slope through a field of tawny wild grass and disappeared over a low ridge, fifty yards away, leading to the quiet place where the great oak stood, where Meg planned to spend her day in contented solitary observation and industry.

Meg pulled her truck into the little clearing, parked it under a tree, and shut off the engine. Immediately the rushing water of the river filled the air with a soft, steady, peaceful sound. She got out, walked a few paces to the center of the clearing, stopped there and opened all her senses to the gentle impressions of nature. The air was strikingly different here from the hot dry air of the ranch; there was a dampness, a fragrance of foliage, the coolness of running water and the shady woods.

The sun was just over the top of the jagged east wall of the canyon now, its slanted beams playing on the water along the far side of the river. Soon it would be time to go to work, Meg thought—but for a few minutes still she had a legitimate excuse for idleness and dalliance.

She walked quickly down to the edge of the river and sat down on a low rock, tested the water by trailing her fingers in the swift current, and shivered with the small delicious shock of icy coldness.

Somewhere near the center of the stream there was the sudden stealthy splash of a trout breaking the surface in pursuit of an insect; Meg looked up with quick excitement, imagining that she almost caught sight of the elusive silvery flash. The sunlight was moving farther out on the water now, catching tiny droplets of spray and turning them into sparkling short-lived rainbow fragments. Meg's eye then drifted downstream, following the pull and thrust of the powerful current, the leaping of water on top of water in froth and foam—melted snow from the high fastness of winter, running now to the warm plains.

The artist resolved again, as she had done many times before, to paint the river someday, as soon as she felt equal to the challenge. The peculiar difficulty, she thought, is not color, nor texture, nor composition. It is the trick of capturing the feeling of *motion*, and stopping it in mid-air, which in the case of turbulent water is particularly—

The train of thought came to a sudden jarring stop. Her eye had fallen upon a patch of color in the dense brush some twenty or thirty yards downstream, and had hung there absently for a moment before it registered in her mind that the color—a bright vibrant rose—did not represent a natural element in the landscape. Now her conscious attention shifted abruptly, focused on the spot, and quickly identified a metallic painted surface.

Meg got up and walked to the edge of the clearing to get a closer look. As she approached the place she noticed what seemed to be fresh depressions of tire tracks in the weeds, raised her eyes to follow them, and realized with a shock that she was looking at a car.

It was a small sports car, almost completely buried from sight in the thick underbrush, and was tilted perilously downward at the edge of the steep bank along the river, as if it had gone out of control and stalled in that most unlikely spot.

Meg stood quite still, and stared. It crossed her mind that someone could be inside, injured, perhaps unconscious. Perhaps dead. Her pulse quickened in a kind of subdued excitement that she tried to suppress. Suddenly the natural quiet of the lonely place was disturbing to her; the atmosphere that had seemed soothing and peaceful a few moments before now seemed heavy with menace, vaguely frightening.

She took a few cautious steps toward the vehicle, and recognized the distinctive shape of an expensive foreign car—the name of which she could not call to mind—and as she drew a little closer she saw in the shadowy interior a gaudy custom-made upholstery of simulated leopard skin. She paused again, still a few steps away, and gazed at the elegant, apparently undamaged, apparently abandoned car, and felt an insidious chill creeping up her spine. She tried to shake off the feeling. Not really fear, she told herself, just a hint of uneasiness, or wariness—it's such an odd thing.

Well, I *must* investigate, she thought. Someone may really be inside, and desperately in need of help.

She went on, made her way to the side of the car, cupped her hands over the window to block reflections, and peered inside. It was empty. The window was rolled up tight and the door locked.

She stood for a moment in perplexity, and realized with a blink of surprise that what she was feeling now was disappointment. She thought of Bart's friend Carl Gallagher, who had joined the County Sheriff's Department because of his love of excitement and adventure, and who in five years as a deputy had never been involved in anything more dramatic than the apprehension of an occasional petty thief.

A mischievous notion suddenly touched Meg's mind: If I could find something gruesome here, I could rush off and notify Carl, and we could get our pictures in the paper, and be interviewed by a TV newscaster, maybe. *Then* wouldn't Carl be happy! She smiled at her frivolous thoughts and dismissed them, stooped and looked inside the car again, hoping to spot some detail that would provide a clue.

Then from somewhere close by a quiet voice said, "Good morning."

Meg gasped and whirled.

A young man was standing at the edge of the clearing. He was about Meg's age, tanned and slender, with wide-set gray eyes and sandy hair that tended to swirl around his head like an unruly mop. He wore dungarees, a multicolored sport shirt, and a pair of binoculars suspended from his neck by a strap. He stood with his feet wide apart, looking at Meg and smiling brightly.

Meg stared. The chill gripped her again—this time, unmistakably, fear. She swallowed hard, tried to return the young man's smile, and spoke in what she hoped was a firm voice.

"Hello."

They gazed at each other in silence, for what seemed to Meg an absurdly long time.

"This your car?" she said finally, and with consternation heard the tremor in her voice that betrayed her fright.

"Yep. Some fancy buggy, huh?" His tone was casual and cheerful. He started unhurriedly toward her. "Well, no, not precisely *mine*. It's really my uncle's car. My Uncle Harry's."

Halfway to the car he stopped short and began to study Meg's face. She stood rooted to her spot, staring at him fixedly, with wide eyes. One hand was at her throat, the other tightly gripping the handle of the car door.

"I wouldn't own a car like that," the young man said softly. "It's not my style at all. Even if I could afford it." His sunny smile broke out.

Meg smiled weakly. The young man continued to observe her, and his face became solemn.

"You're afraid of me, aren't you?"

Her hand fluttered, and she gave a nervous little laugh. "It's . . . you know, it's just rather . . . strange."

"I didn't mean to frighten you," he said. He started to retrace his steps toward the clearing. Once there he turned and looked back at her. "Don't be afraid. I won't hurt you, really."

She had to strain to hear him. The odd quietness of voice seemed to be a fixed characteristic of his speech. She felt a slight easing of inner tension, but made no move to follow him out to the clearing.

38

In a moment he laughed and threw up his hands. "What can I do to convince you I'm harmless?" He looked around, searching for an idea. "Tell you what—I'll walk up the road and give you room, then you can come scooting out of there and run get in your truck and zoom away! Okay?" He waved to her, smiling, and walked away and out of her field of view.

Meg stood still for half a minute longer, then cautiously edged forward to the clearing, walked to the side of the road, and looked up and down. The young man was sitting cross-legged on the ground at the roadside, fifty yards away in the uphill direction.

He waved to her again. "Quick!" he called. "Run to your truck and make your escape!"

She suddenly felt foolish. All trace of fear drained away. She walked toward him with a smile that conveyed apology. "Hey, I'm sorry. It was just so . . . crazy, sort of, coming upon a car in the brush like that. I wish you'd tell me what *happened*. I'm dying of curiosity."

He sat where he was without moving until she came up to him. "Well, I tell you. I can't talk so hot when I'm sittin' on the cold, cold ground." He extended his hand toward her. "Help me up?"

Uneasiness returned. She made no move.

He sighed. "And I can't talk to you at all if you're going to go on being afraid of me, like a ninny."

She gazed down at him. His eyes are kind, she told herself. Open and honest, and free of deviousness.

Almost without realizing it she held out her hand to him. He took it and came up lightly to his feet, and they stood facing each other, eye to eye—almost exactly the same height—his smile reflecting delight at his little victory, her smile reflecting his. He still held her hand.

"Hey . . ." he breathed, in his very quiet voice. "I think we're gonna be friends, don't you?"

5

The morning matured. Miles to the southeast of the Hannah ranch the blue-and-purple cloak of mist on the massive mountain escarpment fell away, and features emerged crisp and clear in the distance—cliffs, crevices, stands of evergreen along lofty ridges, needlepoints etched on a brittle sky, and silvery slivers of old snow and ice hanging in steep protected places, hiding from the sun. The tall cottonwoods and sycamores bordering a shallow brook that ran through the ranch grounds came alive with the conversations of birds. The great mountain shadow retreated; the sunlight crept across the yard and bathed the house in light and warmth.

A car, moving unhurriedly, came up County 15 from the direction of the state highway, slowed, and turned onto the ranch road—a big black-and-white sedan, on its roof a shiny red rotary flasher identifying a law enforcement agency vehicle, on its door the gold emblem of the County Sheriff's Department.

The driver, the only occupant of the car, brought it to a stop in front of the house and got out. He was lean and muscular, in his early thirties, with a sharp face that was deeply lined from a sun-and-wind existence. His crisp tan uniform, his stiff-brimmed hat set at a carefully determined angle on his head, and the great gleaming badge of his office all were part of his orderly personality. He looked around the grounds, saw no sign of life, went to the front door and knocked. After a patient wait he knocked again.

Then the door opened and Bart Hannah squinted out into the bright morning glare. He was bleary-eyed and unshaven, in his undershirt, and fumblingly closing the zipper on his pants.

"Hey, Bart! Did I wake you up?" The deputy sheriff's voice was loud and hearty. He took off his hat and grinned through the screen door at the man inside. "Holy mackerel! Didn't mean to disturb your beauty sleep!"

" 'S all right, Carl. Come on in." Bart held the door open. "I was just gonna have a little hair o' the dog. Join me?"

"Oh, no, thanks, I'm on duty," Carl said. "I'll just have a cup o' coffee if you've got one."

"Good 'nuff," Bart mumbled. He led the way to the kitchen.

Carl sat down at the kitchen table while Bart lifted the lid of the coffee pot, peered in, and muttered, "Shit!" He rinsed the pot and started to measure fresh water.

"Don't bother on my account," Carl said. "I can only stay for a minute, anyway."

"Sit tight, it'll be ready in no time," Bart said. After setting up the coffee pot he got out a bottle of bourbon, poured himself a jiggerful, and yawned mightily.

Carl watched him. "Meg sleepin' in this morning, too? Jeez, you guys musta tied one on last night."

Bart made a sour face. "You kiddin'? Meg believes in that early-to-bed-early-to-rise crap. Sundays, holidays, don't make no difference. She was up and out o' here this morning at the crack o' dawn. Couldn't even take time to make some coffee, for Christ's sake."

"Where's she off to?"

"Up the canyon, paintin' a goddam oak tree."

Carl smiled, and Bart responded with a helpless shrug. "Yeah, I know, Carl. I'm married to a nut. What can I do?"

"You've got a nice little lady there, Bart. Don't knock it."

"I ain't gonna knock it. Hell, I can't even knock it *up*."

Bart grinned at the chortling laugh he drew from the deputy sheriff at this. He sat down at the table, eyed the other man with a squint, and spoke in a broad cowboy drawl.

"Wall, now, Sheriff, what brangs you hyar? Don't tell me yo're out chasin' varmints on a Sunday mornin'!"

Carl chuckled. "No, kind of a slow day, as usual. Nothin' much on the books but a dern stolen-car report, from the May-field office." He took a paper from his shirt pocket and began to read the vital statistics. " 'Seventy-seven Porsche. Rose-colored. License number—"

Bart produced a sharp whistle. "Holy Jesus! Who the hell in Mayfield owns a *Porsche?!*"

"Fellow by the name of Emmons. Harry Emmons."

"Emmons . . ." Bart frowned. "Sounds a mite familiar."

"Wealthy fellow. Owns a wholesale hardware business."

The coffee started to boil over, and Bart uttered a curse and jumped to take care of it. The deputy's eyes crinkled with amusement.

"Meg's gonna give you hell for messin' up her stove."

Bart snorted. "Shit! Meg ain't got the gumption to give a flea hell." He poured two cups of coffee and returned to the table. "I'll give *her* hell when she gets home, for goin' off without fixin' my breakfast."

Bart tossed his jigger of whiskey in a gulp and slurped the scalding coffee. "Ah! What a combination! Fixes me up for the day." He stared thoughtfully out the window. "Emmons. Yeah, yeah. Emmons' Hardware and Mercantile, or sump'm like that. I think I know the place."

Carl picked up the stolen-car report again and studied it. "Let's see. Rose-colored Porsche. Has some kind o' fancy leopard-skin upholstery, it says here. Ought to be easy to spot."

"Christ, what *is* this guy Emmons, a fag?"

"Not hardly. Fella in our Mayfield office told me Emmons just about single-handedly supported the local whorehouse before he got married, 'bout a year ago. Wife's a former actress or somethin'. Stacked to beat hell, they say."

"Be goddamned!" Bart breathed. His eyes were gleaming. "Hey, Carl, speakin' o' whorehouses—when we gonna pull that little job?"

Carl shot him a quick look and tried to suppress a grin. "What job?"

"You know the job, you bastard! You're gonna deputize me, and we're goin' down to Caxton and bust Madam Angel's house, and take our pick."

Carl shook with silent laughter. "I was only kiddin', fella. I can't deputize you, I'm only a deputy myself."

"You chicken, you said we'd do it one o' these days."

"One o' these days, yeah. Someday when I'm off duty, drunk, and in the mood to lose my job. Right now I'm supposed to be *on* duty, sober, and out lookin' for a rose-colored Porsche with leopard-skin upholstery."

"How long's it been missing?"

"Don't know. Emmons came home from a business trip last night and found it gone."

"Hell, whoever took it's probably in L.A. by now."

"Or God knows where. But I'm supposed to be out lookin' for the damn thing, so . . ." Carl finished his coffee and got to his feet. "Want to drive around awhile?"

"No, thanks. I got to pull my tractor engine apart and find an oil leak, and get the damn thing back together again." Bart walked with the visitor out to his car.

"If it ain't one thing it's another, eh?" The deputy got into his car and cranked it up. "By the way, where'd you say Meg was?"

"Up on the Cutler place, by the river, paintin' some dumb oak tree. Why?"

"I'll be cruising up that way. Maybe I'll stop by and say hello."

"Never mind hello. Just tell her to get her sweet ass home in time to cook supper."

The deputy gunned his engine. "Thanks for the coffee," he called. "And keep your eyes peeled for a rose-colored Porsche, will you?" He waved to Bart and pulled out.

Bart watched until the car turned right up County 15, then went back into the house.

6

She pulled gently at her hand. He looked down at it, still holding on, gazed for a moment at her gold wedding band, and let go. They walked back along the road together, toward the clearing.

"Are you going to tell me what happened?" Meg asked.

"Oh, uh . . . sure." He kicked playfully at small pebbles on the roadway. "But it's hard to talk to somebody whose name I don't know."

"It's Meg. Meg Hannah."

"Meg . . . Meg . . ." He tested the sound of it. "Is that short for Margaret?"

She nodded.

"I like it," he announced. "It fits you. Nice and warm. Not flashy, but not drab, either. Sort of . . . comfortable."

"Thank you."

"You live around here, Meg?"

"We have a little ranch about fifteen miles back, my husband and I. It's the first place you come to after you turn off the state highway."

"Kids?"

She shook her head. After a moment she glanced at him. "What about you?"

He took a long breath, as if pondering a problem. "The name's Lonnie Hayward. I live over in Mayfield—used to, anyway. Right now I don't much live anyplace. I'm on my way to . . . to somewhere else."

Meg gave him a quizzical look. "That's a little vague."

He grinned. "I know."

They stood again in the clearing, near the spot where the car had plunged into the brush.

"Come on, now," Meg said. "Tell me what happened here."

Lonnie Hayward laughed softly. "That Porsche—it's a heck of a car, but you know, it's got one serious engineering flaw. When it runs out of gas, it won't go anymore."

Meg gaped at him. "You ran out of gas," she said. "Does that mean you have to go careening off into the woods?"

He shrugged. "Didn't want to cause a traffic hazard on the road."

"There's plenty of room here in the clearing. Besides, that road's practically deserted this time of year. There are no houses up the canyon, except a few summer vacation places around Cedar Lake."

"I know about Cedar Lake," he said. "My uncle owns a house up there. Fact is, that's where I was headed." He reached out and touched Meg lightly on the arm. "Say, you're not going up that way, by any chance, are you, Meg?"

" 'Fraid not."

"Okay. Just thought I'd ask."

"Well, I'm certainly not going to leave you stranded here." She put a finger to her lips and frowned thoughtfully. "Let's see, how shall we handle this? I could drive you back to the Cutler place, and you could phone for help—" A new idea struck her. "Wait, I know! I'll phone Bart. He has a tractor, and he'll—"

"Bart?"

"My husband. I'll see if he won't bring his tractor and pull your car—"

He put up his hand and brought her thoughts to a stop. "Wait, Meg, wait. I just thought maybe, if you were on your way up the canyon, I'd ask you for a ride. That's all. Nothing else."

She stared at him. "Don't you want to get the car pulled out of the brush?"

"No. I mean, not yet. First I've got to . . . well, I can't explain it to you now. Not just standing here like this." He glanced at her with a sudden smile. "And, anyway, two can play at this curiosity game. What the heck are *you* doing here?"

"I was on my way up the path over there." She pointed across the road. "Just over that ridge there's a big old oak tree. I'm painting it."

45

His face lit up. "Painting? Do you paint?"

"Yes. A little."

"Hey, that's great! I've always been interested in art, but I've never met a real live professional before."

She smiled, faintly embarrassed. "I'm not really professional."

"Could I watch you work?" he asked eagerly, then answered his own question. "Naw—artists don't like to be watched while they work."

"If you never met one, how do you know *that?*"

"You mean . . . I could?"

"Sure. I'm flattered out of my mind when anybody's even a little bit interested."

"You're kidding. How could anybody not be interested?"

She laughed quietly and made no attempt to explain. They walked over to Meg's truck.

"Nice lookin' buggy," Lonnie said.

"Now *you're* kidding," Meg said. "It's homely as sin—but it's mine."

"Runs nice, though. I heard it purring up the grade."

Meg thought of something puzzling. "Hey . . . where were you when I drove up?"

"By the river. Upstream a little way."

"Doing what?"

"Sitting on a rock. Chewing on a piece of grass. Counting the trout jumps. Watching a red-tailed hawk circle over the river. Wondering what he was doing there—red-tails don't usually *fish.* Wondering what *I* was doing there." He glanced at Meg with what she thought was a touch of shyness. "I guess what I was really doing was waiting for you to come along."

She dismissed this with a quiet smile and began to reach into the flatbed of the truck. "Well . . . what *I'm* supposed to be doing is getting my paint things set up."

"Let me help you." There was a boyish eagerness in his offer.

"Thank you."

Suddenly he stared at the sky and lifted his binoculars. "Look! There he is again. See?"

Meg followed his gaze upward to a large broad-winged bird turning effortlessly on the air currents high over the canyon floor.

46

Lonnie trained his binoculars on him. "What a beauty! A young one, but fully grown." He took off the glasses and thrust them into Meg's hands, his eyes shining with excitement. "Take a look, Meg. Just *look* at him. He's really a beaut."

Meg put the binoculars to her eyes without much interest, wanting to be polite. "I don't see anything," she said.

"You have to adjust them to your eyes," Lonnie said. He put his hand over hers and guided her fingers. "Adjust them here . . . and here."

Then she uttered a small gasp and went rigid. Without warning the insignificant speck of life in the sky loomed in her vision larger than life—a great fierce predator, gliding silently just beyond reach, his hooked beak cutting the air like the prow of a pirate ship, his cold eye seeming to stare directly at Meg.

"Oh, my gosh!" She held her breath, transfixed. "What kind of a bird did you say that was?"

"Red-tailed hawk. See the reddish color on his tail?"

"No. Just looks beige to me."

"Wait till he turns at an angle, so you can see the *top* of his tail."

As she held the glasses to her eyes he stood close beside her, watching for her reaction. It came in a few seconds.

"Oh-h-h-h! Yes, I saw it!" After a moment she lowered the glasses and gave Lonnie an astonished look. "His tail really *is* red!"

He laughed. "I know."

She put the glasses back to her eyes and continued to watch the circling bird. "There! I saw it again. It's a beautiful shade of . . . almost a rusty rose."

"Uh-oh. There he goes!"

Abruptly the hawk broke out of his leisurely spiraling pattern, elongated his body, and launched himself into a straight glide that carried him down the canyon at high speed. Within a few seconds he was gone. Meg lowered the binoculars.

"He's hunting, you see," Lonnie explained. "Small rodents, rabbits, things like that. He evidently wasn't doing any good here, so he decided to move on. He didn't like *our* presence, besides. And excuse my male chauvinism—I call it a he, but it could just as well be a she." He squinted off into the distance down the canyon where the hawk had disappeared. "Anyway, it's a magnificent creature. One of the most successful, most well-adapted predators in North America."

He turned to Meg, and the light of excitement in his eyes was bright with a strange intensity. "Imagine it if you can, Meg. Just imagine having that kind of . . . *freedom!*"

She stared at him in silence and shook her head, uncomprehending.

He smiled suddenly and shrugged. "Oh, well . . ." The strange light in his eye changed to casual amiability. He took Meg's easel and paints out of the back of the truck. "Lead on, lady."

They crossed the road and went up the path to the crest of the low ridge, then down the other side, and shortly arrived at the secluded hollow where the great oak tree stood. Following Meg's directions, Lonnie set up the easel, fumbling with the screws and joints and laboring mightily, but insisting on doing it himself. Then he backed off and appraised the big oak tree before them.

"That's a superb white oak. One of the finest I've seen."

"I thought it was called live oak."

Lonnie chuckled. "Westerners mostly call all oaks live oak. This happens to be a California white oak. And a beautiful specimen it is."

"My goodness, Lonnie, you know so *much!*"

"Naw." He grinned. "I'm just showing off my smattering of ignorance for you."

She put her canvas in place, unfolded a tiny portable stool she had brought along, and opened her paints. The light was not yet quite right, but no matter—she had an audience; he was eager to see her work; she was eager to show it. She went to work while he examined her canvas intently, squinting and frowning, moving this way and that, studying it from every angle. Finally he nodded, and issued a weighty pronouncement.

"It's good."

She smiled up at him. "How do you know?"

He remained serious. "I don't know how I know, Meg, I just know. I can feel it. Your work has imagination. It has mood, it has sensitivity. Most of all, it has individuality. It's not any old painting, it's *your* painting."

48

"Thank you, sir. I'm deeply flattered."

"Flattery? Not at all. The truth is never flattery."

She mixed her colors and got on with it. He walked around behind her, observing. She became self-conscious, found it difficult to concentrate, but persevered. After a while he knelt on one knee beside her stool and watched while she touched the canvas delicately with the brush.

"Aren't you cluttering up the background a bit? Seems to me you might spoil it with too much detail."

She looked at him with a glint of merriment in her eye. "Ah ha! A brand new art critic is born!"

He brought his eyes away from the canvas to meet hers, and they smiled at each other, very close.

"You're beautiful, Meg," he said suddenly. The quiet voice was almost a whisper.

"So are you." She touched the tip of his nose with her brush. "Except for that funny green spot on your nose. Is that a birthmark, or what?"

He rolled over in a quick backward somersault, as agile as a small boy, and bounded to his feet. "No, by my troth, 'tis no birthmark!" He stood tall and declaimed to the countryside. " 'Tis a *love*mark, as God is my witness! 'Twas put there by a most angelic lady, as a sign by which I know her heart is mine, as mine is hers. 'Twill stay there always, I swear, for never, never will I wash my face again!"

She smiled, watching his antics. "My goodness! You sound like Shakespeare!"

He struck a theatrical pose and stared at the top of the oak tree.

"But soft! What light through yonder window breaks?
It is the east, and Juliet—"

Her delighted laughter rang out. He abruptly collapsed like a rag doll, did another somersault, and her laughter pealed after him. He came up grinning, the spot of green paint miraculously intact on the end of his nose.

"Come here, you idiot," she commanded.

"And why, pray?"

"I want to wipe that paint off."

Gingerly he put a finger to the sticky place on his nose. "Nay. Thou shalt not."

"I'll give you something better than that," she said coaxingly. He stroked his chin thoughtfully. "Careful, Hayward," he muttered. "It could be a trap." He pondered a moment longer, then nodded. "I'll risk it." He scampered forward and knelt beside her.

She wiped the paint from his nose with a cloth, then planted a feather-light kiss on the spot, and smiled into his eyes. "There. See?"

His face turned solemn as he gazed back at her. "It *was* a trap," he murmured. He came closer to her, until his lips were almost touching hers. "I've fallen in love with you, Meg."

She blinked at him in astonishment. "What?!"

"Could you say you love me too?"

She gave him a playful little push. "Go on, now, stop your nonsense. I have work to do."

He leaped to his feet and ran around to the other side, knelt again, and clasped a hand over his heart.

> "*I take thee at thy word,*
> *Call me but love, and I'll be new baptized.*"

She scorned him. "That's ridiculous! We're perfect strangers. I can't call you love—I hardly know you well enough to call you Lonnie."

Again the sudden solemn look, appearing like an unnatural cloud in a clear sky, and the oddly soft voice. "We're not strangers, Meg. I've known you for a long, long time. Longer than I can remember."

She gazed at him with a slight frown, half charmed and half puzzled.

"If only it hadn't taken us so long to find each other," he whispered. "Pray God it's not too late."

They held each other's eyes for a moment in a spell of suspense. Then abruptly Meg pulled back and pointed.

"You go over there and sit quietly, like a good boy, and stop bothering me. Otherwise I'll never get my work done."

He rolled on the ground and moaned, and stared at the sky.

> " 'Tis torture, and not mercy. Heaven is here
> Where Juliet lives, and every cat and dog
> And little mouse, every unworthy thing,
> Lives here in Heaven and may look on her,
> But Romeo may not."

She gave him a severe look. "Control yourself, Romeo. Go on over there and be quiet now."

He crawled on his hands and knees to the spot she had indicated, a few feet away, sat up and locked his hands around his knees and gazed off into the distance.

"Good." She nodded, and resumed her work. After a few minutes she glanced curiously in his direction.

His eyes were still fixed in space. "Am I being quiet enough?"

"Too quiet. You're making me nervous."

He cocked an eye at her. "Can I talk to you, then?"

"Yes. But no Shakespearean recitations, please."

"In that case, ma'am—let me call your attention to one of the world's most interesting birds." He pointed toward the lower part of the sky to the right of and beyond the oak tree. Meg looked in that direction and saw a small bird hovering miraculously in a fixed spot in the air, a hundred feet above the ground, its wings a blur of rapid fluttering.

"Oh!" She reacted with a start of recognition. "I've seen *those* before, around the corral." She reached for Lonnie's binoculars and trained them on the bird. Almost as if on cue it folded its wings and dove, plunging swiftly toward the ground, and disappeared. "Oh, darn!"

"Right about now," Lonnie said, "there's probably one less field mouse in the world."

"What do you call it?" Meg asked.

"The kestrel. Also called the sparrow hawk, by people who don't care about accurate names—there's nothing sparrowlike about *that* bird. What it is, really, is a falcon. A true falcon, a miniature replica of the peregrine."

"The what?"

"The peregrine falcon. The big fierce bird, famous in falconry since ancient times. Unfortunately an endangered species in the U.S. now. Very rare."

"Tell me about it."

51

"Be glad to." He lay back on the grass and told her about it while she worked on her canvas.

"Tell me more," she said then. "Tell me about lots of different kinds of birds."

He laughed with the warm delight that a shared enthusiasm brings, moved closer to her, and launched into a lengthy rambling discourse on the physical and behavioral characteristics of various kinds of birds, common and exotic.

At last she put down her paintbrush and gazed at him, entranced. "It's funny. I've seen birds all my life, of course—I mean, I've been aware of them, more or less. But until today I've never really *seen* them."

"Sure. You've been like most people. Birds are not things you see without effort, the way you see buildings and mountains and billboards. They don't just spread their plumage before you and hold still for your convenience. They have to be looked for— that's part of what makes them interesting."

She picked up her paintbrush again. "Tell me some more," she commanded.

"I'm tired of talking." He lay back on the grass and put his hands behind his head. "You tell *me* some things."

"I don't know anything."

"Tell me about yourself."

"I'm not interesting."

"Careful—you're speaking of the girl I love."

"Now, don't start *that* again." Playfully she pointed her paintbrush at him.

Lonnie came up on an elbow and gazed at her. "Seriously, Meg. Tell me about yourself. I want to know about you."

She sighed. "Oh, all right." She resumed her work and began to talk.

"I was born and raised on a small ranch down near Caxton. Just Mom and Dad and me—no other kids. My dad wanted so much to be a successful rancher. He liked to talk about how he thought it was the noblest of human endeavors to provide foodstuffs for his fellow man. Dad was a smooth talker. I never could figure out whether he was really sincere about all that fellow man stuff or not. But anyway, I guess he wasn't very good at ranching, because we were always kind of hard up, even though everybody seemed to think we had pretty good land.

"Well, I went to Caxton High School, and suffered through four years as a social misfit and permanent wallflower—"

Lonnie snorted. "You, a wallflower?! I don't believe it."

"It's true. I was so horribly shy and backward that when anybody spoke to me I practically curled up and slid through the cracks in the floor. Really, I was a case! But I consoled myself with my painting, and after high school went on to Grange Junior College. I had the idea of switching to a four-year college later, and majoring in art. Then, after my first year at Grange, the ranch went broke, so I left school and got a job, to help out. Soon after that my dad died suddenly, and Mom immediately sold the property and moved to town. I found out then for the first time that she'd always hated the ranch. I'd always thought of Mom as a happy, contented person—it was a big shock to discover how little I had known about her.

"Anyway . . . pretty soon I quit my job and got married, and . . . well, here I am."

She cast a glance at her listener. "You see? I *told* you it wasn't interesting."

"That's because you left out the interesting part," he said.

Her eyes widened in surprise. "What do you mean?"

"Why did you go and get married and bury yourself on yet another ranch, instead of going on with your studies?"

She started to reply, stopped, became hesitant. "Well, that's . . . that's kind of hard to answer, I guess."

"Yeah. The interesting part is always the hard part."

She dabbed absently at her canvas. "There were a couple of reasons. To begin with, when Bart and I were first going together he was an up-and-coming young sales representative for an agricultural-machinery outfit—tractors, and all that. He had visions of being in the West Coast office in San Francisco soon, and naturally I had visions of being in an ideal spot to carry on with my art studies from there. Then, shortly before we were married, he got a chance to buy a choice piece of property at a really good price—and he did an abrupt flip-flop and became a rancher instead."

"That was before you were married, you say—so it wasn't too late."

"Yes, it was. I was mad about the guy, I thought. He could do no wrong, as far as I was—"

Lonnie leaned forward and interrupted. "You were mad about the guy, you *thought?*"

"I mean . . ." Meg's hands fluttered nervously. "I was mad about the guy."

Lonnie lay back on the grass again and closed his eyes. "What was the other reason?"

"Well, that's it. Bart was just . . . somebody superspecial." Meg put down her paintbrush and turned to look at Lonnie, and spoke with a sudden surge of interest in her subject. "You see—I have to go back a ways to explain it—when I was a freshman in high school, Bart was a senior and a big man on campus."

Lonnie chuckled. "Ah!"

"There were two b.m.o.c.'s. Bart, and another boy named Rick Jennings. All through school they had been rivals, but Rick always seemed to be a step ahead. He was number one, Bart was number two. Rick was student-body president, Bart was vice-president. Rick was the star of the football team, Bart was his understudy. All the girls pined for Rick's attention, but if they couldn't get it they were happy to settle for Bart's. Poor little me, I would have swooned dead away if I'd had so much as a glance from either one."

With his eyes still closed Lonnie smiled faintly. "What fools we mortals be," he murmured.

"Lonnie, have you ever been a shy, awkward, tongue-tied freshman girl, sick in love with two senior heroes, neither of whom knew you existed, and unable to decide which was the more wonderful?"

"No, and if I play my cards right I never will be."

"Then you probably can't imagine what it was like for that same girl years later, as an insignificant sales clerk in the local five-and-dime, to find herself the center of attention of *both* those two great heroes."

Lonnie groaned. "God, Meg! What a lurid past you have!"

"Don't laugh. It was pretty heady stuff, believe me. Turned *my* poor head, anyway. First it was Bart. He'd been living with a girl named Rita for a year or so, scandalizing all the old-fashioned local folks. Then Bart and Rita broke up all of a sudden, and Rita promptly married a cousin of Bart's, a fellow who's as unlike Bart as anybody could be. And, strangely enough, Bart did

54

the same thing—that is, he went looking for a girl as unlike Rita as he could find. That was me."

"Let me see if I can guess the rest," Lonnie said. "Rick came around and tried to muscle in. And Bart and Rick fought it out for you, and people came from miles around to witness the titanic battle between the two ferocious—"

Meg laughed and shook her head. "Wrong. Except for the first thing. Rick *did* try to muscle in. Well, gosh, I was so thrilled by all that unexpected attention I was plumb out of my mind for a couple of weeks. But then I came to my senses. I realized it was a game Rick had played for years, just for his own amusement—anything Bart touched, Rick would come and take it away from him. Rick came home on summer vacation from college, found Bart spending time with a lowly salesgirl, and figured it was just another round of the same old game. Right away he tried to move in on me, just to beat Bart out."

"Wait," Lonnie said. "*Now* I can guess the rest. You felt sorry for poor Bart, because Rick had always beaten him at everything. So you married Bart just to put Rick in his place for once."

The glint of sly amusement in his eyes brought no response in kind from Meg. Her face remained grave.

"That's not true," she said very quietly. "You see, Bart was not playing around. He was serious. He really wanted to marry me and settle down." She seemed to become distressed, picking nervously at her nails, and searching for the right words. "He was . . . he was very *nice* to me. In those days."

Quickly she picked up her brush and started to paint again, stuck her brush into the wrong paint, and made a grimace of annoyance. "Darn!"

"Meanwhile, your art studies—down the drain. Too bad." Lonnie shook his head glumly.

Meg busied herself cleaning her brush. There was an angry frown on her face. "Well . . . I don't see why I should be telling you all this, anyway. It's really none of your—" She stopped.

Lonnie got up and went to her, and knelt on the ground beside her little stool. "Business." He finished the sentence for her.

She ignored him.

"I'm sorry, Meg."

"What are you sorry about?"

"I got you started on a subject that upsets you. And I'm sorry. I don't want you to be upset."

She made no response. The frown remained in place.

"I didn't mean to pry into your private life. I was just interested in the question of your development as an artist, and I guess you just . . . overreacted a little."

She gave him a sharp look and resumed painting.

"Don't be angry, Meg."

Still no response.

"If you don't forgive me I'll go jump in the river and drown myself."

She turned her dark eyes squarely on him and said, "Now, *that* would be overreacting."

Instantly they were laughing together, the laughter quickly degenerating into childish giggles, and in the momentum of this sudden burst of good humor he leaned forward and put his arm around her. "You're so nice, Meg. I think you're the most—"

"Ah-ah-ah!" She waggled a warning finger at him.

He withdrew his arm and sat back on his haunches. "Okay. I promise I won't tell you how serenely lovely I think you are, how it makes my heart ache just to look at you, how I'm overwhelmed by thoughts that until now I'd have considered unbelievably corny—like how I knew the first instant I saw you that you were the very girl I've been dreaming about since I've been old enough to think about girls—no, Meg, I won't tell you any of that stuff. I promise."

"Good," she said primly. "See that you don't. Because I'm a married woman."

"Yes, ma'am, I know that."

"And I don't fool around."

"No, ma'am!"

"Especially with crazy guys who recite Shakespeare at odd moments and babble about birds and drive cars off the road for no good reason."

"I don't blame you."

She fixed him with a stern school-teacherish look. "And, furthermore, the morning is almost gone, and I haven't accomplished a thing!"

"Want me to leave?"

The stern look faded. "No. I want you to sit here while I work, and tell me your life story."

He made a face. "God! How boring!"

"I told you mine."

"Well, if you insist." He stifled a yawn and gazed off into space. "But first I must have a nap," he announced. "Suddenly I'm overcome with an irresistible drowsiness."

"Fine. Now maybe I can get something done."

He got to his feet and went to a small tree close by, and stretched out on his back in the shade beneath it. He raised his head and cocked an eye at Meg. "You can work in blessed silence for a while. And when I wake up I'll amuse you with carefully selected autobiographical anecdotes, mainly droll in nature, which I'll make up as I go along."

She smiled at him and turned to her canvas.

After twenty minutes, hearing no sound from him, she looked around and saw that he was indeed fast asleep. She put her brush down and tiptoed quietly to where he was, and stood looking down at him. He was flat on his back, arms and legs spread out in total relaxation. In the tranquillity of sleep his boyish face seemed like the face of a child. An unruly lock of blond hair fell over one eye. Meg bent down and extended her hand, meaning to push the hair back, then hesitated, and withdrew her hand without touching him. She gazed intently at his face for a long quiet moment.

"Crazy man," she whispered.

She tiptoed back to her easel and went on with her work.

7

Bart had another straight shot of whiskey with a second cup of coffee, then fixed himself a large breakfast of ham and eggs. After that he checked the weekly TV guide to see if there were any good games on that day. Nothing. He went out the back door, glanced briefly at the sky to check the weather, then went on to his toolshed next to the garage, where his big silent ailing tractor stood. For a moment he scowled at the mechanized monster. Then he picked up a wrench and went to work. A long time later the tractor parts were strewn on the toolshed floor, and Bart was covered with grease and sweat. Time for a break. He put down his tools, wiped his face and hands with a rag, and returned to the house. After a quick trip to the bathroom he went to the kitchen and took a can of beer out of the refrigerator. As he pulled it open the telephone rang. He strolled to the phone alcove, slumped into the little chair there, and took a long slow pull on his beer before he picked up the phone.

"Hello?"

Rita's voice came to him, soft and husky. "How you doing, big fella?"

Bart relaxed with a grin. "Hi ya, sexpot. How's the girl?"

"Barely alive. Herbie's still out like a light."

"Herb's gettin' to be a late sleeper in his old age."

"Not really. But last night was a big night."

"Hmph! I didn't think it was so damn big."

"I mean after we got home. The dear boy was hornier than I've seen him since we got married. Practically tearing my clothes off before we got in the house. By the time he was through with me I was black and blue, and begging for more."

"Aw, cut the crap, Rita."

"No kidding, it was really—"

"I don't want to hear about your goddam love life."

The throaty laugh. "What's the matter, big fella? Jealous?"

"Hell, yes, I'm jealous."

"Aw-w-w! Isn't little Meggie taking care of you, sweetie?" Suppressed amusement quivered in Rita's voice.

"Listen, I get what I want, when I want it. Trouble is, she makes me so damn mad, half the time it's no fun."

"That's what you get for having such a foul temper."

Bart squirmed in irritation. "Look, I wake up this morning thinking, okay, I'm gonna talk to Meg real nice. Patch things up. But you know what the first sound is I hear? That goddam tin Lizzie truck of hers, rattlin' off up the road."

Rita laughed again. "Good heavens! Where's she gone to?"

"Where d'ya think? Up the canyon, to paint that damn oak tree of the Cutlers'. She's making a lifetime project out o' that stupid thing. I swear to Christ, Rita, you don't know what I have to put up with around here."

"Aw-w-w! Poor baby!"

"Damn right. I deserve a little sympathy."

"How long do you think she'll be out today?"

"Oh, hell, she won't be home until dark, you can bet your life."

There was a moment of silence.

"No kidding?" Rita said.

"Listen, Rita, I wanted to tell you—I'm sorry about last night."

"What do you mean?"

"About all that business I started and couldn't finish."

"You're not remembering right, sweetie. *I'm* the one who started it. And it wasn't your fault we couldn't finish. Meg was the monkey wrench."

"The silly bitch."

"Hey . . . you didn't beat up on her, did you?"

Bart expelled his breath in exasperation. "Stop worrying about Meg. You're not her mother."

"Well, *did* you?"

"Hell, no! I told you, I've never laid a hand on Meg."

"You better not, you bastard."

"Listen, don't ask me that dumb question again. I'm tired of it."

"Well, I worry about little Meggie. She seems so . . . helpless, sort of. Herbie worries about her, too, I can tell you."

"Is Herb sore about last night?"

"Christ, no, are you kidding? Herb's the realist in the crowd. He knows he could no more have Meg than he could fly to the moon."

"No, I mean . . . about you and me playing around."

"Does Herb mind about you and me playing around? I'll tell you the truth, sweetie, I wish to hell I could answer yes to that. Actually, he can't get over thinking of me as basically your property. He's just grateful to have your permission to set up housekeeping with me."

"Yeah." Bart sounded glum. "I sure fixed Herb up good when I introduced him to you. Wish I could fix myself up that well."

"Hey, big fella . . . you're really going to be home all day by yourself, huh?"

Bart sighed forlornly. "Looks like it."

There was another short silence. Rita's voice came back lower, and huskier.

"Well, look, why don't I, uh . . . see if I can get away for a little while this afternoon? Maybe come over and see you?"

"Hey . . . !" Bart breathed. "That's a hell of an idea!"

"It'll take some doing. I'm supposed to be working in the church raffle this afternoon."

Bart groaned.

"But listen, I'll, uh . . . I'll work on it. Maybe I can figure out something."

Bart took a swig of beer. "You can do it, Rita. You can figure out anything you put your mind to. I always did say you were damned smart, for a female."

"You do say the sweetest things, Bart." Rita's voice was laced with acid.

"So get to work on it, huh? Don't fool around."

"Okay." Rita sighed. "Sometimes I think I tend to bite off more than I can chew—"

"Aw, hell, Rita, you're so damn *much* woman—you could take care of Herb and me both and have plenty of energy left over for church raffles."

"Well, I'll see what I can do."

"Early, okay? Don't make it too late."

"You just hang loose, sweetie. And don't keep a hard on waiting for me, because I can't promise anything, understand?"

Bart chuckled. "Is it all right if I just keep my fingers crossed?"

"Listen, I gotta go now, Herbie's stirring around. See you later." She hung up.

Bart slapped the phone back in its cradle and grinned at it. "You sweet little slut, you," he murmured.

He finished off the beer and tossed the can into a wastebasket. Then he went back outside and attacked his tractor again with a burst of new vigor.

8

For a long time Meg had worked steadily, frowning at the sticky paint with fierce determination, willing it to take on shape, pattern and purpose, and in the course of her labors had reached a level of concentration that shut out the awareness of all things except the slowly evolving creation on the canvas before her.

Then abruptly she stopped, closed her eyes for a moment, sagged in weariness on the little stool, and allowed the tense muscles of her arms and back to rest. She turned to look toward the place where Lonnie had gone to sleep, and was startled to see that he was sitting up, leaning against the trunk of the tree and watching her.

"Hello!" she called. "Have a nice nap?"

He got slowly to his feet and came toward her, and stood behind her, examining the painting. He nodded approval. "That's great, Meg. I see you work much better when left alone."

Meg leaned back and surveyed her work, and pursed her lips. "I'm not quite satisfied with it. It's too bright. I think I'll darken the green tones down a bit."

"Well, okay. That's fine. A real artist probably never should be quite satisfied. But it's good, Meg, it works. You've created something more than just the likeness of a tree in a field. You've captured a mood."

"I have? What mood?"

He squatted beside her and gazed at the painting with half closed eyes. "Peacefulness. The tranquillity of nature undisturbed. A kind of fragile dreaminess . . . a remembrance of some lazy summer day in childhood, long ago."

She was charmed. "Really? That's nice."

He was surprised. "You mean you didn't know that? You're the one who did it!"

"Tell you a little secret—half the time I don't really know what I'm doing. A lot of it is just blind groping. And some of my best things are sort of . . . accidental, more or less."

He smiled. "Admirable of you to admit it. But it's a measure of your talent that you can turn out something of value anyway, even if you *are* groping. You're good, Meg, and that's a fact. You have a marvelous gift."

"Thank you, sir."

He stood up and went to where his binoculars were lying on the ground, picked them up and slung them over his shoulder. He turned and gazed down at Meg, and his eyes were solemn. "You keep it up, you hear? Keep working. Keep trying. Keep on being just a little dissatisfied. And one way or another you'll get there, Meg, even without the advanced training. Someday you'll be a famous artist. I predict it."

He raised a hand and gave her a quick little wave. "And now, kind friend—adieu."

She stared at him in alarm. "What?!"

"As the old song says, I can no longer stay with you."

"Why not?"

"I've got to move. It's sheer madness that I've lingered here this long."

She was up and standing before him, her eyes pleading. "Ah, don't go, Lonnie. I've got stuff for lunch in the truck. We could have a picnic."

His faint smile spoke wistfulness. "I'd like that, Meg. But . . . there's no time. I've got to go now, this minute."

"Go where? For heaven's sake, what's the hurry all of a sudden?"

"Want to get up to my uncle's cabin at Cedar Lake before nightfall. It's a ways off. Got to get moving."

"But you promised to tell me about yourself."

"There's no more time, Meg. Sorry."

"Well. You mean this is . . . goodbye? Just like that?"

He searched her eyes with earnestness. "Ah, Meg, I'd be the happiest man in the world if you'd come fly away with me. Maybe if I switched from Shakespeare to Marlowe—"

He caught her hand suddenly.

> "*Come live with me and be my love,*
> *And we will all the pleasures prove . . .*"

He broke off with a soft laugh and dropped her hand. "But you probably wouldn't go for that, would you?"

"No, I'm afraid not."

"Thought not. So . . . I guess it's goodbye, then."

She fixed him with a frown, and a glint of disapproval in her eye. "You know something, Lonnie? You really don't make a lot of sense. You're going to leave your uncle's car stuck in the brush down there, do absolutely nothing about it, and go ambling on your way!"

He was unperturbed. "Don't worry about the car, Meg. It's unimportant. And look, do me a favor, will you? Don't tell anybody you saw me." He took her hand again and held it for a moment, and gave it a gentle squeeze. "So, adieu, kind friend. And somewhere along the way I'll hang my heart for you on a weeping-willow tree."

He turned and started up the path, and she watched until he reached the crest of the low ridge and began to drop out of sight down the other side, then ran after him. At the top of the ridge she stopped and called.

"Lonnie? Wait a minute."

He looked back at her and waited.

"You're not . . . you can't just . . ." Her hands fluttered toward him in a gesture of frustration. "What makes you so *crazy?*"

He took a few steps back toward her, and when he spoke his voice was somber.

"I waited a long time for you, Meg. I knew I'd find you, sooner or later. But I didn't know you'd go and get yourself married to some guy named Bart before we ever had a chance to meet. That was foolish of you, you know? I wish you hadn't done that."

He came a little closer, his eyes riveted on hers. "Why did you do it, Meg? You can't be in love with a guy named Bart. Didn't you know I was out there somewhere, wandering around looking for you? Didn't you think—or hope—that someday, somehow, we'd find each other?"

She shook her head, in a daze. "Well, I'm . . . I'm sorry. But is that any reason to run off like this?"

His gaze wandered up toward the high canyon walls in the distance.

64

*"Night's candles are burnt out, and jocund day
Stands tiptoe on the misty mountaintop—"*

"Oh, Lonnie, for heaven's sake, will you *stop* that?!"
He looked at her with eyes that burned intensely. His voice
dropped to an almost inaudible level.

"I must be gone and live, or stay and die."

Abruptly he turned and walked rapidly away from her. When
he reached the road he continued without pause, going up toward the distant pine and cedar forests of the high altitudes. He
did not look back.

Meg stood motionless and watched him until he was out of
sight, and continued to stand on the path for a full minute, staring at the empty roadway. Then she turned and walked very
slowly, eyes on the ground, back to her easel, and sat down on
the little stool in front of it. She gazed vacantly at her painting.
Keep working, he had said. Keep trying. Keep on being just a
little dissatisfied. She picked up her brush, freshened the paint,
and began to apply light touches to the canvas. After a few moments she paused and cocked her head to one side, as if listening. The voice she heard was gossamer, as disembodied as the
whispering movement of the soft breeze through the leaves of
the great oak tree.

Heaven is here where Juliet lives . . .

It drifted by, and was gone again. She tried to continue working, stopped again in a little while, sighed, and let her brush
hang limply at her side. She allowed her tired eyes to drift away
from the painting and off across the treetops into the restful
blue distance. The phantom voice caressed her ear again.

Call me but love, and I'll be new baptized.

It seemed impossible to work any longer. She put her brush
down.
A shadow moved in eerie silence across the sunlit ground at

65

her feet. She looked up quickly, startled. The red-tailed hawk was there, banking steeply against the bright sky. Hanging there, broadside, he seemed to hold Meg for an instant in his cold eye—then he wheeled and beat his powerful wings toward the rock cliffs on the far side of the canyon.

Night's candles are burnt out . . .

Meg was gripped in a sudden inexplicable chill. "There's no time," she said, in a whisper.

She put her hand to her mouth and gnawed fretfully at a knuckle, and shivered in the hot midday sun.

What is it, what *is* it? she thought.

I must be gone and live, or stay and die.

Without any kind of conscious decision she began to put away her paints. Then she lifted her canvas, holding it away from her to avoid smearing, and gathered up the paints and the little stool and the easel and started awkwardly up the path toward the road. With each step she felt an urge to haste that rose and swelled within her and threatened to burst out in an unreasoning panic. In vain she tried to suppress it. She walked faster, faster still, then gave in and allowed the mysterious urgency to overwhelm all control and sweep her away. She ran— wildly, recklessly, almost fell on the rocky path, ran on all the way to the truck, with the ungainly easel banging painfully against her legs. With a determined effort to be careful she put away the canvas, then flung the other things helter-skelter into the flatbed. She was panting; she leaned against the side of the truck for a moment to catch her breath, then got into the cab and started the engine. It coughed and sputtered and protested, but after a few seconds settled down to a steady obedient chugging, ready to go.

Meg pulled her vehicle out onto the blacktop and turned it to the right, and began the long climb toward the mountains.

9

A little past noon Bart got the greasy parts of his tractor back together again and drove the big machine rumbling and clanking out onto an empty field east of the house, for a trial run. Once across the width of the field, which was bordered on the opposite side by the county highway, and back, and Bart was perspiring under the bright midday sun, though the air of early spring remained sharp and cool. After completing one round trip he stopped and climbed off the tractor and made some fine adjustments, climbed back on and headed across the field again. At the far side he made a right turn along the edge of the field parallel to the road. Then, squinting into the distance, he brought his ponderous iron monster to a stop and sat waiting, with the engine idling.

Carl Gallagher's patrol car approached down the blacktop highway and glided to a stop opposite Bart. "Hey, I see you got her running," Carl said. He had to raise his voice over the noise of the tractor.

Bart nodded. "You just back from the Cutlers'?"

"Turn that damn thing off," Carl yelled. "Can't hear a word you're sayin'." He parked the patrol car off the road, got out, and crossed to Bart's side.

Bart killed the tractor engine and climbed down, and walked over to the fence. "You just back from the Cutlers'?"

"Yep. Didn't get a chance to see Meg, though. They said the place where she's painting is on up the county road about another mile above their turnoff."

"That's right."

"I didn't get up that far."

"Why not? Thought you were supposed to be patrolling."

"Well, the Cutlers insisted on me having Sunday brunch with

'em. I was just goin' to have a cup of coffee, but then this sexy Mexican gal that does their cookin' brings in a plate of hot blueberry muffins." Carl grinned. "You know how *that* is."

Bart grinned back. "How what is? Blueberry muffins, or sexy Mexican broads?"

"Both. This gal—Melita, or somethin' like that—starts in tellin' me about how her boyfriend keeps roughin' her up, and what should she do about it. Mrs. Cutler shoos her back to the kitchen, says stop botherin' the sheriff, he's got more important things on his mind. I say yes, right now I'm in the middle of crackin' an international spy ring. But you know me—soon's I get time I'll go back and straighten out Melita's love life."

"Bet you will." A deep earthy chuckle rumbled up from within Bart. "You need any help, just let me know."

A car was coming down the road from the direction of the canyon. The two men suspended their conversation to watch it approach. Bart said, "Ike Peterson. My neighbor, just up the way." As the car went by he and Carl exchanged waves with the driver, then continued to watch until the car was out of sight and the roadway again empty.

"Haven't seen a rose-colored Porsche go by, have you?" Carl said.

Bart chuckled. "Oh, sure. Five or six of 'em."

The deputy sheriff took off his hat and wiped his head with a handkerchief. "Damn, it's beginnin' to warm up, you know it?"

"Come on in for a beer," Bart said.

"Can't do it." Carl patted his belly. "Too many blueberry muffins. Besides, right in the middle of the meal Lieutenant Cole starts squawkin' on the radio. I damn near upset the Cutlers' table, gettin' out to the car to answer. Lieutenant says I should get back on Highway Seventy-eight and stay there. So I had to skedaddle on back. That's why I didn't take the time to run on up and see Meg."

"What's with Highway Seventy-eight?"

"We got some fresh dope on the Emmons case. Old man Emmons called back and said he thinks the car must have been taken by his nephew—young fella by the name of Hayward. He works for Emmons, in fact lives in a garage apartment right on the place. Well, when Emmons came home from his business

68

trip last night and found his nephew and his wife's car both gone, he figured they must be together."

Bart had a puzzled frown on his face. "But you didn't have anything about this nephew in your first report, did you?"

"No, and that's the very question Lieutenant Cole put to Emmons a while ago—how come he didn't mention the nephew in the first place. Emmons said he figured we'd just think it was a family quarrel and not take it seriously if we knew it was his nephew in the car. He wanted to have the kid arrested, scare him a little, teach him a lesson, maybe. Then later on he got to thinkin' that might not be such a hot idea. Hayward's a quiet, moody, temperamental type, he says. Very unpredictable. Has to be handled with care—whatever *that* means."

"Bet your boss was plenty pissed about all that."

Carl laughed. "I can just hear Cole now, rumbling at Emmons, wantin' to know how in thunderation he expects us to locate his car if he deliberately withholds information."

"You say it's the wife's car?"

"Right. She's quite a sex-bomb, they say."

"Yeah, you told me. Used to be an actress, you said."

"Actress is what some people say. Other people say she's an ex-stripper."

Bart produced a low appreciative whistle. "Hey . . . that's even *more* interesting. But what's all that got to do with Highway Seventy-eight?"

Carl pulled a long weed at the roadside and began to chew on it. "Well, Emmons is sayin' he thinks maybe Hayward might head for the coast, and west on Seventy-eight is the only direct route from this area—assuming he came this way."

"Why the coast?"

"Because Hayward's been talking for a long time about gettin' himself a boat and sailin' off to the South Seas or someplace. Emmons thinks he might try to trade the car off for a boat, or some damn fool thing like that. I don't know, it don't make much sense to me."

Bart snorted. "Anyway, it's a dumb idea to think he'd come this way. From Mayfield there's a hell of a lot more direct route to the coast—"

"Yeah, I know that. You know it. Everybody knows it but the

lieutenant. He says for me to get on Seventy-eight and stay there."

Bart's face clouded with a scowl. "That Emmons must have you guys on his private payroll. I can just see you goin' all out like this if I lost *my* car."

"I'm just a peon, Bart. I do what I'm told. More or less." Carl grinned. He threw down the weed, which he had chewed to a pulp, and started back to his car. "Well, guess I'll cruise on out Seventy-eight to the county line and back. Then maybe I'll drop by and take you up on that beer."

"Fine, Carl, but listen, uh . . ."

With his car door open the deputy paused and waited.

"If you notice a dark-green Chevy station wagon parked at the house when you come back by—keep going, okay?"

"Oh. Private business?"

"Right. Private business."

Carl studied Bart's face and read something there. He thought for a moment. "Let's see, now . . . what hot-blooded broad around here drives a dark-green—"

"Never mind, peon. Just do as you're told." Bart smirked at the deputy and gave him a significant wink.

Carl tipped his hat with elaborate courtesy, got into his car and cranked it up. "If she's got a friend," he called, "remember me."

Bart laughed and gave a quick wave as the patrol car moved off, then climbed back onto his tractor.

10

He had covered an incredible distance, it seemed to Meg. After driving for several minutes she began to wonder what had become of him. Could he have gotten a ride with someone else? Unlikely. There had been a few other cars on the road—local canyon residents, mostly, on their way down to the flatlands for shopping or Sunday socializing—but nothing going uphill. Had he left the road altogether, and taken one of the wilderness trails? She leaned over the steering wheel and searched the empty pavement that stretched before the truck, and tried to ignore the irrational feeling of anxiety gnawing at her from within.

Then unexpectedly she saw him. He stepped out from behind a roadside boulder fifty yards ahead and stood watching as she approached. She pulled to a stop beside him, and he stepped up to the window and gazed at her with that strange solemnity she had come to recognize.

He seems to have two faces, she thought. One boyish and playful and lighthearted, the other as somber as a Puritan. Nothing in between.

"Come on, crazy man," she said. "Get in."

He got in, and Meg drove on. They traveled a minute or so in silence. Then he spoke, in his quiet voice.

"So. I don't have to hang my heart on a weeping-willow tree, after all."

Without looking at him she said, "Mr. Hayward, can I just ask you one simple question?" Her voice was sharp.

"As long as you keep it simple. I can't handle complex things."

"Just answer yes or no. Did you *expect* me to come after you?"

He answered without hesitation. "No, Meg, I didn't. I really didn't, and that's the truth." He glanced at her with a small tentative smile. "But . . . I was sure hoping I'd be wrong."

She kept her face stern and her eyes straight ahead. "Is this cabin of your uncle's one of those around Cedar Lake?"

"On beyond there. On a little road that winds up the side of Hale's Peak."

"And you thought you were going to walk there today?!"

"As far as I could get today. The rest of the way tomorrow. Or the day after. Or never. What does it matter . . . ?" His voice trailed off into emptiness.

"And sleep where, in the meantime? On the ground?"

He shrugged, without interest. "I suppose."

"Dressed like *that?!*" Her disapproving glance took in his thin cotton sport shirt. "You know what the temperature is like up here at night? Honestly, Lonnie, you're crazier than I thought!"

He looked at her with meek, mute patience, like a schoolboy taking a reprimand from the teacher.

Meg gripped the steering wheel tighter and kept her eyes resolutely on the road. "Boy, you really take the prize! Spouting Shakespeare, and lecturing on the behavior of birds, and dumping cars off the road and leaving them, and heading for the mountains in your shirtsleeves! I just can't figure you out!"

"Let's not try to figure each other out, Meg. Let's just enjoy each other's company."

"*I'm* not hard to figure out," she said, and that made him laugh.

Then the solemn look returned. "You're angry again," he said. "Don't be angry, Meg."

She glanced at him and saw the gentle pleading in his clear gray eyes. She smiled, without meaning to—she had meant to hold on to her scolding mood a little longer. His somber expression brightened instantly. He smiled back at her and relaxed in his seat, and began to watch the passing scenery.

The road turned upward in earnest, and climbed away from the canyon floor along the steep east wall, and the little river became a sliver of twisted metal foil, far below. On the slopes ahead, among scattered oaks and stands of aspen, a few pine trees signaled the transition to higher altitudes. The air grew sharper, and pungent with the fragrance of distant evergreens.

Suddenly Lonnie leaned forward and pointed. "Hey, look at that!"

Meg caught a glimpse of blue-gray wing movement that streaked across the road ahead and was gone instantly.

"Another red-tail?" Meg asked.

"Not *that one.* Cooper's hawk."

"What's the difference?"

"Plenty. The red-tail's a buteo. Heavy-bodied, broad wings and tail, a high-soaring bird. The Cooper's is what's called an accipiter. Smaller and lighter, short rounded wings. A quick agile flier, darts through the forest faster than you can follow with your eye. I've had a Cooper's hawk zoom over my head so close I felt the fanning of ,his wings. Sounded like a miniature cyclone."

Lonnie squirmed in his seat, becoming animated again with the excitement of his favorite subject.

"We human beings think we're mobile, trudging around on our two feet, sitting inside of machines and moving up and down narrow strips of concrete. We don't know what mobility is. We can't even imagine the meaning of the word 'freedom.' "

"We can fly, though, same as birds," Meg said. "We have airplanes."

Lonnie gave her a pitying look. "When you're in an airplane, Meg, how do you feel? Do you feel *free?* In an airplane I feel more imprisoned than I do anywhere else in the world. Only a submarine could be worse."

Meg smiled and conceded the point. She glanced at her watch. "Hey, it's way past lunch time. Keep your eyes open for a good picnic spot."

Lonnie twisted suddenly to look through the rear window of the truck at the long down-slant of roadway behind them. "There's a car coming," he said. There was a strange low urgency in his voice.

Meg checked her rear-view mirror. "There's a car coming. What about it?" She looked at Lonnie. He was sitting in a half crouch, staring straight ahead. His right hand gripped the door handle, and the knuckles were white with tension.

The large late-model four-door sedan came up behind them, moving fast. At the last second it pulled out to the left and roared past Meg's chugging truck in a rush of chrome and power. In the car was a densely packed group of bright-faced teen-agers, several of whom grinned amiably at Meg and Lonnie as they went past.

Meg smiled. "Kids, going to find some snow to play in." She glanced at Lonnie again, and her smile faded. She returned her eyes to the road.

"Thought you were going to jump out and run for your life," she said.

Lonnie made no comment.

In a moment she said, "Are you watching for a nice place for a picnic?"

He stirred restlessly and fiddled with his binoculars. "Uh, Meg . . . could we just eat while we drive along? Would you mind?"

She frowned at him. "Why are you in such a hurry?"

"Well, it's a long way. And I suppose you'll want to get back before too late."

Meg blinked and stared vacantly ahead. "Yes. Naturally I'll have to get back." Her voice was flat. Without warning she pulled the truck to the side of the road and stopped.

Lonnie looked at her in alarm. "What are you doing?!"

"You drive, and I'll fix the lunch."

He turned and peered again through the back window. "Okay. Quick—coast is clear." He got out and ran around to the driver's side, and Meg slid across the seat. Lonnie studied the controls of the unfamiliar vehicle for a few seconds, then got it under way.

Meg pulled a large brown shopping bag from behind the seat and opened it, and a few minutes later handed Lonnie a sandwich. "Nothing fancy, I'm afraid. Just bread and cheese."

Lonnie smiled his thanks. "Fancy enough for me." He ate ravenously, clutching the sandwich in one hand, steering with the other. Meg fixed a sandwich for herself.

"What did you mean a minute ago—the coast is clear?" she asked suddenly. "Is it against the law to change places?"

He shook his head, smiling. "Speaking of coast—that's where I was heading at first, to the coast. Changed my mind at the last minute, and decided to come up here for a day or two."

"What for?"

74

He studied Meg for a moment, and his face became solemn again, and thoughtful. "Tell me something, Meg. Do you think our lives are governed largely by chance? Or do you believe in fate—predestination, or whatever?"

Meg shrugged. "I don't know. Never thought much about it. Why?"

"It's funny. I knew I wanted to come up here, but for the life of me I couldn't have told you why. *Now* I think I know the reason. It was to meet you."

He looked at her for so long that she shook her head in alarm and said, "Hey, watch the road!"

He obediently turned his eyes forward. "Do you think that's crazy, Meg?"

"You're crazy, all right. I've known that all along."

He laughed and held out his hand for more food. She stared in astonishment—her own sandwich was not yet half eaten.

"When did you eat last, crazy man?"

"Let's see . . . what's today, Sunday? I think it was lunch Saturday."

Meg looked at him quickly, and saw that he was not joking. She prepared another sandwich and handed it to him.

They reached the high plateau of dark-green forest—stately spires of ponderosa pine and Douglas fir through which the road wound like an aimless stream, cutting a narrow canyon—and soon left the county highway to follow an even narrower road that skirted Cedar Lake. Several acres of what in the summer was a sparkling blue sheet of fun and recreation, dotted with small boats and streaked with the contrails of water skiers, now lay steel-gray and forbidding, and ringed with dirty melting snow. Around the deserted lake they went, to the far end, and off the encircling road onto another, still smaller, that led up-hill steeply past a few lake cottages and into the high wilderness flanking Hale's Peak, a bald rounded promontory miles to the southwest. The pavement ended abruptly, signaling the traveler to go no farther except for a serious purpose, and was replaced by a pair of ruts that twisted and turned over exposed roots, rocks and potholes. Lonnie drove with concentration now, communicating expertly with the game little truck, urging it on. Meg

75

held on grimly, wondered how much farther, resolved not to ask.

As if reading her mind, Lonnie glanced at her with a quick smile and said, "Not too much of this. Only about seven miles from the lake to the cabin."

"Seven miles," Meg repeated. She hoped the dismay didn't sound in her voice.

A long time later Lonnie eased the truck to an idling standstill at a hairpin curve. "There it is," he said. He pointed upward through the windshield.

Meg leaned forward and gazed openmouthed at a rustic cabin perched incredibly on the side of a rocky cliff, hanging, it seemed, almost directly above their heads. She leaned back and looked at Lonnie in amazement, and some relief.

"Your uncle really believes in getting away from it all, doesn't he?"

"Actually, no. Hardly ever comes here."

Lonnie put the truck in gear and drove on, very slowly. "Only a hundred feet to go." Soon he turned sharply to the left and maneuvered the vehicle off the road and onto a little bridge of heavy weatherbeaten planks spanning a ten-foot-deep ravine.

As the planking rumbled and creaked under the truck Lonnie smiled and said, "You'll like it up here, Meg. It's very quiet and peaceful."

She was amused. "Funny the way you said that. Anybody would think we were moving in—"

A deep muffled crunching sound rose up as if from within the earth, and burst forth in an agonized screech—the sinews of old wood, tearing asunder. Meg gasped, clutched wildly at Lonnie, and clung to him desperately. Solidity went out from under them, became airy space, and vanished; the world tilted insanely. A violent shudder—the truck was being held and shaken in the jaws of a gigantic and angry beast—then a jarring thud, and all was still again.

Mentally Meg checked her body for injury. She was still in her seat, half sitting, half lying. The hood of the truck slanted insanely upward toward the blue sky shining between the lace-like foliage of pine trees. The engine had quit and left them in eerie silence. Lonnie reached for the ignition switch and shut it off.

Meg continued to hold on to him. "What happened?! Earthquake?"

"The bridge gave way. You all right?"

"I . . . I think so." She looked around anxiously, not daring to move. "Did I scream?"

"Tell you the truth, I don't really know." He reached for the door handle and tested it gingerly. With an effort he disengaged himself from Meg's clutches. "I'll have a look around," he said. "You sit perfectly still. Don't move."

Cautiously he opened the door, stuck his head out, and inspected his immediate surroundings. Moving with delicate care, he climbed out, looked around, inched his way a few feet up along the steeply slanted edge of a shattered bridge beam, returned, and reached into the truck cab toward Meg.

"Okay, give me your hand. Slow and easy, now. Don't make any sudden movements."

They stood on the edge of the ravine and surveyed the damage. The front wheels of the truck were on solid ground, having made the crossing safely. The rear wheels were buried in a jumble of splintered planking. What remained of the bridge tilted at a grotesque angle down toward the right side.

"Those planks *looked* strong enough," Meg said.

Lonnie walked a short distance along the ravine embankment, squatted and peered down at the underside of the bridgeworks. Then he returned and stood beside Meg. "It wasn't the planks. One of the support pilings on the right side buckled. Evidently just snapped in two, like a matchstick."

Meg gazed at him blankly. "What do we do now?"

"Well, we, uh . . ." He turned his eyes up toward the little cabin on the precipitous slope above them. "We go up to the house and make you comfortable. Then we send me back down here to make a study of the engineering problems involved, and to come up with a solution."

He gave Meg a cheerful smile and took her arm. "Don't you worry, I'll get your truck back on the road in no time. I'm sure it isn't damaged." He led her up a narrow winding path that climbed through brush and vines, around tree trunks and rock outcroppings, toward the high cantilevered front porch of the cabin.

"You're lucky, Meg. You're just lucky you're with a fellow who once, when he was about eight years old, spent the better part of a summer making an exhaustive study of the dynamics of bridge design. 'Course, he was working with mud at the time, instead of wood, but that's okay, the principle's the same."

He led her by the hand up the intricate path, turning frequently to look at her. "Don't worry, Meg. Just don't you worry."

"I won't worry, Lonnie, I promise." She laughed lightly, to reassure him, and said, "I believe in you, crazy man."

She was surprised by the lighthearted sound of her own voice, and by the words she heard herself say.

11

In the afternoon Bart put his tractor away and went into the house, pulled off his grimy work clothes, and plunged into a hot shower. A little while later, freshly scrubbed and shaven and wearing only undershorts, he went through the kitchen for another can of beer, went on into the living room and turned on the television set, and slumped in an armchair.

The little screen displayed a commentator interviewing the newly appointed chief of a federal agency. In meticulously enunciated syllables the commentator asked an inane question; the government man replied at length, expanded copiously, digressed freely, exhibited a marvelous mastery of the glib marble-smooth jargon of the professional public figure, and said nothing.

Bart growled a curse, leaned forward and flicked the selector knob, and produced a medium two-shot of Joan Crawford and a tall handsome leading man. Miss Crawford's clothes said 1940s. Her face was tense with emotion. Bart flicked the switch again. *Sports in Review* was presenting an indoor swimming meet. Bart watched the women's hundred-meter free-style event, following with eager eyes the lithe young female bodies as they slid like pretty dolphins through the water. When the announcer urged him to stay tuned for a men's event, to follow right after this message, he switched again. A fervent-voiced evangelist was collecting souls for Jesus. Another flick of the switch. A matronly lady was demonstrating how ridiculously easy it was to bake a prize-winning cake, if you'd only buy her brand of flour, accepting no substitutes. . . .

Bart cursed again and went on around the dial, and stopped again on Joan Crawford. She was in close-up now, and her eyes were brimming with tears. Bart grimaced, leaned back in his chair, put his feet on the coffee table, and resigned himself to watching Joan suffer.

Tires grinding on the gravel driveway outside intruded on the incessant audio drivel of the television. Bart opened his eyes with a start, blinked, and looked around the room. A wildlife documentary was on the little screen before him. Joan Crawford was gone, replaced by a family of hippos wallowing in a muddy African river.

Bart glanced at his watch and scowled. "Goddam!" He slapped the TV set off, got up and half stumbled to the front windows, and peered anxiously out. A slow smile crept over his face. He moved quickly, wide awake now, across the room to the front foyer, listened for the click of high heels on the stoop, then pulled the door open.

Rita put her hands on her hips and laughed loudly when she caught sight of Bart's gaily colored shorts. "My Lord, sweetie, you didn't have to go and get all dressed up, just for me!"

She was wearing tight-fitting black slacks and a thin lime-green shirt, which was pulled up high in front and knotted under her breasts.

Bart held the door open for her. "Jesus, Rita, couldn't you get here any sooner? It's late!"

She came inside, stepped up to him and slipped her arms around his neck. "I'm *here*, big fella. And I brought all my equipment with me. What the hell more do you want?"

His arms went around her. One of his large hands roamed over her bare lower back, the other slipped under the waistband of her slacks.

"What did you do about the church raffle?"

"Sent Herbie to fill in for me. Naturally he grumbled, said he wouldn't do it, but of course you know Mama always has her way. I told him I had some important, uh . . . charity work to do."

Bart chuckled. "This is the right place for *that*. I'm a needy case, if there ever was one. But, Christ, it's so late! Just my god-dam luck for Meg to come home, right when I'm deep in the heart o' Texas."

80

Rita laughed in his ear. "So live dangerously," she murmured. "A little risk only makes it better." She pressed herself close to him, pushing her breasts against his bare chest, and pulling his lips down over hers. When they came up for air she murmured in his ear again. "You know what I told you about what Herbie did to me last night, sweetie? All lies. Wishful thinking. Gross exaggeration, to say the least. Only you can make me beg for more." Her lips nibbled at his earlobe. "Only you."

Bart was breathing hard, but still complaining. "Just wish you'd gotten here earlier."

Rita pulled back to look at him, her green eyes flashing. "Hell's bells, buster, I did the best I could. Do you want it dangerously, or do you want it not at all?"

Both his hands were under her slacks, gripping her buttocks and pulling her hard against him. "I want it without interruption, goddammit."

She pulled his hands out of her clothes and took a step back "Look, why don't you call the Cutlers? Meg's probably sitting in their living room right this minute, having a nice polite chat about the painting, and wondering if the old skinflints are going to spring for a cash purchase."

Bart's eyes lit up. "Hot damn! That's the second great idea you've had today!" He moved immediately toward the telephone alcove.

Rita glided past him into the living room and sat down on the couch, where she could watch him while he phoned.

"You can tell her you hope she's having a nice day," she called to him. "Tell her to enjoy herself, and not to worry about rushing home to fix supper. She'll appreciate your kindness. You give happiness to others, sweetie, and you'll find it brings happiness to you too." She gave him a sweet coquettish smile.

Bart laughed soundlessly as he consulted the phone directory. "You're a whiz, Rita. Sometimes I think you've got a man-sized brain in that gorgeous head." He dialed the number, leaned against the wall with the phone tucked under his chin, and waited.

"Hello, Mrs. Cutler? . . . Hi there, this is Bart Hannah. . . . Bart Hannah. You know, Meg's husband? . . . Yes, ma'am, that's right. . . . Oh, fine, thanks. How are you?" Bart's voice dripped with geniality. "That's good. And Mr. Cutler? . . . Good, glad to hear it. . . . Say, Mrs. Cutler, I was wondering, is Meg there?"

He gripped the phone tensely. His gaze was riveted on Rita as he listened. Suddenly his eyes widened.

"Oh, I see. . . . Well, I guess that means she's still out there, hard at work." He laughed with great good humor. "You know Meg, Mrs. Cutler. She's never satisfied with a painting. She'll stay out there making last-minute touch-ups till it's plumb dark!" He grinned across the room at Rita and winked.

Rita smiled. Her hands went quietly to work, untying the knot in her shirt.

"Yes, ma'am, I know she meant to finish it today. I remember, she told me. . . . Oh, my, yes, she certainly is. *Very* serious. If she says she's gonna finish it today, she's gonna finish it, you can bet. . . ."

The knot was undone. Rita's hands moved up the shirt front, unbuttoning.

"You were gonna do what? . . . Oh, well, gee whiz, Mrs. Cutler, that's real nice of you. . . . Oh, I know Meg would enjoy staying. She doesn't get a chance to have supper out that often. . . . No, no, no, I don't mind, not a bit! I like for Meg to have a good time. She deserves it."

Rita slipped her shirt off and leaned back on the couch. Her great bulbous breasts thrust themselves at Bart, rising and falling. Bart stared at them.

"Listen, uh, Mrs. Cutler. I don't want to keep you . . . you tell Meg when she shows up, uh . . . just tell her I said not to worry about havin' to hurry home, or anything like that. She should relax and enjoy herself. I'll get myself some supper. . . . Oh, no, ma'am, no problem, not at all. She shouldn't give it a thought, tell her. Okay?"

Rita stood up, kicked off her shoes, and began to push her slacks and panties down together, very slowly, giving her hips a languid undulation to help the process. Her smile reached across the room to Bart, her moist red lips blew kisses. Bart squirmed.

"That's fine, Mrs. Cutler. . . . Like I said, it's uh, it's real nice of you. And I hope you like the painting. . . . Well, she's worked real hard on it, I know that. . . . What? . . . Oh, yes, ma'am, I *know* she is, Mrs. Cutler. You're right, I *am* a lucky man. A very, *very* lucky man." His shoulders shook with another silent laugh as he winked at Rita again.

Rita stepped delicately out of her garments and reclined on the couch with a deep voluptuous sigh. She spread her arms alluringly above her head and gazed at Bart.

"All right, Mrs. Cutler, I sure will. . . . Yes, ma'am." A trace of impatience was creeping into Bart's voice. "Thank you. . . . Yes. G'bye."

He hung up, and sat still for a moment, letting his hungry eyes drift slowly up and down the ravishing pink body on the couch. His mouth opened, his lips pulled back, baring his teeth.

"Hot *damn!*" he breathed.

"C'mere, big fella," Rita's husky voice whispered.

He moved like a panther toward her, and left his shorts in the middle of the living room floor.

12

The straight-line distance from the bridge to the front steps of the cliffside house was about a hundred yards, but the serpentine footpath that connected the two points was twice that in length, and consisted of roughly equal parts of horizontal and vertical progression. Meg and Lonnie were flushed with exertion as they climbed the steep steps to the front porch of the house and stood on that windswept platform and looked out over the ocean of evergreen forest below them. Meg's truck was a miniature far below, half hidden under tree foliage. The disks of its headlights stared sightlessly at the sky, like the eyes of a wild creature held in a trap.

Lonnie waved his arm toward the vista before them. "See, Meg? Isn't it beautiful up here? *Isn't* it?"

"Yes, indeed. It certainly is."

"You don't seem very enthusiastic. Where's your artist eye?"

A light gusty wind, unfelt down at the road, was moving unobstructed across that high exposed place and through the treetops, creating the whisper of surf on a distant shore. Meg hugged her arms and shivered slightly.

"It's chilly. I guess I'm not in the mood to appreciate beauty right now."

"Come on. Let's get you inside." Lonnie pulled a large ring of keys out of his pocket, inspected its contents, picked out a key and applied it to the heavy padlock on the front door. A grin creased his face as he pushed the door open and stood aside for Meg to enter. "Come into my parlor, said the spider."

Inside, Meg stood in semidarkness while Lonnie moved about opening drapes and blinds. Then she continued to stand still examining her surroundings.

The interior of the house was relentlessly rustic, its knotty-pine walls and furniture of rattan and redwood displaying an easy comfortable informality. One large, central all-purpose room occupied more than half of the total area of the house. At one end of this room, to the right, a high wall housed an enormous fireplace; at the other end a doorway opened into a compact kitchen. On the far side of the room, opposite the front entrance, a short set of stairs led to an exposed banistered hallway on a split-level elevation, along the far side of which three open doorways revealed a pair of small bedrooms and a bathroom between.

Meg smiled her approval. "Mm-m-m. It's really nice."

"On behalf of Uncle Harry, who spent a mint on this place and practically never uses it, I thank you." Lonnie came and stood beside Meg, and they continued to inspect the room.

"Lacks only two things," Lonnie said. "Books, and art." He smiled at Meg. "Uncle Harry and his bride are not exactly intellectual giants. Nor are they beacons of cultural illumination in this darkling world."

He moved to the front door. "You make yourself comfortable, Meg. I'll go down to the truck and check out the damage. See you later."

Meg walked slowly around the house, looking at everything with a childlike curiosity. The identical bedrooms were almost bare of furnishings except for double beds, which were stripped to the mattresses. Closets in each room were secured by padlocks similar to the one on the front door. The kitchen was a model of compact functional efficiency. The window above the sink displayed a breathtaking panorama of space—the wide forest, rolling in green billows down the mountain slope, and, directly beneath, a nearly perpendicular rock cliff that fell away toward the road, far below. At the rear of the kitchen a small Dutch door looked out on a tiny back-yard area that showed traces of having once been a landscaped garden, now gone to weeds from neglect. Beyond that, a path disappeared into the forest toward the upper reaches of the mountain.

Meg went back to the main room, stood in the center of it and gazed about, and tried to imagine the people who maintained the luxury of this remote mountain retreat and made little use of it. Idly her eye fell on another item, hanging on the wall in a far corner, which had somehow escaped her attention. A telephone. For a full minute she stared at the gleaming black instrument. Then she moved indecisively in that direction, reached for it, hesitated, withdrew her hand, reached for it again and picked it up, and put it to her ear.

Dead silence. It was disconnected.

Quickly she put the phone back on the hook and turned away, went across the room and sat down in a chair near the fireplace, and gazed pensively into its dark cavernous interior.

After a long time Lonnie came back up the path from the road. He was carrying Meg's easel and the nearly completed painting, and was moving with meticulous care to avoid scraping the canvas surface on low hanging branches. When he arrived at the house he looked up and saw Meg sitting at the top of the steps, watching him. He smiled.

"Just saw an acorn woodpecker," he announced, and started up the steps. "Black and white, with a brilliant red crown right on top of the head. Wait'll you see one, Meg. Fantastic."

"What are you going to do with the painting?" Meg asked.

"Thought it would be fun to see how it looks inside, since the place so badly needs a little art." When he reached the porch he leaned the canvas and the easel against the wall of the house.

"Then, too, I figured you wouldn't want to leave it out overnight."

Meg looked up at him, startled. "Overnight?"

"Feel that wind? It's getting cold and damp. And take a look at that cloud creeping in. I got a feeling we're gonna be socked in here."

"Oh, but, Lonnie, listen . . . I've got to get home, you know? I can't just . . ." Meg's hands fluttered nervously.

Lonnie sat down beside her. "Look—might as well be honest about it—the truck's disabled. Rear axle's busted. We can't go to the neighbors for help, there *are* none. We can't call anybody, the phone's not connected. We might try walking down to Cedar Lake, but it's a rugged two-hour hike, and the way this weather's building . . ."

86

Meg stared at him without speaking. He became embarrassed, apologetic.

"Ah, Meg, I feel rotten about this. I owe you a whole string of apologies. You're in some kind of a jam now, and it's my fault. I shouldn't have let you—"

"Nothing's your fault, Lonnie."

"I should never have let you come all the way up here."

"But I wanted to. Really. It was fun."

"And I should have checked that old bridge before trying to cross it. It's been threatening to fall down for years."

Meg laid a soft hand on his arm. "Let me tell you what happened to me a minute ago, Lonnie. I was looking around in the house, and I saw the phone. For some reason it was the last thing I noticed, after I'd looked at everything else. And all of a sudden this strange, awful feeling came over me. Sort of . . . pressure, or tension, or something. I knew I ought to pick up that phone and try to call my husband. And that nice mood I was in before, that feeling of, of . . ."

"Freedom?"

"Well, whatever—a nice feeling. Suddenly it was going to be taken away. That phone seemed to be an evil thing, threatening me. I didn't *want* to use it. Then when I picked it up and discovered it was dead . . . you know how I felt then?"

"How, Meg?"

"I felt good. I felt *relieved.*"

Lonnie beamed at her. "That's wonderful!"

"That's terrible!"

"Yes, it's terrible too. It confirms what I thought. You have a bad marriage."

Meg stiffened and withdrew her hand from his arm. "It doesn't confirm anything of the kind."

"But it shows you've still got a spark of discontent down deep somewhere. As long as you keep that spark of discontent alive you've got a chance of breaking out of your personal prison—"

"Oh, that's nonsense! It just shows I'm an addle-brained idiot who doesn't know her own mind."

"It proves you're happy being with me, Meg, as I am with you. We belong together."

"You're crazy. I'm sorry to keep using that same old word, but everything you say just sounds crazy to me."

"Look at me, Meg." His quiet voice became almost a whisper. "Even though I met you only a few hours ago, I know I love you. There's not the slightest doubt in my mind about it. And that doesn't seem crazy to me at all."

"Why, Lonnie, that's just—" She put her hand over her mouth and giggled like a schoolgirl.

"Crazy," he said.

"Right." Laughter rippled forth, and was suppressed again immediately. "I'm sorry, I wasn't laughing at *you*, Lonnie."

His solemn expression remained unchanged. "And if you could free yourself from those tight blinders you're wearing, you'd see you feel the same way about me. If you didn't you wouldn't be here."

"Lonnie, listen to me." Her hand crept back onto his arm. "I admit I wanted that phone to be dead, so I wouldn't have to use it, though I know it was wicked of me. And I admit I'm enjoying all this. I think it's exciting to be involved in . . . in an adventure. But something's not right about it, Lonnie. And I'm not going to get one bit more involved than I am right now, as long as I don't know exactly what I'm involved *in*." She paused, and again withdrew her hand from his arm. "Or who I'm involved *with*."

"Just me, Meg. It's just you and me now."

She searched his face. "Who *are* you?"

He smiled. "You know me. Crazy man. Remember?"

She would not respond to his smile. "No, I don't know you. I never saw you before in my life until nine o'clock this morning. And so far what I've learned about you is your name, and the fact that you have several peculiarities like spouting Shakespeare and lecturing on birds and running cars off roads—"

"And trucks into ditches."

"What else do I know? I know that when we were driving up the mountain you got terribly nervous every time another vehicle appeared behind us."

"You mean those kids? I always worry about kids in cars."

"It wasn't just them. There were several other cars after that, and you acted the same way every time."

"Well . . ." He shrugged. "These winding mountain roads make me edgy, I guess."

"You're running away from something, Lonnie."

He picked at the sole of his shoe and avoided her gaze.

"What are you running away from?"

He leaned forward, put his elbows on his knees, and stared across the treetops to the far horizon. His face had gone somber. "I think we better make a dash for Cedar Lake," he said.

"Why?"

"It's the only way I know of to get you back to civilization."

"Lonnie?"

"You do want to get back to civilization, don't you, Meg?"

"I suppose so. Eventually."

He kept his eyes straight ahead. "I don't think you ought to stay here tonight."

"Lonnie, listen—"

"They'll be looking for you. They'll be coming here."

"They won't know to come here."

"They'll find the Porsche. They'll put two and two together and figure it out. They'll come after us, Meg."

"We haven't done anything wrong. *Have* we?"

"Come on." He stood up abruptly, still evading her eyes. "I've got to get you down to Cedar Lake, so you can call your husband and be enfolded in your nice, safe, orderly life again."

"It's going to storm. You said so yourself."

"Storm or no storm, it's the only way." He picked up her canvas.

She got to her feet and stood before him, forcing him to look at her. "I don't want to go."

His face went hard. "You've got to."

She took the canvas from him and put it down again. "I won't."

"Things could get nasty, Meg. You might get hurt."

"Why should I? Will *you* hurt me?"

"Of course not! I *love* you."

"Well, I'm going to stay."

"Meg, you . . ." He squirmed with exasperation, and groped for words. "Why are you being so stubborn?"

"You're in trouble, Lonnie. I want to help you. Please?"

He shook his head, unable to answer. Her eyes clung to his, held them tenaciously.

"Please, Lonnie, just let me try, at least. Won't you let me try?"

He nodded weakly. "All right."

"Tell me, then. Tell me everything."

The wind was rising, pushing a bank of sullen clouds across the sky. A sudden gust of icy air rattled the windows of the cabin and whistled around the eaves. Meg shivered. Lonnie picked up the canvas again.

"Let's go in," he said. He took Meg by the arm and led her toward the front door.

13

Daylight faded into a gray dusk.

Rita sat up and switched on the lamp on the end table next to the couch. She glanced at her watch, and a look of alarm swept over her face. She reached for her clothes, gathered them in her arms, and fled down the hall to the bathroom. Bart sniffed, mumbled something unintelligible, and turned heavily onto his side, facing the wall.

Rita was back, fully dressed, in two minutes. She leaned over Bart and shook him. "Come on, fatso, get up. It's so late. . . . God, Herb's going to kill me!"

She hurried across the room to the phone alcove, picked up the phone and dialed a number. While she waited she gazed appraisingly at the thick nude male body on the living-room couch.

Bart rolled over on his back, stretched, and produced a mighty yawn.

"You know, you're putting on a few extra pounds you don't really need, sweetie," Rita said. "Meg's feeding you too well. You better watch it."

Bart slapped his belly and grinned at her. "Hey," he murmured. "Put the phone down and c'mere."

Rita spoke into the phone. "Hello, Herb? Hi, sweetie. I got delayed a bit, but I'll be home in a few minutes, okay? . . . Were you worried about me? . . . No? . . . Not a teeny little bit? . . . Well, thanks a lot. . . . Oh, I stopped by Marcia Dunham's for a while, then we went over to see some friends of hers—you know how it is with us girls. When we get to talking, time doesn't mean a thing. . . . Don't panic, sweetie, you'll get fed, for God's sake. How'd the raffle go?"

Rita listened for a while.

Bart kept grinning at her from across the room. "Give ol' Cuz my regards," he said impishly.

Rita began to look bored. "Okay, Herbie, tell me about it when I get home, huh? I'll be there in fifteen minutes. Okay. 'Bye."

She hung up.

"C'mere, baby," Bart said.

Rita was fuming. "Here I was worrying about Herb worrying about me. Does he give a damn? Hell, no, he's worried about his dinner. Honest to God, you men are all alike."

"C'mere, I said."

"Cut it out, Bart. I've got to go."

Bart scowled. "You're no damn fun anymore. Guess you're not as young as you used to be."

"For Pete's sake, I'm a married woman! I've got to go take care of my responsibilities."

"All right, goddammit. Go, then." He turned on his side again, his back toward her.

Rita went to the front door. She stood holding the doorknob for a moment, gazing at Bart.

"You want to say thanks for the service?"

"Thanks, old lady."

She went out quickly and closed the door behind her with a sharp slap. A few seconds later her station wagon roared away, droned off down the long slope of land, and a silence descended on the Hannah ranch.

Bart lay still for a long time. Finally he got up, moving very slowly, scooped his shorts up off the floor, and headed for the bedroom. In a few minutes he came back up the hall, fully dressed, went into the kitchen and turned on the light. He opened the refrigerator and stared frowning into it, studying its contents.

"Why is there never anything to eat around here?" he grumbled under his breath.

Then the phone rang, its loud jangle startling in the quiet house. Bart grimaced with annoyance and went to answer it.

"Hello?"

"Hi, old buddy."

"Oh, h'lo there, Carl."

"I saw the station wagon when I passed by, so I did like you told me, and kept goin'."

"That's a good fella."

"Business get taken care of okay?"

"You bet your boots. Uh . . . you got a rain check on a free beer."

"Thanks."

"Fact, if you want to come by now, you can get a free ham sandwich to go with it. I'm havin' supper alone tonight."

"Alone? How come?"

"I got softhearted and gave Meg the evening off. You know, you gotta treat 'em nice these days. Domestic help's hard to find." He chuckled.

"Well, thanks anyway," Carl said. "But I'm home now, and Lois is about to feed me fried chicken. I'm fat and happy."

"Okay, another time. How'd it go today?"

"Great. Glad you asked." Carl's voice went low and confidential. "Caught me a criminal. A real baddie."

"Yeah? Who?"

"Teen-age girl, hitchhikin'. A sex-pot like you never saw."

"Be goddamned!"

"Picked her up and gave her a ride. Told her hitchhikin's against the law in this county, and I ought to arrest her."

"Holy shit! She *believe* you?"

"Well . . . she persuaded me not to arrest her, let's put it that way."

Bart cackled with laughter. "You son of a bitch! I *knew* there must be fringe benefits to that sheriff work! Gimme the juicy details."

"Uh . . ." Carl's voice dropped to a whisper. "Tell you later. Know what I mean?"

"Hey, Carl, find out if she's got a girl friend, huh?"

"Still tryin' to get deputized, eh, pal?"

Bart shook with laughter again. "Only tryin' to do my duty as a citizen, to aid and assist law enforcement officers in any way I can—"

"Sure, sure, sure. I'll find out if she's got a friend just as soon as your, uh . . . business associate in the green station wagon comes up with a friend for me."

"You got yourself a deal. By the way, anything new on rose-colored Porsches?"

"Not much. I was talkin' to Lieutenant Cole when I came in a while ago. He said he was tryin' to reach Emmons all afternoon, wanted to pump him for a little more information, if he could. But he hasn't been able to reach the old boy at all. Turns out Emmons took off in his airplane again, without tellin' anybody when he'd be back."

"He flies his own plane?"

"So they say. We're told Mrs. Emmons is out of town, too, visitin' friends in San Francisco. We found out Emmons departed the Mayfield airport for Frisco early this afternoon, so he must have gone to pick wifey up, and I guess tell her the happy news about her car. And right now that's all we know about the whereabouts of any of 'em."

"Hm-m. Funny case." Bart was beginning to grow restless.

"Cole says to hell with it. We're gonna put it on the back burner until something definite develops."

"Hey, listen, Carl, I'm gonna grab a bite to eat, huh? I'm starving."

"Right. I gotta go, anyway. Told Lois I might take her to the evening church service."

"You do that. You need it, you dirty old man."

Carl laughed. "See you later, pal."

Bart fixed himself a massive sandwich, opened a can of beer, and sat down at the little kitchen table. He took a large bite of the sandwich, chewed vigorously, washed it down with a gulp of beer, and paused to produce a deep belch.

"Meg's feedin' me too well," he mumbled, addressing the kitchen floor. "Like hell! I'd starve if I had to depend on her."

He was halfway through his sandwich when the phone rang again.

"That'll be the mouse," he said. He let it ring three times before he got up, and as he went unhurriedly to the telephone alcove he screwed up his face and mimicked Meg's voice: "Hello, Bart? I'm sorry I'm so late. Have you found anything to eat?"

In his own voice he growled, "You dumb broad, you're always

94

late, and you're always sorry. What a drag!" He picked up the phone and answered gruffly, "Hello."

His face registered mild surprise. "Yes?" Instantly his manner became polite. "Oh, hello again, Mrs. Cutler. How's everything? . . . Oh, that's all right, no trouble at all. . . . Uh, no, she's not here yet. When did she leave your place? . . . What's that? . . . You mean she hasn't even *been* there?"

He frowned at the floor as he listened, and shifted the phone from one hand to the other. "Wait a minute, Mrs. Cutler, let me get this straight. You haven't seen Meg today? Not *at all?*" The surprise on his face had deepened into bafflement. "That's funny. That's very funny."

He glanced at the windows in the living room. "Well, hell, I mean—excuse me—it's pitch dark out, she *can't* still be painting. . . . Who did? . . . Mr. Cutler? . . . Did he look around thoroughly? . . . Across the road by the river, too? . . . No sign of her at all, huh?"

Bart's eyes roamed restlessly around the room as he listened. He switched the phone to the other hand again. "Well, I tell you, Mrs. Cutler—my guess is she probably sat there and worked till it was so dark she couldn't tell green paint from red paint. It'd be just like her, y'know. . . . Yes, ma'am, she sure is. . . . Then, since it was so late, she prob'bly just headed for home, instead o' goin' by your place. . . . What time was Mr. Cutler out there?" Bart checked his wristwatch. "Well, yes, it *has* been a long time. . . . That old truck of hers could've acted up, I guess. Or she might have had a flat. . . . Oh, no, that wouldn't be any problem for Meg. She's changed many a flat tire."

Bart took a deep breath, and made a decision. "Tell you what, Mrs. Cutler. I'll hang around a little while, and if she don't show up I'll drive on up there. But I expect she'll come barreling into the driveway any minute now. . . . Yes, ma'am, I'll get back to you later, or Meg will. . . . Fine. Thanks for calling. . . . G'bye."

Bart set the phone gently back on the hook and stood there for a moment, frowning. "Goddam crazy dame!" he muttered. "I'll give it to her good when she gets here." He went back to the kitchen, picked up his half-eaten sandwich and the can of beer and returned to the living room, and set his food on the coffee table. He switched on the television set, flicked the selector knob several notches, and sat down.

Seven-thirty. Time for *You Said a Mouthful,* that fun-filled laughter-packed game show that'll test your IQ while it tickles your funnybone. Watch our contestants match wits with celebrities, folks, and maybe win an all-expenses-paid trip to fabulous Las Vegas. . . .

Bart finished his sandwich and beer while he watched, then got up and went to the kitchen for another beer. He returned to the living-room couch, put his feet up on the coffee table, and tried to relax. After a while, during a commercial break, he got up and went to the front windows and peered out into the darkness. He did not return to his seat when the program resumed, but continued to stand, staring out, seeing nothing but his own reflection in the glass.

"Goddammit, Meg," he whispered. "Where the hell *are* you?"

He stood motionless for several minutes. Then he turned from the window and went down the hall to the bedroom. He opened a closet, groped on a top shelf for a moment, brought down a snubnosed revolver and stuck it inside his shirt. Then he strode rapidly through the house and out the back door, went to the garage and got into his car. The engine exploded into life in a few seconds; the car moved out of the garage and with a screech of tires leaped away, throwing gravel. The tires screamed again at the junction of County 15 as Bart swung to the right without slowing down and pushed the car up the blacktop strip toward Stag River Canyon.

In the living room the fun-filled laughter-packed game show was winding up in a tumultuous orgy of hilarity.

14

The sun hung precariously on the edge of Hale's Peak, flung out spectacular radiations of splendor past a battery of glowering clouds, faded, and sank from view. The interior of the mountain cabin was shrouded in semidarkness, the bright-golden knotty-pine walls rendered gray and gloomy. Around the eaves of the house the wind continued to chase itself in intermittent gusts, giving off a dismal wailing.

Meg sat huddled on the long low couch facing the fireplace and hugged herself, rubbing her arms for warmth. Shortly Lonnie came in through the kitchen, carrying an armload of firewood, and smiled encouragement at her as he went by.

"Sit tight, you'll be warm in a jiffy."

In a few minutes he turned to her again, his face beaming cheeriness and reflecting the light of a crackling fire. "There. That's better, isn't it?"

Meg smiled and nodded, kicked off her shoes and curled herself comfortably on the couch, feet tucked under her. Lonnie stood before her and delivered a brisk little lecture.

"Now, Meg, maybe you're wondering about the necessities of life around here. There's no fuel for the stove, no electricity, no phone, and all that. But never fear, survival is possible. There are stacks of canned goods in a cupboard in the kitchen, and we can heat the cans right here in the fireplace. It won't be a gourmet experience, but it won't be starvation either. There's no bedding or blankets, but there are good sleeping bags, so no problem in the sleeping department. Let's see, what else? Oh, yes, I know what you're thinking—the most critical of all essentials of life is missing. Television. Crippling, I admit, but again I urge you, do not despair. I've heard that certain primitive tribes in the interior of Borneo have been existing for centuries without television and appear to be perfectly healthy and happy. Poor things, they don't know any better. Anyway, your host for the evening is none other than Lonnie Hayward, who, for all his unfortunate tendency to craziness, is a genial and charming fellow nonetheless, and will endeavor without cease to make your visit pleasant, comfortable, and enjoyable. Any questions?"

Meg shook her head gravely.

"All right. So now that necessities are under control, we can turn our attention to aesthetics." He picked up Meg's painting and held it against the wall next to the fireplace, and studied it at arm's length while he held it in place. "Maybe a little more to the left, huh?" He moved it a few inches. "There, that's it. Beautiful. Really dresses up the wall."

He examined the picture in detail, cocking his head from side to side and squinting. "I've said it before, Meg, and I'll say it again—you've got talent. Lots of it. Your work has tone, it has structure. It has—well, what can I call it? Character. It has character."

He lowered the canvas and leaned it against the wall. "So much for praise. Now the criticism." He paced up and down before Meg as he continued.

"Meg, I think your work is too constricted. Too orderly, too well-behaved. Some artists lack discipline—you're overly disciplined. You need to bust loose from your inhibitions, forget about caution, let your imagination run. Stop being timid. Open the doors wide and let something wild and daring come rushing in, something passionate. Develop a love of . . . freedom."

He came and stood in front of the couch, and gazed down at her. "That goes for your life as well as your art, Meg. You could do it if you tried."

She sat up, reached out and touched him on the arm. "Lonnie?"

Instantly he knelt at her feet and beamed at her.

> "She speaks.
> Oh, speak again, bright angel! For thou art
> As glorious to this night, being o'er my head,
> As is a winged messenger of heaven."

She put a finger to his lips. "When are you going to stop talking about *me* and start talking about *you?*"

98

He captured the finger with a deft movement and kissed it. "Oh, 'bout a week from Thursday, if the weather be good."

She retrieved the finger. "Be serious, Lonnie. You're a mystery, and it troubles me. I want to *know* about you, and you promised to tell me."

"Oh, we'll get around to all that trivia later. Right now we're discussing something important—your potential for artistic growth." He came up off the floor and sat beside her. "Now, the question I want to raise is, how does your husband Bart feel about your work?"

Meg shrugged. "I don't know how he feels about it. I guess he thinks it's okay."

Lonnie looked pained. "He thinks it's *okay?* Is that an *opinion?*"

"It's a nice hobby for me, he thinks. Gives me something to do. He doesn't seem to mind it."

"That's nice. He doesn't seem to mind it. Does he encourage you?"

Meg frowned at him. "What are we discussing, my artistic life or my personal life?"

"Both. They're inseparable, you know."

"I don't think so."

"You're not answering the question. Does he encourage you?"

"Well . . . no, not really."

"Has he ever urged you to continue your training? Study with somebody big in the field?"

"How could I, living way out here on a ranch? I'd have to be in San Francisco, or Los Angeles, or someplace like that. I explained all that to you before."

"Yes, I know. Bart made a last-minute decision to be a rancher."

"That's right. And you can't be a rancher in the city."

"No, you sure can't. So . . . that's it. No chance for you."

She said nothing. She had begun to make a minute examination of her fingernails.

"Does that bother you at all, Meg?"

"Well, sure. Sure it bothers me."

"Does it bother Bart?"

"Why should it? He thinks I'm a good enough painter already."

"Is he proud of you, do you think?"

"I don't know. I guess so. We don't really talk much about—"

She pulled up in mid-sentence and gave her questioner a suspicious look. "Lonnie, what are you trying to prove?"

"That you have a bad marriage."

"Isn't that a little silly? Just because my husband doesn't appreciate art?! I don't know anything about *his* work either, even though I was born and raised on a ranch. When Bart and his cousin Herb Duggan sit around talking about their cattle, and the best kinds of grazing grass, and the government's policy on beef prices, I don't understand a word they're saying. Am *I* proud of *him*? I don't know, I never thought about it."

"That's what I said. You have a bad marriage."

She bristled. "You're being very unfair. You're trying to pretend it was Bart's fault that I didn't go back to school. That's not true at all, it's my own fault. He didn't *force* me to marry him. The reason I didn't go back . . . the *real* reason I didn't go back . . ." She faltered.

"Go on, Meg."

"Was because I lost my nerve. I just didn't have the . . . the . . ."

"The guts?"

"Yes. The guts. Even in that dinky little junior college there were people around me who seemed to have so much more to offer than I did—gosh, if I felt inferior in a little pond like that, what would become of me in a *big* pond?"

"Poor Meg. You had everything you needed except one simple ingredient. A little encouragement. What a shame."

She looked away from him. "I don't want to talk about this anymore."

He sighed. "I'm getting you upset again. And I'm sorry again. But I love you, and it makes me unhappy to see *you* unhappy—"

"Suppose you just let me be the judge of my happiness or unhappiness, will you?"

"Sure. You be the judge of it." He got up and started walking aimlessly around the room. "I'm just trying to goad you into *making* a judgment. It won't do me any good if, five years from now, you decide I was right. I'll be long gone. I want a decision by sunup tomorrow."

She gaped at him, astonished. "A decision about what?"

He gave her a long solemn look. "Meg, tomorrow morning either we're going to make our break together or we're going to say goodbye."

"Make our *break?!* Lonnie, you're just . . ." Words failed her.

" 'Crazy' is the good old reliable word, in case you've forgotten it. Listen, Meg, let me tell you what I'm dreaming of. You wanted me to tell you about myself. All right, here's the most important part. I've got my eye on something that's going to spell freedom for me—for *us*, maybe. Something that, next to a bird, is the most free-moving thing in this world. It's a sailboat. A thirty-nine-foot ketch. Trim, beautiful, and brave. Rides the ocean like a feather, without a trace of effort. It's going to be my home, Meg. My boat and I are going to run before the wind and follow the seabirds, all over the world, and be as free as they are."

Meg shook her head in hopeless incredulity. "Ah, Lonnie, Lonnie. 'Crazy' is the word, all right."

"Wait, Meg, I have to tell you about this boat. You see, for the past couple of years I've been going down to Diamond Bay almost every weekend, working in a boat shop, taking sailing lessons, generally learning the seafaring art. I'm just about ready. Then about a year ago I spotted this boat and fell in love. Just as I did with you, Meg—fifteen minutes and I was a goner. It was lying in the marina, neglected and shackled, just begging to be liberated. Owned by some lazy landlubber who didn't know what to do with it. Well, all of a sudden, a miracle—it was up for sale, and the price was ridiculously right. I went that very day and made a down payment, and I've been making monthly payments ever since. Sometimes I go down to the harbor and just sit and look at it, all black and silver and sleek and raging to get loose and leap off toward the horizon. It'll soon be mine, Meg."

He paused and gave Meg an intense look. "Say the word, and it'll be ours."

Meg was staring at him. "What's the name of it?"

"Well, I don't know yet. Maybe I'll call it the *Albatross*. Right now it's lying there all miserable, with a phony name painted on its bow. The *Nellie D*. That's an insult. Who would name a noble thing like that *Nellie?* The first thing I'll do when

I take possession is paint over that obscenity and put a real name on."

"But why the *Albatross?*"

"Because he's such a great flier. The albatrosses knew the world was round a long time before man ever did. For thousands of years they've been sailing around and around the world over the southern ocean. They know they can leave a feeding ground and fly eastward and eventually come back to that same place, and they do it all the time, over and over again. Think of it, Meg! The wandering albatross has a wingspan of eleven feet. *Eleven feet*—can you imagine it? It sails on the west wind, knowing no fear because it has no enemies, feeling no restraints, no self-doubts, encountering no impediment, facing the rising sun and the curve of the sea horizon—the freest, most blessed spirit of all the earth's creatures . . ."

His voice had gone distant and breathless; he stood as if transfixed, gazing at Meg. Slowly he moved back to the couch and sat beside her.

"They're the greatest of the seabirds, Meg, and that's what I admire most in the world—the seabirds. I'm going to go and follow them. And I want you with me."

They sat silent for a moment while her grave eyes studied him. Then she shook her head.

"I don't like albatrosses," she announced.

Lonnie reacted with surprise. "Why not?"

"Because I had to read *The Rime of the Ancient Mariner* in high school, and I hated it."

Lonnie laughed. "Oh, come on! Don't hold it against the poor bird just because Coleridge made up a phony legend about it."

"I don't care, I don't like it," Meg said stubbornly.

"Okay. You name the boat, Meg. What shall it be?"

She pondered. "How about . . . the *Dolphin?*"

Lonnie made a face.

"The *Mermaid?* The *Flying Cloud?* Something like that?"

"Ordinary names for ordinary boats. They wouldn't do for *our* boat."

"Because it has to be a bird, doesn't it? I think you'd turn into a bird if you could."

"They have what I want, Meg. The ability to roam over the surface of the earth at will, and look down in pity on us poor creatures who are chained to the ground in a lock-step regimentation that lasts from birth to death."

"That's a mixed-up view of life, Lonnie. You shouldn't let yourself be envious of inferior creatures."

"Meg! Remember that magnificent red-tail we saw this morning? Could you really look up at a thing like that and feel *superior?*"

"To tell the truth, I felt a little afraid. He looked like a killer."

Lonnie smiled. "He *is* a killer. He can't help that, Meg, that's nature's way. The things to admire are the beauty, the grace, the marvelous mobility of flight. Most of all, the mobility. That's where the seabirds are the champions of the world. Take the arctic tern, for instance. Have you heard about the arctic tern, Meg?"

She permitted herself a soft indulgent smile. "I don't believe so."

"The arctic tern breeds in the Arctic and winters in the Antarctic. That's a bland enough statement, isn't it? Nothing to get excited about, right? But think a minute—do you know what that means? It means ten thousand miles of migration, over open ocean. A round trip is *twenty thousand miles* a year. How's that for mobility? How's that for *freedom?*" Lonnie's eyes shone. "That's what I want, Meg. Nothing else will do."

Meg sighed. "So . . . the boat has to be a bird, then."

"Definitely."

"A seabird?"

"Absolutely."

"Well . . . why not just call it . . . the *Seabird?*"

He gazed at her for a moment without answering. Then he took her hand and held it.

"That's beautiful, Meg. Our boat has a name now. It's called the *Seabird.*"

"Oh, no, it's not *our* boat," she said quickly. "It's *your* boat."

"Come with me, Meg. Just you and I and the *Seabird,* soaring over the ocean—"

"Stop it, Lonnie!" She pulled her hand away from him.

103

"You're not a bird, you're a human being, and you ought to plant your feet on solid ground and face up to reality."

"What's 'reality'? Reality to you may be pure fantasy to me. What most people call reality I find depressing. Just plain *boring.*"

"But you have problems that need to be solved. You can't just run away from problems."

"Why not?"

"Well . . . because."

He shook his head and smiled. "You don't understand, Meg."

"No, I don't. You promised you'd tell me and let me try to help, but you continually change the subject and talk about everything else you can think of, instead."

Lonnie got up and went to the fireplace, shook up the faltering fire, and threw on more wood. He glanced toward the front windows and said, "Look at that weather!"

The wind had ceased, had given up its mournful wailing and wandered off across the unseen mountain ridges. It was replaced by a relentless icy rain that stroked the windowpanes and made a soft caressing sound.

"Are we going to have a discussion about the weather now?" Meg said.

"Absolutely not, Meg. There are more important things to think about, as you have so rightly pointed out. And the most important one of all is . . ." The bright boyish grin suddenly lit up his face. "Supper!"

He danced across the room and disappeared into the kitchen. Meg sighed, got up and followed him, and stood in the doorway while he rummaged on his hands and knees in a far corner, making a fearful clatter, his head inside a low cupboard. From the darkness he called to her.

"Hey, Meg, light up one of those candles for me, will you? Over there, above the sink."

She lit the candle and knelt beside him. His head came out of the cupboard for a moment, and his eyes met hers over the little diamond point of light between them. He smiled.

"Hey, this is fun, isn't it? Aren't you having fun, Meg?"

She returned his smile, then quickly suppressed it and tried to look severe. "Yes, it's fun. But when are you going to start telling me about yourself?"

104

"Pretty soon. Right now you tell me something about *yourself*."

"What?"

"Which do you prefer—chicken and rice, spaghetti, or cornedbeef hash?"

15

Bart's big car roared into the compound of the Cutler ranch house and jerked to a stop, its heavy chassis lurching forward and rocking several times on its soft suspension. By the time it had settled to stillness Bart was out and halfway up the front walk to the house.

The tiny elderly woman stood silhouetted in the doorway, peering out through the screen at the man approaching.

"Is that you, Mr. Hannah?" Her voice was thin and piping, and as frail as her body.

The man bounded up onto the porch and into the light, and his face was so grim that the woman shrank back.

"Yes, ma'am, Mrs. Cutler. Bart Hannah. You folks still haven't heard anything from Meg?"

"Why no, Mr. Hannah, nothin' at all. Like I told you on the phone, we were so lookin' forward to—"

"Can I use your phone, Mrs. Cutler?" Bart opened the screen door without waiting for an answer. The woman stepped back hastily to make way for him.

"Certainly, Mr. Hannah. Just in the dining room, there, in the corner. Melvin, show Mr. Hannah where the phone is."

A thin bony gray-haired man, no larger than the woman, stood in the darkened living room. Behind him, in a corner, a gigantic television console displayed costumed dancers in kaleidoscopic images of red and yellow and orange, and filled the room with bouncy brassy music.

"Why, sure," said Mr. Cutler. He shuffled unhurriedly toward the dining room. "Right this way, Mr. Hannah. Be more than glad to—"

"I can find it, thanks," Bart said. He went past the old man, nodded curtly to him, and continued on through a large double doorway into the dining room.

Mrs. Cutler followed him, and Mr. Cutler came along behind. They found the visitor already dialing the phone.

"I declare, we were so disappointed when Meg didn't come, Mr. Hannah," the woman said. "We had a simply lovely supper—ham and potato salad—I thought Melvin was goin' to make himself sick. Melvin, pull a chair over for Mr. Hannah, so he don't have to stand like that."

Bart stared at Mrs. Cutler while he held the phone to his ear and waited. Mr. Cutler pulled a chair away from the dining-room table and put it next to the visitor. Bart ignored it.

The woman's voice piped on. "My goodness, I sure do hope your Meg ain't had no kind o' trouble, Mr. Hannah. I never did think it was fittin' and proper for a young girl like her to go traipsin' off to all sorts o' lonely places by herself, like she does—"

Bart pressed the phone button down with his finger and muttered, "Damn!"

"Who you callin', Mr. Hannah?" the woman said. "Maybe you don't have the right number. Melvin, bring the phone book—"

"I'm calling home," Bart said. "Thought maybe Meg might've gotten past me some way."

"Well, I declare, I just can't imagine . . . Maybe she decided to do something else today, Mr. Hannah, 'stead o' paintin', like maybe visitin' friends someplace, and forgot to tell you."

Bart's eyes were roaming restlessly around the room. "Say, is that phone book handy? I need it after all."

"Why, yes." The woman looked around, trying to think. "Melvin, where's the phone book?"

"I'll get it," Mr. Cutler said, and shuffled back to the living room.

Mrs. Cutler called after him, "And turn that television down! Me and Mr. Hannah can't hear ourselves think!"

Bart sat down in the chair. Mrs. Cutler came closer and gazed down at him.

"Mr. Hannah, I bet you ain't had a bite o' supper. Can I fix you a plate? Some nice ham and potato salad?"

"No. No thanks, ma'am."

"We had just worlds of it left over. I'd be so happy to fix you a nice—"

"I had supper, ma'am. I'm not hungry."

"Well, maybe a cup o' coffee, then. A cup o' coffee and a nice piece o' cake."

Bart pressed his lips together. He stared in the direction of the living room. "What do you suppose is keepin' Mr. Cutler?" he muttered.

Mrs. Cutler's voice rose to a piercing screech. "Melvin! Where's that phone book, for heaven's sake?"

Melvin reappeared and handed Bart the phone book. "Dang thing dropped down behind the TV set."

Bart flipped furiously through the pages of the directory. Mrs. Cutler stood over him and watched.

"Who you lookin' up, Mr. Hannah? Maybe it's a number I know."

"Carl Gallagher. The deputy sheriff."

"Oh, yes!" Mrs. Cutler beamed. "Sheriff Gallagher was here, just this morning. Such a nice man he is!"

"He'll be off duty now," Mr. Cutler said. "And he lives down around Caxton, I b'lieve."

"That's right," Bart said.

Mr. Cutler frowned. "That'll be a toll call."

Bart found the number and reached for the phone. Between dialings he glanced at the other man. "Don't worry about it, Mr. Cutler. I'll pay."

Mrs. Cutler's hands fluttered in embarrassment. "Oh, well, don't give a thought to *that*, Mr. Hannah. Melvin didn't mean, uh . . . After all, the important thing is to find Mrs. Hannah, isn't it? My goodness! I'd feel just awful if anything happened to that dear sweet girl, right here on *our* property—"

"Hello, Carl?" Bart let out a long breath of relief. "Thank God I caught you. Thought sure you'd gone to church."

Mrs. Cutler sat down at the dining-room table, folded her hands in her lap, and prepared to listen. Mr. Cutler sat down opposite her.

"Yeah, well, listen, Carl, I got two things to tell you. . . . You listening? . . . Come on, cut the horseplay, Carl, this is no joke. Meg's missing. . . . That's right. Missing. She came up

108

here to the Cutler ranch this morning, to paint. . . . Yeah, you knew about that. Right. Well, she never came home. . . . Yeah, I'm at the Cutlers' now. They haven't seen hide nor hair of her. . . . No, nothing. Mr. Cutler was out there earlier, and I've just come back myself, had a good look around. Absolutely nothing. . . . What? . . . Oh, it's an old oak, 'bout a hundred yards off the road. . . . Yeah, yeah, I *know* she shouldn't—we ain't got time to go into *that* now. . . . Wait a minute, listen. Item number two. I found the rose-colored Porsche. . . . Yeah, you heard me right. The Porsche. . . . There's a spot up there where the road dips down close to the river, by a kind of a little clearing. . . . You know the place? . . . Well, it's right in there. Off the road, in the brush. Hidden. . . . Yeah, but listen, Carl, I know that must be where Meg parked her truck, 'cause it's real close to where she was painting—I mean *real* close, right across the road. And, you know, I just can't help thinkin'— it don't take a Sherlock Holmes to put two things like that to-gether, does it? There's no doubt in my mind, Carl, the son of a bitch that took that car, uh . . . he, uh . . ." Bart's face twisted with a mixture of rage and another emotion he could not have named. "He's kidnapped my wife."

He gripped the phone with both hands, and the knuckles were white with pressure. There was a long silence while he stared at the floor, listening.

Mrs. Cutler was moaning softly. "Oh, Lord! May the Lord have *mercy* . . ."

With his ear glued to the phone Bart raised his eyes and stared absently at the woman; she stammered and fell silent.

"Yeah, I will, Carl. . . . Don't worry, I've got hold of my-self. . . . But hurry, will you? I mean, you'll come on up, too, won't you? I know you're off duty now, but, hell . . . Good. Thanks, pal. I'd do the same for you, I swear. . . . Okay. I'll meet you at the Cutler turnoff. . . . Right. And hurry."

Bart hung up the phone and gazed at his spellbound audience of two. " 'Scuse my language," he mumbled.

Mrs. Cutler was wringing her hands. The piping voice became quavering. "Oh, merciful heavens, I just can't *believe* it! That poor, poor girl—Mr. Hannah, do you really think she's been *kidnapped?*"

Mr. Cutler leaned forward toward Bart, frowning. "Mr. Hannah, you say you found that car the sheriff was lookin' for today?"

Bart glared at the old man. "I expect you heard what I told Sheriff Gallagher, Mr. Cutler."

"Where was it?"

"Just like I said. In the brush, close to that clearing next to the river."

Mr. Cutler slapped his knee. "Well, now, that's danged funny. I looked around over there, and I didn't see no car. Somebody musta jes' put it there—"

"Cold," Bart snapped. "It was stone cold."

Mrs. Cutler sobbed quietly and produced a tiny handkerchief, and sniffled into it. "Oh, I just pray to the Lord that poor dear child is all right."

Mr. Cutler pointed a finger at Bart and presented a new line of thought. "Well, now, lookee here, Mr. Hannah—the way I see it, there ain't necessarily no connection between your little woman and that dang car in the brush. F'rinstance, Mrs. Hannah might 'a' gone too close to the river, maybe decided to go swimmin', or somethin'." Mr. Cutler's weatherbeaten face wrinkled in a grin. "Why, I 'member a couple o' weeks ago I dropped over there when she was s'posed to be paintin', and there she was at the river, in her bare feet, wadin'. Just like a little kid—cutest dang thing you ever saw—" Mr. Cutler's grin disappeared abruptly. "Well, what I mean to say is, you know, that river's mighty swift this time o' year, and, well . . . she, uh, she might 'a' got careless."

Mrs. Cutler wailed. "Oh, dear Lord, dear merciful Lord!"

Bart regarded Mr. Cutler with a cold eye. "Your theory don't account for Meg's truck bein' gone, does it?"

The old man pondered. "No, by dang, it don't. Guess you're right. Mr. Hannah, I think you hit it. This looks like a clear-cut case o' kidnappin'."

"Oh, that poor sweet baby." Mrs. Cutler buried her face in her handkerchief.

Mr. Cutler slapped his knee again. "Well, now, wait a minute, by dang. Could be she went into the river like I said—or maybe went for a long walk and got lost, or somethin' like that—then this here bad guy comes along, y'see, in this stolen car, and he sees Mrs. Hannah's truck, and he figures he'll switch vehicles, to throw the cops off his trail. Y'know, come to think of it, I saw somethin' very much like that on TV not long ago—there was this fella robbed a bank, y'see, and he stole this car and lit out across the desert—"

"Oh, yes," Mrs. Cutler said. "I remember that. It was on *Private Eye*, wasn't it, Melvin?"

"Yeah. You ever watch *Private Eye*, Mr. Hannah? Thursday nights at nine?"

"Bruce Gordon plays the private eye," Mrs. Cutler said. "He's *such* a good actor, so *realistic*."

"Ordinarily nine o'clock's a mite late for us," Mr. Cutler said. "But we make an exception for *Private Eye*. That's one dang program we jes' wouldn't miss—"

Bart stood up abruptly. "Listen, thanks for your help, folks. Sorry to barge in on you like this."

Mrs. Cutler was on her feet, protesting. "Why, my goodness, Mr. Hannah, you're not bargin' in. You *know* we're concerned, and want to help."

Bart was edging toward the living room. "Well, that's mighty nice—"

Mrs. Cutler caught his arm and clung to it. "Anyway, I don't want you to leave without havin' a bite to eat. Melvin, go get the ham and potato salad out of the refrigerator, and let's fix a plate for Mr. Hannah."

"Oh, no thank you, ma'am. I got to be goin.' " Bart disengaged himself from the woman's grasp and backed away.

Mrs. Cutler's eyes twinkled at him. "I bet if you got a whiff of my ham and potato salad you'd change your mind pretty quick."

Mr. Cutler joined in. "Y'know, Mr. Hannah, Pearl's potato salad won a blue ribbon at the county fair couple o' years ago. Maybe you heard about that."

Bart forced a quick smile. "Bet it's good, all right. But I got to go—I promised the sheriff I'd meet 'em at the road. Anyway, I had a ham sandwich before I left the house."

Mrs. Cutler's eyes lit up in delight. "Fancy that! Did you hear that, Melvin? Mr. Hannah had ham for supper, too!"

Bart had succeeded in reaching the front door. "Thanks again, folks," he said hastily. "G'night." He went across the porch and leaped down the front steps.

The Cutlers followed him out. Mrs. Cutler waved her damp handkerchief at him.

"You'll let us know what happens, won't you, Mr. Hannah? We'll be so worried."

Mr. Cutler went out to the top of the steps. "Now, don't fret about that toll call, Mr. Hannah," he called. "You got enough on your mind right now. I'll send you a note on it, soon's I get the bill."

"Oh . . . yeah. Thanks, you do that." Bart opened the door of his car and slid behind the wheel.

Mrs. Cutler went around her husband and down the steps and part way to the car. "And if there's anything we can do to help, Mr. Hannah, just anything at all, don't you hesitate . . ."

Bart gave her a nod and quick wave, cranked up the engine and gunned it, and drowned out the piping voice.

16

They ate a supper of corned-beef hash and applesauce, on paper plates balanced on their knees, sitting on the couch, which Lonnie had pulled closer to the fire. Outside, the sleet was forming a crystalline buildup on the windows, and the cold was creeping through the house.

Meg praised their meal extravagantly, declaring it to be one of the most excellent in her experience. When they were done Lonnie collected the paper plates and the empty cans, disposed of them in the kitchen, returned, and flopped down cross-legged on the floor at Meg's feet. She had pushed off her shoes again and was curled up on the couch.

"Now, then," she said. "Begin."

Lonnie gave her a blank look.

"Don't play dumb, young man. Don't give me that innocent look and say, 'Begin what?' Your story. I want to hear it. I want to know about you."

He shrugged. "All right. You asked for it."

"And asked, and asked, and *asked*."

He got up and stirred the fire, and put more wood on. When he returned to his seat on the floor by the couch he hunched forward and stared into the flickering blaze, not looking at Meg again, and began to speak in a voice so detached and distant that Meg had to strain to catch his words.

It's kind of a dreary story, Meg. I'll try to keep it brief and to the point. I was an only child—just like you—grew up in a little crossroads community way upstate. My father was a traveling man, out of town most of the time. Finally deserted us, when I was about five or six years old. I don't remember him very well.

When I was fourteen my mother married again. Earl, my stepfather, started right in trying to be a pal to me. It didn't work. He wasn't very good at it, and I guess I didn't really want a forty-year-old pal, anyway. After a while he switched back to his real style and started harping on me to buckle down and work. Give up all foolishness and frivolity, he said, and work, work, work, if you ever hope to make anything of yourself.

I couldn't understand that. I never was a frivolous kid. At that age I was already gone on birds, making studies of spring and fall migrations, and writing up my observations—even had an article published in a nature magazine. I thought I was already making something of myself. But Earl saw all that as a foolish waste of time.

Once, when I was about sixteen, we had a big row. I had lined up a summer job for myself as a junior counselor in a boys' nature-study camp, and Earl wanted me to go to work in a local produce-packing plant. The nature-study camp would be great experience, but the packing plant would pay a little more. Earl said the pay was the important consideration. I disagreed. He started yelling at me, and I yelled back, and my mother started crying—it was a mess. That night I packed my duffel bag and ran away—or tried to. The cops caught up with me next morning, thirty miles down the road. I wasn't taken home. I was taken to the police station, and there was my mother, and Earl, with a bandage around his head. They were having a big conference with the police about whether I ought to be booked for assault or let off because I was a minor.

That was the first time I had this . . . this very *peculiar* experience. They were saying I had attacked my stepfather, had hit him with a poker. I didn't know what they were talking about—I had no recollection of any such thing. I remembered the argument, and I remembered running away, but nothing in between. I figured the whole thing was staged. Earl was putting on a big act, to scare me.

Well, they let me off. But it was pretty clear that Earl and I weren't going to hack it, living in the same house. So then my mother fixed it up for me to go and live with Uncle Harry and Aunt Wilma, in Mayfield. Uncle Harry was my mother's older brother, and he always had a great fondness for her. That's got to be why he agreed to take me in—can't think of any other reason. He and Aunt Wilma were childless, and not exactly young anymore, and they sure didn't need a hard-to-handle teen-aged boy around. But they tried very hard to do right by me, and I tried, too, so it worked out fairly well. Uncle Harry was aloof, and hard to know—still is—but he's decent. Aunt Wilma was kind and gentle, a really good woman. By the time I graduated from high school my mother and Earl had picked up and moved back East, and I didn't feel any great loss. Soon after that Aunt Wilma died suddenly, and that hurt me a lot worse.

I had one little bit of trouble my senior year in high school. I went out for track, and the coach was a stiff-necked Prussian type, who believed in crew cuts and strict military discipline. Needless to say, I blew it right off—had a big row with him over his fanatical insistence on conformity and my unwillingness to conform. He told me I was off the team.

Then I had that funny experience again. They hauled me into the principal's office and accused me of attacking the track coach. Some other kids testified as witnesses, said I threw a punch at him. Coach must have thrown one back, because I had a painful bruise on my head and didn't know where it had come from. The thing was, I didn't remember anything about it. I denied everything, but no use—I was suspended from school.

That little episode shook me up—I mean about the memory failure. The first time, I thought I'd been framed, but now, again, the same peculiar thing—I just couldn't figure it at all.

Meg stirred, leaned forward toward him. "Didn't you try to get help, Lonnie? You must have known you needed help."

He shook his head. "It was my secret. I didn't want anybody to know."

"That was foolish."

He continued to stare into the fire and went on with his story.

Well, eventually I got back in school, and finished without any more trouble, and then went on to State College, with the idea of majoring in ornithology. I liked college, enjoyed the lively give-and-take of ideas, and all that. But the ornithology thing was a mistake. I loved the beauty of birds, but I couldn't develop any passionate interest in the details of their anatomy. The tibia, the tarsus, the caudal vertebrae, the cervical and inter-clavicular sacs—my God, I thought, this isn't what I'm after at all. It seemed to me the purest form of beauty in nature was be-ing reduced to something hateful by the dull, dry scientific ap-proach. I kept thinking of that poem by Whitman, where he tells of hearing the astronomer in the lecture room explaining the universe in terms of charts, diagrams and figures, of becom-ing tired and sick, and rising and going out into the night air, and looking up in perfect silence at the stars. I gave it up and changed my major to drama.

Quite a switch. I got into Shakespeare, and a whole new world opened up. The wisdom, and the fantastic poetry, and those godlike, larger-than-life characters, and every word they spoke eloquence, engraved on stone. I did well. Toward the end of my second year I got the opportunity to play Romeo in a de-partmental production. Not bad, for a sophomore.

But—time for trouble again. The director was a visiting pro-fessor, someone who'd done professional work and who wore his reputation like a cloak of royalty. You could say he was authori-tarian to a fault, you could say he was arrogant and dictatorial, a little Caesar—it would all be understatement. He wanted the actors to move and speak with all the programmed precision of automated devices, and to hell with spontaneity. All the mem-bers of the cast except one grumbled and knuckled under. Guess which one put up an argument.

My downfall was the sword fight between Romeo and Tybalt. The director wanted it choreographed like a ballet. Romeo thrusts *here*, Tybalt parries *there*, Romeo feints *thusly*, the ac-tion moves upstage left, where at a certain moment Romeo scores the mortal hit like *so*, and Tybalt sinks down and dies on *this* spot, marked by chalk. I couldn't stomach it. There were these two fiery-tempered young bucks fighting to the death, and the action was no more than a pretty dance, as orderly as a min-uet, without a trace of fury or desperation. One night after re-hearsal I went to the director in private and told him I thought the whole thing was absurd. He was offended, of course. He said I lacked the discipline to be an actor. I told him he lacked the imagination to be a director. He got furious, turned red in the face, began to shout.

116

Then there I was, in the middle of another one of those . . . experiences. I have no idea how that argument ended. All I know is the police came and dragged me out of my room that night, took me to the station, and booked me on suspicion of assault with a deadly weapon. The director was in the hospital with a four-inch-deep sword wound in his chest.

Meg gasped. "Oh, my God! I can't believe it! What did you do?"

I just stood there, gaping. I couldn't believe it, either. My memory lapses aside, I didn't see how it was possible—I think it would be all you could do to push one of those blunted stage swords four inches into a tub of butter. But there it was. They finally decided it was an accident, with the probability of criminal negligence involved. I got off with a year's probation. And I was thrown out of school.

That was several years ago. I sort of broke up after that, went into a shell, became a recluse almost. It's hard to describe how I felt about myself. "Afraid" is the word, I think. I was afraid I would never be able to trust myself to behave rationally under stress, so I began to avoid people altogether. Uncle Harry let me come back, even invented a job for me, until I could make up my mind about what to do with myself. So I moved into a little apartment over the garage and became caretaker, auto mechanic, and general handyman around the place. Uncle Harry's a pretty wealthy man, big in wholesale hardware, and the place I'm talking about is a big, plush, walled-in country estate, just outside Mayfield. Harry was spending a lot of time away from home since Aunt Wilma died, and it wasn't a bad idea to have somebody living in.

Well, I settled in and kept myself busy, and in my spare time roamed around in a wooded arroyo out behind the estate grounds, compiling a catalog of bird species native to the area. Gradually I began to feel a little more at ease with myself, but it was about a year before I felt like venturing out much. Then I started going down to Diamond Bay, and pretty soon got hooked on sailing, and found my boat—*our* boat, the *Seabird*—and fell in love for the first time in my life, as I did today for the second.

The fire was getting low. Lonnie got up and poked it, stirring the coals, then added fresh wood. He glanced at Meg as he returned to his seat on the floor.

"How do you like it so far? Not exactly a barrel of laughs, is it?"

Meg had been lying quite still, listening, her eyes dark and grave. Now she reached out and smoothed his hair lightly with her fingertips.

"You poor, foolish, stubborn guy. After all that, you *still* didn't try to get any help for yourself?"

He gave her a wry smile. "What, and ruin a good soap opera? This is the way the story goes, Meg. You want to tune in for the next episode, or do you want to forget the whole thing?"

She sighed. "Go on, crazy man."

Last year Uncle Harry brought home a new bride. He'd been working overtime making a reputation for himself as a lecher since Aunt Wilma died—having himself a fling before old age set in, I figured. At first it was just around Mayfield. Then he started flying to San Francisco—Uncle Harry flies his own airplane, y'see—he started going to San Francisco for weekends, two or three times a month. And one time he brought the new Mrs. Emmons back with him.

Betty's about half Harry's age—young enough to be his daughter is the way the local gossips put it, of course. She's a good-looking blonde, very glamorous, very . . . well-upholstered, as Uncle Harry likes to say. Her clothes are expensive, flashy, and a couple of sizes too small. Too small in all the right places, Uncle Harry says. Harry's quite a quipster. He loves to sit and watch Betty walk around, and he pinches her bottom a lot, especially in front of company.

He introduced her as an actress. I took it he was using the term in the loosest possible sense, but that was okay with me. The gossips around Mayfield say she was a stripper, known in the bay area as Betty Boswell, the Bubble Girl. They say she used to walk around the stage wearing nothing but a clear plastic sheath filled with colored bubbling water. I wouldn't know about

118

all that, never having seen her at work, but I thought it was rotten the way people gossiped about her. So she *is* half Harry's age and married him for his money—so what, if it works? He was happy, that's certain, and she was too, far as anybody could tell. What else matters?

Anyway, Betty moved right in and took charge of the money-spending department. Thinking up things she wants is one of her special talents. Uncle Harry loves to buy things for her, and she never, never runs out of ideas. When they were in San Francisco not long ago she saw that rose-colored Porsche on a showroom floor and sighed wistfully, and Harry bought it for her on the spot—even had the upholstery ripped out and replaced with that fake leopard-skin stuff, because that's what she wanted. She was happy as a baby with a new toy, and he was happy because she was. I'd just about decided they were the perfect couple, a match made in heaven.

And of course you know something's got to go wrong with all that. What went wrong was, Betty started to get bored. Uncle Harry's not lively enough at his age to keep her entertained. She began to make eyes in my direction. Funny thing is, I'd come to like Betty quite a lot, as a friend. She'd discovered I was a drama student once, and she wanted to talk theater with me. At first I did it just to be polite, but I found out pretty quick that she knew plenty—a lot more than I did. We had some great conversations.

Uncle Harry got jealous. He started being cold toward me, discouraging me from coming to the house. That hurt, because Betty and I had done nothing to justify his jealousy and, as far as I was concerned, had no intentions to. But Betty had intentions. She started hanging around whenever I was working, and acting cute and cozy. I couldn't blame Uncle Harry for not trusting us, even though I still felt injured about it. I began to make a conscious effort to avoid Betty. It didn't help.

One night, when Harry was working late at the store, Betty came out to my apartment and went to work on me in earnest, and seduced me. God! That sounds silly, doesn't it? I'm a grown man, I can make my own decisions about things like that, right? Well, to tell you the truth, I'm not all that sexually experienced —absolute putty in the hands of an expert like Betty. She took off her clothes, and took off mine too, and ordered me to make love to her, and I did as I was told—simple as that. Afterward Betty got dressed and patted me casually on the cheek and said, "Till next time, darling," and left.

I felt bad. I felt terrible, I felt worse than I'd ever felt before about anything. There I was, trying to work up a good case of righteous indignation about Uncle Harry's suspiciousness—and, boom, all of a sudden Harry's *right*, and I'm a lousy sneaky s.o.b.

Next day I went to see Uncle Harry at the office and told him I'd decided to leave. I thought I'd go on down to Diamond Bay and start working full time at the boat shop where I'd been going on weekends. I'd already made substantial payments on the boat I wanted, I told him, and I figured I'd be able to pay it off in a couple more years. I said I deeply appreciated all he'd done for me and I hoped I could make it up to him someday.

I thought he'd give me a lecture about how foolish and irresponsible I was, but he didn't. What he did instead made it a lot tougher for me. He said he had tried for the sake of his sister my mother to be a good foster father to me, but he was afraid he hadn't shown much talent for it. He said furthermore he'd been having some suspicions about me lately, but now he realized he'd been doing me an injustice. Then he said that since I was determined to go, he was going to turn over to me a little savings account he'd started for me some years ago. It would amount to seven or eight thousand dollars, he said. He hoped it would help.

Help?! I was floating on air! I wouldn't have to spend another year or two paying on the *Seabird*, I could have it soon and be gone! I'd be free! I practically got down on my hands and knees to Uncle Harry, thanking him. Naturally, when he asked me if I'd mind staying on a couple of weeks longer, until he could find somebody to take my place, I said sure, be glad to.

I went away thinking Uncle Harry was an absolute prince— and then I thought about Betty, and I felt lower than a worm. I swore to myself if she came around me again I was going to tell her to get lost and stay lost. Well, she came around, and I told her. She laughed and put her arms around my neck. I pulled her arms off me and told her to leave me alone. She pouted. She said, "You're not really serious about leaving, are you?" I said I couldn't wait to be gone. She turned nasty, started cursing me. I took her by the arm and led her to the door. She screamed at me, accused me of having ruined her virtue, said I'd be sorry, she'd fix me good. But at least she went.

That was about a week and a half ago. Then, last Wednesday, Uncle Harry flew Betty to San Francisco to spend a few days with some old friends, and went on to Reno, on business. The arrangement was that he'd return home on Monday and go back to San Francisco to pick up Betty later next week. So I was home alone for a few days.

Well, Saturday afternoon I was out in the arroyo, checking out the bird population, when suddenly there's Betty, coming toward me from the house. She was all smiles and sweetness. She'd come back on the bus, she said, and taken a taxi from the station. She guessed she'd become a small-town girl, she said, didn't enjoy the city anymore. Had to get back. Wanted to see me. Wanted to give me another chance. She came at me, with her seductive smile and her perfumed hair, and her fingers climbing up and down the back of my neck.

I pushed her away. It didn't have any effect. She kept smiling, kept coming at me. One last chance, she said. I pushed her away again.

"All right, then," she said. "You might as well know that on the way to San Francisco I had a talk with Harry about you. I told him I thought he ought to know that you'd made improper advances toward me. He was very upset, you can imagine. I said I think he'd be a fool to give you that big fat going-away bonus, and all the time you trying to lay his wife right under his nose. . . ."

I couldn't believe my ears. I just stood there, staring at her.

She started smiling again. "It's still not too late," she said. "I can tell Harry it was all a misunderstanding." She waited. "How about it?" she said. I told her to kindly go to hell.

"All right," she said, "that's it. I'm going to tell Harry that I came home today because I wasn't feeling well, and *you*—" she took hold of her blouse at the collar and ripped it, ripped it all the way down the front, so it was hanging in tatters "—you tried to *rape* me."

Lonnie fell silent. Meg watched him, waiting.

"What happened then, Lonnie?"

He was staring into the fire and did not answer.

"Lonnie, do you . . . do you not *remember?*"

He turned an absent, preoccupied look on her. "Oh, I know what you're thinking, Meg," he said suddenly. "That's what I was afraid of, too, of course. That's why I just stood there for a minute, paralyzed, afraid to make a move. Then I think I did the only sensible thing. I ran. I ran from Betty as if she were the devil incarnate. I ran back to the house and got in her car and drove away."

He looked at Meg and went on hastily, as if in response to a question he read in her eyes. "Why did I take Betty's car, you're wondering. Why did I even have keys to her car? I have keys to all the cars, because I do routine auto maintenance. But Harry's car was at the airport, where he leaves it when he goes off in his plane, and my old jalopy was up on blocks with the crankcase drained. I took Betty's car because it was the only one available at the moment. I couldn't fool around, I had to get out of there fast, before something bad happened. I drove and drove, trying to decide what to do. I wanted to get down to Diamond Bay, but I was afraid Betty would have the police looking for me, so I figured I'd better stay off the main roads and hide out somewhere for a while. Then I thought of this place. But by the time I got up into Stag River Canyon I knew I wasn't going to make it. I was running out of gas, and I had no money, no wallet, no credit cards, no nothing. The car shut down just as I cleared the crest where the road drops down along the river. I let it roll as far as the little clearing, then I pushed it off into the brush. Saturday night I slept under a tree—or mostly lay awake under a tree. Sunday morning you came along."

He gazed in silence at Meg for a moment before continuing. "I've just got to believe that Saturday night was the low point in my life, Meg. Sunday morning the upward turn began. And meeting you was the thing that did it."

"Lonnie . . ." Meg searched for words. She placed the warm palm of her hand against his cheek and held it there. "What can I say? What can I do to help you?"

He took her hand in both his own. "If you were with me, Meg —that's all the help I'd ever need."

She shook her head in puzzlement. "But how could I be with you if I don't understand you?"

"I've tried to be truthful, to tell you everything I know."

"But I still don't understand. Why did you feel that running away was the thing to do? Why did you have to go and turn yourself into a . . . a *fugitive?*"

He sat silent, head down, examining Meg's fingers. Then he released her hand and got slowly to his feet. The fire had burned down to a last flickering remnant of life. Lonnie bent over it, stirred it with the last remaining sliver of firewood, then tossed the stick onto the coals.

"That's the last of the dry wood," he said. "Now we either freeze or crawl into our sleeping bags." He glanced at Meg, and his look was blank and guarded. "Where would you like to sleep, Meg? In one of the bedrooms?"

"Where are you going to be?"

"Right here, on the floor."

"I'd like to be here, too."

"Thought maybe you'd prefer privacy."

She came and stood beside him and touched him on the arm. "I want to be with you."

He did not look at her; his gaze remained on the smoldering fire. "Aren't you afraid to sleep next to a crazy man?"

"No. Besides . . . I think we still have an awful lot to talk about. Don't you?"

He raised his eyes to her then. "I hope so, Meg. Because time's running out for us."

"Don't say that," she whispered.

He smiled suddenly and gave her arm a gentle squeeze. "I'll get the sleeping bags."

She watched him go up the short steps to the split-level hallway and into one of the dark bedrooms. Then she turned and stared down into the feeble glow of the dying fire. Her eyes were somber.

17

Two sheriff's cars, one following tightly behind the other, swung off Highway 78 onto County 15 and headed south at high speed toward Stag River Canyon. They passed the turnoff to the Hannah ranch to the right, and a minute later, to the left, the road to Ike Peterson's place, the only other habitation besides the Hannahs' at the lower end of the canyon. After that, open country, leading up into the wide canyon mouth. In the darkness ahead a cold misty rain began to swirl in microscopic droplets, fogging their windshields; the cars reduced their speed only slightly.

In fifteen minutes, at the outer limits of the lead car's headlight beams, the ostentatious sign of the Cutler ranch rose out of the night. And beside the sign, parked in the right angle where the Cutler turnoff met the highway, a car. Deputy Sheriff Carl Gallagher recognized it as that of his friend Bart Hannah. He pulled his vehicle to a stop at the side of the road, and the car following rolled up behind.

Bart's face, ghostly pale, was immediately hovering outside Carl's water-speckled window. The deputy climbed out and grabbed his friend's arm.

"You all right, Bart?"

"Jesus! Thought you guys would never get here!"

"Came as fast as we could. Believe it or not, the lieutenant was on the phone with Mr. Emmons while I was tryin' to reach him with *your* message. Any further developments?"

Bart shook his head impatiently. "I've told you all I know. Now we gotta *do* sump'm, and do it *fast*."

Carl held on to Bart's arm. "Just take it easy, pal. Don't panic. These things usually seem worse than they really are."

They were joined by two other uniformed men from the second car, and the four stood in a tight huddle on the dark rain-damp roadway.

Carl struggled with introductions. "Uh, Bart, uh . . . lemme introduce my boss, Lieutenant Cole of the Sheriff's Department. And, uh, Sergeant Mulray. This here's Mr. Hannah, gentlemen."

Bart shook hands with the men, returned their mumbled greetings, and searched their faces intently, waiting. Lieutenant Cole, short, round-faced and tending to stoutness, stepped up to Bart and took charge.

"Mr. Hannah, I understand you have some information as to the whereabouts of the automobile allegedly stolen from the premises of Mr. Harry Emmons' residence, in Mayfield, sometime Saturday."

Bart glanced impatiently at Carl. "Yeah, it's down the road here a piece." He jerked a thumb over his shoulder. "But I'm more interested in the fact that my wife is missing. I'd rather talk about *that*."

"We're coming to that, Mr. Hannah. Could you describe the exact location and condition of the car?"

"It's pulled off into the brush, in a little clearing by the river. I don't know what condition it's in, I didn't look at it that close."

"Hm-m-m." Lieutenant Cole took a moment to ponder. Bart shuffled his feet restlessly.

"Now, as to your wife. I'm told she was in this vicinity today, engaged in some sort of sketchin', or drawin', or such like. That correct?"

"Yeah. Painting."

"Painting?"

Bart attempted to pantomime it. "You know—landscape painting."

"Alone?"

"Yes, alone."

"Are you sure, Mr. Hannah? Completely alone?"

Bart scowled at the short man before him. "It's not a group activity, Lieutenant."

The sheriff stiffened his back and increased his height by a quarter of an inch. "I realize that, sir. I'm tryin' to determine the exact circumstances under which she, uh, she, uh . . ."

"Look, why don't we just get a move on?" Bart snapped. "Let's find her first and determine the circumstances later."

The sheriff's height increased by another quarter of an inch. "I have a little experience in matters of this kind, Mr. Hannah. Fourteen years' worth. I can tell you for a fact that the fastest way to proceed is to move deliberately, and to avoid hurry. What you do is, you examine all the known facts first, develop a theory, and then follow it through, instead of rushin' off wildly in six different directions."

Bart exhaled noisily and shuffled his feet again.

"Now, then. As to the site of Mrs. Hannah's, uh . . . painting activity. Where would that be?"

"Down the way here, about a hundred yards off the road. I'll show you—"

"And her car?"

"Truck. A wheezy old Ford pickup."

"Missing also, I understand?"

"Right."

"Where would it have been parked? By the roadside?"

"Probably in that little clearing, close to where the Porsche is."

Lieutenant Cole frowned. "So these two, uh . . . occurrences —they're in the same location?"

Bart huffed with annoyance. "Christ, I thought that was understood! They're all part of the same thing!"

Cole put up a hand. "Not so fast. We'll determine that in due time. Now, how far is this place from here?"

"A mile, maybe."

Lieutenant Cole deliberated. "Well, I think the next step is for you to lead us to the location, so we can have a look around. You ride with Sergeant Gallagher. Sergeant Mulray and I will follow."

"Quick thinking, Lieutenant," Bart said. The sardonic sneer on his face came and went too rapidly for the sheriff to catch.

The little group dispersed to the cars. Bart got in beside Carl and slammed the door hard, and muttered, "Christ, what a windbag!"

Carl eased his car out onto the road. The misty rain was coming harder now, glittering in the headlights.

"Listen, buddy, lemme give you a hint," Carl said. "Cole's a

126

first-class windbag, all right. But he's also a first-class law enforcement man, and—".

"Law enforcement man, shit! We need a detective. This is a *case*, for Christ's sake!"

"He can do the job. Just try to keep it cool, and let him handle it."

Soon Bart leaned forward in his seat and peered through the windshield. "Here we are. Just ahead, on the right."

The two cars pulled off the road, and the men reassembled in the little clearing. Somewhere just beyond the tight perimeter of illumination from the car lights the swift current of the river roared invisibly in the darkness.

"Over here," Bart said, and led the way toward the brush on the far side of the clearing. The sheriffs' flashlights probed the dripping foliage and found the little car, its rose-petal surface gleaming bright with wetness in the incongruous setting. Bart hung back waiting, pacing restlessly in the clearing, trying to ignore the rain. At length the other men came out of the brush.

"It's locked up tight," Lieutenant Cole said to Bart. "Can't get inside."

"I know," Bart said dryly.

"All right, let's go have a look at Mrs. Hannah's painting site."

Bart led them across the road and up the little dirt path to the great oak tree, and again paced on the soggy ground and cursed under his breath, while the uniformed men made a minute search of the area. Then Lieutenant Cole led the procession back to the roadside clearing and went to his vehicle. He called to Carl.

"Sergeant Gallagher, suppose you and Mr. Hannah climb in the back of this car for a few minutes, so we can have a little conference." When they were all seated Lieutenant Cole turned partially in his seat to address the others.

"Now, first of all . . ." He cleared his throat noisily, fished for a handkerchief, and blew his nose. "Damn that cold rain," he muttered. "First of all, Mr. Hannah, we don't seem to have pinpointed any firm evidence that Mrs. Hannah was even in this vicinity at all today. Secondly—"

"What the hell is *that* supposed to mean?" Bart growled.

"Secondly, assuming she *was* here, it's nothing more than conjecture that she actually came in contact with anyone connected with the Emmons vehicle. However . . ." The sheriff paused to blow his nose again. "In view of the fact that a viable alternate theory does not readily suggest itself, I think for the time being we will proceed on that one—that she *was* here, and came in contact with the automobile thief, or thieves, who then abandoned the Emmons car and appropriated Mrs. Hannah's vehicle for the purpose of throwin' us off the scent . . ."

Bart leaned back in his seat and huffed with exasperation. Lieutenant Cole paused at the disturbance and backtracked to pick up his train of thought.

". . . for the purpose of throwin' us off the scent, and, in the process, abducted Mrs. Hannah as well."

"Congratulations, Lieutenant," Bart said. "That's what I've known for a couple of hours. Now could we get these damn cars moving and start a *search?*"

Cole's small eyes, set close together in a broad flabby face, observed Bart without expression.

"I understand your impatience, Mr. Hannah. You're concerned about your wife's safety. Believe me, sir, we are also. But, again, I think we should take a moment to review all the facts we have so far, before rushin' off helter-skelter. For instance, this car over here in the brush. I'm not sure how much you already know, but—"

"I know about the Emmonses," Bart broke in. "The Porsche is Mrs. Emmons' car, and Mr. Emmons thinks it was taken by his nephew."

"Right. Young fella by the name of Hayden."

"Hayward," Carl Gallagher corrected.

Lieutenant Cole shot a cold glance at him, then continued, to Bart, "That's the theory. But that's not all there is to it. I got another call from Emmons, about an hour ago. He was callin' from San Francisco, and what he said seems to throw some new light on the subject. He had flown to Frisco this morning to pick up his wife, who was visitin' friends. Well, he had trouble locatin' the friends, and when he found 'em they said Mrs. Emmons had left the city Saturday morning to return to Mayfield, by bus. He'd been callin' home, but hadn't been able to reach her. I told him I wasn't surprised, because we've had his place under observation, and I know there ain't nobody there. Now

Emmons has stopped worryin' about the car and is worried about his wife.

"So I did some quick checkin' around. Ed Atkins, the taxi driver in Mayfield—the only one there is—tells me he picked up Mrs. Emmons at the bus depot Saturday afternoon and took her home. Are you sure it was Mrs. Emmons? I ask him. Certain, says Ed. No mistakin' *that* doll. My favorite fare, he says. Best damn tipper in town."

Bart was leaning forward, listening intently. His interest had been captured. "So what do you make of it?"

"What I make of it is, young Hayward and Mrs. Emmons have run off together."

Bart's eyebrows went up. "You think so, uh?"

"In the first place, Mrs. Emmons is a very good-lookin' woman, they say, and much younger than her husband."

"Yeah, I've heard."

"And, second, Emmons sort of halfway hinted that he's had some suspicions about his wife and young Hayward. He didn't come right out and say it, but I could tell it was in the back of his mind. And, third—well, just look at the facts. We know Mrs. Emmons came home Saturday afternoon. We know Hayward lives on the place, and was probably there alone when Mrs. Emmons arrived. *Next* thing we know, they're both missing."

Cole permitted himself a little chuckle and took time out to blow his nose again. "Seems pretty clear, don't it?"

After a short thoughtful silence Bart leaned back in his seat. His attention span had expired. "Well, that's all fine, Lieutenant. But, dammit, I'm still just interested in gettin' on with lookin' for my wife—"

Cole held up a hand. "But think about it, Mr. Hannah. I'll bet you had visions of your wife bein' the victim of a rapist, or some such thing. But if Hayward is already travelin' with a woman, that danger would appear to be considerably diminished. Am I right?"

From behind the wheel Sergeant Mulray contributed a thought, in a flat expressionless voice. "Maybe Hayward and Mrs. Emmons killed Mrs. Hannah and dumped her body in the river—"

"All right, that'll do, Mulray!" Lieutenant Cole snapped.

Sergeant Mulray gulped and reverted to silence.

Bart ran a hand through his hair. "Christ Almighty, this is ridiculous! Could we for God's sake get a move on now?!"

"That's exactly what we're gonna do," Cole said. "I got a man standin' by at the Mayfield airstrip, to catch Emmons when he shows up. It's just possible he could give us a hint as to what Hayward might have had in mind, headin' up this way. Meanwhile . . ." He turned his beady eyes on Carl. "You've been on all day, Sergeant Gallagher. Can you stand a little overtime?"

"Hell, yes," Carl said quickly.

"All right. You and Mr. Hannah patrol up Highway Fifteen to the Cedar Lake turnoff, take the turn and check around the lake area. Sergeant Mulray and I will continue on up Fifteen to the end of the road, then double back and regroup with you at the lake. Sergeant Mulray, get out your pad and pencil. Mr. Hannah, what's the license number of your wife's truck?"

"Oh, ah . . ." Bart closed his eyes and frowned, then squirmed, then shrugged. "I can't recall offhand."

"Color?"

Bart pondered. "I'd say . . . dung color."

Sergeant Mulray gravely wrote it down.

"All right," Cole said. "Let's go."

Bart and Carl got out and went back to Carl's vehicle. The other car moved out, and Carl pulled his out after it. The rain had degenerated into occasional light flurries, with somewhat improved visibility. They rode in silence for a few minutes, then Carl glanced curiously at his companion.

"You see what I mean about Cole, Bart? He starts off so slow you think hell's gonna freeze over before anything gets done, but first thing you know he's got it all organized. He's a pretty good one."

Bart made no reply.

After another minute or two Carl spoke again. "Don't sweat it, buddy. This is a dead end, you know. Either way, to the end of the highway or to Cedar Lake, it's a dead end. There ain't no place the son of a bitch can hide. We'll have 'im in no time. You'll see."

Bart sat motionless, staring out past the monotonous swinging of the windshield wipers, into the darkness ahead.

130

"Carl?"

"Yeah, buddy?"

"I'm scared, Carl." There was a tremor in his quiet voice. "I want my little mouse back."

18

The icy rain had ceased as quietly as it had begun, and gone the way of the wind. In the main room of the mountain cabin the gray remains of the fire gave off listless curls of smoke, and from time to time a feeble crackle. All else was silence.

Meg came down the short steps from the upper-level hallway, carrying a candle. She crossed the room and set the candle on a small table near the couch. She was alone. Two sets of pads and sleeping bags were laid out on the floor in front of the fireplace. Quickly Meg undressed to the skin, put her clothes in a neat folded stack on the couch, then slipped into one of the sleeping bags and lay still.

In a few minutes she heard a light step on the front porch, and Lonnie came in, carrying a flashlight and shivering from the cold. He came across the room and stood looking down at Meg.

"Good," he said gravely. "I see you know proper sleeping-bag technique."

"What do you mean?"

"It's not smart to wear clothing in a bag. Restricts free movement, and makes you colder rather than warmer."

Meg hugged the covering snugly around her neck. "Where were you?"

"Went to check the truck once more, to see if everything was secure. Also wanted to give you a chance to, uh . . . crawl in." He smiled down at her, and walked away, out of her view.

In a few minutes he snuffed out the candle, and what remained was a soft near-darkness that was tinted with a rosy glow from the fireplace. Meg heard him shuck off his clothes then, and dimly saw the outline of his body as he slid into his sleeping bag.

They lay quiet for a little while. Lonnie rolled onto his stomach and propped himself on his elbows, and peered in Meg's direction. She could see his eyes shining with liquid reflection of the residual light.

"Hello," he said.

"Hello."

"How do you feel? Warm enough?"

"Fine." As her eyes grew accustomed to the darkness she saw his face more clearly. He seemed very close.

"I feel a little strange, though," she said.

"In what way strange?"

"Well, I'm not exactly in the habit of spending the night with strange men."

"Certainly not *crazy* strange men."

"I wasn't going to say that."

"I know you weren't. Now that you think maybe it's literally true, it seems a poor subject for joking, doesn't it?"

"Don't talk like that. You have problems, Lonnie—that's all right, everybody has problems. But they can be solved, if only you're willing to face them."

He rolled onto his back and put his hands behind his head. "Better not spend so much energy worrying about *my* problems. Better worry about your own."

"*Mine?*"

"How are you going to explain all this to that macho husband of yours, for instance?"

Meg uttered a little gasp. "My God! I haven't thought about Bart for hours!"

Lonnie laughed gently. "I think that poor fellow made a mistake, marrying you. A hawk can't mate with a pigeon—even birds know better than that. However, out of sheer magnanimity, I'm willing to take you off his hands."

Meg didn't answer. Lonnie came up on his elbows again and looked at her. He put out a finger and touched the tip of her nose.

"Hey, poker-face."

She refused to banter. "We're going to be serious, Lonnie."

"Are we, now?"

"Yes. And we're going to stick to the principal subject."

"Which is?"

"You."

"How flattering."

"Now, I've been doing some thinking."

"How marvelous!"

"And what I think is . . ." She could see the gleam of his teeth as he grinned at her. "Are you going to be serious or not?"

The grin disappeared. "I'm serious, Meg. I'm so serious it's giving me a headache. Tell me what you think."

"I think that as soon as the sun is up in the morning, no matter what the weather is like, we're going to walk down to Cedar Lake and go straight to the nearest telephone. I'll call Bart and try to explain things to him, and you'll call Mrs. Emmons and tell her you're sorry about taking her car, and—"

"We don't have that much time, Meg." His voice had gone low and solemn, and the sound of it stopped her abruptly. "When the sun is up in the morning we won't need to walk to Cedar Lake and call anybody. They'll be *here*."

"All right, then. We'll go out to meet them, and we'll say—"

"Just a minute, Meg. It's not quite that simple. When they show up I'm going to stop them before they get to the door. I'm going to stop them just long enough to find out one thing I need to know. If it's good we'll open the door and go out to meet them, and I'll explain that it was all an accident, and no fault of yours, and maybe I'll even consider going back and facing up to my problems, the way you think I should. But if it's bad I'm going to kiss you once and say goodbye, and that'll be that."

"Find out *what*, Lonnie? You talk in such riddles."

"I'm sorry. I can't explain it to you any better than that. And if I have to go I'll have to go fast, there'll be no time."

"But how *can* you? Where can you go from here?"

"Out the back and over the mountain. I know a trail—and it leads in the right direction, too. Toward the coast."

"Lonnie, you can't mean that. You're in trouble, and you've got to go back and make things right. You can't mess up everything and then just . . . run away and leave it."

"You said something like that before, and I said why not, and you weren't able to tell me why not."

"Because it's mean, that's why not. And you're not a mean person."

He lay back and was silent for a little while. "Seems to me

I've never made any unreasonable demands on life," he said at last. "All I've ever wanted was to be left alone, to do the quiet things that give me joy . . ."

"You're like a child, Lonnie."

"But everywhere I turn, people lie in wait for me with traps and snares, plotting to take away my freedom."

"Even me?"

He reached toward her in the darkness, and her hand came out from under the covers and found his.

"Not you, Meg. Not you. You're trying to help, I know, and I'm grateful. You're kind, and you're good—that's why I love you."

"Please stop saying that."

"Come with me, Meg."

"Lonnie, please . . ."

He was up again, leaning close, his eyes burning into hers. "If you'd come with me I could get hold of my life and make it work, and develop some meaning, some sense of direction."

"I'm not *free* to come with you, Lonnie. I can't just—"

"If you loved me, we could break out of all the entrapments, *all* of them, and fly away together. The wide world could be ours."

"Stop it, Lonnie." She pulled at her hand. "Please, stop it."

He held her fast for a moment, then relaxed his grip. Her hand flew to safety under the covers. When Lonnie spoke again the vitality was gone from his voice.

"All right, Meg. You call the shots. What is it going to be for us? Is this all? Shall we call it a day and go to sleep now? Then don't say good night, say goodbye, because that's all there will *ever* be."

"Lonnie . . ." There was a quavering in her voice. "Oh, Lonnie, I don't want you to go. I don't want to say goodbye."

"Then come with me, Meg."

She shook her head in anguish. "Don't do this to me, please. I don't know how to cope with . . . something like this." Tears sprang to her eyes. She covered her face with her hands. "Why does it affect me this way? Why does it *matter* so much?"

"Could it be that you love me a little, Meg?"

His hand moved on her bare shoulder, slid around behind her back, pulled her gently toward him. She dropped her hands

135

away from her eyes and stared. He moved closer, his lips almost touching hers.

"Could it be, Meg? Just a little, maybe?"

Her hand crept upward and touched his face. A soft sob caught in her throat.

"Don't cry, Meg." He pulled her closer still, and his voice became a whisper in her ear. "The last thing in the world I want to do is make you unhappy."

"I'm sorry. I just . . . don't understand what's happening."

"It's not always possible to understand. Sometimes you just have to let yourself—"

Suddenly he pulled back and looked at her and laughed softly, and she turned her tear-damp face up toward him in wonderment.

"Aren't we funny, Meg? Isn't this a good joke? Neither of us able to handle his own problems, but both busily trying to give guidance to the other."

He laughed again, and she started to laugh with him, but the laughter turned to sobs, and the floodgates of tears were opened.

He stroked her forehead, smoothed her hair, and pleaded, "Don't, Meg. Please. It just makes everything so much tougher."

"I can't help it. I just wish . . ." She bit her lower lip and struggled for control.

His hand came down caressingly along the curve of her throat, his fingers entwined themselves in her hair. "What do you wish, my angel?"

"I just wish we'd met a long time ago. We could have helped each other so much, we could have been so *good* for each other. Now it's too late."

Again his arm went around her and pulled her toward him. With his lips brushing the lobe of her ear he spoke in breathlessness and urgency. "No. It's never too late for people who love each other, and we love each other, Meg, you know we do."

He was lying at the edge of her sleeping bag now, out of his own, and his naked body pressed against the hidden softness of hers.

"You're so beautiful, Meg, I want you so very much. It's *not* too late for us—there's still a chance, if you'll only admit we love each other."

She closed her eyes and followed with all her consciousness the course of his lips as he kissed her ear, her hair, her throat and shoulders. One of his hands had found its way beneath the sleeping bag and crept over a breast and held it, caressing with infinite tenderness. He was breathing heavily, and his breath fell scalding on her skin, and sent hot electric impulses thrusting through her tingling body. Her breasts heaved upward against him, under his hand, her chest rising and falling with her own deepening gulps of breath.

Suddenly she was aware of something tight and rigid inside and all around her that was dissolving and falling away, loosening invisible bonds. A fantastic image of herself as a newborn butterfly emerging from the long imprisonment of the cocoon rose before her eyes, in resplendent beauty. Her arms came up out of the coverings and hung in space for an instant before descending and sliding languidly around Lonnie's neck like soft silken cords. She breathed a long sigh and lifted her face toward him, seeking. Their lips came together, open, hungry, eager, devouring each other ravenously.

"Yes," she whispered at last. "Yes." Her moist eyes shone close to his, her eyelashes fluttered against his cheek.

He pulled back once more and looked at her with a fierce intensity, and held her face between his hands. "But, Meg, you've got to know this—there's one thing I will have no part of. I'll have no cheap, hasty one-night stand with you. We're not playing around, and we're not Romeo and Juliet either. I want to take you in my arms and make love to you, to have you for my own, but I want you permanently, not just for a passing moment. If I can't have you on those terms, then send me away. Let me lie alone and nurse my misery."

"Oh, dear sweet crazy man." She smiled with tender sadness and kissed him. "That's all so foolish. You can't set conditions on our lovemaking—we're *already* making love."

He groaned in helplessness and buried his face in the curve of her neck. "Oh, Meg, Meg . . . can't you see . . ."

"My poor head is hurting, Lonnie. I can't think anymore." Her hand moved quietly down along the side of her sleeping bag, opening the zipper.

"But it's important, Meg. We've got to have an understanding—"

"Sh-h-h." She touched his lips with a fingertip. "Darling, don't talk so much. Come in out of the cold."

She lifted the covering that lay over her, and the warmth of her body enveloped him like a soft cloud of incense. Revealed, vivid, almost luminously visible in the darkness, her beauty lay open for his ravishing.

He came in to her, his taut body entwining itself in hers, his hands moving in adoration over the soft and lovely treasures, his lips following tremblingly, and stopping at the nipples of her breasts, one after the other, and feeding there like a suckling child. She held his head, stroked his hair, pulled him closer against her. And soon she opened herself to him completely, spoke his name again and again in a soft moaning chant, clutched and held him with all her strength, and went spinning off into a mindless joy that was like nothing she had ever known before.

Time, being not relative but absolute, and insensitive to those who consume it, moved heedlessly on and left them far behind. They could not have guessed at the extent of its orderly and passionless progression, the number of degrees by which the clockwork stars shifted their arc above the evaporating swirls of cloud that clung to the topmost points of the mountains.

Long afterward Meg lay quiet and limp with exhaustion in her lover's arms, eyes closed, barely conscious, incapable of movement or the formation of a rational thought. She could feel Lonnie's gentle breath soft and regular on her shoulder. He stirred slightly in the darkness, half turned, and was still again.

And as she sank toward the oblivion of sleep she heard his murmuring voice, very faint and from a far distance, and could not tell whether it was real or imagined:

> "I am afeard,
> Being in night, all this is but a dream,
> Too flattering-sweet to be substantial."

She floated away, and behind her eyes there danced a vision of a bright blue sun-dazzled waterscape, and pretty white sails moving toward an infinite horizon across the cool ocean.

138

19

Cedar Lake. A beach-house and juke-box community whose life blood was daytime summer recreation for middle-aged vacationers and throngs of tanned teen-agers. In mid-March it slumbered still in winter hibernation, soggy, chilled, and desolate. Toward midnight the misty rain had ceased, and invisible wisps of fog floated in icy ghostlike silence over the dark surface of the lake, across the road that encircled it, and between dilapidated cottages, service stations, and hot-dog stands, all locked up and lifeless. At one point the road skirted a broad parking area overlooking the lake. On the other side of the road was the Lakeside Lodge, a massive wooden-frame structure with a wide veranda, the community's largest building. A sign near its entrance proclaimed its name and the promise that it would be open May 1.

Deputy Sheriff Carl Gallagher's patrol car made the three-mile trip around the lake perimeter road once, then a second time, more slowly. After the second trip it turned off the main road and wandered at a snail's pace in the labyrinthine maze of narrow residential roads that cut through the forested slopes uphill from the lake. At length it returned to the parking area opposite the Lakeside Lodge, and stopped under the dismal circle of illumination of a solitary street light at one end of the empty lot. The two men in the car sat for a moment in heavy silence.

"Nothin'," Bart muttered. "Not a goddam thing."

"Why, hell, we just barely scratched the surface," Carl said. "We're gonna have to get reinforcements and go over those little back roads up there in the woods with a fine-tooth comb. Might take a while. Might take a day or two to cover it thoroughly." Carl's optimism had weakened appreciably.

Bart heaved a despondent sigh. "How about tryin' to raise Cole again on your radio, see if he's got anything."

"Take it easy, Bart. We just talked to him a few minutes ago. He'll check in again soon."

Bart sagged in his seat and stared miserably out at the lamppost bathed in its own pale light. Ignoring Carl, he talked to himself, speaking in a low mutter. "Why the hell did I let her do it? She was always goin' off to crazy lonesome places, all by herself, where a good-lookin' babe like her's got no goddam business bein'. She's got spunk, that gal. Never scared of anything. But I shoulda known better, for Christ's sake. I'm her husband, goddammit, I'm supposed to take care of her." He shook his head in a surge of anger. "Damn!" he growled, and slammed his fist repeatedly into his open palm. "Damn, damn, *damn!*"

Carl put a hand on his friend's shoulder. "Tell you what, ol' buddy. Why don't you crawl in the back seat and stretch out, maybe catch a couple o' winks. Might as well, this waiting game could get tough—"

"To hell with it!" Bart flung himself out of the car. "I'm gonna take a walk."

He slammed the door and walked away toward a low stone wall on the far side of the parking lot, bordering the lake. Carl watched him go. Then he slumped in his seat, leaned back against the headrest, and yawned. In a few minutes his eyelids drooped toward closing.

Bart walked the quarter-mile length of the parking lot along the lakeside edge, paused for a minute and listened to the sleepy lapping of the black water just beyond the stone wall, then walked slowly back again. The cloud cover was gradually dispersing, revealing a cold moon that tinted the darkness with a faint pallor. Bart put a foot up on the low wall, cupped his chin in his hands, and stared out over the pale gray sheen of the lake.

"Hang in there, little mouse," he murmured. "I ain't goin' home without you."

In a few minutes Carl opened the door of his car and called to him, "Hey, Bart! Cole on the horn."

From across the deserted field of blacktop Bart could hear the staccato crackle of the sheriff's radio. He ran toward the car. When he got there the radio was silent again.

140

"Well, what'd he say?"

"Said for us to stay put, he'd be here in a minute. Said he's got some fresh info that'll help us move forward on this thing."

"What is it? Did he spot somethin', or what?"

"Said he'd explain when he gets here."

Bart exhaled explosively and slapped his forehead. "Jesus H. Christ! The son of a bitch sure loves to be mysterious! Call him back and find out what the hell he's talkin' about!"

"Easy, Bart. He'll be here in a couple o' minutes."

It was a quarter of an hour before the lights of Cole's car came into view far down the lake shore. Bart, pacing around Carl's car and fuming, stopped and watched the other vehicle creep toward them, and scowled.

"Don't get in a hurry or anything, fatso," he muttered. "Jus' take your own sweet goddamn time."

Lieutenant Cole's car pulled up next to Carl's, and Cole rolled down his window and spoke to the deputy. "You and Mr. Hannah crawl in this car, Sergeant Gallagher. We got a little wait yet."

Carl got out of his car and got into the other one. Bart leaned down and glared at the sheriff through the window.

"What the hell you got, Cole? What are we waitin' *for?*"

Cole didn't bother to look up. "Climb in, Mr. Hannah. Make yourself comfortable." He rolled up the window.

Bart swore softly and got into the car.

"Now, the situation is this," Cole said. "A little while ago we had a report from the Mayfield office. Mr. Emmons is back from San Francisco. Our man at the Mayfield airstrip met him when he came in, and gave him the news about Mrs. Emmons' car bein' found. And his reaction was most interesting, most interesting indeed."

Cole shifted his position to look directly at Bart in the back seat. "My hunch is proving to be sound, Mr. Hannah."

"What hunch?" Bart growled.

"There's evidently some significance to the car bein' on County Fifteen. Young Hayward, with or without Mrs. Emmons, was on his way to a particular destination. That destination, Emmons believes, and I am fully inclined to agree—"

"Get to the point, will you?!" Bart snapped.

"That destination was undoubtedly the summer house Emmons owns, right here in this area."

"Jesus Christ! Where?!"

"Back up in the woods someplace, above Cedar Lake."

"But where, goddammit! *Where?!*"

"That's what we're waitin' to find out. A couple of our men are bringin' Emmons up here now so he can show us the place."

"God Almighty! Couldn't he give you directions by radio?!"

"Emmons thought it was too complicated to describe. He wanted to come in person and lead the way."

Bart leaned back in his seat and groaned.

"I fully sympathize with your impatience, Mr. Hannah," Cole said placidly. "But our men didn't feel they ought to argue with Emmons, under the circumstances."

"Under the circumstances, shit! While we sit here jawin' and twiddlin' our thumbs, some son of a bitch is doin' God knows *what* to my wife!"

"Mr. Hannah. . . ." Lieutenant Cole made a concentrated effort to maintain his own patience. "These little forest roads up here above the lake are treacherous. Some of 'em are still impassable this time of year. We could get lost, or stuck, or both, and be unable to do anything at all. Now, how would you like *that?*"

Carl laid a hand on Bart's arm. "Calm down, buddy. We're makin' progress, you've got to admit."

"They'll be here . . ." Cole switched on the interior light and consulted his watch. "Within half an hour." The sheriff reached hastily for his handkerchief, got it up to his face just in time to cover an enormous sneeze.

"Start the engine and turn on the heater a few minutes, Mulray," he said to the driver. "I'm freezin' my ass off."

Sergeant Mulray complied.

Bart rested his forehead in his hand and stared at the floor of the car. "Oh, Lord," he moaned. "Oh, Lord, I can't believe this."

When the lights of another car became visible across the water, following the lake shore road toward them, Lieutenant Cole checked his watch again. "Thirty-six minutes," he announced. "Not bad, eh?"

A third Sheriff's Department car came into the parking lot and moved up near the others, and the four waiting men got out of Cole's car and converged on the new arrival. The tall stiff-backed young deputy driving the third vehicle got out and came around his car toward Cole.

"Got here as soon as we could, sir," he said smartly.

"All right, Ogilvie." Cole went past the deputy and squinted into the interior of his car.

There were two passengers—another deputy in the back seat and, in the front, an elderly man in a bulky fur-collared coat, with a felt hat pulled down tight on his head. The elderly man climbed out of the car.

"You're Mr. Emmons, I take it," Cole said to him.

"Yes, I'm Emmons," the man said curtly. "You Sergeant Cole?"

"Lieutenant Cole," said the sheriff. He extended his hand. "Pleased to meet you, sir."

He waved in the direction of the other men around him. "This is Sergeant Gallagher here, and Sergeant Mulray. And this is Mr. Hannah. He's the gentleman who discovered the Porsche."

Emmons ignored the deputies and nodded gravely to Bart. "Much obliged, Mr. Hannah."

Bart shrugged. "Forget it. I wasn't lookin' for your car, I was lookin' for my wife. Still am."

"And I'm looking for mine." Emmons turned intense bushy-browed eyes on Lieutenant Cole. "It's quite a ways up to the cabin, Sheriff. Shall we get moving?"

"I suppose you're acquainted with the circumstances of Mrs. Hannah's disappearance, Mr. Emmons, and the possible involvement with—"

"Yes, yes, I've heard all that. Let's get going, shall we?"

"Just a minute," Cole said. "There's somethin' you might as well know right now. I'm operatin' on the theory that your wife and your nephew ran off together, and that they took Mrs. Hannah's vehicle when their own became disabled, and that they—"

Emmons emitted a loud snort. "That's a hell of a lot of theorizing, Sheriff."

"And a hell of a lot of time wastin'," Bart muttered.

Cole stood his ground. "I want you gentlemen to understand a couple of important points, and understand 'em good." He scowled at each man in turn and spoke with deliberate slowness.

"First, this is a deadly serious case. I'm assumin' that Hayward is a desperate character, capable of anything, and I intend to take precautions accordingly. Second, this is a paramilitary operation we're conductin', and I—*I*—am in complete command. Is that clear?"

Emmons sniffed. "Nobody's questioning your authority, Lieutenant. But your assessment of my nephew is faulty. He's a nut, but a harmless one, I can assure you of that."

"*You* may be sure of it," Cole said stiffly. "As for me, I will make no such dangerous assump—"

"Jesus Christ!" Bart exploded. "Why don't we just *go!*"

The sheriff gave him a cold look. "Naturally, Mr. Hannah, that's exactly what we're goin' to do."

Cole turned to his deputies. "Now, as to deployment. Sergeant Ogilvie, you and your man lead the way, with Mr. Emmons. Sergeant Mulray and I will follow you. Sergeant Gallagher, you and Mr. Hannah bring up the rear." He looked hard at each man as he spoke. "Have your arms at the ready, men. All right, let's move out."

They went quickly to the cars, and the caravan got under way, snaking out of the parking lot and along the deserted lakeside road.

"About time," Bart grumbled. He sat huddled in the seat next to Carl, staring straight ahead. His hands, clasped tightly together between his knees, worked torturously against each other, making the knuckles white with pressure.

"Don't give up, little mouse," he said in a whisper. "I'm comin' to get you."

20

Meg drifted back into wakefulness gradually and stared blinking into black space, unable for a moment to focus her mind and fix the place where she was. Remembrance returned with a rush; she reached out to touch Lonnie, and discovered he was not there. Then she became aware of a dim light on one edge of the darkness, and turned her head in that direction. The two windows overlooking the little front porch of the mountain house were silvery gray squares set in the dark wall, and from them pale slanted beams of light formed a pair of parallelograms, distorted images of the windows, on the floor. Meg frowned in cobwebby confusion, trying to puzzle out the nature of the cold illumination, then recognized moonlight. At the same instant she made out Lonnie, huddled quiet and still in a chair by one of the windows, gazing intently out. The window before him was wide open, and through it an icy current of outside air flowed over the sill and across the floor.

He must have heard her stir, or noticed the change in the soft regular sleep-rhythm of her breathing, for he turned and looked in her direction. She raised herself on an elbow and pushed her loose hair back from her face.

"Lonnie?"

She could not see his face clearly in the darkness, but his eyes shone with startling brightness. He was fully dressed. When he spoke his soft voice seemed detached and floating.

"Hello, Meg. Hello, my love. I'm glad you're awake. I was lonely."

She sat up in her sleeping bag, and shivered as the cold touched her bare shoulders, and frowned toward Lonnie, trying to force her eyes to adjust to the darkness.

"I can't see you very well. What are you doing?"

"Doing?" He seemed to ponder the question. "Why, waiting, Meg. Waiting, and remembering."

He put something he was holding down on the window ledge and came to her, and took her in his arms.

"Remembering last night. Our first night together, our first lovemaking. I'll remember it all my life."

He kissed her on the neck, and his hands moved gently over the smooth skin of her back and shoulders, beneath her flowing hair.

She murmured in response, and slid an arm around his neck. "Not *last* night, darling. It's *still* night. Take off your clothes and come back to bed."

He kissed her again, now on the mouth, but the kiss was quick and guarded; he held back, not letting it grow.

"It's morning now, love. It will be light soon. There is no more time."

She pulled back just far enough to meet his eyes. "Then, for heaven's sake, Lonnie, listen. I will make my commitment to you—but not to run away. If you'll go back and face up to your troubles honestly, I'll stand by you. Will you do it?"

"I can't, Meg. I don't know how."

"Just be honest. Tell them everything you've told me. If your Uncle Harry was willing to give you all that money as a going-away present, he ought to be willing to pay for some . . . some professional assistance."

She felt him stiffen. "You mean a psychiatrist?"

"I don't know—whatever is necessary."

"You really *do* think I'm crazy, don't you?"

"No. You're *not* crazy. But you've got problems that are just too big for you to handle by yourself."

He disengaged himself from her gently and got up, and stood looking down at her with a strange expression, and she clutched at her sleeping bag and pulled it close around her, feeling suddenly exposed.

"Please, Lonnie." She reached out and took his hand, and turned pleading eyes up to him. "If you'll do it I'll be with you, and we'll see it through together. I swear it."

For a long moment he gazed down at her, without speaking. Then he pulled his hand out of her grasp and went back to his seat by the window. He picked up the object he had laid on the windowsill and leaned forward, resuming his vigil, gazing out over the silent forest. The moonlight caught a hard metallic glint. And Meg saw that the thing he held in his hand was a gun.

She sat motionless, staring, feeling her throat tighten. Before she spoke she made a conscious effort to control her voice, to make it loose and casual.

"Lonnie, why do you have a gun?"

He did not respond. He sat silent, looking out the window.

She came out of her sleeping bag and reached for her clothes, and dressed as quickly as she could, shivering and fumbling in the darkness and the cold. When she was dressed she went across the room and pulled up a chair next to Lonnie, and sat down.

"Where did you get the gun, Lonnie? Have you had it all the time?"

"Oh, this?" He looked at the compact automatic, turned it over in his hand, examined it as if he were seeing it for the first time. "Oh, no, I wouldn't own a thing like this. It's part of Uncle Harry's collection of toys."

"May I have it, please?" Meg held out her hand. "Give me the gun, Lonnie."

He gazed at her with a musing smile and leaned back in his chair.

"You know, Meg, when I was a drama student, I used to get this funny thought, right in the middle of a play. Just when the plot was thickest, when it seemed impossible that the characters would ever extricate themselves from the sticky situation they'd gotten themselves into, I used to think, wouldn't it be fun to forget the script now and have each character do and say what he would do and say under those circumstances in real life, with nobody knowing what was going to happen next, or how it was all going to turn out? I have that feeling now, Meg. It seems to me we're reciting our lines and dutifully acting out our parts to a predetermined ending—helpless puppets, with no control at all. The plot was worked out long ago, the play written, and set in unchangeable type."

Lonnie's right hand, holding the gun, rested on the windowsill. He lowered his head and with his left hand gripped his forehead.

"And, God!" he breathed. "God, how I wish we could throw away the script!"

Meg stared at him and shook her head in hopeless incomprehension. Then her eyes drifted down to the gun. Her hand stole toward it.

"Lonnie, would you please just give me that—"

He lashed out suddenly, thrusting her hand back with a violence that made her gasp. There was a fury in his eyes, and a hard edge on his voice that she had not heard before.

"Follow the script, Meg. Nobody gave you the right to meddle with it. The script has it that you're a nice person, one of the very nicest people ever. You were a good little girl when you were a child, minded your mother, never got your pretty dresses dirty, always said please and thank you. In school you sat at the front of the room, prim and straight in your desk, and raised your hand promptly when the teacher asked a question. You have never been in trouble once, not once, in your whole life. Don't start now."

For the first time since the morning, ages before, when he had surprised her by the river, Meg felt uneasy, in the presence of a stranger.

"Funny you should say that to me now. After . . . all this."

"There's nothing here you have to take any blame for, Meg. You're in the clear completely. You can tell a good story—you can even choose between several versions. Why did you come here? You felt sorry for a poor miserable wretch who needed help, or the wretch kidnapped you. Why didn't you return, or call? Truck broke down, and the phone is out of order. Or you were a *prisoner*, for God's sake. The sleeping bags on the floor, so cozy and close together? You had no choice. Was there sex? Take your pick. Say no, or say yes, I forced you."

"Lonnie, don't." Meg turned her eyes away from him, trying to escape his strange mood.

"You have no problem, Meg. You can go back to your Bart and go right on being a nice well-behaved housewife. Nothing has changed."

"I see. And what about you?"

"I'm the fugitive, the heavy in the play. You're good, virtuous, faithful—I'm a renegade. We'll each play out our parts, like well-disciplined actors."

148

"But the gun—there's nothing in the script about a gun."

"Oh, yes there is. It's a very important prop."

"It's not good for anything, except to make things worse than they already are."

"Look, Meg. When our friends and relatives show up here I want to be able to greet them with some simple gesture of ceremony, however makeshift. I don't have a cannon for a formal salute—" he waved the pistol playfully—"so this little toy will have to do."

"And when they come—what then?"

"When they come I'm going to let them know I'm armed, and that they are not to enter until I say so. And in a very few minutes of polite conversation—from a safe distance—I'll probably find out what I need to know. Then we can turn over another page of the script, and go on."

"Find out what, Lonnie?"

He shook his head. "I can't explain it exactly, Meg. But it'll all come clear to you—"

"Oh, Lonnie . . ." Her eyes pleaded with him. "Put that horrid gun away, and when they come we'll walk out of here to meet them, and we'll see this thing through peaceably. Everything will be all right, you'll see."

He took her hands in his and gazed at her earnestly. "I doubt that the script will turn out to read that way. But however it reads, whatever happens, my angel, you'll know I love you, have always loved you, all my life, even though I found you only yesterday."

"Yesterday," she whispered. "That was so long, long—" She caught her breath and trembled.

He held her and rocked her in his arms, kissed her gently on the temple and stroked her hair, while she clung to him and sobbed quietly in an agony of helplessness.

"Oh, I just wish I could . . . if only I could understand . . ."

"Never mind, love," he murmured in her ear. "You are one of those blessed people who are too good to understand evil things, who are too—"

He went suddenly rigid. She raised her tear-dampened face and looked at him inquiringly.

"Listen," he whispered.

Far down across the deep predawn silence of the wilderness

something harsh was intruding, beating against the cold still air, faint, but telegraphing itself distinctly—the grinding of automobile engines laboring in low gear on a steep mountain road.

They sat very still, hardly breathing, listening to the alien sound.

"They're coming," Lonnie said.

Deliberately, unhurriedly, he disengaged himself from Meg, turned away from her, picked up the gun, hunched forward over the windowsill, and stared fixedly out.

Meg got to her feet and stood over him. Her fingers twisted themselves tensely around each other, her eyes were burning bright.

"Lonnie, you're making a dreadful mistake."

"Go back," he said quietly, without looking at her. "Get back away from the windows."

She backed away from him, went to the far end of the room near the fireplace, sank down on the couch, and was lost in the gloom.

The engines ground on somewhere far below, coming closer, becoming more insistent, rising more and more powerfully out of the moonlit tangle of forest. Lonnie sat motionless, waiting, his eyes straining to catch the first visual corroboration of what he was hearing.

Finally, after several minutes, it appeared. A pair of tiny white dots of light, far down the mountainside, blinking in and out among the trees—there, not there, there again. And another pair—then a third. Out of sight momentarily behind a curve, but still present in their relentless grinding, on and on, and back into view, higher and closer, now overwhelmingly real and recognizable. Three cars. Those behind splashing light on the ones ahead, illuminating the gold emblems and stark black-and-white design that proclaimed the authority and officialdom of the Grange County Sheriff's Department.

Lonnie rested his forearms on the windowsill and watched the weaving lights of the motorized caravan come around the final bend and approach the collapsed bridge. The pistol in his hand glinted dully in the pale light of the moon. His fingertip stroked the contoured metal of the gun barrel with a gentle steady movement.

150

21

The men in the trailing car couldn't tell why the caravan had come to a halt. Carl pulled up the handbrake and let his car idle in the narrow dirt road, rested his hands lightly on the top of the steering wheel, and waited with placid patience. Bart leaned forward and peered through the windshield at the cars ahead.

"What's the goddamned holdup?" he muttered.

Lieutenant Cole got out of the second car in line and walked forward to confer with the men in the lead vehicle. In a few seconds he returned hurriedly to his own car, scrambling to get out of the glare of its headlights and gesturing to Sergeant Mulray, the driver, with energetic handsweeps in the air. Mulray shut off his engine and doused the lights. The lead car had already gone dark. Carl quickly took the cue and did the same.

"Jesus, what's fatso Cole up to now?" Bart said.

Carl rolled down his window as Cole came toward him.

"All right, men, this is it. We've got 'im." The sheriff's voice rang with a hard crispness that sounded unfamiliar to Bart.

"What d'ya mean?" Bart said.

"The Emmons cabin is just up ahead. And a pickup truck is in the ditch, Mr. Hannah. Probably your wife's."

Bart peered frantically into the dim labyrinth of forest foliage ahead. "Where, for Christ's sake?! I don't see a damn thing!" He got out of the car and slammed the door and started forward, half stumbling in the darkness.

"Hold it!" Cole barked at him from across the top of the car. "Don't move until I tell you."

Bart froze in his tracks from sheer surprise. Carl got out of the car, and Cole turned to him.

"Sergeant Gallagher, come on up forward, and bring your rifle."

When Carl was ready Cole started forward and beckoned to Bart. "All right, Mr. Hannah. Move slowly and carefully, and don't make any unnecessary noise."

Carl followed Lieutenant Cole, and Bart came behind, muttering to himself.

In a moment the company had assembled at the edge of the ravine that bordered the road and stood gazing down at the dark silent hulk of Meg's truck, hanging grotesquely half in and half out of the earth amid split planks and shattered beams, like the sea-washed remains of an old shipwreck.

"Son of a bitch!" Bart breathed.

"That your wife's truck, Mr. Hannah?" Cole asked.

"Sure as hell is. What's left of it."

Cole turned to Emmons, who was standing beside him. "Where's the house?"

Emmons pointed upward through the overhanging branches of trees. "Up there."

Cole craned his neck to look. "Holy Christ! What holds the damn thing up?"

The house was clearly visible, bathed in moonlight and hanging above them, jutting from its cliffside perch. No sign of life could be seen.

Lieutenant Cole squinted up at the house, down at the truck, up at the house, and down at the truck again. He rubbed his chin thoughtfully. "Best I can make out, the bridge collapsed when they tried to cross. The truck appears to be disabled."

Bart snorted. "No kiddin'!"

Harry Emmons stared glumly down at the wreckage. "I'm embarrassed by this, gentlemen. I knew that bridge was in need of repair, but I had no idea it was *that* bad."

"That's not all you've got to be embarrassed about, Mr. Emmons," Cole said brusquely. "If you'd mentioned Hayward to begin with and told us about this place, we'd have been here twelve hours ago."

"Why, I never would have thought he'd come *here*—"

Bart exhaled with explosive suddenness. "To hell with this!" he growled. He looked around the group. "Anybody got a flashlight?"

152

"Sh-h-h!" Cole hissed at him. "Keep it quiet, goddammit! No lights."

"Who the hell do you think you're foolin', Cole?" Bart rasped. "You think they don't know we're here?"

"No lights," Cole said firmly. "Not unless you want to turn yourself into a perfect target."

"Target for what?" Emmons demanded. "I told you, my nephew's harmless. He'd never try to shoot anybody."

The sheriff gave Emmons a look that dripped with professional disdain. "Right. Thanks for the information."

He walked away from the others, went a few steps along the edge of the ravine. When he found a good vantage point he stopped and gazed up at the house, and rubbed his chin again.

"Don't see any signs o' life," he mused. "I just wonder . . ." He turned to the others. "Mr. Emmons, how far does the road go above here?"

"Only a couple of miles, to a locked gate, where the National Forest lands begin. Beyond that point is a fire patrol road that goes around to the other side of the mountain."

"Any more dwellings up that way?"

"No, none."

Cole stared absently at the other men, absorbed in his thoughts. "Y'see, the question is," he said finally, "did Hayward actually stop here, or did he abandon Mrs. Hannah's vehicle and continue on up the hill on foot—"

"The question is," Bart said, "why are we just standing here? Why don't we just go on up to the goddam house and find out?"

Cole arched an eyebrow at Bart. "You ever serve in the armed forces, Mr. Hannah?"

"No, why?"

"Good thing. In a combat situation you'd last about ten seconds."

Bart stepped toward the sheriff, his jaw jutting belligerently. "Listen, Lieutenant, I'd like to know just what the hell you're gonna do. If anything."

"Why, I'm gonna consider all possibilities, and then I'm gonna come up with a plan."

"Great. And while we fuck around here waitin' for you to come up with a plan, the son of a bitch has plenty o' time to stroll out the back and escape. I say we storm the place. All of us at once."

"You tired o' livin', mister? If we rushed madly out in that moonlight, we'd be dead men. This situation calls for subtlety."

Bart almost spat his disgust. "Subtlety, shit! If you guys are too chicken to go up there, I'll go myself!" He turned away abruptly and felt for footing along the dark edge of the ravine. "If I can find a way across this goddam ditch."

"Stay right where you are, Hannah." Cole's voice was low and hard.

"What?"

The sheriff stepped up to Bart and almost pushed his short stout bulk into the taller man. "Now you listen, mister, and you listen good. This is a police action here. That, as I've tried to explain, is a military-type operation. I'm the ranking officer, and I'm in charge, you got that? I'm in charge."

"All right, goddammit. Be in charge."

"I mean to. And if you delay this operation another two seconds with your yappin', I'm gonna put you under arrest."

"You can't do that."

"Try me."

Bart hesitated. "Well . . . all I want to know is, when are you gonna *do* sump'm?"

"As soon as you shut your trap long enough for me to collect my thoughts."

Bart grimaced, and shuffled his feet. The trap, for the moment, was shut.

Cole turned his attention to Harry Emmons. "Now, then, Mr. Emmons. Is there an easy way across this ravine?"

"There's a little pedestrian bridge, a short ways up." Emmons pointed uphill.

"Any way to get around to the back of the house?"

Emmons shook his head. "As you can see, nothing but these steep slopes on either side."

"All right. I'm gonna go across and work my way up the hill as far as I can get and try to establish verbal contact. The rest of you wait here. Sergeant Mulray, you and the other deputies keep me covered. Show me the bridge, Mr. Emmons."

Emmons led the sheriff thirty yards up along the ravine to a small footbridge half hidden under low-hanging foliage. As Cole started to feel his way across, Emmons touched him on the arm and stopped him.

"I was just thinking, Sheriff—maybe it would be better if I tried to make contact. I'm the boy's uncle, and I'm positive he bears me no ill will. I believe I could talk to him more easily than you could."

"Sorry." Cole shook his head. "It's my responsibility."

"But, Sheriff, it would make better sense—"

"It's my operation, Emmons, and it's my responsibility. I can't allow civilians to expose themselves to danger while I stay under cover."

"But I keep telling you, the boy's not dangerous, he's just a little bit—"

Cole turned away, started to move across the little bridge. "Go on back with the others," he said to Emmons over his shoulder.

The sheriff worked his way slowly and cautiously up along the lower part of the path that led to the cabin. Despite his bulk he moved with quickness and agility, crouching low, scurrying from the shelter of a tree trunk to the protection of a boulder, trying to keep himself within shadowy areas, out of the moonlight glare. Halfway up the path he stopped behind a rocky outcropping, craned his neck around the edge of it and peered up toward the dark silent cabin. He looked back down the slope. The other men were safely out of sight under the dense growth of trees that lined the ravine. He turned his gaze back up to the house and stood quietly examining it in detail for a full minute. There was no sound, no movement. Moving with careful stealth, he started forward again.

Immediately a man's voice rang out from somewhere within the house.

"That's far enough. Sta, right there."

Quickly Cole moved back to the shelter of the rock.

"Who are you?" the voice called out. "What do you want?"

Cole cupped his hands over his mouth and shouted back. "Lieutenant Cole, Grange County Sheriff's Department. Will you identify yourself, please?"

The reply was unhesitating. "My name is Lonnie Hayward."

"What are you doing here, Mr. Hayward?"

"I'm minding my own business, Sheriff. What are *you* doing here?"

Cole's eyes had continued to roam over the house, searching for the location of the voice. He now settled on the open window facing onto the front porch.

"Mr. Hayward, we've had a search on for you for something over twenty-four hours. I'd appreciate it if you'd come down here, I want to ask you a few questions."

"Can't do it," the answer came. "Talk to me from there."

The voice sounded rational, relaxed, even casual. Cole edged cautiously forward a few steps.

"Don't come any closer, Sheriff," the voice said sharply.

Cole retreated again. He rubbed his chin, adjusted his hat, glanced back down the slope, and squinted up at the window, trying to penetrate the square of darkness within.

"You had some questions, Sheriff?" the voice said.

"Yes, well . . . First, Mr. Hayward, are you the nephew of Mr. Harry Emmons, of Mayfield?"

"I am."

"Did you depart from the Emmons residence sometime Saturday, driving the small sports car that belongs to Mrs. Emmons?"

"I did."

"Did you abandon that car on County Highway Fifteen, in the Stag River Canyon?"

"Keep it up, Sheriff. You got everything right so far."

"Did you then confiscate the truck that we see disabled down below?"

"Ah, too bad, Sheriff. You goofed. All I did was hitch a ride."

"Mr. Hayward, that truck belongs to a lady by the name of Mrs. Margaret Hannah. Can you tell me anything about the present whereabouts of that lady?"

"Sure can. She's right here with me."

"Is she, uh . . . is she all right?"

"Absolutely in the pink. Just a minute, see for yourself."

Cole watched and waited. Presently the door of the house opened, and the slim figure of a young woman appeared dimly on the shaded porch and stepped forward to an area of full moonlight illumination.

Lieutenant Cole stared up at her. "Are you Mrs. Hannah?"

Meg spoke out in a clear steady voice. "Yes, I am Mrs. Hannah, Sheriff. And I am perfectly all right."

Down below, concealed beneath the branches of trees beside

the ravine, Bart peered up toward the house, sucked in his breath sharply when he recognized Meg's voice, closed his eyes for a moment and trembled slightly.

"Thank the Lord, thank the Lord!" he said in husky whisper.

Carl grabbed him by the arm and gave it a quick squeeze, and grinned at his friend in the darkness.

A short distance away, standing alone by the footbridge, Harry Emmons huddled in his elegant fur-lined topcoat, gazed frowning up at the unfamiliar young woman on the porch of his mountain retreat, then shifted his eyes to the sheriff on the slope below her.

"Ask about *Betty*, damn you," he muttered under his breath. "Find out about Betty."

And far across the valley, above the dark velvet-green mantle of forest to the east, the first soft tint of dawn light touched the sky along the icy mountain ridges.

22

Meg kept her eyes fixed on the broad-brimmed hat that marked the sheriff's position behind the rocks, halfway down the slope. Though the man's face was hidden by the hat, Meg knew he was watching her closely. After a brief deliberation the sheriff spoke to her again.

"Mrs. Hannah, would you step down here, please, so I may speak with you?"

Behind her, close to her ear, Lonnie whispered, "Tell him no, you can't."

Meg hesitated a few seconds. "I'm sorry, Sheriff, I'm afraid I can't do that."

"Why not?"

"It's just . . . it wouldn't be practical right now."

The sheriff was silent for a moment while he studied her. "Mrs. Hannah, am I to assume that you're a hostage?"

Again, from behind her, whispered instructions: "Yes. Tell him yes."

This time Meg's hesitation was more prolonged. The fingers of her hands twisted together in suppressed tension. "For the time being, I think you'll have to assume that, yes."

The sheriff raised his head a little higher and pushed his hat back, and suddenly Meg could see his wide beefy face, pasty-pale in the moonlight.

"Mrs. Hannah, I'm here to take Mr. Hayward into custody, one way or the other. I hope he can be persuaded to come down out of there with his hands up, because if he won't, we'll just have to take the place by force, and somebody might get hurt."

Meg struggled inwardly to retain composure, and hoped that desperation would not sound in her voice.

"Sheriff, please don't try to force your way in here. Mr. Hayward is a . . . a disturbed person. If you'll just wait patiently until I've had a chance to talk to him a little while longer, I'm sure we can work something out. Just be patient, please."

The sheriff seemed to be thinking it over. He looked back down the hillside, then up to the house again.

"All right, Mrs. Hannah. We'll wait fifteen minutes."

"Thank you."

Meg was aware of Lonnie standing very close behind her, and his hand on her arm.

"That's fine, Meg," he whispered. "Now come back inside."

She allowed herself to be led back into the house. Lonnie closed the door quickly and put his arms around her.

"You were great, my love. Poised, cool, serene—beautiful."

She looked at him bleakly. "And bewildered."

He kissed her lightly on the cheek. "Never mind. You pacified 'em for a few minutes. And a few minutes is a lot of time right now."

He sat down in the chair by the open window again, and resumed his watch. "This Lieutenant Cole seems like the cautious conservative type. That's good. Wouldn't want to contend with any trigger-happy heroes."

Meg sat down in the chair beside him. "What's supposed to happen next, Lonnie?"

He stared fixedly down the slope. "Don't really know yet, Meg," he said softly. "Haven't read the script."

Suddenly he frowned and crouched forward until his chin was almost resting on the windowsill. "Hey—enter a new player, upstage left."

Meg stretched to look out, over Lonnie's shoulder. A gray-haired man in a fur-collared topcoat was moving up the lower section of the path toward the sheriff. He was making no effort to conceal himself.

"It's Uncle Harry," Lonnie said.

"He was out of town, wasn't he?" Meg asked.

"He was—but of course if he got word that I'd been a bad boy, he'd come running. And I guess he got word."

They could see Lieutenant Cole gesticulating frantically at the other man. Emmons kept coming, paying no attention. As he neared Cole's position the sheriff rushed out and grabbed him by the arm and pulled him off the path into partial concealment behind the rocks.

Lonnie, watching, chuckled softly. "Cole thinks he's dealing with a desperado here. Strange it doesn't occur to him to wonder why I haven't already taken several perfect opportunities to plug him."

In a moment the sheriff peered out from behind the rock shelter. "Mr. Hayward? Are you there?"

"At your service, Sheriff," Lonnie called back cheerily.

"Mr. Hayward, your uncle Mr. Emmons, is here with me "

"I know."

"Well, we'd like to question you on one more point, please Is there anybody else with you, besides Mrs. Hannah?"

"No. Nobody."

"In that case, Mr. Hayward, we'd like to know if you can give us any information as to the whereabouts of Mrs. Emmons."

Lonnie sat very still, and did not reply. He glanced over his shoulder at Meg, then turned back quickly to face the window. The sheriff's gruff voice came at them again.

"Mr. Hayward? What about Mrs. Emmons? Can you tell us where she is?"

Lonnie laid the pistol, carefully balanced, on the windowsill, clasped his hands tightly together between his knees, and rocked gently back and forth.

Meg watched him, and felt a slow chilling horror rising within her. She laid a hand on his shoulder.

"Answer him, Lonnie," she whispered. "Answer . . ."

Lieutenant Cole persisted. "Mr. Hayward? Do you understand the question? Where is Mrs. Emmons?"

Lonnie stood up and grasped the window ledge with both hands, and thrust his head out.

"I don't know." He flung the statement with vehemence down the hillside.

"When did you last see her, Mr. Hayward?"

"I don't remember."

"You didn't see her Saturday, when she returned home unexpectedly from San Fran—"

"No! No!" Lonnie was shouting. "I have *not* seen her!"

Then he slumped back into his chair, clasped his hands to-

160

gether again, and stared across the pale sky toward the far eastern ridge, where the dawn light was rising.

Meg reached toward him, touched him timidly on the arm with her fingertips. "Lonnie . . . that's a lie." There was a quiver in her voice.

He kept his eyes locked on space. "It doesn't matter, Meg. There's no point in going on with this dialogue, anyway. I've found out all I need to know."

Meg took him by both arms, tried to pull him around to look at her. He would not meet her eyes.

"No, Lonnie, you haven't found out *anything*. It's more of a mystery than ever—"

"Mr. Hayward?" The harsh sound of the sheriff's voice seemed suddenly closer. "Try to recall, Mr. Hayward. When was the last time you saw Mrs. Emmons?"

Lonnie grabbed his gun and peered intently down the slope, searching. The sheriff had moved up a short distance farther, was now crouched behind another rock, closer to the house.

Lonnie rested the butt of the pistol on the windowsill, with the muzzle pointed in Cole's direction.

"Go back!" he yelled.

Cole crouched lower, but stayed where he was. His speech became tight with urgency.

"Grant me one minute, Mr. Hayward. I want to let you know where you stand—this is for your own good, believe me."

"All right." Lonnie held the pistol in place and glanced at his wristwatch. "You have exactly one minute. Use it well."

"Mr. Hayward, it's a known fact that Mrs. Emmons returned to her home on Saturday afternoon, at a time when you were probably there alone, and she hasn't been seen since. And about that same time, for some strange reason, you drove off in her car, and later attempted to conceal it in the brush, by the side of the road. But you haven't seen Mrs. Emmons, and you know nothing of her present whereabouts. Is that correct?"

"Go on," Lonnie said. "You've got forty seconds."

"And *you've* got some very serious charges buildin' up against you, Mr. Hayward. And your present behavior ain't helpin' your case one little bit. Now you better come out o' there peaceably, surrender your weapons, and accompany me back to town. If you try to resist arrest you'll only make things a whole lot worse for yourself, I promise you. My deputies have this place surrounded, and it's only a matter of minutes before—"

"Your deputies have nothing surrounded, Sheriff. Your deputies are cowering in the shadows, down by the ravine. I suggest you go cower with them."

"I'm warnin' you, Hayward, you're makin' a very serious—"

"Your minute is up, Sheriff. I'm giving you another thirty seconds to get back down the path, or I'll open fire."

Cole crouched lower still, until he was completely hidden behind his rock shield.

Then Harry Emmons was out from behind the rocks farther down the slope. His eyes were fixed steadfastly on Lonnie's window. He came up the path toward the house, taking one slow deliberate step after another.

"Go back!" Lonnie shouted. He leaped to his feet and thrust his pistol far out the window.

He could hear Lieutenant Cole whispering frantically at the other man, "Get down, you fool! Take cover!"

Harry Emmons planted himself in the path, feet spread apart, and called out, "Lonnie my boy, you've got to tell me—where is Betty?"

Lonnie forced his words between clenched teeth. "I told you— I . . . don't . . . know."

"You've *got* to know. You're the only one who could have—"

"Go *back!*" Lonnie bellowed. He raised his weapon and aimed it straight at the man on the path. "Get back down the path, or I'll fire!"

From behind him Meg gasped. "Lonnie—no!"

Emmons held his ground. "You won't shoot me, Lonnie. I'm your uncle, your own flesh and blood—"

Cole rasped at him, "For God's sake, Emmons! Get *down!*"

Lonnie fired. The blast echoed deafeningly through the little house. The bullet slammed against the rocky hillside with a vicious tearing sound and careened off harmlessly into space.

There was a scrambling on the path. Cole lunged at Emmons, grabbed him by the arm and half led, half pulled him stumbling down the path to the protective covering of the trees, yelling hoarsely at the hidden deputies, "Hold your fire! Hold your fire!"

Then silence.

162

Lonnie stared down the deserted slope for a minute, then slumped into the chair by the window. The gun hung limply at his side. At length he raised his eyes to Meg, standing rigid as a statue in the center of the dark room.

"No harm done," he said softly.

Meg remained silent.

He got up and went toward her, slowly and with caution, as if she were a wild creature, easily frightened. Weakly he tried to smile.

"I was just bluffing, Meg. I wouldn't shoot anybody, you know that."

As he stepped closer to her she moved back a little, almost shrank from him, and he saw that she was indeed like a wild creature and held something akin to terror in her eyes.

23

The moon was fading before the slow rising light of dawn, the sky and the earth below growing gradually brighter.

Lieutenant Cole pulled Harry Emmons back across the footbridge to the shelter of the trees, both men struggling to maintain their footing and cursing under their breath. Carl was there waiting for them and took Emmons by the arm as if to help. Emmons thrust him roughly away and wrested free from Cole's grasp.

"Get your hands off me, you bastards!"

Cole confronted him. "All right, Emmons, I'll give you the same damn lecture I gave Hannah. I told you to stay down here and keep out o' sight—"

"This is my property, Sheriff, and I'll—"

"Goddammit, when are you civilian numbskulls gonna get it through your heads that this is a *military* operation, and I'm in charge—I'm in *charge*, and you'll damn well do what I tell you!"

Emmons brushed his hair back and regained some composure. "Look here, Sergeant Cole, Lonnie Hayward is my—"

"Lieutenant. *Lieutenant!*"

"Sorry. Lonnie Hayward is my nephew, Lieutenant. I know him well. He wouldn't shoot me."

"He came damn close!"

"Nonsense! He fired into the ground. You saw it yourself—"

Cole turned away, muttering and churning in anger. Then he planted himself in front of Emmons again and shook a finger in the other man's face.

"Now I'm gonna give you a firm order, and if you don't obey it I'm gonna place you under arrest. I want you to go and get in Sergeant Ogilvie's car and stay there. And I want Hannah to do the same. I'm sick and tired o' you know-it-all amateurs gummin' up the works—"

He stopped abruptly and looked around. "Where's Hannah?"

Carl Gallagher answered. "He's down in the ravine, inspecting the truck."

"Good!" Cole growled. "Maybe it'll fall on 'im." He turned to another deputy. "Sergeant Ogilvie, I want you to take Mr. Emmons and Mr. Hannah on home. And ring up Headquarters and tell 'em—" Cole stopped again and glared at Carl. "Goddammit, Gallagher, I said where the hell is Hannah? Tell 'im to get his ass up here."

"Right, Chief." Carl hurried off to the ravine.

Cole turned back to Sergeant Ogilvie. "Tell H.Q. we got a shootout situation here, we need reinforcements. And contact the forestry people and get 'em up here. Maybe they can help us get around to the other side o' the mountain, so we can approach the place from behind."

"Gotcha, Chief," Sergeant Ogilvie said smartly, and started for his car.

Harry Emmons stood still. "Lieutenant Cole, I must say I resent this," he said stiffly.

The sheriff glowered at him. "I must say I resent it, too. I resent havin' to send one o' my badly needed men away just to get you and Hannah out o' my hair. I resent this constant carpin' and meddlin' and second-guessin' from both o' you, preventin' me from doin' my job."

"I don't care to be treated like a child," Emmons huffed.

"You were sure *actin'* like one, out there darin' that young kook to take a shot at you."

"This is my property, Lieutenant. That's my nephew holed up in there, and it's my wife who's missing. It seems to me the least you could do is allow me to participate—"

The sheriff held up a hand for silence. He was no longer paying attention to Emmons, but was staring into the dense shadows in the direction of the ravine.

"Hold it," Cole muttered. "Sump'm's funny here." He walked rapidly away.

Carl Gallagher was on the other side of the ravine and was crouched behind a tree, peering up the hillside toward the house.

He turned and looked back across toward Lieutenant Cole, and on his face was a glassy smile that revealed embarrassment and worry.

Cole stepped to the edge of the ravine. "What's goin' on?" he demanded. "Goddammit, Gallagher, *where's* Hannah?"

Carl swallowed hard. "Hate to tell you this, Chief, but . . ." He pointed up the slope. "He's up there."

"For Christ's sake, up where?" Cole bent low to find a clear line of vision through the overhanging foliage.

"About three quarters of the way up toward the house, over by that big rock to the left."

Cole spotted him. "Well, I'm a son of a bitch!"

He sat down at the edge of the ravine and slid down into it on his backside, and scrambled laboriously up the opposite bank. Carl clutched at him and helped him climb out. They stood in a half-crouch behind the tree and stared up at the dark figure of a man hugging the base of a massive boulder on the jagged cliff-side above them.

"Jesus H. Christ!" Cole rumbled. "I'll just be goddamned! I absolutely give up!"

Carl attempted an explanation. "He had some kind of an idea in his head, Chief. A while ago, when you and Emmons were up there, he kept sayin' he thought you were wrong to go up along the path—"

"Oh, Lord!" Cole moaned. "I should've asked the son of a bitch for *instructions!*"

"He said he thought you ought to be over this way, toward the left. Said he bet he could sneak all the way up to the house that way, without bein' seen—"

"Well, goddammit, why didn't you tell the stupid jerk to shut up and mind his own damn business?!"

"Chief, I been tellin' him ever since we were down at the Cutler ranch to just relax and let *you* handle this. Bart's a stubborn, headstrong guy—but, Christ, I never thought he'd try anything like this!"

"Is he armed?"

"Not that I know of. But I don't really know for sure."

"Look at 'im—the perfect target. Hell, Hayward couldn't miss from that distance, even if he *is* a lousy shot."

Carl turned an anguished face to his superior. "I didn't know

166

what the hell to do about it, Chief. I started to call to him, tell him to get the hell back down here—but then I figured maybe Hayward won't see him, maybe he'll make it. If we called to him it would alert Hayward, and Bart wouldn't have a chance."

"Yeah, you're right." Cole shook his head somberly. "Has to be a hero," he muttered. "Has to be a goddam hero, even if it kills him."

They watched in silence for a few minutes. Behind them, across the ravine, Emmons and the other deputies had formed another tight silent group of watchers.

"There he goes again, movin' up closer," Cole said. "Wonder what the dumb bastard thinks he's gonna do when he *gets* there."

Although the mountain air at dawn was chill, perspiration stood out on Carl's face. He took out a handkerchief and wiped at his brow. "What'll we do, Chief?" He searched Cole's face anxiously for guidance.

Without taking his eyes off the slope the sheriff took Carl by the arm and issued some clipped orders.

"Get back across the ditch and tell Ogilvie to be sure and keep a sharp eye on Emmons, so *he* don't try to pull another stupid trick. These two assholes seem to have a competition goin', to see which one can get killed first. Then go back to the car and see if you can get Headquarters on the horn. Tell 'em we're in a state o' siege up here, that we're dealin' with a homicidal maniac, and we got a couple o' lunatics on *our* side, which don't help matters at all. Tell 'em we need help and we need it fast."

"Yeah, but, Chief, that's not goin' to help Bart right *now*."

"Him? We can't help *him*. All I can suggest for that idiot is prayer. If you feel like wastin' your breath."

Carl hesitated. "Yeah, but—"

"Get goin'," Cole snapped.

Carl scrambled down into the ravine and climbed the other side.

Lieutenant Cole leaned against the tree and stared up at the man on the rocky hillside above him.

"The damn fool," he muttered under his breath. "Let 'im get his silly ass shot off. I don't give a good goddamn."

He took off his hat, wiped his brow, and with a heavy sigh of

167

weariness sat down on the pine-needle-covered forest floor, his back against the tree trunk. He kept his eyes fixed on the rugged landscape between himself and the lofty cliffside house. It was a scene that was becoming noticeably brighter now with the approach of daylight.

"I couldn't help it," Cole mumbled to himself. "There's no way I could stop the son of a bitch." He sighed again.

"It's not my responsibility anymore   not my responsibility

24

The edge of the sun broke like a jewel over the jagged ridge to the east and sent scattered shafts of light fanning through the murky blue-gray mist of the forested slopes below. Far up on the opposite side of the valley the Emmons cabin remained partly in shadow. Inside, the light was dim; the big main room retained a somber semidarkness.

In the center of the room Meg stood, tense and rigid, and stared at Lonnie. Her eyes were bright with an undefined anguish.

Lonnie moved tentatively toward her. "Meg . . . why are you looking at me like that?"

She turned and retreated to the couch at the far end of the room, sat down stiffly on its edge and hugged herself, rocked gently back and forth, and gazed into the dark fireplace.

Lonnie followed and knelt beside her. "What's the matter, Meg?"

"I'm suddenly very cold," she murmured.

He started to put his arm around her, but she pulled away from him.

"Don't. Leave me alone, Lonnie."

"Meg, Meg, my angel . . ." His voice was pleading. "Don't turn against me, please? I need you now. I need you. . . ."

She continued to gaze into the fireplace and said nothing.

"What's wrong, dear heart? Is it the gun?" He glanced at the weapon he still held in his hand. "Pay no attention to it. I didn't hurt anybody when I fired, and I didn't intend to. I was just bluffing, don't you know that?"

He put the gun on the floor and gave it a shove under the couch.

"There—it's gone. You can forget all about it. I won't be needing it anymore, anyway. It'll be a little while before the troops down below gather up their nerve for another advance, and by then . . ."

Quickly she turned her eyes to him.

"By then I'll be gone."

Pain clouded her eyes. "Lonnie . . ." Her hand went out and touched him on the cheek, and hovered there. "You don't remember, do you?"

He remained motionless, staring at her.

"You don't remember about . . . about Betty."

He went limp, sagged back on his haunches, and gazed bleakly at the floor.

She leaned over him, clutching him by the shoulder. "Tell me, Lonnie. Is it true? Tell me."

"It's true," he said quietly. "I don't remember."

She closed her eyes. A kind of numbness seemed to flow over her.

"God knows, I've tried, Meg. I've probed, and groped, and searched my mind, over and over. It's just . . . not there."

There was a moment of silent misery, shared but unexpressed. He went on.

"That's what I had to wait for our visitors for. That's what I had to find out. There was a page of the script missing, and they had it. And I had to wait for it, because I had to know . . . I had to know . . ."

Impulsively she hugged him and put her cheek tightly against his. "Lonnie, you still don't know. Nothing is . . ." She struggled for words, fighting to preserve hopefulness. "Nothing is *certain*."

He seemed not to hear. He took her hand and held it in both his own and looked up at her, and his face was serenely calm.

"I must go now, Meg. Will you come with me?"

She found a last reservoir of optimism. "Oh, listen, Lonnie. I don't know what crazy conclusion you're jumping to, but it just doesn't make sense. I'll bet Betty felt so humiliated when you . . . when you rejected her . . . she probably decided to just sneak away and pretend it never happened." She managed a little smile. "That's what *I'd* do—I'd crawl into a hole so fast you'd—"

"Stop, Meg. Time has run out. Will you come with me?"

Her face contorted. She put her head down in her hands and bit her lip, trying not to cry. Lonnie came up on the couch beside her and took her in his arms.

"Don't say no, Meg. You'll kill me if you do. If you can't say yes, say maybe, possibly, I'll think about it—anything but no. Because I'll wait for you, I swear I will."

He kissed her on the temple, on the eyes, felt wetness, cradled her head on his shoulder and stroked her hair. "Darling Meg, give me your answer. Anything but no, anything . . ."

"I can't," she whispered. "I can't."

"Just say maybe, at least, and think about it for a day or two. I'll wait for you at the *Seabird*. You can find it easy—it's the *Nellie D.*, remember, and it's lying in the marina at Diamond Bay. Meet me there. Anytime, day or night, just come there and I'll see you, I'll come to you and take you in my arms . . ." He lifted her face with a finger under her chin. "I'll take you on the *Seabird*, my angel, and I'll love you for as long as it takes to sail to the stars and back."

She gazed at him in hopeless misery, through the shimmering of tears.

"Say maybe," he whispered. "Please. Just say maybe."

She nodded, mouthed the word soundlessly. *Maybe.*

"Thank you." He smiled, and plucked a tear from her cheek with the tip of a finger, and put it to his lips.

"Now, no more crying, because there's no time for anything but a smile, a kiss, and farewell. If we come together again, it will be for always. If not—well, then, what we've had is better than a lifetime of ordinary things."

She clung to him, unable to speak, and he held her close, with his lips caressing her neck and throat, and his murmuring voice sounding soft as a dream in her ear:

"*Ah me, how sweet is love itself possessed*
When but love's shadows are so rich in joy!"

With a desperate effort she pulled herself back and found her voice again. "Lonnie . . . you must *not* do this."

"Will you tell me you love me before I go?"

"If you try to run they'll kill you. They'll just shoot you down."

He laughed gently. "I know these mountains so much better than they do—they'll never catch up with me."

She shook her head vigorously, almost as if in anger. "But it's . . . it's . . ."

"Crazy." He took her face between his hands. "Will you tell me you love me? Please tell me. It will give me the strength I need."

She was trembling, choking with silent convulsive sobs.

He leaned forward and kissed her with infinite tenderness on the lips, then released her and got to his feet.

"Goodbye, Meg. Till we meet again, by the *Seabird*."

Her tear-streaked face turned upward, beseeching. Her hands went out, seeking to grasp and hold him. "Don't, Lonnie. Don't, please."

"I must be gone and live," he said. "Or stay and—"

An electric tension crackled mysteriously in the room.

"*Or stay and die*," he finished in a whisper.

Meg had stiffened suddenly. A hand flew in quick panic to her throat. Her wide eyes were riveted on the open window behind Lonnie.

He froze for an instant, sensing danger, then whirled, looked into the barrel of a snubnosed pistol and, behind it, framed in the window, a man's face, squint-eyed and glowering.

"Put up your hands!" the man shouted.

"No, Bart! No!" Meg was on her feet and flying across the room, her arms outstretched and the palms of her hands raised facing her husband.

"Get out o' the way, Meg, goddammit!" he bellowed at her. His face was twisted with intense ferocity. He raised the pistol higher, trying to aim past Meg.

She waved her arms at him frantically and screamed, "No, no! Stop it!"

Somewhere behind her, a quick movement. Bart's gun shifted, following it.

"Stay where you are!" he roared. "Put up your hands, or I'll fire!" He was halfway into the house, astraddle the windowsill.

Then his jaw dropped in astonishment. Meg was moving toward him, her eyes fixed on his weapon, her hands reaching for it.

He threw up a protective arm. "Jesus Christ! What are you—"

She got past his guard and grasped the muzzle of the gun. Bart pushed at her roughly, spitting curses. She held on. He was in the room now, his fierce eyes burning with rage.

The sound of quick movement again in the shadows of the room—running feet, toward the kitchen.

Bart advanced on Meg, snarling. "Crazy bitch! Leggo!"

She caught a glimpse of his free hand coming toward her in a blur—then recoiled involuntarily as something struck her on the side of the head. She staggered, gasped, groped for balance. The room spun wildly, her ears rang. Through the ringing she heard heavier, more violent movement, more running feet, something crunching against something else—then the deafening report of the gun firing, obliterating all other sensations of sight or sound.

Meg tried to scream, but her voice had ceased to function. She tried to look around, to see what was happening, but her muscles refused to respond. Straight ahead of her a peculiar geometric pattern formed dimly—then she realized with a small shock that she was lying on the floor.

There was more movement, the sounds of struggling, unseen, but appallingly felt through the vibrations in the floor. Then Bart yelled again, from somewhere farther away, and this time in a bellowing fury: "Halt, you bastard! *Halt!*"

There was a strange moment in which nothing moved, nothing made a sound. It was shattered by the vicious crack of a gunshot—another, then a third.

Meg tried to get up, but found herself held fast in the grip of a mysterious paralysis, though her mind raced feverishly.

Oh, God . . . how awful is the sound of gunfire inside a house.

Running feet again—heavy footfalls, rushing past her. She rolled her head from side to side, and saw the floor of the room tilting away from her at an impossible angle, as if the house had turned on its side. A large square of light flooded the room, a patch of daylight sky shone in her face, as the front door was flung open.

"Hey, you guys get up here! Quick!"

Is it Bart yelling? He sounds so strange.

Then his face loomed into view above her. His hand slipped under her head and lifted it up.

Easy, Bart, please. My head hurts. I hurt all over.
She groaned softly.

"Meg, Meg—are you all right, honey? Speak to me, sweet-heart. Are you all right?"

Strange—stranger than before. His voice is gentle now.
Suddenly a dark terror rose in her throat and filled it. She stared up at Bart wild-eyed, and fought to hold back panic.
What happened to Lonnie?

"I'm sorry I had to hit you, baby," Bart was saying. "Jesus, you were actin' so crazy, grabbin' the gun and all . . ."

Never mind, Bart. Just tell me what's happened.

"My God, what you must've been through, baby! I've been out of my mind with worry!"

Heavy footsteps on the stairs outside, and across the porch, and suddenly the floor of the room was creaking under the feet of many men—a hundred—an army, it seemed to Meg. She tried to turn her face away from them, but they were on all sides, milling about. Far above her, unfamiliar male eyes hovered and peered down at her in frank, offensive curiosity. She felt a sting of resentment.

"Honey, talk to me," Bart was pleading. "Say sump'm."

She tried to say, "I'm all right." It came out a soundless whisper.

"Is she hurt?" a gruff voice said.

"Can't tell yet," Bart said. "Get back, goddammit. Give her room to breathe." He was cradling her head in his hand and stroking her brow.

Oh, Bart, leave me alone, please. If somebody would just tell me where Lonnie is . . .

Other voices asked the question for her.

"Where's Hayward?"

"What happened, did you plug him?"

"Christ, you guys really move fast, don't you?" That was Bart, growling. "Took you five minutes to get up here!"

Somebody growled back at him. "You're a crazy damn fool, Hannah. You're lucky to be alive right now—tryin' to act like a goddam hero."

"Well, *somebody* had to make a move, goddammit! You chicken-livered bastards were all set to wait for hell to freeze over."

"All right, cut it," the gruff voice snapped. "Where the hell's Hayward?"

"Out the back."

Some of the feet scurried off, fanning through the house.

"Did you plug 'im?"

Meg's hand groped, clutched at Bart's sleeve. *Oh, please, please* . . .

"Hell, no," Bart grumped angrily. "The son of a bitch was too damn fast. Got clean away."

Meg closed her eyes and felt the aching muscles of her body go limp.

Bart held her face between his hands. "Meg, honey, are you all right? *Say* sump'm, will ya?"

A chord of sweet harmonious music seemed to rise up out of the depths of the earth and inundate her like a wave of soft surf on a warm sandy beach. She floated lazily. The tiresome male voices rumbled on, but became muffled and incoherent, mercifully drowned beneath the rolling water.

Dear God, thank you, thank you. . . . Now I can rest.

She sighed gently, and fainted.

25

For what seemed like a lifetime she drifted detached from all thought, feeling or sensibility, through infinite nothingness in which there was neither darkness nor light, comfort nor pain. At last she came up in the world again, in a world of kaleidoscopic dream-images that melted silently from one to the next, with blackness in between; scenes distorted and disjointed, viewed through a miraculous X-ray lens that stripped the veneer from all surfaces and laid bare the hard bony structure beneath. All things were alternately stark and then diffused by a soft protective blur. Faces floated in a white mist; voices reached her from far away, then rang with detestable intimacy in her ear.

She was on her feet somehow, groping in her fuzzy mind for orientation and equilibrium, and being led down stairs and down, down an endless steep rocky path, and, on either side of her, large hands held her elbows unnecessarily tightly, as if trying for some ludicrous reason to lift her off the ground.

On one side: "There, there honey. That's a good girl. Easy, now." That was Bart.

On the other: "If you feel sick or anything, Mrs. Hannah, just let us know. You can rest anytime."

The gruff voice she had heard before and felt menaced by— now a quiet reasonable voice, and surprisingly comforting. Who was it? Mental exertion was unbearable—she concentrated on the simple task of trying to focus her eyes on the ground before her, to see where she was going.

Then she was sitting in a car, a large unfamiliar car, with thick black leather upholstery that smelled of stale cigar smoke. On her right, Bart, putting his arm around her and trying to pull her close to him, and patting her arm ceaselessly, and murmuring, "There, there, honey. Everything's all right now. I've got you. Just relax."

On her left side another man, a stout man, who wheezed softly from exertion, and whose wide buttocks spread on the seat and touched her. She sat rigid and stared straight ahead.

Someone cranked up the car, and the motor roared. The vehicle lurched into motion.

The stout man on her left spoke, and as he did the smell of old cigar smoke increased intensely. She recognized the gruff voice—now, in these close quarters, not comforting, but unpleasantly grating on the ear.

"Mrs. Hannah, I'm sure you don't feel up to talkin' very much, but if I could just ask one or two questions while we drive down the mountain—"

"I want to go home," she heard someone say, and recognized her own voice, faint and tremulous.

"You'll be home soon," the gruff voice said. "But first I'd like to get a brief statement from you. We need to determine if we can the exact extent of criminal culpability on the part of—"

Close to her ear on the other side she heard Bart's growl: "Let her be, Cole, goddammit! Can't you see she's in no condition?"

To her, with cloying gentleness, he whispered, "There, there, honey. You don't have to talk now."

A little trembling rose in her throat; she felt a wild desire to burst into tears. Resolutely she suppressed the feeling, and closed her eyes. Bart pulled her head down on his broad shoulder. She kept her eyes closed for a long time, while around her fragments of conversation floated in and out of her hearing.

". . . have Sergeant Ogilvie stop and get the Forest Service people on the ball. . . ." "And shouldn't we contact the Jackson County Sheriff's office, Chief? . . ." "Yeah, the other side of the mountain's in Jackson County, ain't it? . . . Ought to be able to intercept Hayward without much trouble, not too many ways he can go, after all. . . . The F.B.I.? Hell, no, not if *I* can help it. This here's *our* show, goddammit. . . ." "Yeah, but, Chief, there's kidnapping involved here. . . ." "Well, I guess we'll just let Inspector Gregory worry about that. . . ."

Meg opened her eyes and raised her head, wanting to say no, no, there's no kidnapping. . . .

Bart pulled her head back down on his shoulder, saying, "There, there, honey, don't fret yourself. Just take it easy. There, there."

Oh, Bart, please stop saying there, there, honey. . . .

She closed her eyes again and let the droning of the car's engine wash over her and drown out everything.

Then she was at home, taking a shower and changing her clothes, and trying to rest for a few minutes, but without a moment of privacy, with Rita Duggan there, hovering, trying to be helpful and comforting, with the men from the Sheriff's Department sitting impatiently in the living room waiting, and Bart coming to the bedroom door to see if she was ready to go.

Go where? She didn't understand, but couldn't summon the energy to ask.

A long time later she was sitting in a cafe with Bart and Carl Gallagher, staring at a soiled tablecloth, and being served lunch. Next to her Bart wolfed a huge platter of ham and eggs and hotcakes and made a joke about having missed breakfast that morning. Meg toyed with her food. Bart watched her closely and said, "Eat up, baby, you must be starved. Eat up."

She smiled wanly, ate a little, sipped a cup of coffee, and waited, not knowing what she was waiting for.

She and Bart were left alone for a minute while Carl went to the cigar counter. Bart leaned toward her and spoke in low conspiratorial tones.

"Are you all right, baby? Were you hurt?"

She shook her head. "No."

"No what?" he said impatiently. "All right, or hurt?"

"I'm . . . I'm all right. Not hurt."

"You're not exactly bubbling over with information, are you?" Bart said, a trifle peevishly. He leaned closer still and whispered, "You can tell me, honey. I'm your husband. I won't tell anybody. Did the bastard rape you?"

She raised her eyes and looked at Bart—looked at him directly for the first time since he'd come through the window of the cabin. His broad earnest face seemed unfamiliar. He looked like a stranger.

178

"I wasn't hurt, Bart. I wasn't harmed in any way. And I wasn't kidnapped either."

"Well, never mind," Bart said. He turned his attention back to his plate. "You're prob'bly still in shock or sump'm. Don't even remember what happened exactly."

"That's not true, Bart. I remember everything. I was *not* kidnapped—"

"Never mind, I said," he snapped. "There's plenty o' difference of opinion on that subject. The sheriff guys think it's a clear-cut case if there ever was one."

"Bart, really, I—" Something told her to stop. Something said, why bother?

"Case of what?" Carl said, having returned to the table.

"Kidnapping." Bart drummed his fingers on the table, his anger renewing itself and making him restless. "Damn lucky thing for that son of a bitch I didn't catch him. I'd 'a' killed him for sure."

Meg stared into her coffee cup, and wondered how long this day would last, and how long it would be before she could be alone.

"Eat your lunch, Meg, dammit," Bart was saying. "I'm payin' for that food, so come on, eat up."

She swallowed hard and closed her eyes.

Lonnie, Lonnie, my darling . . . where are you now?

Then there was Inspector Somebody-or-other—she didn't catch the name. She sat in a cramped, dingy office and studied the innumerable scratches and scuffs on an old worn desk top and, tiring of that, gazed at the portrait of the governor of the state, on the wall behind the desk. The governor gazed back at her with immensely dignified impersonal eyes; he had no intention of coming to her aid, that was clear.

The inspector, on the other hand, scrutinized her with eyes that were sharp, shrewd, probing, and anything but impersonal. The inspector was handsome in an unappetizing way, with a lean hawklike face and wavy hair meticulously groomed. He asked trivial questions in a smooth, soothing, professional manner. Meg listened curiously to her own voice talking about herself, and thought, How uninteresting I am. How ordinary.

My name is Meg Hannah. Yes, Margaret. Meg is for Margaret. I am twenty-three years old. Yes, I have lived in this area all my life. I was graduated from Caxton High School, attended Grange Junior College for one year, and was employed for two years at Maybrey's Variety Store, before my marriage. My present address is . . .

What has all this to do with anything?

Who? Alonzo Hayward? Oh, the fugitive. Yes. No, I never knew him before. I never saw him before I met him last—let's see, Sunday it was—was that yesterday? Or the day before?

Alonzo Hayward. How strange. I don't know anybody named Alonzo. His name is Lonnie. He is Lonnie, and he is my love. . . .

The circumstances. Yes, well—I was painting in the canyon, Stag River Canyon, that is, and—painting. Painting a picture, a landscape. Watercolor. Yes, I do, frequently. Yes, alone. I've never had any kind of trouble. The canyon is a very quiet secluded place. . . .

The inspector had come around the desk and was leaning over her. He smelled of expensive men's cologne, and his eyes were soft. He was wondering aloud how an attractive young woman like her—a beautiful young woman, really—could consider such a solitary activity safe.

I wonder, my dear Mrs. Hannah, the inspector was murmuring, if you have any idea how tempting you would be to a sex-crazed . . .

The inspector's velvet voice seemed peculiarly lacking in staying power; it faded. Past the man's shoulder and through the unwashed window of the little office Meg could see traffic going by on the street outside.

All you dull people, in all those dull cars . . . have you ever dreamed of the wild and wonderful world that can be seen through Lonnie's eyes? No, of course you haven't. Only I have. . . .

The inspector had gone back to his seat and was addressing her in a more official tone.

Oh, excuse me, Inspector. What was the question? Abduction? I can't tell you anything about an abduction. There was no such thing, that I know of. No. No, I wasn't. I offered Mr. Hayward a ride and drove him up to the Emmons cabin. Yes, voluntarily. No, he did *not* assault me, or threaten me, or mistreat me in any way. No, I wasn't frightened, or suspicious. Why should I have been? Captive? No, definitely not, I was not held captive. And I was not held as a hostage. Well, yes, I guess I did tell the lieutenant I was, but—no, I didn't, really. I only said that because I . . . I didn't know how to explain to him. . . . How could I have explained to him about Lonnie . . . I mean Mr. Hayward . . . under those circumstances? . . . It was very difficult. . . .

Oh, how could any of you ever possibly understand? You are earthbound. What do you know of the sea and the sky?

It went on and on. At length the inspector heaved a sigh, got up and came around the desk and leaned over her once more.

My dear Mrs. Hannah . . .

Oh, no, I'm not your dear anything, Inspector.

. . . extremely distraught, and exhausted from your experience, he was saying. So I am going to let you go now. We'll go over all this again later, after you're feeling better. I'm sure you understand. This is a serious matter, and we have to make a thorough investigation, you see. There are many unanswered . . .

Yes, all right, Inspector. Thank you very much.

I could do a portrait of you, Inspector. And those cold eyes of yours would be fierce and cruel, the eyes of a predator. The eyes of a red-tailed hawk.

Then home. Home at last, and somehow the sun was low in the west, somehow the dreary hours of the day had dragged by.

She stood for a moment gazing up at the darkening shadows in Stag River Canyon to the south, and then up at the faint blue line of the high pine and cedar spires on the mountain ridges, far beyond. Soft evening clouds hung there, brooding over the quiet earth.

Where are you now, my love? Are you cold, hungry, miserable? Are you afraid? Do you ache for me, as I ache for you?

Bart led her into the house. She stumbled to her bed and lay down fully clothed, curled up on her side, and closed her eyes tight.

From somewhere far away she heard Bart say, "Hey, honey, get undressed, for Christ's sake. That's no way to sleep"—and heard no more.

181

26

It was a little while after dark when headlight beams swung in from County Highway 15 and illuminated the Hannah ranch road, and a moment later the tires of the Duggans' big green station wagon churned the gravel of the driveway and rolled to a stop. By the time Herb and Rita were out of the car the front door of the house was open and Bart was standing on the front stoop, waiting for them.

Rita walked rapidly toward him, studying his face and asking, "How's our girl, Bart?"

"Out cold." He sounded peevish. "Came home, flopped down on the bed, and hasn't moved a muscle since."

"Poor baby." Rita's voice went soft in sympathy. "She must be simply devastated."

Bart glared at her. "How about me? How do you think *I* feel, not knowin' all that time where she was, or what the hell happened to her?"

Rita patted him on the cheek. "Another poor baby."

"And you know sump'm?" Bart went on. "I *still* don't know what happened to her."

Herb had gone to the rear of the station wagon and lifted out a cardboard box covered with a tablecloth. He came up the walk, carrying the box. "How's Meg?" he said to Bart.

Rita answered him. "We don't know yet, sweetie. Take the food on into the kitchen, will you? I'll be right there."

Herb went in. Rita paused in the doorway and looked closely at Bart's glum frowning face.

"Don't worry, sweetie. She's just exhausted, that's all. She'll be all right."

Bart would not be comforted.

"All the way home I kept beggin' her to talk to me, tell me exactly what happened and how it happened. 'I'm your husband,' I said, 'you can tell me.' She just kept shakin' her head and gazin' off into the distance and sayin', 'I don't want to talk about it now, I don't feel like talkin',' and things like that. She's actin' mighty damn peculiar, if you ask me."

"Well, nobody's asking you, sweetie. And, anyway, she's not acting peculiar, she's acting perfectly normal."

"Well, Jesus, I don't see—"

"She's had a hell of an experience, for God's sake. Be patient, give her a little time to recover. Just tell yourself she's back, and she's safe—that's the important thing."

Bart nodded. "Yeah, you're right. That's the important thing. I got my little mouse back."

Rita smiled, and patted him on the cheek again. "I brought supper. Are you hungry?"

"When have you seen me when I wasn't hungry?"

"You're not hungry about as often as you're not horny, which is never."

Bart laughed. "Goddam, Rita! You can always find a way to cheer me up, I swear!"

"So how about a little appreciation? Wasn't that sweet of me to bring supper?"

Bart grinned, leaned toward her and kissed her on the ear. "You're a peach, baby."

"And don't you forget it, you sexy bastard," she murmured, and went inside.

Some time later a Sheriff's Department patrol car rolled into the Hannahs' driveway and stopped behind the Duggans' station wagon. Immediately Bart was in the doorway of the house, waving a greeting.

"Carl! Glad you could make it."

Carl Gallagher, looking like an altogether different person off duty, was dressed in white slacks and a Hawaiian print sport shirt. He came up the front walkway ahead of his wife, then turned and waited for her.

"I believe you've met Lois, haven't you, Bart?"

"Sure!" Bart beamed at the woman.

Lois Gallagher was short and dark-eyed, with a soft round face and an hourglass figure—prominent bust, waspish waist, and full hips—that was well accented by a tight tailored dress. She held out her hand and said, "Nice to see you, Mr. Hannah."

"Nice to see *you*, Lois, honey," Bart said genially. "And the name's Bart." He leaned down and kissed her on the cheek.

Lois blinked in surprise.

"Well, how you doin', old buddy?" Carl said. "Completely recovered?"

Bart chuckled. "Hell, yes! Good as new."

"Lieutenant Cole said he'd try to drop by in a little while, pay his respects."

"Great! Christ, I feel so good I'll even be civil to *that* ol' windbag!" Bart laughed and looked at Lois, and she responded with an uneasy smile.

"Hope it won't be too big of a crowd," Carl said. "I see you've already got company."

"Aw, no, no company. Just my cousin Herb Duggan and his wife. You folks ever met the Duggans?"

"Don't think so," Carl said. "But seems to me I've seen that green station wagon before." He grinned slyly at Bart and winked.

Bart ignored it.

"Well, my goodness," Lois said. "We haven't asked about the most important one. How's Mrs. Hannah?"

"Oh, she's fine," Bart said offhandedly. "She's havin' a nap right now, she'll be with us in a little while." He held the door open. "But, what the hell, we've got enough for a party already. Come on in."

In the living room Bart made quick introductions. Rita, lounging on the couch and nursing a drink, smiled at Lois Gallagher and patted the seat next to herself.

"Come sit here, sweetie. Bart will fix you a drink, and you and I can be envious together."

"What'll you have, Lois?" Bart said.

"Just a soft drink, please. No alcohol."

"Aw, c'mon!" Bart roared. "We're celebratin' tonight, this is a party!"

Lois looked apprehensive. "Well . . . maybe just a weak bourbon and ginger ale."

184

"Atta girl!" Bart took Carl's order and started for the kitchen. "Not too much whiskey in mine," Lois called after him. Bart laughed.

Lois crossed the room and sat down gingerly next to Rita on the couch.

Herb waved Carl to a chair. Carl sat down and gazed in undisguised fascination at Rita. Rita smiled languidly at him and sipped her drink.

"What is it we're supposed to be envious about, Mrs. Duggan?" Lois said stiffly.

"Call me Rita, sweetie. Everybody does." Rita smiled some more and sipped.

"We're envious about the fact that while we're living dull uneventful lives, yearning for a little excitement and slowly dying of boredom, a great big dramatic thing happens to Meg. To little Meg Hannah, of all people!"

Lois shuddered faintly. "My goodness! I certainly don't feel inclined to be envious of *that*! It must have been simply terrifying for her."

"Oh, I don't know." Rita shrugged. "She's safe and sound, after all. And just *think* of having a thrilling adventure like that to brag about for the rest of your life!" She leaned her head back and gazed at the ceiling. "God! Why can't anything like that happen to *me*?"

"My goodness!" Lois said.

Bart returned with drinks for Lois and Carl, and stood watching as Lois took a cautious sip.

She produced another little shudder and frowned at Bart. "Oh, my, that's much too strong for me." She held the glass out to him.

He chuckled and sat down next to Rita. "Good for you, sweetheart. Brings out all those hidden charms you didn't know you had."

Rita patted Lois on the knee. "Drink up, sweetie. You don't want to be a party-pooper."

Lois sipped, looking worried.

"What were you sayin' about an adventure?" Bart said to Rita.

"I was telling Lois how I'm all curled up with envy over

Meg's luck. *She's* going to be the center of attention for months now, while *I*, who pant passionately for every particle of attention I can get—*I'm* going to be ignored!"

Bart grinned at her. "I bet you'd have given that jerk Hayward more than he bargained for, wouldn't you, hot stuff?"

"You know me," Rita said. "I'd have turned him every way but loose."

Carl laughed loudly, causing Lois to glare at him.

"Damn right I know you." Bart leered at Rita and pinched her on the thigh.

"My goodness!" said Lois. She took a healthy swig of her drink.

Carl was leaning forward in his chair, watching Rita, never having taken his eyes off her. "Funny thing, Mrs. Duggan—"

"It's Rita, sweetie," she said, smiling at him.

"Oh, uh . . . yeah." Carl blushed. "I was gonna say, Rita—I don't recall meeting you before, but soon's I saw that green station wagon outside I knew I'd seen *it* before. Fact is, seems to me I've seen it *here*."

"Rita and I come over quite a lot," Herb said brightly. "Bart and Rita and Meg are old chums from school days, y'know? And Bart and I are first cous—"

"Yeah, he knows all that, Herb," Bart growled. His eyes bore into Carl's.

Carl raised his glass toward Bart, smiled, and said, "Cheers, ol' buddy."

Bart glared at him.

"Say, we got lots o' spaghetti left over," Herb said, addressing Lois. "Would you folks like some?"

"It's terrific," Rita said. "Herbie makes it himself."

"Oh, no, thank you, we've had dinner," Lois said.

Bart said, "Herbie, I think Rita's real lucky to have you for a wife."

"We have a perfect marriage," Rita said. "I wear the pants, Herbie wears the apron."

Herb grinned.

Lois leaned forward and looked past Rita at Bart. "Carl told me about what you did, Mr. Hannah, breaking into that cabin and all. That was an awfully brave thing to do."

"The lieutenant was plenty p.o.'d about it," Carl said.

"Well, I think it was wonderful," Lois said.

Bart gave a modest little shrug. "Oh, it wasn't anything, really. My wife was in danger. . . ." A dramatic, faraway look came into his eyes. "There are times when a man has to do—what a man has to do."

"Oh, I think it's just thrilling!" gushed Lois.

"I think I might be sick," muttered Rita.

"How's your drink, sweetheart?" Bart said to Lois. "Ready for a refill?"

Impulsively Lois drained her glass, gasped, and handed it to Bart.

Bart chuckled, and leaned across Rita and patted Lois on the knee. "Good girl," he murmured. Lois giggled.

Rita gave Bart a cold look. He ignored her. His gaze lingered boldly on Lois, openly appraising the large breasts and ample hips.

"Hey, Carl, you mean to say you leave this sexy babe at home unguarded while you go on patrol?"

"Sure do," Carl said amiably. "You think it's dangerous?"

Bart's eyes remained on Lois. "Just tell me when you're goin' out again, and how long you'll be away."

Carl laughed raucously. Lois turned scarlet.

"You bastard," Rita said quietly. She handed Bart her glass. "Take your lecherous eyes off the lady, and go fix us some more drinks."

Bart took the two glasses and his own and started across the room. He glanced at Carl as he went past. "I could use a little help in the kitchen, Carl. Bring your glass, and Herb's."

Herb got up quickly. "I'll help, Bart."

Bart pushed him back down in his chair. "Not *you*, Herbie." He gave Carl a quick signal with his eye as he left the room.

Carl followed Bart into the kitchen and watched in silence while the host busied himself with the drinks. In a moment Bart glanced at him with a slight toss of the head that said, Come closer.

Carl came closer. "What's on your mind, Bart? You sore about me talkin' about the green station wagon?"

"Naw, naw!" Bart dropped ice cubes in the glasses with elaborate care. He spoke in low tones, without looking at Carl. "What d'ya think o' Rita?"

Carl nodded. "Some dish."

"You bet your sweet ass, some dish. That's only half of it."

"That right?" Carl's eyes gleamed. "So tell me the other half."

Bart counted out more ice cubes. He worked very slowly.

"She's hot as a firecracker, pal. Ready for action, anytime, anyplace. All you gotta do with Rita is snap your fingers, and she'll drop her panties and spread her legs." Bart held a jigger glass up to eye level and poured whiskey.

"Snap your fingers, huh?"

"Right."

Carl edged closer. "Uh . . . whose fingers?"

"Yours. Mine. Anybody's. You know the old saying—she only fucks her friends—"

"And she ain't got no enemies?"

"That's the story."

"Mighty interesting." Carl pondered. "Why are you telling me all this, buddy?"

"Well, I was thinkin'—how'd you like to arrange a little swap party sometime?"

Carl's face reflected confusion. "I don't get it, Bart. You're tryin' to sell me on Rita—but she ain't yours to sell."

Bart gave his friend a look of superior amusement.

Carl stopped looking confused and started looking astonished. "*Is* she?"

"Let's put it this way, pal. Rita will do *anything* for kicks. And she'll do anything I tell her to."

Carl's eyes shone with admiration. "What an operator!"

"Yeah. So how about it?"

Confusion returned. Carl frowned and shook his head. "Lemme see if I read you right—you mean you got the hots for *Lois*?"

Bart chuckled. "Hey, don't put your little woman down, pal, just because you're *used* to her. Have you backed off and taken a good look lately?"

"What are you talkin' about! Have you taken a good look at *Meg* lately? That doll puts 'em *all* to shame!"

Bart shrugged. "Well, that's how it goes, y'know?" He had finished making the drinks and was now wiping each glass with a napkin. "Familiarity breeds—what is it?"

"Contempt."

"Worse than that. Boredom. You and I are sufferin' from the same damn problem, pal. That's why they invented swap parties."

"But what about Herb? What about Meg?" Carl's eyes suddenly widened with a titillating idea. "Hey! Don't tell me those two—"

Bart laughed. "Not a chance! That's the cross Herbie has to bear. He wants Meg so bad he can taste it, but she's straight as a mother superior. There's no way I can help *him*. But I can help *you*." He gave Carl a long hard look. "Think about it."

Rita's vibrant, throaty laugh floated in from the living room.

"I am," Carl said softly. "I *am* thinkin' about it."

"In the meantime, don't get annoyed if I play up to Lois a little, okay? Just testin' the ground, you might say."

Carl nodded absently.

"Hey, Bart!" Rita yelled. "You guys playing with each other in there? Where are those drinks?"

Bart grinned. "I'm tellin' you," he whispered, "that gal's a million laughs." He picked several glasses. "Help me carry these in, will you?"

Carl stood for a moment in the kitchen after Bart had left. Slowly he shook his head. "What an operator!" he said again, under his breath.

A while later another patrol car drove into the Hannahs' driveway and pulled up alongside Carl Gallagher's car, and Lieutenant Ed Cole, crisp and neat in a fresh uniform, stepped out and went up to the house. He rang the doorbell, waited, scowled darkly when he heard the sound of raucous laughter from within, muttered, "What the devil's goin' on?" and rang again.

Finally the door was opened by Herb Duggan, who stood with drink in hand and stared fuzzily out at the sheriff.

Cole stared back. "Mr. Hannah in?" he barked.

A light dawned on Herb. "Oh . . . you must be Lieutenant What's-it."

"Cole. Lieutenant Cole, Sheriff's Department. May I come in?"

"Hell, yes, come on in, join the party." Herb held the door open and grinned at the sheriff. "You shoulda brought a date, though. We're short of women as it is—"

Cole had walked past him and into the living room.

Bart was sitting next to Lois Gallagher, his arm extended behind her along the back of the sofa. He was talking to her in an undertone, close to her ear. Lois sipped her drink and smiled at him across the rim of her glass.

Carl Gallagher sat in a chair that he had pulled up close to Rita, at the other end of the sofa. He was telling her a funny story and was supplying the laughter to go with it. Rita wasn't listening. Her eyes were dull.

She smiled at Cole when he appeared in the doorway, and said, "Hi, there," in her most flirtatious voice.

Carl looked around, and his jaw dropped. He bounded to his feet and went toward Cole. "Glad you could make it, Lieutenant." He glanced nervously at Bart, who was whispering in Lois' ear. "Lieutenant Cole's here, Bart."

Bart glanced up, got unhurriedly to his feet, and came toward the sheriff, grinning.

"Well, well, if it ain't the mastermind himself! Nice of you to stop by. We were just havin' a drink or two, by way of celebration. What'll you have?"

Cole's face was stone. "Nothing. Can't stay. Just thought I'd inquire as to Mrs. Hannah's condition."

Bart's eyebrows went up. "Her condition?" He shrugged. "Well, she's doin' all right, I guess. No thanks to the do-nothing Sheriff's Department."

"What's that supposed to mean?"

Bart chuckled. He swayed slightly. "Forget it, Sheriff, ol' buddy." He grabbed Cole by the arm. "I'm feelin' just too damn good to fight with anybody tonight. C'mon, have a drink with us."

Cole detached himself from Bart's grasp. "No, thanks."

"Jesus Christ!" Bart's temper flashed. "Unlimber a bit, why don't you? You gonna be a stuffed shirt all your life?!"

"Mr. Hannah, would it be possible for me to speak with Mrs. Hannah for a few minutes?"

"What the hell for?"

"Inspector Gregory asked me to check and see how she was doin' tonight. It's nothin' urgent, but—"

"That's good, because you can't see her."

"Why not?"

"Because she's asleep, that's why not."

"Asleep?" Lieutenant Cole gazed around the room. "With all this goin' on?"

"Hell, yes, with all this goin' on. She's bombed out. Don't you think she's got a right, bein' raped all night by some god-damned sex fiend while we sat around in cars discussin' strategy—"

"That's not accordin' to your wife's testimony, Mr. Hannah."

Bart's face flushed with anger. "Goddammit, why don't they teach you cops a little sump'm about human psychology, for Christ's sake! Can't you see through that? Don't you know it's because she's ashamed and embarrassed to talk about it? *I'll* get it out of her, don't worry. She can't keep anything from me—"

"You're full of crap, Bart." It was Rita, and her voice was flat and hard.

Bart glared at her. "What d'ya mean by that?!"

"Meg said the guy didn't harm her, and I think she's telling the truth."

"Ho-ly Christ! Anybody else want to put in a half-assed amateur opinion?!"

Rita was sitting up straight, and her green eyes were flashing. "*Your* opinion's about as amateur as an opinion can get, you stupid jerk!"

Bart moved toward Rita and fixed her with a fierce scowl. "What the hell would *you* know about rape? The woman who gets raped is the woman who tries to *resist*. And resist, baby, is sump'm you've never done in your life—"

He closed his eyes just in time. Rita's drink splashed in his face, and an ice cube struck him on the bridge of the nose.

Herb came hurriedly across the room, almost stumbling, took the empty glass out of his wife's hand and whispered to her, urgently, "For God's sake Rita, calm yourself, will you?"

"What do you mean?" she said, with perfect serenity. "I *am* calm."

Lois Gallagher sat paralyzed, staring at Rita, her eyes wide with astonishment.

Herb turned anxiously to Bart. "You all right, buddy?"

Bart was wiping the whiskey off his face. "Yeah, sure," he mumbled. Gingerly he felt his nose, and rubbed it.

"Gee, I'm sorry," Herb said.

"*I'm* not," Rita said.

Lieutenant Cole cleared his throat and spoke forcefully. "Mr. Hannah."

Bart turned back to the sheriff.

"One or two things I want to say, then I'll be goin'. First, I think it's mighty inappropriate for you folks to be havin' a party here tonight. Whatever it was that happened to Mrs. Hannah, it's pretty certain she was deeply disturbed. The least you could do is let her have a little peace and quiet."

"I guess I can run my household without your advice, Sheriff," Bart snapped.

"But you're absolutely right, Lieutenant," Carl said hastily. "Lois and I were just leaving."

Cole ignored Carl, kept his eyes on Bart. "And, second, Inspector Gregory wants you to have Mrs. Hannah stand by for a possible summons back to Headquarters tomorrow."

"Goddam! What the hell for? Meg gave her testimony, for Christ's sake! Now you guys go and do your job and catch that bastard Hayward, and leave us alone!"

"Mrs. Hannah's testimony was somewhat vague, to tell the truth. Inspector Gregory says she was obviously in a state of shock. He wasn't altogether satisfied."

"Harassment!" Bart growled. "You're harassing her, that's what you're doin'!"

"Come, come, Mr. Hannah! This is a serious case. Hayward is still at large, and one person, Mrs. Emmons, is still missing. Don't forget that."

"If you bums were half as good at catchin' criminals as you are at hounding innocent people—"

"Oh, one more thing, Mr. Hannah. It's distinctly possible that charges may be brought against *you*."

"Me?!"

"For your high-handed behavior at the Emmons cabin this morning, takin' the law into your own hands, as it were."

Bart exploded. "Jesus H. Christ, *listen* to this shit! I saved Meg's *life!* I did it myself, because nobody else had the guts to make a move! And now I'm bein' accused—"

"We'll discuss it later, Mr. Hannah. At Headquarters."

Cole turned on his heel and started for the door, then paused and looked back. "Please convey my regards to Mrs. Hannah," he said. "For some strange reason I find I'm developing a great deal of admiration for her." His eyes roamed over the assembled company. "And a certain amount of sympathy."

He went out, and Bart stood in the center of the room, staring after him.

Carl nervously cleared his throat. "Come on, Lois. We got to be goin'."

Lois was already on her feet. She touched Bart on the sleeve. "It was *so* nice talking to you, Bart." Her voice was soft and girlish. "Do tell Mrs. Hannah we're sorry not to have seen her. I hope she's feeling fine again by tomorrow."

Bart suddenly grasped Lois' hand and gazed at her feelingly. "You know, it's just a shame how seldom we've seen you folks. You and Carl will have to come over for an evening real soon, okay?"

Lois glowed. "Oh, we'd *love* to!"

Bart gave her hand a gentle squeeze before releasing it, and winked at her. Lois blushed and glanced quickly at Carl.

After perfunctory goodbyes, Carl and Lois were gone. Silence descended on the room. Herb looked from Rita to Bart, and back to Rita.

"Well . . . guess we ought to be goin' too, honey." It was more a question than a statement.

Rita didn't move. She was leaning back on the couch, watching Bart. "You go warm up the car, sweetie. I'll be right with you."

"Hell, the car don't need warming—"

"Go warm up the car, dammit," Rita said sharply.

"Oh." Herb hesitated, then shuffled toward the front door. "See you, Bart," he said quietly. "Give our love to Meg, hear?" He went out.

Bart turned toward Rita, and they gazed at each other for a long silent moment.

Rita locked her hands above her head and gave him a bland smile. "Well, you did pretty well tonight, I'd say, considering all the handicaps you had to put up with. I figure you'll have little Lois in the sack within two, three weeks, at the most."

Bart shrugged and looked sheepish. "Aw . . . I was just kiddin' her."

"The thing I can't figure out is what kind of a deal you made with Carl. Surely you didn't pretend you were going to fix him up with Meg! Even *you* couldn't tell *that* big a lie."

A cunning grin crossed Bart's face and disappeared quickly. He rubbed his nose and frowned.

"You gave me a hell of a whack, y'know."

"Just luck. Probably couldn't do it again."

"You didn't even say you were sorry."

"I said I wasn't. Remember?"

Bart pouted, rubbing his nose. "It hurts."

Rita laughed softly. "Aw, poor baby!" She held out her arms to him. "C'mere, baby."

Bart went to the sofa and sat down beside her. She put a hand behind his head, pulled it down and kissed him lightly on the bridge of the nose.

"There. Now it's all better." Her voice was sultry.

Immediately his arms were around her and pulling her close. Their open mouths came together hard and ground on each other. Then Rita pulled back.

"That's all, big fella. No more."

"Aw, Rita . . ." Bart's hand was moving up and down her hip.

"I said no more, Bart. Now or ever." Abruptly she slapped his hand away and got to her feet.

He stared up at her, astonished. "What?"

A serene smile suddenly lit Rita's face. "Tell you how it is, sweetie. I figured out something about myself tonight. And I'm glad, because now that I know this, maybe I can do something about it. Maybe I can help myself a little."

Bart got up and moved toward her, his hands seeking her body. "Aw, don't go gettin' psychological on me, baby. We got better things to talk about—"

"No, wait, Bart, listen to this. It's interesting." She fended off his groping hands and retreated a few steps. "I figured out what it is about you that's always aroused me so. You know what it is? It's your meanness. That's what does it to me, believe it or not— your goddamned hateful son-of-a-bitchin' *meanness*."

Bart made an impatient face and reached for her again. "Aw, cut it out, Rita."

She darted to the front door, stood there poised for flight, and looked back at Bart with a new light shining in her eyes.

"Can you feature that, Bart? All that time we were together I kept thinking, if only you weren't so god-awful mean, I could really love you, I could marry you and be a faithful wife forever. What a laugh! What a crock! It just struck me tonight that the only time you really turn me on is when you're being nasty. Hell, nobody can live a whole lifetime like that. When I threw that drink in your face, what I really wanted to do was tear my clothes off and grab you and go at it hot and heavy. But when you're being nice, the way you were trying to be with that Lois dame, you don't thrill me at all. You absolutely bore me to *death!*"

Bart moved toward her again. His face had gone hard. "Lower your voice, goddammit. You'll disturb Meg."

Rita threw back her head and laughed. "Oh, brother! *Now* you're being considerate of Meg—how very touching!"

Suddenly Herb was standing outside the screen door, peering in. "Coming, Rita?" he said very quietly.

"Coming, Herbie."

Rita beamed a shallow smile toward Bart. "Do give our love to dear sweet Meg. And, you know, I think I'll take a cue from Lieutenant Cole. Include our sympathy while you're at it." She patted Bart playfully on the cheek and walked out, and Herb caught Bart's eye and let a sober weighted look rest on him for an instant before turning away.

Bart stood still until he heard the Duggans' station wagon drive off. Then he closed the door softly, turned and went back into the living room and sat down. He gazed broodingly at the floor.

"I'll be damned," he muttered. "I'll just be goddamned."

27

She struggled in a dim wasteland of half-dreaming, half-waking, and reached out restlessly, groping in the darkness. There were voices somewhere, muffled, but reverberant in a vast chamber, and rising and falling in random spurts. There was laughter at times, raucous and abrasive, and movement—doors opening and closing—and once it seemed the voices turned rough and strident, and rose in anger—but always muffled, veiled, and unintelligible. In her mind garish comic-strip-colored images glowed vividly, came up painfully close to her eyes, receded, were pushed aside by other images, and fell away silently over an invisible precipice.

Then gradually individual faces became recognizable, and words distinguishable.

Bart's face, contorted with a strange mushy-soft smile, drifted around her, bobbing like a child's toy balloon, his unseen hand stroking her cheek, his voice flowing like syrup in her ear: *There, there, honey. There, there. . . .*

The stout gruff-voiced sheriff, smelling of cigar smoke—stiff-necked, pompous, but meticulously correct and courteous, and somehow reassuring—appraising her quietly from a distance.

The faces of other men, strangers, some of them very young, staring at her with brazen, hard-eyed curiosity.

Rita, regarding her with motherly sympathy and murmuring, *Poor baby, poor baby.* She was clinging to Bart's arm.

But nowhere Lonnie. Nowhere that gentle sensitive face, and the pensive eyes, soft with melancholy and dreaming. Her hands roamed aimlessly in the dark wilderness, trying to find him, to touch him.

Suddenly there was the inspector. Cool, suave, oily-smooth,

his computer-operated smile turning on and off like an electric sign. She sat stiff and still in an enormous chair and waited.

Your full name, Mrs. Hannah? Your date of birth? Your place of residence? Your innermost thoughts, Mrs. Hannah, your secret dreams, if you please? Your entire biographical history, since you were a baby?

She sighed wearily. Oh, Inspector, you do tire me so.

Oh, so sorry.

But he came closer, shockingly close, and was garbed in the somber robes of a judge.

Then let me get straight to the point, Mrs. Hannah. Why did you go out alone? To be picked up?

Certainly not. I went out to paint.

But you allowed yourself to be picked up.

I was not picked up. Mr. Hayward wanted to go up to the mountains. I decided to take him.

Why?

Why? Well . . . because he was nice to me, that's why.

Was that so remarkable?

It was much more than remarkable. It was miraculous. Nobody has ever been that nice to me before.

The piercing eyes of the inspector looked right through her clothes and examined her body. The eyes gleamed. They liked what they saw.

I find that hard to believe, my dear.

I find it hard to believe, too, Inspector. And I'm still not your dear.

And I'm not the inspector, the man said. It was Bart.

I'm your husband, for Christ's sake. You can tell me, baby. Did that bastard rape you?

No, no, no! He loved me—he *loved* me!

Is that so goddamned remarkable?

Bart, I've never been loved like that before. I've never been *loved* before. Not ever. I'm sorry, Bart.

The son of a bitch. He not only got into your body, he contaminated your mind.

Leave the poor baby alone, sweetie, Rita's voice said. Her eyes swam into view, superimposed themselves on Bart's.

Well, goddammit, why won't she tell me the truth? I'm her husband, she can tell me—

Go away, Bart, Rita said. Bart's eye screwed themselves up into a ferocious frown and slid over the precipice. Rita glided closer and smiled at her.

Somebody's got to look after you, you poor helpless child, so it might as well be me. Now, then. I'm a woman, so you can tell me. What happened?

He loved me, Rita. And I loved him.

You can trust me, sweetie. Just tell me everything.

That's everything. Isn't that enough to be everything?

Poor baby. Why can't you just play around with other people's husbands, like I do? So nice and easy, so uncomplicated, y'know? Now, you take Herb, for instance. He's really a very sweet guy. Come here a minute, Herbie.

Herb's boyish face beamed at her from behind Rita's eyes.

You see how cute he is, sweetie? He's a hell of a lot of fun in bed, too, take it from me.

Herb grinned, and hung his head sheepishly.

All right, Herbie. Go out and play now. We'll call you if we need you.

Herb vanished.

Thank you just the same, Rita. But I'd really rather not—

You'd rather not what? the woman's voice said. It was a strange voice, silky, but ice cold. She had never heard a voice like that before. It was frightening. She searched for a face to go with it, but there was none. The darkness was blank.

Who are you?

I'm Betty Emmons, don't you know me? I'm Betty the Bubble Girl. Everybody knows Betty the Bubble Girl. I'd like to tell you about me and Lonnie.

Why are you hiding? Where are you?

The hard silken voice laughed. *That's a good question, where am I. I wish I could tell you, I really do. All I can tell you is about me and Lonnie—*

No, no, tell me about yourself. Where are you?

Lonnie's a darling boy, really. So gentle and sweet-natured. But of course you know that already, don't you?

Please, just tell me where you are.

It's too morbid. I don't like to talk about it.

Please. I have to know.

He didn't mean to do it, I know he didn't. He just lost his head. He's really a very sweet boy.

Do what? What did he do?

Sometimes I feel sorry for men, you know what I mean? The way they're always lusting after us gals—must be tough on 'em. Anyway, Lonnie was mad about me, much more than he ever could be about you, you silly. Once he'd tasted my body, he couldn't stand to be without it. But he was tortured by these stupid guilt feelings, y'know? That's why he did what he did to me. Men are such idiots. It was awfully foolish of him, and not at all necessary—

But what did he do? What did he do?

I don't like to say it. It sounds so terrible when you just say it out loud.

But I've got to know. Tell me, *tell* me!

You're tiresome, the way you keep saying everything twice. He killed me, if you must know. Bashed my head in with a rock, and left me lying in the dry wash.

A scream rose in her throat. She struggled desperately to fight it back.

I don't believe you.

I wouldn't kid you, honey. Why should I kid you?

Oh, no, I don't believe you. You're a liar, you're just trying to make trouble for Lonnie, to get even with him. You're a bad person. Go away and leave me alone.

You better listen to me, kiddo. You could save yourself a lot of grief. It could happen to you too, y'know. Lonnie's an angel, but sometimes the wires in his head get crossed up, and he does funny things.

No, no, no! You're lying! Go away!

You know what the worst part about it is? I'm lying there in the sand all twisted up like a rag doll, with my skirt up to my waist, and my mouth open, and my eyes full of dried blood. Damned unflattering, believe me. I'm an unholy mess—

You're lying, lying, lying!

She felt herself rising, straining forward with outstretched hands, wanting to locate the source of the horrid voice, to find the hidden face and claw at it until it was silent.

The voice vibrated with a shrill laugh.

You can't touch me, you silly little bitch. I'm beyond touching. . . .

She struggled frantically in the darkness. The icy laughter rang louder, floated around her, jangled tauntingly in her ear.

Get away from me! Leave me alone, please!

She heard her own voice, strained and high-pitched in hysteria. The laugh became louder, deafeningly loud, and hideous.

Oh, Lonnie, Lonnie, where are you? Help me, *help me!*

The pent-up scream within her found explosive release. All the images leaped before her eyes, whirled madly, and melted away into a gray featureless landscape wrapped in total, blessed silence.

28

Bart went down the hall on the run, flung open the bedroom door, and switched on the light. Meg was sitting on the edge of the bed, gripping the bedcovers with both hands. She was disheveled and wide-eyed, and staring at some mysterious point in space far beyond the confines of the room. When the light struck her she closed her eyes tight and brought her hands up to cover her face.

"What's the matter, baby?" Bart sat beside her on the bed and put his arm around her. "Wake up, you're havin' a nightmare. Wake up, now."

He squeezed her shoulder gently, and rubbed her arm. "There, now, it's all right, baby. Bart's got you. You're safe now, home again and safe. Just relax."

He pulled her hands down away from her face and lifted her chin, looking at her closely. "You okay now?"

"Yes." She managed a whisper. "Yes, I'm all right."

"Jesus, you were yellin' to beat hell. Must've been some godawful nightmare."

Her eyes drifted aimlessly around the room. "Where am I?" she said dully.

"Why, you're home, baby. Don't you know your own home?" He hugged her close to him, rubbing her arm and shoulder. "What the hell were you dreamin' about?"

She shook her head. "I don't remember."

"Well, now, you just relax and let Bart take care of you. Everything's all right now. Ol' Bart's gonna take care of his little mouse, just don't you worry."

His hand on her shoulder moved down over her back, around her waist, up and down, massaging gently, and exerting a constant subtle pull toward him.

"Ol' Bart knows what's good for his little mouse, yes he does." His voice had gone mushy. He leaned close and nibbled on her ear.

She jerked back. "What's happened, Bart?"

"What d'ya mean, what's happened?"

"Did they catch him?"

"Who, Hayward? Naw. That stupid jerk Cole couldn't catch his own grandmother. But don't let it worry you, baby. Your good ol' hubby's lookin' after you now. That bastard won't ever be able to come near you again."

His hand had slipped under her blouse, and was roaming over the warm skin of her back, caressing, constantly moving. She had stiffened and was leaning away from him. He put his free hand on the side of her head, pulled her face toward him, and kissed her hard on the lips. She continued to strain against him.

"Come on, baby, loosen up," he said. "You're home now, nice and safe."

She tried to get up. He held her, pulled her back.

"Hey, where you goin'?" His voice remained soft, but carried a sharp hint of impatience.

"Something's bothering me, Bart. I've got to ask you . . ."

"Okay, shoot."

"What about that Mrs. Emmons? Have they found her?"

He shrugged. "Not that I've heard." His hand was moving on her back again.

"But have they made a thorough search, do you think? I mean, all around the estate grounds?"

"I don't know. Who cares?"

His hand became suddenly still. He frowned at her. "Hey—do you know something about the Emmons dame?"

"Oh, no, I was just . . . just curious."

He sat back and gave her a hard look. "I don't see why you should be so damn curious about those people. They don't mean anything to us."

"Well, I was just—"

"Lemme tell you something, Meg. Those are not our kind o' people, see? They're low class, that's what they are. Not our kind at all. I want you to put 'em out o' your mind, you hear me? Low class. Anybody that would let a sex maniac like that

202

Hayward live on his place—probably screwin' the wife any ol' time he felt like it—"

"Bart! What are you talking about?"

"I got the straight dope from Carl. He knows all about the Emmonses. You know what that dame was before she hitched onto old man Emmons? A stripper in Frisco, that's what."

"I don't see what that has to do—"

"You just forget about 'em, I said. They're not our kind." His hand was around the back of her head, pulling her close again. "*I'm* your kind, baby, and you're mine. That's all that matters for us." His other hand was busy on the buttons of her blouse.

She pushed him away, clutched at her blouse, and held it closed.

"Bart, you just . . . you don't understand anything about me, do you? You don't know that I'm . . . I'm . . ."

"You're what? What the hell's the matter with you, anyway?" It was a demand, gruff and angry.

"I'm troubled."

"You're troubled. Too goddam bad, you're troubled. What about me? Here alone all day yesterday, goin' half out o' my mind, not knowin' whether you were alive or dead, or what. How do you think *I* felt?"

"I'm sorry. I didn't mean to cause you so much trouble and worry."

"Seems like you ought to be crawlin' on your hands and knees, beggin' forgiveness."

"I said I was sorry."

"Big deal, you're sorry. I bust my ass findin' you, then risk my goddam life breakin' in that place to rescue you. For what? You give me a blank look and say, what's all the fuss? You weren't kidnapped, you went up there voluntarily. The poor guy needed a ride, and you felt sorry for him. For Christ's sake, what kind of a stupid-ass story is *that?!*"

Meg sat stony-faced. Bart rushed on, warming up.

"Just be honest about it, that's all I ask. I wouldn't mind if you wanted to go out and get picked up once in a while and get laid, just for kicks. There's nothin' wrong with that. Hell, sometimes I feel like foolin' around a little myself. People need variety now and then, women as well as men. But, for Christ's sake, just level with me. I'll be big about it, I'm open-minded."

Meg was staring at him now, her eyes wide with wonder, as if she had never seen him before. It fed his anger.

"Well, don't just sit there like a dummy, goddammit. Let's have it. Level with me."

"Bart, I'd like very much to level with you. But I can't think of a way to tell you how it really was. It's just not possible."

"Now, what the hell does *that* mean?!"

"You couldn't even begin to understand. You wouldn't know what I was talking about."

He huffed in exasperation, got up and strode angrily around the room.

"Jesus Christ! The great feminine intellectual! It's just a waste of your time to try to talk to a dumb, ignorant . . . what? What would you call me?"

Her eyes were following him around the room as he paced.

"Crude," she said quietly. "Crude is what you are."

He stopped and glared at her, fierce-eyed.

"Well, ain't that just great! Crude. That's the thanks I get for all I've done for you! I took you out o' the five-and-dime and married you, when no other man would even *look* at you twice. I've given you a nice home, and I've been a good provider. And I damn near get myself shot, rescuin' you from a sex maniac. But all that don't matter. All you can say is, I'm crude."

He went toward her, and she shrank back from him.

"All right," he said, "out with it. I wanna hear everything, even if I'm too damned crude to understand. So start talkin'."

His words came out iron-hard, between clenched teeth.

She tried to avoid his eyes. "Please, Bart, let's stop this."

"Come on. Tell me sump'm I don't know. I wanna be educated."

She got up and started to move past him. He stopped her by putting a hand on the back of her neck and holding her in a tight grip.

"Don't be stingy, Meg. God knows you're stingy with sex, but that don't mean you have to be stingy with all that swell knowledge you have."

She tried to move, but he held her fast.

"You're hurting me, Bart."

"With all those terrific adventures you been havin' lately, you musta learned a lot o' good stuff. So come on. Share."

204

She made a quick movement and stepped out of his grasp, and when he started to reach for her again she was facing him with a burning in her eyes that looked like defiance.

He grinned. "Hey, what d'ya know! Little Miss Mousey's beginnin' to show some spunk!" He moved in a little closer. "Come on, Miss Mousey. Tell me sump'm good. Educate me."

"Did you know that young eagles can't fly?" she said suddenly.

He stopped and stared. "What's that?"

"Young eagles don't know how to fly. They have to be taught by their parents. They have to be taught to hunt too. Did you know that, Bart?"

"What the hell's *that* got to do with anything?"

"You know those scrub jays that hang around the yard, squawking all the time? Did you know they're killers?"

"What?"

"Killers. A jay will attack and kill a lizard ten inches long and eat it on the spot. Bet you didn't know that."

He started to move toward her again, and she retreated until she was standing with her back against the wall.

"Oh, I know lots of interesting things *you* don't know, Bart. Did you know that little bird they call the sparrow hawk is really a falcon? A real, genuine falcon, in miniature. Isn't that amazing?"

Bart moved closer, staring at her, his breathing becoming heavy with the pressure of growing anger. Meg put her hands out protectively.

"And, Bart, did you know that hummingbirds migrate across the Gulf of Mexico? Fifteen hundred miles, nonstop. Can you believe that?"

He growled at her. "What is all this goddam crap you're babblin'?"

"Interesting things, Bart. Things you don't know anything about."

"What the hell did that son of a bitch *do* to you?! Did he make you crazy?!"

"What he did, Bart, what I did, the thing that happened to me during that one day and night of my life—*that's* something you don't know. And you never will."

His anger welled up and broke the surface. "Why, you bitch . . ." His fierce eyes came closer still, impaling her.

"You're gonna tell me everything, goddammit, every gory little detail, or I'm gonna *beat* it out o' you. You got that?"

"Yes, Bart. Everything. Did you know the wandering albatross has a wingspread of eleven feet, and it flies around and around the world, over the southern ocean?"

He seized her by the arms and shook her. "Stop that stupid crap, you hear me? Talk sense!"

She pushed against him and held herself rigid, and when the shaking ceased, gulped new breath and continued, her voice firm and steady still.

"And have you heard about the arctic tern? It flies twenty thousand miles a year, from the Arctic to—"

"Shut up, goddam you! I don't want to hear it!"

He shook her again, and increased the pressure on her arms until he saw the corners of her mouth twisting downward, reflecting pain.

But she went on. "Oh, the seabirds, Bart—they're the wildest freest living things on earth . . ."

Bart's face was a twisted mass of rage. He flung Meg backward and away from him with a force that sent her crashing against the wall. She stood still, with closed eyes, panting. But when he approached her she looked at him again, and the blazing spirit was undiminished.

"And we're going to follow them, Bart. Lonnie and I. We're going to follow the seabirds, and be free . . ."

Bart drew back his hand to strike. His eyes were bulging, his face scarlet.

"I'm warning you, Meg. Shut your . . . goddam . . . mouth!"

For an instant they were frozen in time and space, staring unbelievingly at each other. Then Meg's voice rose like the cry of a wild thing.

"Go ahead! Hit me!"

Bart held his threatening stance, trembling, hovering on the outermost edge of control.

"What are you waiting for?" she screamed. "Hit me, hit me!"

Slowly he lowered his arm. The wild fury was draining from his face and being replaced by a slack-jawed look of dismay and astonishment. He reached toward her, and she shrank back from his touch.

206

He whined, "Meg, baby . . . what's goin' *on* here? What's happening to us? Where's my sweet little mouse gone?"

His fingertips touched her arm, and she flinched and drew back farther. Her wide eyes were fixed on him in trancelike intensity. "How come you're lookin' at me like that, baby? You look like a wild animal caught in a trap."

He reached again, got a hand on her shoulder, but she slipped out of his grasp and moved quickly to a corner. Again he moved toward her, slowly and cautiously.

"Aw, baby, listen, I'm sorry, you hear? I didn't mean to rough you up. I just couldn't stand it, the way you kept on jabberin' all that crap. It sounded like crazy talk, it didn't make any sense. But I know you don't go around talkin' nonsense, and that's what made me mad, see? I knew damn well what you were sayin' made a lot o' sense, but I couldn't figure out what it meant, 'cause it's something I'm not a part of. I can't stand for you to have something that leaves me out, y'know what I mean?"

He stopped an arm's length away from her and smiled.

"Don't hold it against me, baby, and I won't hold anything against you either, huh? Is it a deal? I know you didn't mean all that crap about goin' off to follow some stupid seabirds or whatever, and you know I never meant to hurt you, 'cause what I really want to do is take care of you. That's my job."

He held out his hand, palm up, beckoning. "So come on, baby, let's forget the whole thing. C'mere and gimme a kiss, and be my sweet little mouse again."

She stood rigidly still and unresponsive, staring at him.

"Come on, Meg," he coaxed gently. "Don't you *know* me, for God's sake? Don't you know who I am?"

Her hunted-animal eyes watched him warily. She held herself tensed and ready.

"Meg, baby, I'm your husband. You're my wife. And I want you to *act* like a wife. I missed you when you were gone. Now you're back, and I want to hold you in my arms again and let you know you're safe and sound, I'm takin' care of you, and everything's all right . . ." His outstretched hand was almost upon her.

"Don't touch me, Bart." She spoke with a slow mechanical deliberation. Her voice was hard, her eyes were pinpoints, cold as midnight.

Bart gaped at her. "What? Did I hear you right?" Astonishment grew in his face. "You're tellin' me not to *touch* you? Not to touch my *wife?!*"

He took another small step toward her. She raised her hands defensively, and her words thrust at him like daggers.

"Don't touch me!"

He stared, his eyes narrowed to slits. All the muscles of his body became tight as spring steel, preparing for action. But something held him back.

"Meg . . ." His speech came in a hoarse rasp and quivered with a turmoil of suppressed emotion. "I've let you get away with murder around here for too long, too damn long. I've given you the very best a man can give a woman—my love and devotion, my name, all my worldly goods—I've protected you and kept you and taken good care of you and let you do exactly as you please. And what have you given me in return? Abuse, that's what. You insult my friends, you turn up your superior little nose at everything I say or do, you live in a secret little world of your own and shut me out of it. I'm just the guy who pays the bills, that's all. Hell, I even have to beg you for a little sex once in a while. Well, I'm tired of it, Meg. We're gonna make some changes around here now. Some real . . . big . . . changes."

Without warning he lunged for her, got both her wrists in his hands and held her helpless. She gasped and began to struggle. He held her easily and watched her, and gradually his face was lit by a new light. The anger had given way to something more remote, more instinctive—the primitive delight in combat.

"Oh, you wanna be a wild woman, huh? Okay, fine, be a wild woman. Let's have a little wrestling match, then—I can handle you on that level, easy."

He pulled her up close, worked his arms around her and crushed her to his chest. She twisted from side to side, seeking escape. He held her fast, ignored her frantic struggling, and planted quick kisses on her neck between whispered words. "You might as well stop tryin' to fight me, baby, 'cause I'm gonna have my way. I'm gonna have me a wild woman, and when I get through with her she'll be tame as a kitten—"

Somehow she had worked one arm loose from his bear hug. His face contorted suddenly with a grimace as sharp fingernails clawed at the flabby flesh of his cheek. He snapped his head back, trying to evade the attack, and groped for her hand—and the nails caught him again, just under an eye.

"Ow-w-w! God*dam* you!" He released her and took a step back, roaring with pain and rage, and clapped one hand over the wound. With the other he grabbed at Meg as he saw her darting past him. He caught her by the shoulder, held on tenaciously, and fought to recapture her flailing hands.

"You bitch, I'll kill you!" he bellowed. "I'll tear you apart!"

"Maybe you'll kill me . . ." Her words came out chokingly, half smothered in gasps of desperate exertion. "But you will . . . *not* . . . *have* . . . *me!*"

From somewhere deep within her an ultimate surge of energy burst forth that was beyond anything she herself could have imagined. Bart felt himself falling backward, realized with an instant of shock that his frail adversary had pushed him off his feet. His arms swung out wildly, seeking balance. He staggered against the bed, regained control, looked up in time to see Meg fly across the room and disappear into the adjoining bathroom.

The door slammed shut. The lock clicked.

He stood in the center of the room in a half-crouch, clenching and unclenching his fists, his breath coming in heavy panting gulps. Gradually some degree of calm returned. He approached the bathroom door and spoke in a voice that was low and even and tightly controlled. "Meg? I'm gonna count to ten. If you don't come out o' there and apologize to me by then I'm goin' outside and get my crowbar and break the door down. And if I have to do that, Meg, I'm gonna beat you up. I'm gonna beat you up good."

He counted, with slow ponderous deliberation, reached the count of ten, and stood there for a moment longer, having had no response to his ultimatum.

"All right, bitch. Don't say I didn't warn you. Now you're gonna get it."

He strode rapidly out of the room, down the hall, through the kitchen—and stopped abruptly there when he heard a noise. Another door had slammed shut, and the thud of wood against wood was followed immediately by a metallic sliding sound: the bolt lock on the bedroom door.

He stood still, frowning, momentarily overcome by indecision.

Then he turned and walked back along the hallway and stood in front of the door to the bedroom.

The master bedroom. He thought of the architectural drawings, replete with specifications and scientific precision, that he had pored over with the building contractor at the time the house was built, just before he and Meg were married—that spacious chamber, with the private bathroom adjoining, was labeled the master bedroom. He had been delighted with the term, had referred to it often in conversation, and had titillated himself by thinking: It's called the master bedroom because it's the place where the master receives the rewards of his rank, where the master lies in luxury between silky sheets and feeds on the fruits of love served up by his eager and willing and adoring woman.

Well, those neat drawings of the floor plan don't show it the way it really is, he thought. The damn architects may know all about structural strength and square footage, but they don't know nothin' about human orneriness. *Female* orneriness.

"Master bedroom, shit!" he muttered.

He tried the door; it was locked, as he already knew. He rattled the knob angrily, suddenly pounded with his fist on the door—closed his eyes and pounded blindly, concentrating on the simple act of making noise. Suddenly he was aware of sounds on the other side of the door. He stopped pounding and listened. There was movement inside, muffled scrapings across the thick carpeting—furniture being moved. Something thudded against the inside of the door.

She's barricading, he thought.

"Meg? Meg, cut it out, will you? Lemme in."

He was appalled by the sound of his own voice. It was not hard and commanding, as he had intended, but weak and tremulous, almost pleading. He tried again.

"You open that door, Meg, or, by God, I'll bust it down, I'm not kidding you."

It was no good. I don't convince myself, he thought, how can I convince *her?* He decided to try a different approach.

"All right, goddammit. If that's the way you want it, fine, that's the way you'll have it. You're not *worth* busting an expensive door for. You can stay in there and rot, for all I care. You think I give a damn? You think I'll go and sleep on the couch, and be lonesome? Well, I got news for you, baby, I *don't* give a damn, and I *won't* sleep on the couch. You know what I'm gonna do? I'll tell you what I'm gonna do. I'm goin' down to Caxton, to my old favorite hangout, Madam Angel's, and I'm gonna sleep with a nice friendly gal who knows what it's all about, which is more than *you* know."

He waited and listened. The movements in the bedroom had ceased. All was quiet.

"You hear me, Meg?" His voice had risen to an unnatural shrillness. "I'm goin', you hear me?"

There was no response. He put his ear to the door and listened intently. Total silence within.

"All right, that's it." It was a mumble, more to himself than to Meg.

He turned on his heel and moved with long angry strides down the hall, through the kitchen, out of the house, slammed the back door as hard as he could, went to the garage and got into his car. He sat there in the darkness for several minutes, not moving.

Then he got out of the car and went quietly back to the house. He walked with slow dragging steps, and with head bowed. He went into the living room, stopped and looked aimlessly around. The lamp on the end table next to the couch was on, the only light in the room. Some flimsy pink garment, draped over a chair, caught his eye. He walked over and picked it up. It was a thin cardigan sweater that belonged to Rita. She had forgotten it. He turned it over in his hands, looked at it without interest, then tossed it aside. He went over to the lamp and switched it off, and sat down on the couch in darkness. In a moment he reached up and turned the lamp on again.

He sat on the edge of the couch and stared with dull eyes at nothing. He cocked his head, frowned with intense concentration, and listened. The house was frozen in silence. With the fist of one hand he suddenly slammed a savage blow into the open palm of the other.

"I want my mouse, goddammit," he muttered. "I want my little mouse back."

For two or three minutes he sat hunched forward, his forearms on his knees, his eyes fixed on a point on the floor. Then he lay down on the couch, on his stomach, and buried his face in the cushions.

The pale sunlight of morning penetrated the Hannahs' living room in slanted beams that moved in a slow silent progression, inch by inch, across a wall, over the carpet, up the side of the couch, and onto the face of the sleeping man. The steady monotonous rhythm of Bart's snoring was disrupted. He stirred, sniffled, snorted, opened his eyes briefly and blinked, and turned over, hiding from the invading light. A few minutes later he rolled over onto his back and frowned at the ceiling. Slowly the nerve ends of his mind came alive, and went to work reviewing the turmoil of thoughts and feelings that had caused him to bury his face in the couch some hours before and prepare to spend a night of sleepless torment. He noticed with a grimace of irritation that the lamp next to the couch was still on, but made no move to turn it off.

He lay still for a long time, thinking. Then laboriously he sat up and gazed around the room, his early-morning frown carved deeply in his brow. After a few minutes in this intermediate position he yawned mightily and got to his feet, and walked in a listless shuffle out of the room and up the dark hallway, and stood again, as if to double-check the accuracy of his recollections, before the closed door of the bedroom. The master bedroom.

He had hoped that in the light of day a clear and simple solution to his problem would occur to him, but so far none had. He stared dully at the door for a while, then turned away, shuffled back down the hall and turned into another doorway, next to the kitchen.

"Thank God for two bathrooms," he mumbled, and closed the door.

Fifteen minutes later the phone rang. Bart came naked out of the steaming bathroom, rubbing himself with a towel, and rushed to the phone alcove.

"Hello."

"Hey, Bart? Carl."

"You're up early," Bart said.

"What d'ya mean? It's eight-thirty. You sleepin' in late this morning?"

"Yeah, I guess you could say that."

Carl chuckled. "Heavy action last night, eh?"

"What was it you wanted, Carl?" Bart snapped.

Carl cleared his throat awkwardly. "I just wanted to let you know that I had a talk with Cole a while ago, and I think I've got him talked into forgetting about that little, uh . . . insubordination thing."

Bart grunted. "Thanks."

"And Cole says Inspector Gregory has agreed to lay off Meg, at least for the time being. Cole thinks we have a good chance to pick up Hayward today, and that's who we want, anyway, not Meg."

"That's good. What's the news on Hayward?"

"There's a hot tip from over by Soda Springs, down on the west side o' the mountain. There was this strange-lookin' young guy comin' around, askin' people for somethin' to eat. Fits Hayward's description to a T. We've got a couple o' cars high-tailin' it over there now."

"Hey, listen, Carl, when you catch the son of a bitch, see if you can fix it for me to be in on the interrogation, will you? I got a few questions I'd like to ask, and I guarantee you I'll get the answers out of 'im."

Carl laughed.

"Oh, and Carl—you remember what we were talkin' about last night?"

"What?"

"*You* know. I was tellin' you all about Rita's talents?"

"Oh, yeah."

"I mean, have you ever seen a sex-pot like that, Carl? No kiddin', that gal just *radiates* heat, man. She's ready all the time—I mean *all* the time."

"That a fact?"

"So, listen . . ." Bart lowered his voice slightly and cupped his hand over the mouthpiece. "How about that little get-together I suggested? Just you and me and Lois and Rita. We'll drive down to the coast some weekend and have an all-night orgy. What d'ya say?"

"Uh, look, Bart—how about if I bring another date?"

"You mean, not Lois?"

"Not Lois."

"Why? What's the matter?"

"I just don't see Lois in that kind o' scene. She's not the type."

Bart laughed. "Oh, man, them's famous last words! Those female-type people can fool you. Believe me, I've found that out the hard way. You take a meek timid little mouse like Meg, for instance. You wouldn't think she could surprise a wise ol' man o' the world like me, now, would you? Well, I got news for you, pal, she's *loaded* with surprises. She's got a lot more gumption than I ever gave her credit for. You know sump'm, Carl, I've been blind. I haven't fully appreciated that girl."

"Well, congratulations. Glad to hear you're wising up at last. But with all this talk about orgies, I got a feelin' you're still not appreciating her."

"Aw, come on!" Bart scoffed. "Playin' around between *friends* is all right. It's this takin' up with *strangers* that burns me. I'll teach Meg better'n that, by God. When I get through with her, you can bet your ass she won't ever do *that* again!"

There was a pause before Carl spoke again. "Say, Bart, none o' my business, but . . . seems to me there's a tiny bit of confusion about exactly what went on between Meg and that guy Hayward—"

"Goddam right, there's confusion! I'll level with you, Carl, the girl's got me baffled. She's actin' mighty damn peculiar."

"In what way peculiar?"

"Aw, just sort of—unfriendly, you might say."

"Can I offer a bit of advice?"

"Offer all you want. I ain't sayin' I'll take it."

"Treat her gently, Bart. She's a thoroughbred, that girl is."

"Yeah? How do *you* know?"

"Christ, everybody knows it but you, seems like. You can tell just by lookin' at her. High-strung and skittish. You don't abuse a thoroughbred like you would a mule, fella. You handle it with care."

Bart enjoyed a good laugh. "Okay, buddy. You ought to know. You're as good a judge of horseflesh as anybody."

"Well, I got to go," Carl said. "Talk to you later."

"Hey, how about the party?"

"I'll, uh . . . I'll think it over."

"Do that. And, Carl—gimme a chance at that bastard Hayward, will you? Just five minutes. I'll work him over good."

"Don't be silly, Bart."

"No kiddin', Carl. I mean it."

"We haven't *caught* him yet. Just relax. I'll keep you posted."

"Okay."

"And give my best to Meg."

Bart laughed again as he hung up. He took the towel and went to work rubbing his hair, still wet from the shower.

"Give my best to Meg," he mumbled. "Hell, I'm still tryin' to give *my* best to Meg."

He started back toward the bathroom, and the phone rang again.

"Son of a bitch!" he growled, and hurried back to the phone alcove.

"Hello? . . . Oh, yes, Mrs. Cutler. How are you? . . . Fine, fine, couldn't be better. . . . Yes, ma'am, everything's under control. Everything's just great. . . . Yes, she's fine, just fine. . . . No, apparently not. No harm done. . . . Any what? . . . No, no moral outrages, nothing like that. . . . Well, I can't tell you any details, I don't really know a whole lot myself. All I can tell you is, I climbed up this steep cliff to this cabin, see, and I looked in and I saw this bas—this fella holdin' on to Meg, tryin' to use her as a shield. . . . Oh, yeah, he had a gun, all right, he was a regular gangster or sump'm. Well, I got mad. I just saw red. I climbed in the window and knocked the gun out o' his hand and laid him low with one blow. 'Course, when the dangerous part's all over the sheriffs come bargin' in, actin' like they did it all. Then, to top it off, while I was lookin' after Meg, danged if the dumb sheriffs don't let the guy get away! Can you beat that? . . . Yeah, well, that's the way it is. You can't depend on anybody to do a job right these days. . . . Meg? Oh, she's still asleep. She's all tuckered out, naturally. . . . No, I couldn't do that, Mrs. Cutler. I wouldn't want to disturb her, y'know? Tell you what, I'll have her call you the minute she has a chance. . . . Well, I don't exactly know *when*. Soon as she has a minute. . . . Yeah, sure will. . . . No, I won't forget. . . . Yes, all right, Mrs. Cutler. G'bye now."

Bart hung up. "Drop dead, you gabby ol' biddy," he growled at the phone.

He went back to the bathroom, and came out again in a few minutes with his pants and shoes on. He stood in the hallway for a moment and gazed thoughtfully in the direction of the closed bedroom door. Then he went back to the telephone alcove. He picked up the phone and paused, and struggled with indecision. It passed. He gripped the instrument firmly and dialed.

Herb answered. Bart made an effort to sound cheerful.

"Hi, there, Cuz. How's the boy? . . . Fine an' dandy, jes' fine an' dandy. Could I speak with your charming wife a minute? . . . What? . . . Naw, she's not up yet. Still flaked out. Just like a little kid, y'know, so damn glad to be home. . . . Yeah, right. Say, could I speak to Rita a minute? . . . Oh, nothin' important. Just want to ask her sump'm. . . . What d'ya mean, *what?* It's personal. I need some advice from her. . . . No, I *can't* ask you. I need a *woman's* advice. . . . Hey, cut the crap, Herb. Call Rita to the phone, dammit!"

Bart's attempt at cheerfulness had flown.

Rita came to the phone. "H'lo, Bart." She sounded subdued.

"Hey, what the hell's with Herb? Givin' me a hard time about talkin' to you—wantin' to know what *about*, for Christ's sake!"

"Oh, he's just a touch cranky this morning. We had a little spat last night."

"Well, that's just too damn bad. You tell him I'll give him a spat right across the kisser if he fucks around with me."

"Tell him yourself. He's listening on the extension phone."

"Jesus Christ!" Bart roared. "Get off the goddam phone, Herb!"

There was a soft click on the line.

"He's off," Rita said. "Now you can tell me how much you love me."

"Goddam silly-ass bastard! What's eatin' him, anyway?"

"Well, to tell you the truth, sweetie, Herb's decided after all this time to start objecting to the, uh . . . what he calls 'peculiar' relationship that exists between you and me."

"Well, I'm a son of a bitch!"

"Herb would agree with you completely on that."

"Why, he never would've even met you if I hadn't introduced him! Hell, you never would've *looked* at a pipsqueak like Herb if I hadn't talked him up to you!"

"Is that so?!"

"The ungrateful bastard. I'll kick his teeth in, next time I see him!"

"That might not be for some time."

"What d'ya mean?"

"Herb thinks it would be better if we didn't see you and Meg so much. He thinks we ought to cultivate some new friends and, as he puts it, develop a new life style."

Bart blew noisily into the phone. "Why, that's the biggest pile o' crap I ever heard! Stupid, just plain stupid! And since when are you lettin' that silly jerk tell you how to live your goddam life?"

"Since never. But for once Herbie's come up with a good idea, and I'm going along with it."

"You mean you *agree* with him?"

"I sure as hell do."

Bart snorted. "Hmph! Thought you said you had a spat!"

"Oh, this was after the spat, when we were kissing and making up. And, mm-m, brother, did we *ever* kiss and make up!"

"Aw, shit!"

"Thanks, sweetie. I knew I could count on you for an intelligent civilized reaction."

"Listen, Rita, cut it out, will you? I got to talk to you about sump'm important. I'm in deep trouble."

"Send me your T.S. card in the mail, and I'll punch it for you and send it back."

"Come on, Rita. I need your help, no kiddin'. Don't let me down."

"All right. Tell Aunt Rita what's bothering you."

"Well, it's . . ." Hastily Bart pulled up a chair and sat down. "It's Meg. Sump'm's wrong with her, Rita. I don't know what it is, but she's—she's different."

"What happened? Did she turn you down last night?"

"Worse'n that. She won't even let me come near her."

"Well, good Lord, that's a girl's privilege, once in a while—"

"She locked me out o' the bedroom."

"She . . . locked you out of the bedroom?"

"That's right. Bolted the door and barricaded it with furniture."

Rita's soft throaty laugh sounded tauntingly in Bart's ear. Angrily he shifted the phone from one hand to the other, and glowered.

"What's so goddam funny?! That's not normal behavior, sump'm's *wrong* with her!"

"Let me see, now. She locked you out, and you *didn't* bust the door down?"

"No, I didn't. Hell, I think she's mentally disturbed or sump'm. I wouldn't wanna make it worse, y'know?"

"Hey, maybe there's hope for you yet, sweetie. Maybe someday you'll get beyond the cave-man stage after all."

"But, listen, Rita . . . what am I gonna do?"

"Well, now, let's reflect soberly on this matter. We know something happened to Meg. We don't know exactly what, but we darn well know *something* happened, something very much out of the ordinary. Whatever it was, it's going to take her a while to get over it. You're just going to have to develop a new virtue, sweetie. One you're not overly familiar with. Patience."

"Trouble is . . ." Bart groped for words. "Trouble is, I think I *know* what happened. I got it figured out. That guy Hayward didn't pick her up—she picked *him* up. They went to that cabin and shacked up, and they dumped the truck into the ditch so the whole thing would look like an accident. Can you picture that, Rita? Little Meg, doin' a one-night stand!"

"I not only can't picture it, sweetie, I think you're full of crap, as usual."

"All right, so *you* tell *me*."

"In the first place, and you know it as well as I do, a one-night stand just isn't Meg's style. You just better hope it's no more serious than that. I got a feeling it could be a lot worse."

Bart gripped his forehead. "Well, goddammit, what, then? What *is* it?"

There was a moment of silence on the line. "Have you considered the possibility that Meg may have *fallen in love?*"

218

Bart's breath exploded in exasperation. "Oh, for Christ's sake! Big help *you're* turning out to be!"

"Okay, pay no attention. I'm only a woman, right? What the hell would *I* know about how a woman's mind works?"

Bart's fingers twitched nervously on the phone. "Oh, Lord, Rita, you gotta be kiddin'. Do you really think it could be sump'm like *that?* I mean, Jesus, Meg's not *available* for falling in love. She's a married woman!"

"All right, all right. Just let me give you my theory. The way I see it, Meg's a shy, timid little waif, easily frightened, easily pushed around. Unhappy most of the time, but too scared to open her mouth. Now, you're in the habit of treating her like a little puppy dog, scratching her behind the ears one minute and the next minute giving her a swift kick in the rear. I think what happened is, she met a guy who treated her *nice.* Believe it or not, fella, that could be pretty heady stuff for a girl like Meg. It just totally flipped her out, that's all. Now, what I think *you* should do is pull a big surprise and treat her even nicer. It might just work a miracle."

Bart was squirming with impatience. "Aw, Christ, what are you talkin' about? I *do* treat her nice. Hell, she locked me out o' my own damn bedroom, and I didn't lift a finger!"

"You're not getting the message, sweetie. I mean treat her real, *real* nice. Treat her like a queen. Treat her . . . as if you *loved* her."

"How the hell am I supposed to do that if she won't even let me *see* her?!"

"Is she still locked in?"

"Hell, yes. The bitch. What I oughta do is bolt the goddam door on the outside and make her beg to get out."

"Okay, smart-ass. You already know all the answers, so what are you asking *me* for?"

Bart slumped. "I don't know any answers, Rita. I need you to help me. Just tell me what to do and I'll do it."

"All right, then. You go in the kitchen and fix Meg a nice breakfast on a tray. Make it look like something from room service at the Heavenly Hilton. I mean the fanciest, most beautiful breakfast your creative mind can dream up. Then go knock softly on the door and say breakfast is served, milady, and say you'd like to come in and tell her how sorry you are about being such a god-awful beast all this time, and you're going to turn over a new leaf, blah-blah-blah. You can do it. Lay it on thick, and be so sweet that little Meg'll wonder why it took her so long to notice what a big lovable teddy bear you are."

Bart frowned mightily and gripped his forehead. "In other words—lemme see if I read you—she's made my life pure hell for the last twenty-four hours, and I should go in and apologize for it and fix her a special treat as a reward for her lousy behavior. Is that right?"

"That is exactly right, buster. If you value your marriage, that is. If you want to keep Meg."

Bart stared glumly at the floor. "Damn it all to hell—I *do* want to keep her."

"Well, then, hop to it. And good luck."

Bart thought about it for a moment longer. He sighed. "Okay, kiddo, I'll give it a try. Can't hurt, I guess. And thanks. I appreciate your advice, even if I don't understand it. You're a pal."

"Yeah. Well, see ya around, sweetie."

"Hey, listen, Rita, if I get things patched up okay, can you and Herb come over for a drink this evening?"

"Boy, you've really got a short memory, haven't you? Already forget what I told you a minute ago?"

"Christ, you guys ain't really serious about that?!"

"Never more serious in our young lives. Listen, Bart. You've got some work to do on your marriage, and I've got some to do on mine. Let's hope it's not too late for either of us."

"Come *on!* Cut the crap, will you?"

"See you in the funny papers, big fella."

"That corny expression went out with high-button shoes."

"So did *that* one."

"Aw, Rita, listen—"

There was a gentle click on the line, then silence. Bart sat holding the phone to his ear for a long time before hanging up.

30

The job took him forty minutes. But when it was done he stood back and looked at the results and grinned with satisfaction and some pride. A sterling-silver tray and matching set of serving dishes that had been a wedding present, and never used, stood polished and gleaming, laden with culinary attractions, and ready for presentation, including a crowning touch of elegance that had occurred to him in a flash of inspiration at the last moment—a red rosebud in a slender vase.

Bart nodded with approval. Fit for a king, he thought. No, a queen. He picked up the tray and headed for the bedroom.

In front of the door at the end of the hall he paused and pondered the mechanics of his task. Carefully he set the tray on the floor. He composed his features, mentally arranged his vocal chords to produce a soft gentle tone, and knocked.

"Meg?"

There was no response. He knocked again.

"Meg? Good morning, honey. I have a treat for you."

He waited and listened. Stillness within—no sound, no movement.

"Open the door, sweetheart. I have your breakfast all ready. Breakfast in bed—how's *that* for a treat? And it ain't even your birthday!"

Silence. Bart frowned. He felt a rising of annoyance, and fiercely repressed it.

"Aw, come on, honey, lemme in. You'll be glad you did. This here's very fancy room service, believe me."

As he stood there waiting, and the silence beyond the closed door remained unbroken, he felt impatience growing rapidly, reinforced now by the low dark rumblings of anger, and knew that deep within him powerful forces were stirring and would not be long controlled. Abruptly he turned away from the door, walked down the length of the hall and stood for a moment at the far end. Then he returned. He knocked again, sharply.

"Meg!" His voice was still low and even, but gentleness was abandoned. "Meg, open this door."

He waited a few seconds. "Please, Meg. I don't want to be mad at you anymore. I'm sayin' please to you, do you hear me? I'm sayin' *please*."

After another short wait he called out commandingly, "Meg, you get this door open in thirty seconds or I'll break it down."

Mentally he counted off the allotted time, and felt all restraint and reason draining away with it. He stared at the door, gulped his breath in short hard pants, and began to tremble.

The dam burst. He shouted, and the pent-up rage that forced its way out turned the shout into a maniacal scream, "God*dam* you, you female devil! *Now* you're gonna get it!"

He hurled himself forward, and his words were lost in the crunch of his shoulder against the door. Again and again, and the paneled door splintered, but resisted stubbornly, with a heavy weight against it on the inside. The furious battering continued, and with each blow guttural words were ground out between clenched teeth. "You . . . rotten . . . bitch . . . I'll break . . . every bone . . . in your . . ."

Then the opening was wide enough, and Bart forced his bulk through, past the large heavy chest of drawers that had been pushed against the door. He stood still, panting heavily, as his eyes searched the room.

Meg was not there. The bed was made, as if not slept in.

Bart rushed to the adjoining bathroom, opened the glass door of the shower stall and looked in, returned to the bedroom, flung open the closet doors and probed with his arms among the stacks of clothing on the racks. He whirled about, his eyes darting, seeking some clue. With a sudden thought he dropped down on his stomach and peered under the huge bed. Back on his feet, he stood for a moment gazing dumbly down at the rips in the carpeting that had resulted from his forcing the door open against the furniture barricade.

Then he saw the clue—it fairly leaped at him, and his mouth dropped open in astonishment that he had not noticed it immediately: the open window. Wide open, and the screen removed, leaving a great unnatural gaping hole of empty space.

Bart swallowed hard and stared. He rushed forward and leaned far out of the window, as if to test with his body if the space was as empty and open as it appeared to be. On the ground below the window, leaning grotesquely against shrubbery, was the screen. Bart's eyes fixed on it for a moment, then drifted up in an imaginary retracing of a route of flight—across the yard, past a low wooden rail fence, through an empty field of arid scrub land beyond, and, beyond that, to the blacktop strip of County Highway 15.

Bart shook his head. "No," he whispered hoarsely. "No, it can't be." His face was ashen-pale, and twisted with an unthinkable panic.

"Meg! Meg!" His shout rolled out across the silent landscape and seemed to echo mockingly through the house behind him.

He went out the window, leaping to clear the screen and the bushes, sprawled on the ground, got up and ran blindly, as if trusting to instinct to lead him somehow in the right direction. He clambered over the rail fence, ran through brush, stumbled and recovered, on and on, climbed another fence, scrambled across a ditch and onto a road—his own road, leading to the highway—and ran on, not knowing his destination, but impelled by a mindless sense of urgency.

At the county highway, two hundred yards from the house, he stopped and stood in the middle of the road, panting in desperate, choking exhaustion. Perspiration ran off his head, down his face, into his eyes. He shook his head furiously, wiped at his face with his hands, and squinted up the blacktop strip that shimmered with heat under the morning sun. The road converged to nothingness in the distance, toward the shadowy walls of Stag River Canyon. He whirled and peered in the other direction, down toward the junction with the east–west highway, two miles away, and found the same quiet desolate emptiness.

He shouted again. "Meg! Meg! Where are you?!" With all his strength he hurled her name at the sky.

"Meg!"

His cry was lost in space, absorbed like a single drop of rain in a boundless desert.

He slumped, acknowledging defeat. He turned and walked very slowly, his dragging feet scraping the pavement, back toward the house. When he had gone fifty yards he sat down on a rock at the side of the road, stared at the dusty ground before him, rested his bowed head in the palm of his hand, and wept.

31

The little harbor at Diamond Bay is a rectangle of turgid oily water, enclosed by a jutting of land on one side and a stone breakwater half a mile away on the other, and partially bisected by a pier that lies over the water on massive wooden pilings. It is the homing nest for a swarm of small to moderate-sized vessels, the striking variety among which is a reflection of the hybrid nature of the town itself.

In its half-century of life Diamond Bay has been unable to decide whether to be a vacation resort or a fishing village. It perches at the lower end of one of the countless long shallow ocean-facing canyons that scallop the western edge of the continent, and clings tenaciously to life between forested hills and the gray sea. A short stretch of the highway that runs through it parallel to the coastline is utilized as a main street, on which are clustered motels and service stations and small businesses that cater to vacationers or fishermen or both. From this thoroughfare, to landward, narrow streets climb steeply to residential areas, and, on the seaward side, drop two blocks through a jumble of dilapidated boarding houses, pool halls, bars, and boatyards to the harbor.

At the waterfront end of one of these streets—Mission Street —is a tiny hole-in-the-wall cafe called Oley's Sea Shanty. There is nothing ambiguous about the clientele Oley's means to serve; a hand-painted sign in the window says: "FISHERMEN WELCOME —TOURISTS TOLERATED." Another, smaller sign announces business hours: "OPEN 5:30 A.M. to 9:30 P.M."

Oley is a tall lean leathery man somewhere between fifty and sixty years of age. He is blond and heavily freckled, with curly yellowish hair and bushy brows that overhang clear piercing eyes the color of the North Sea. Most of his business occurs at the extremities of the day; he fortifies the fishermen with enormous hot breakfasts before they go out at first light, and he feeds them when they come in, exhausted, grimy with salt spray, and ravenous, in the evening. Between these periods of peak activity he usually manages to find long stretches of spare time that can be devoted to his favorite form of relaxation—reading the paper. Oley is an insatiable reader of newspapers. He subscribes to a morning and an afternoon edition, and reads every line in both, starting in predawn solitude and finishing in the quiet of late evening when the long day's work is done.

At a quarter past five in the afternoon of a blustery spring day, the cafe was deserted. Oley sat on a little stool behind the counter, reading his paper. Something telepathic clicked in his mind. He turned his head and peered through the plate-glass window, and saw a pair of bearded fishermen coming toward the cafe. They crossed Boardwalk Street, which skirted the harbor parking lot, and walked a few steps up Mission to the cafe. When they entered Oley was already pouring mugs of steaming coffee.

"Hey, you bums!" Oley's voice was hearty and booming. "You're in early today!"

The two men walked past the half-dozen tables in the little room and took seats at the counter.

One of them, a heavyset youngish man, said, "Damn wind out there blows you right off the water."

Oley gave his customers a disdainful glance as he set the coffee before them.

"Sissies!" he snorted. "That's what we got for sailors nowadays. A little breeze comes up, and right away they scurry for home with their tails between their legs!"

The second fisherman, a small, grizzled middle-aged man, gulped his coffee and squinted at the proprietor. "Hey, Oley, how long's it been since *you* been out?"

Oley looked pained. "Listen to this! A crummy fisherman, never been more'n ten knots from shore, daring to question a former merchantman!"

The men on the counter stools grinned at each other.

"You notice he didn't answer your question, Mack," the younger man said. " 'Cause he don't even remember."

"Never you mind how long it's been," Oley said. "The last time I *was* out I rode a typhoon that raised the seas to sixty feet and more—"

Loud groans drowned out his words.

"Don't dish up *that* ol' stale stew again, Oley," said Mack. "Give us some chowder instead."

Oley let go a booming laugh and turned to the big iron chowder kettle. "Oh, Lord, the children they send out to do men's work these days! I've been first mate on ships that neither one o' you bums could get on as cabin boy."

When bowls of chowder were put before them Mack winked at his companion and said, "No damn wonder we get indigestion eatin' here, Al. We always have to take in ten bushels o' horseshit 'fore we can get one lousy pint o' chowder."

Al shook with laughter.

Oley was looking over the men's heads, toward the door. "Clean up your language, boys," he said. "Here comes a lady."

Two necks instantly swiveled.

"Don't stare, dammit, it ain't polite!" Oley growled under his breath.

Al and Mack obediently turned their eyes back to their food, but not before Al had breathed a "Wow!" and produced a low whistle.

Oley quickly took a rag and busied himself wiping an already spotless counter top. He did not look up when the young woman came in and stood hesitantly in the doorway for a moment, then walked to the far end of the counter, away from the other customers, and sat down. Then Oley stopped wiping and looked at her, as if surprised to see her there. His sharp eyes made an instant evaluation.

She was pretty in a quiet way, in her early twenties, dressed in pants and blouse and a lightweight jacket, and carrying a large purse on a shoulder strap. Her long brown hair was tied with a ribbon behind her neck. She sat with her hands in her lap, gazing at Oley—warily, it seemed to him—with dark grave eyes.

A frightened sparrow, Oley thought. This is no woman of the streets. This is class. Somebody who is out of her element right now, for some reason.

He decided he liked her. He went toward her, beaming cheer.

"Good afternoon, ma'am. What'll you have?"

Oley liked her even more when he saw her soft smile.

"I noticed your sign outside," she began uncertainly.

The other two customers were watching her out of the corners of their eyes.

"I'm afraid I'm not a fisherman," she said. "But I'm not exactly a tourist, either—"

Oley treated her to one of his booming laughs. "Oh, pay no attention to that, ma'am. That's just a joke. You're welcome, of course."

And the two fishermen at the other end of the counter grinned at her and nodded, as if to support Oley's statement.

"So, what'll you have?" Oley said.

"Well, I was wondering . . ." The young woman's eyes wandered around the room. She was holding her handbag in a tense grip.

A frightened sparrow, sure enough, Oley thought. He put his elbows on the counter and leaned toward her, and spoke as gently as he could. "The clam chowder's mighty good, ma'am, if I do say so myself. Best sixty-nine-cent bargain in town. Can I serve you a bowl?"

She hesitated. "Well . . . yes, that would be nice. Thank you."

He brought her a bowl of chowder and said, "Coffee?"

"No, thanks." She gazed at the chowder, but made no move to begin eating.

"You want anything else, you just call," Oley said. He started back toward the other end of the counter.

"Oh, excuse me . . ." she said suddenly.

"Yes, ma'am." Oley quickly returned to her and waited.

"Are you, uh . . . Mr. Oley?"

"Yes, ma'am. Gustav Oleson. Some folks call me Gus, some folks call me Oley. I don't know *any*body calls me Mister." He grinned at her.

"Well, I wonder if you could tell me . . ." She glanced toward the men at the far end of the counter and saw that they were openly watching her and listening. She seemed suddenly flustered. She picked up her spoon and idly stirred the bowl of chowder.

"What was it you wanted to know, ma'am?" Oley coaxed.

"Could you tell me where the marina is?" She waved a hand

toward the harbor. "Is that what they call the marina, over there?"

Oley frowned. "I never heard it called the marina. It's just the harbor."

"The marina's down by the breakwater," Al called out. "Them fancy concrete moorings down there along the breakwater—that's what the playboys around here call the marina." He snickered.

"He means the yacht owners," Oley said to the woman. "The idle rich who play with boats like expensive toys. Who ain't got no knowledge of the ocean, nor any respect for it. Who keep the Coast Guard busy hauling 'em home every time the weather blows."

He slapped the counter with his rag. "Us real seafaring men have no truck with such folk."

The young woman nodded. "I see." She took a spoonful of chowder. Seeing that Oley's eyes were still on her, she smiled and said, "It's very good."

"Glad you like it." He continued to observe her. "Anybody in particular you're lookin' for at the so-called marina?"

"Oh, no. Just a . . . a certain boat."

"What boat?"

Again the hesitation, and the quick uneasy glance at the men at the other end of the counter. They were paying rapt attention. She stirred her chowder.

"Well, I'm bein' too nosy," Oley said, and started to move away again.

"Oh, not at all," the woman said hurriedly. "I was just sort of curious about a boat called the . . . the *Nellie D.*"

"The *Nellie D.,*" Oley repeated, without recognition. All three men pondered the question.

"Hey," Mack said suddenly. "Ain't that the ketch belongs to Mister—what's his name—fella that owns the chain o' hamburger stands?"

Al snapped his fingers. "Oh, yeah. Murgison."

"That's it," Mack said. "Murgison's Munchy Burgers."

Oley recoiled. "Please! Do not utter obscenities on these premises!"

"Yeah, I know that boat," Mack said. "It's a derelict. Ain't been to sea in Christ knows how long. Completely run down.

You'll find it way out toward the end o' the breakwater. If it's still afloat."

"Thank you," the woman said softly.

"Come to think of it," Al said, "I believe Murgison sold that boat. Seems like I heard he sold it to some young fella."

"Hmph!" Mack grunted. "No shortage o' suckers in this world. One born every minute, they say."

There was a babble of male voices from the street, and a noisy group of fishermen burst into the cafe, propped their gear against the wall, draped jackets over chairs, occupied several of the small tables and some of the counter stools, and yelled boisterous joking greetings to the two men already there, and to Oley. Each newcomer cast his eye in surprise over the young woman at the end of the counter, appraised her with lively interest, then pretended to be unaware of her.

Immediately Oley was a dynamo of action, fielding shouted orders, slapping steaks on the grill, dipping up chowder, pulling out an endless supply of cold cans of beer from an enormous refrigerator, and constantly engaging in rough good-humored banter with his customers. It was twenty minutes before he was able to pause and draw a breath.

Mack caught his eye and winked at him. "Hey, Oley, your chick flew the coop."

Oley looked toward the far end of the counter and saw that the woman was gone. He went to clear her place, noticed that she had not finished her chowder, found a dollar bill lying beside the half-empty bowl. He returned to lean against the counter near Al and Mack.

"She was a funny one," he said. "A real funny one."

"Yeah. Sure was," Mack agreed.

"Hey, Oley!" one of the other customers called out. "Who's the new girl friend?"

"Yeah, Oley," someone else said. "Where'd an old fart like you ever find a good-lookin' babe like that?"

Oley laughed at the hecklers, but didn't bother to answer.

"You know what she seemed like to me?" he said quietly, to Mack and Al. "She seemed like a frightened sparrow."

Mack and Al both laughed uproariously.

Oley grinned, shook his head in embarrassment, and walked away from them.

32

She walked slowly down the length of the boardwalk that ran along the edge of the harbor, until she came to the landward end of the breakwater. It was a jagged, massive stone-and-concrete structure, extended like the backbone of a giant sea monster two hundred yards long, lolling in the water. Down its center ran a walkway bordered by a rusty iron railing. She stepped up onto the walkway and started toward the outer end.

A number of small vessels were coming into the harbor, retreating before the advance of cold and darkness. The wind was brisk and chilling, the sun fading from golden to pale silver and sinking behind a murky gray fog bank that hovered like a silent menace a mile offshore. She pulled her jacket close around her and gripped the iron railing as she walked.

Toward the far end of the breakwater she began to study the various craft that lay at anchor, bobbing in the choppy water. With fascination she read the names: the *Windjammer*, the *Island Queen*—that's a big one, tall and proud—the *Sea Spray*, the *Rob-Roy*, the *Paramour*. Some were sleek sailing vessels, some sturdy gleaming power boats. The *Joy Rider*, the *Ballerina* —graceful and pretty, that one, just like its name—the *Sunbeam*, the *Wanderer*, the *Nellie D.*

She stopped in her tracks and felt her heart leap as if at the sudden recognition of a dear long-missing friend. She could hardly make out the name—it was nearly obliterated by weather and salt water and time. It rode a short distance out from the breakwater, slowly turning on its anchor chain. Its black-and-silver paint was dingy, faded, and peeling. The man at Oley's had said it was a derelict. That was an exaggeration; it was straining at the leash, moving constantly in the wind with a buoyancy that seemed youthful and eager. He had said it was run down—

that was mercilessly true. It seemed neglected, forlorn, and terribly small. She felt an urge to call out to it, to wave a greeting, to let it know that it was not alone. She wanted to pat it on the side and say, Don't worry, Lonnie will be here soon, and we'll all be together. . . .

There was a bench close by, a heavy iron thing, bolted to the concrete. She sat down there and stayed for a long time, watching the lonesome *Nellie D.* rock gently, aimlessly in the water.

Other vessels were coming into the harbor and being moored, people were disembarking and from time to time walking past her, and she could feel their curious eyes on her, could sense their wondering about her presence; she was a stranger, she was recognized as one, and she felt like one.

Gradually the incoming traffic diminished, and ceased, and the harbor became quiet. Under cover of the fast-fading daylight the outlying fog bank was creeping shoreward. Mercifully the wind had abated, but the chill of approaching darkness crept under her jacket and made her shiver.

She gazed dreamily at the *Nellie D.* and tried to imagine it with a proud new name. The *Seabird.* She tried to picture it gleaming white under a fresh coat of paint, and plowing bravely along with the wild rollers of the open sea, flinging spray before it on the wind. She tried—but the image was blurred, would not come clear.

She got up at last and walked back along the breakwater toward the land. At the boardwalk she stopped and looked in all directions. The harbor was deserted now. In the dusk it seemed somber, somehow sinister. Abruptly islands of garish yellow light appeared along the boardwalk and on adjacent patches of the oil-slick water—tall metal lampposts, like sentinels stationed fifty yards apart, had silently begun their automated nightly duty. Off toward the left, on a little rise overlooking the water, there was a luxurious restaurant, with great picture windows through which an elegant décor, under subdued lighting, could be glimpsed. To the right, the empty boardwalk stretched away toward the pier.

She noticed a slight movement in that direction, and looked closer. A solitary figure—a man, wearing a cap, his jacket pulled up high around his neck—had stepped off the pier onto the

232

boardwalk and was coming rapidly toward her. She could not make out the face, but as he passed under one of the lampposts she caught the soft shine of blond hair between the cap and the jacket collar.

Her heart seemed to stop for an instant. Her hand flew to her throat.

Lonnie? Can it be . . . ?

When the man came a little closer she saw that his lurching shuffle was nothing like Lonnie's light springy step. Inside she felt herself sag, the quick excitement wilt and melt away. The man looked in her direction—another pair of strange eyes, brazenly inspecting her. Hastily she looked away, turning to face the harbor. Behind her the man's footfalls approached, thudding hollowly on the boards, then went suddenly silent. With a stab of apprehension she looked around. The man had stepped off the boardwalk and was crossing a stretch of open sand, going away. In a moment he had disappeared into the gathering gloom.

She took a deep breath and stood for a few minutes in indecision. Then she walked very slowly back out along the breakwater, past the *Nellie D.*, past all the moorings, all the way to the end of the concrete strip, and stood looking down at the dark choppy water.

She imagined that she was standing on the deck of a ship, which was making its way across the watery wastes that extended for thousands of miles to the west and the south. If this were the deck of the *Nellie D.* I was standing on, she thought—of the *Seabird*—I would feel much less secure than I feel now.

A vexatious question intruded upon her mind: *Would I be afraid?*

Oh, I don't want to think about things like that now, another part of her mind said. It's premature.

But, would I?

Just stop that, she told herself crossly. I'd be with Lonnie, and he has a way with things. Anyway, being with Lonnie is more important than being merely safe.

She turned away and walked back as far as the iron bench near the *Nellie D.*'s mooring, and sat down again. The boat was barely visible in the darkness, drifting and weaving without cease. It seemed smaller than ever, and pitifully fragile.

Wouldn't I be afraid? Just a little? The thought nagged at her tiresomely, refused to go away.

I don't know. I've never been on the ocean before. I don't know.

The fog was coming in fast now. It was getting colder.

Suddenly she felt overwhelmed by a desolate loneliness. She huddled down on the bench, pulled her jacket as close as she could, closed her eyes tight, and fought against the rising tears.

33

The day begins early at Oley's Sea Shanty. The fishermen begin to come in around a quarter to six, expecting huge breakfasts instantly. So the lights are usually on an hour before that, and Oley is hard at work, firing up his equipment, mixing mountains of pancake batter, heating gallons of water in the giant coffee maker, generally preparing to cope with the gargantuan appetites his early-morning customers will bring with them.

He noticed when he opened the blinds over the front windows that the fog had lifted during the night and a few stars were dimly visible in the murky darkness above. They would be gone soon; the dawn would bleach the sky in half an hour and wash them away.

Oley worked for a little while in the intense concentration of solitude. He had reached the point where his preparations were under control, affording him the opportunity to sit down for a few minutes, when he heard someone at the door. He looked up and saw the young woman who had visited his place the previous afternoon. She had tried the door, found it still locked, and was standing there with an uncertain expression on her face, looking for all the world like—the whimsical thought occurred to him again—like a frightened sparrow. He hurried to the door, unlocked and opened it, and beamed a wide smile upon her.

"Good mornin', little lady! You're out early today, I see."

She did not return the smile. She seemed nervous and ill at ease.

"Good morning, Mr. Oley. I'm sorry to bother you. I guess you're not open yet—"

"Where did you get *that* idea?!" he boomed.

"Your sign says—"

"For you, little lady, I'm open. Anytime." He stood aside and waved her in.

When she was inside, in the light, Oley looked at her more closely, and his smile turned to a frown.

"Good Lord, you look frozen stiff! Don't you have no heavier wrap than that flimsy little jacket?"

She shook her head. "That's all right. I'm not cold."

"Then how come you're shiverin'?"

She smiled weakly and rubbed her arms.

"Hey—you been out all night?" Oley demanded.

"Oh, no. I got a room at a little hotel, couple of blocks over."

"What hotel? The Bay Shore?"

"Yes, that's it."

Oley snorted loudly. "A flea bag. No place for nice people like you."

"Well . . . I couldn't sleep very much, anyway. I've been walking around for an hour or so."

"Walking?! Where?"

"Oh, just . . . around the marina."

"In the pitch-black darkness?!" Oley's bushy-browed eyes almost disappeared under a stern frown. "My goodness gracious!"

He turned away from her and went behind the counter. She followed and sat down on a stool. Her eyes hung on him while he fussed with his cooking equipment.

"Mr. Oley, I don't want to be a pest, but . . . I'd sure like to have somebody to talk to."

Oley looked at her quickly. He smiled, came toward her, and patted her lightly on the arm.

"Well, you've come to the right place, by golly. There ain't no better listener than me 'tween here and Rio. Now, you just go sit over there at that corner table while I see if the coffee's ready. I'll be right with you."

"You're sure it's not too much trouble?"

"No trouble a-tall! Tell you the truth, it gets a mite lonesome around here sometimes."

She sat down at the table in the corner, and in a few minutes Oley brought a pot of coffee and two mugs.

"Fresh made," he said. "Cream and sugar?"

"Just black, thank you."

He poured the coffee, and she leaned forward and sniffed.

236

"Mm-m. Smells delicious."

"Best coffee in Diamond Bay." He sat down across the table from her, leaned back comfortably, and fixed her in his steady gaze.

"Y'know, I got a daughter 'bout your age," he said. "She's married now, lives up in the Pacific Northwest. I see by that wedding band on your finger you're married, too. I also see your husband ain't taking very good care o' you. If I caught my daughter wanderin' around on the waterfront all by herself at four, five o'clock in the morning, I'd turn her over my knee and give her a good spankin', married woman or no married woman."

She tried to smile, but it flickered feebly, and died. "It's not my husband's fault. I had to get away by myself for a while. I've got . . . things on my mind."

Oley observed her carefully, with narrowed eyes. "I know that," he said quietly.

After a moment he said, "Well, now—why don't you tell me all about it?"

She gazed pensively at the steaming coffee before her. "Mr. Oley . . . you're a sailor, aren't you?"

"Was, for twenty years. Till I took a vow to stay on dry land the rest o' my life."

"What made you do that?"

"Got washed overboard in a typhoon once, four days out o' Manila. Swallowed sea water for twelve hours, clingin' to a piece o' wreckage. Never was a religious man, but I got on real close conversational terms with *somebody* or *somethin'* durin' those twelve hours, and I figure it might've been God. Maybe it was just Neptune. Whoever it was, I made a deal with him. Told him if he'd let me go this once, I'd stay the hell off his damn ocean forever, cross my heart. He let me go, and I'm stickin' to my part o' the bargain."

She smiled. "I'm glad you made it, Mr. Oley."

Oley watched her, and waited. "So, what's that got to do with anything?"

"Well . . . in your opinion, is a thirty-nine-foot ketch a practical boat to go on an ocean voyage in?"

"A thirty-nine-foot ketch. Would you be thinkin' o' that, uh, *Nellie D.*, by chance?"

"Maybe."

Oley rubbed his chin. "Well, that's hard to say. Depends on the boat. Depends on who's doin' the sailin'."

"Seems awful tiny to me."

"Ever heard o' Joshua Slocum?" Oley said.

The young woman shook her head.

"In 1895 Captain Josh Slocum set sail from Fairhaven, Massachusetts, in a sloop called the *Spray*, which he'd built himself, and sailed around the world. Alone. Took him three years and two months. He was the first man to circumnavigate solo. And the *Spray* was thirty-six feet long."

Oley took a sip of coffee and shrugged. " 'Course, Cap'n Josh was not one o' your average amateur weekend sailors. He was a master, and he was a crazy damn fool besides. Now, me, I'd figure a thirty-nine-foot ketch to be a fine craft to go for a Sunday afternoon spin in, maybe out to the Channel Islands and back, thirty miles, round trip. On a *nice* day. But that don't mean nothin' much. It's a well-known fact that I'm a coward." Oley sighed heavily. "In other words—I don't know."

His listener gazed at him for a moment as if deep in thought, then abruptly presented another subject. "Mr. Oley, do you believe in dreams? I mean, do you think it's possible to dream about something that you don't know anything about, and find out later that what you dreamed really happened?"

Oley gave a gentle chuckle. "Well, *now* you're out out o' my territory, for sure. I've heard o' such things—people dreamin' about somebody dyin', hundreds o' miles away, and then finding out it was true. But I don't know, seems to me stories like that all sound alike. I think some little man sits in a dark room somewhere and makes 'em up, two dozen a day."

The young woman listened intently to what he was saying, and went on studying his face after he had finished.

"I don't believe in things like that at all," she said finally, in a firm voice. She sipped her coffee and gazed off into space, as if a troublesome subject had been permanently disposed of.

Oley leaned forward. "What was it you wanted to talk about, little lady?"

She seemed surprised by his question.

"Not boats," he said. "And not dreams. You're nursin' somethin' that's really botherin' you, and you're dyin' to talk about it, but you can't figure out how to begin. Am I right?"

238

She nodded. "I guess so."

"Then I'll help you. I'll get nosy, which is what I do best, anyway."

She nodded again—almost eagerly, it seemed to Oley.

"All right," he said. "Questions one, two and three, in rapid order—who are you, where you from, and what are you doin' in Diamond Bay?"

"Well . . . my name is Meg Hannah. My husband and I live on a small ranch in Grange County, not far from Caxton. And I'm in Diamond Bay looking for a . . . an old friend."

Oley smiled faintly. "Well, well. Meg Hannah. Lives on a ranch in Grange County. Looking for a friend in Diamond Bay. That's quite a lengthy life story."

Suddenly he frowned and stared at her. "Meg Hannah," he breathed. "Meg Hannah . . . sounds familiar."

He sipped his coffee and eyed her thoughtfully. "Who is this friend you're lookin' for?"

"Somebody I met recently."

"Does your husband know where you are?"

"Well, no, not exactly." She began to examine her coffee mug with minute attention. "I left home in the middle of the night last night—no, the night before, I'm losing track of time. All at once I just couldn't stand being there anymore. It seemed like a . . . a jail, and my husband seemed like a jailer. So I ran away."

"How did you get here?"

"I ran down to the state highway, about two miles from our place, and hid in the bushes till morning. Then I started walking toward the coast. Every time a car came by I got out of sight, because I was afraid it might be my husband, looking for me. Finally, about noon, I got a ride in a big trailer truck."

Oley glared at her. "You hitchhiked?!"

"Well, no, not really. I just stood at the side of the road and waved to the driver, and he stopped and picked me up."

Oley shook his head and made noises of disapproval. "Tsk, tsk, tsk!"

"Oh, he was a nice man," Meg went on hastily. "We had an interesting talk, and he even shared his lunch with me. He was amazed that I knew something about trucks—'cause, see, I have a little pickup at home."

Her eyes drifted away for a moment. "Or *used* to have," she added.

Oley continued to study her, frowning. "Meg Hannah," he said thoughtfully. "Grange County housewife. Owns a pickup truck."

He gave a quick nod. "Yep. Now I know why your name sounded familiar."

He poured more coffee. "Tell me somethin', Meg—did your truck fall into a ditch the other day?"

"What?!"

"Were you holed up with some fella in a mountain cabin, and did your husband come with the sheriffs and break in and get you out?"

She sat frozen in astonishment, staring at him.

"And, Meg, this friend you're lookin' for—is he the chap you were with in the cabin?"

She remained silent for a long tense moment. "How do you know so much about me?" she asked finally.

Oley chuckled. "Well, it may come as a surprise to you that you're famous." He winked at her. "Or maybe I should say notorious."

He got up and went across the room, reached behind the counter, and returned leafing through a newspaper.

Meg watched him, wide-eyed. "You mean it's in the papers?!"

"Just happened to see a little item here in yesterday's," Oley mumbled. "Now, let's see, where was it? Oh, yes, here we are."

He scanned the paper, holding it close to his face. "Hm-m-m. Thought I remembered right. It says here Mrs. Hannah was questioned by authorities, and released. It don't say nothin' about Mrs. Hannah gettin' a sudden itch and runnin' off in the middle o' the night. Guess that hadn't happened yet."

Meg held out her hand. "May I see it?"

"Just a minute." Oley folded the paper carefully and gazed down at Meg. "You haven't answered my last question. Is the friend you're lookin' for the fella you were with in the cabin?"

Meg stared at the newspaper in Oley's hand. "Yes."

"Were you thinkin' of running off with this guy?"

Distress gripped her. "Oh, Mr. Oley . . . I'm not thinking at all. I'm just trying to *help* him. He needs help so desperately—"

"You wouldn't be kiddin' yourself a tiny bit, would you?"

She gazed at him without answering. He could see a stubborn streak in her soft brown eyes.

"Who couldn't use a little help?" he said. "Have you ever met anybody who had everything put together so well they didn't need any help at all?"

He sat down again. She reached for the newspaper; he held it away from her.

"Everybody needs help, Meg. Your husband—what's his name, Bart? With a wife who runs off like a wild thing in the middle of the night—*he* needs help. *I* need help. I've been miserable for twenty years, living on land. I want to be at sea, that's the only place I could ever be happy—but I've lost my nerve, Meg. I'm scared o' the thing I love. Don't I need help?"

"I'm sorry, Mr. Oley." Her voice was gentle and sympathetic. "I wish I could help you too."

He chuckled and reached across and patted her hand. "What I'm gettin' at, little lady, is that *you* need help. As much as anybody, and more than most."

"I know. That's why I asked if I could talk to you."

"And I said you came to the right place. Because I think maybe I *can* help *you*, a little. Now read this."

He handed her the newspaper, and pointed to the place.

It was a short article, a few paragraphs only, near the bottom of an inner page. The heading read: "GRANGE COUNTY KIDNAPPING SUSPECT CAPTURED."

Meg sucked in her breath as if stabbed. "*Captured?!*"

She grabbed the paper and read the article through rapidly, then a second time, more slowly. Then she tossed the paper aside, pressed her lips firmly together, gripped her coffee mug with both hands and stared at it, blinking hard.

Oley observed her for a moment in silence. Then he picked up the newspaper and looked at the story again. "About the only thing in this piece that would be news to you is the last paragraph, right?"

He read aloud: " 'The suspect, identified as Alonzo Hayward, twenty-five, of Mayfield, was apprehended in the vicinity of Soda Springs, twenty miles west of the Stag Mountain area, shortly before noon Tuesday.' "

Oley glanced at Meg. "Soda Springs. He was headin' this way, all right." He resumed reading. " 'Acting on a tip, sheriff's deputies discovered Hayward resting in a wooded area along Old Soda Springs Road, two miles west of town, and made the arrest. Hayward surrendered without resistance, and was taken to the Grange County Jail in Caxton.' "

Meg had made a quick movement—a hand over her eyes— and a soft sound that Oley interpreted as a choked-off sob. He put the paper down and sipped his coffee.

"Well, I suppose you think that wasn't very helpful, eh?" he said, after a moment. "I suppose you're thinkin', 'Well, Oley, old boy, if that's your idea of help, thanks a lot. You better stick to clam chowder, and leave helpfulness to somebody else.' "

Her hand gripped her forehead, shielding her eyes. He could tell by the workings of her mouth that she was fighting tears.

"On the other hand, it don't make much sense you wanderin' around Diamond Bay lookin' for somebody who's in jail in Grange County, now, does it? So you might as well give up this foolishness and go on home. Right?"

She had regained control. She wiped at her eyes with her fingers, and sipped her coffee.

Oley picked up the coffeepot. "Here, let me warm that up for you."

"Thanks, Mr. Oley," she said. "I appreciate your advice. But I can't go back home now."

"Why not? You think your husband won't take you back?"

"It isn't that. It's because I've got to help Lonnie somehow. I told him I'd stand by him, and I'm going to."

Oley twisted around and glanced at a wall clock behind the counter. "Lord, time flies!" he mumbled.

Meg made a move to get up. "I'm going now, Mr. Oley. You have work to do, and I'm taking up too much—"

"No you don't." Oley laid a hand on her shoulder and pushed her gently back down in her seat. "We're goin' to thrash this out, by God. Them five-thirty bums can damn well have breakfast at six-thirty for once in their lives. There's a few things in this world more important than fishin'."

He poured himself more coffee and hunched over the table.

"Now let's look at this situation. First—you're havin' an affair with this fella Hayward, right? And because your truck broke down you got found out—"

She silenced him with a vigorous shaking of her head. "That's

242

not how it is at all, Mr. Oley. I drove him up the mountain. The accident happened. We were stranded. Then, during the night, we . . ." She hesitated. "We became very close."

Oley shrugged. "Uh-huh. That's pretty much what I said. Now, second—Hayward's in trouble with the law. The big question is, how much trouble? This article in the paper don't tell me much. Maybe *you* can say. How much trouble *is* he in?"

"I don't know. Nobody really knows. It depends on Mrs. Emmons."

"Ah, yes. The uncle's wife. She seems to be missing, right?"

Meg nodded, looking bleak. Oley pondered.

"Seems to me like maybe Hayward made one o' them classic mistakes—tryin' to carry on with two women at the same time—"

He was startled by her fiery reaction.

"Oh, no, that's not true! He wasn't—*carrying on,* as you put it—with her *or* with me. Nobody understands anything about Lonnie, nobody! That's why I've got to stand by him—I'm the only friend he's got in the world!"

Her voice trembled. She hovered again on the brink of losing control.

"Okay, okay," Oley said hastily. "Don't get in an uproar. I was just speculatin'."

He waited, watching her, while she calmed down. Then he started again. "Now, the way I see it, what you need to do . . ."

She wasn't listening. She was staring off into distance, seeing things he couldn't see.

"He's the kindest, most gentle person I've ever known," she said. Her voice was quiet and far away.

"Well, that may be, but—"

"He's so aware of things. So much in love with beauty. So . . . so *good.*"

Oley sighed. "Okay. Tell me about him."

Meg frowned, and groped for words. "It's hard to tell about him. He's a person who just wants to be left alone, to be free to follow the beautiful workings of nature, to study birds, and admire their flight. He loves birds, because they're so free. They have the kind of mobility he yearns for. He's buying the *Nellie D.,* and he's going to change the name to the *Seabird.* He wants to sail off and follow the seabirds, because they represent to him

243

the very ultimate in freedom, they're the most free-moving things in the world—"

She broke off and smiled, touched with embarrassment. "It sounds a little crazy, I guess."

Oley's quizzical look was noncommittal.

"But it's beautiful, isn't it? Don't you think it's beautiful, Mr. Oley? Because in a way it's beauty he's looking for. The beauty of freedom. It's sort of a . . . clean, pure thing . . . almost like a religious faith. Kind of . . . inspirational. Don't you think so, Mr. Oley?" There was an earnest pleading in her eyes.

Oley started to pour more coffee, and discovered the pot was almost empty. "Well, I tell you what Mr. Oley thinks. Mr. Oley thinks we need more coffee."

He got up from the table. "*And* something to go with it. So you sit still, and when Mr. Oley gets back he's goin' to tell you what he *really* thinks."

He returned shortly with a pot of fresh coffee and a plate of sweet rolls. He refilled both mugs, gestured for Meg to help herself to the rolls, and began to munch on one himself. Meg took one, nibbled at it, and watched Oley anxiously.

"Now as I said before," he began, "I'm a flat-out coward when it comes to sailin', so I won't even comment on the proposition of sashayin' around the ocean in a thirty-nine-foot ketch. Paralyzes my vocal chords just to think about it. But as for all that stuff about the freedom of birds—"

Oley picked a raisin off the top of his roll and daintily popped it into his mouth.

"Pure malarkey. Moonshine. Birds, little lady, are not free. They are anything but. It takes intelligence to be free. It takes an ability to make judgments, and then to make decisions based on those judgments. Now, birds may be beautiful, they may be interesting to watch, because they're fantastic flyin' machines— but intelligent they ain't. On any list of animal life in order of brainpower, you'll find birds way down near the bottom, right above reptiles. Morons, just ahead o' the imbeciles."

Oley popped another raisin. "Oh, sure, the seabirds fly all over the ocean, every which way, just like they owned the dang thing. But that ain't freedom, it only seems like it. You think the seabirds ever had a big conference, listened to scientific papers on the subject, discussed the various points at great length, and decided where was the best place to set up housekeeping and what was the best way to make a living? You think the birds that live on the West Coast ever thought to cruise on over to the East Coast, to see if maybe they might want to make a change?

"No. A bird does what it does because the behavior patterns have been burned into its genes for more thousands of years than man has been alive. It has no more power to say to hell with it and break out of its orbit than a planet has. The only animal on God's earth that stands a ghost of a chance of *ever* reachin' a condition resemblin' freedom is the human animal. And it's got one hell of a long way to go yet to get there. So much for freedom."

Oley took a huge bite of his roll and chomped contentedly. After a moment he cocked an eye toward Meg. She was gazing at him with that streak of stubbornness lurking in her eyes.

"Hm-m. I see you're not impressed with my little lecture," he said. "Well, I'll push on anyway. New subject. There's one character in this story who's had damn little attention so far. Your husband. What about *him?* What's *he* supposed to do, crawl in a hole and conveniently disappear?"

He waited for an answer. Meg evaded his gaze, fastened her eyes on the tabletop.

"Come on," Oley said. "Think about it—is all this fair to *him?*"

"I couldn't help it, Mr. Oley. I didn't *plan* things to be like this."

"Okay, maybe your marriage didn't turn out to be all violins and red roses, the way you thought it would. Hubby ain't a knight on a white horse after all. He's probably a hard-workin', beer-guzzlin', coarse-talkin' cowpuncher, watches television in his undershirt, expects dinner to be ready on time and no excuses. Right?"

Meg smiled in spite of herself. "You're uncanny, Mr. Oley."

"Listen, don't think I don't know the type. I got 'em comin' in here twice a day regular. In droves yet. But it ain't the worst thing in the world." Oley pointed a finger at Meg. "What's the *worst* things you can think of to say about your husband? Think hard."

Meg's eyes went grave and thoughtful. "The worst thing? The worst thing is—he's never loved me."

Oley's bushy yellow eyebrows went up in surprise. "Is that a fact?!" he breathed. He picked up the newspaper again and studied the story.

"It says here—and you correct me if this is wrong—it says here . . ." He read:

"Deputies had previously made an unsuccessful attempt to take Hayward into custody, during the early hours Monday, when they followed his trail to a cabin in the Stag Mountain resort area. On that occasion, Hayward, while holding Mrs. Hannah hostage, opened a deadly barrage of gunfire as the deputies approached, forcing them to take cover. Shortly thereafter Bart Hannah, twenty-six, husband of the hostage, scaled a steep hillside and, despite Hayward's withering fire, gained entry to the house by climbing through a window. In the ensuing struggle, during which several additional shots were fired, Hayward managed to escape."

Oley glanced quickly at Meg and saw that she was fidgeting restlessly.

"Well? Fact or fiction?"

"In the first place, I was never a hostage," she said irritably. "And all that stuff about deadly withering gunfire is ridiculous. Lonnie fired one shot—into the ground."

"All right. Journalistic garbling. But he *did* fire." Oley tossed the paper aside, leaned forward and fixed Meg with a hard look. "I'm askin' you to look at this from your husband's viewpoint. The gunfire wasn't deadly, you say? *Any* gunfire is deadly, if you're somewhere near the receiving end of it. The bare fact is, your husband, who's never loved you, climbed up that hillside and went through the window of that house havin' every reason to believe he could be shot dead at any moment. And why did he do it? Is he tired o' livin'? Twenty-six, little lady, is a rotten age to die."

Meg's stubbornness held firm. "He was never in any danger, Mr. Oley. Lonnie never had any intention of hurting anybody. He had already thrown his weapon down—"

"Beside the point. Your husband couldn't have known all that. The point is that what he did was an act of bravery. And if you've got a fair bone in your body you're goin' to have to admit that it was an act of love."

246

There was a silence between them. Meg sat stony-still, with her eyes lowered.

"Have another roll," Oley said.

"No, thank you."

"How about some more coffee?"

She shook her head. She would not look at him.

"I get the message," he said. "You're tellin' me to leave off the sermonizin', you have no interest in the advice of a washed-up old ex-sailor turned hash-slinger. Well, I've come this far, so I'm goin' the rest o' the way and give you my advice, whether you like it or not. And here it is. The nearest telephone is up at the bus depot. One block over on Boardwalk Street, then one block to the right on Chestnut. You go up there right now and put in a call to your husband. Tell him you're sorry about all your lunatic behavior. Tell him you've come to your senses now, and ask him to please come and get you. Tell him to pick you up right here at Oley's Sea Shanty, and tell him when he gets here Oley's goin' to give him a free breakfast."

She raised her eyes to him then, but the stubbornness was still there. "But I've got to help Lonnie—"

"You ain't gonna help no Lonnie by runnin' away at this point. That's dumb. It'll only make things look bad—like maybe you and him were in cahoots all the time. Go on back and act normal. Then, if there's a trial or somethin', go to court and testify for 'im. Tell 'em what a nice guy he is, just like you told me. That's the only way you can help him."

Meg considered this for a moment. Then she gave Oley a little smile. "I appreciate your taking so much interest, Mr. Oley, really I do. And you're right about . . . some things."

Oley's leathery face crinkled in a grin. "In these days and times, bein' partly right ain't half bad."

He reached across and patted her hand. "So why don't you get goin'?"

She started to open her purse. "What do I owe you for the breakfast, Mr. Oley?"

"You don't owe me nothin'. Mr. Oley enjoyed it more'n you did."

He got up, swept the dirty dishes together in his large hands, and took them behind the counter. When he looked around his visitor was standing in the doorway.

247

She mouthed the words "Thank you," blew him a little kiss off her fingertips, and went out.

He stood watching her through the plate-glass window as she crossed the street and walked rapidly away. Then he went to the door and stepped outside, and breathed deeply of the sharp early-morning air. A pearly glow had spread across the sky as the earth turned toward daylight. Out beyond the breakwater the ocean lay leaden-gray and still.

Pensively Oley surveyed the tranquil scene.

"Missed my callin'," he mumbled to himself. "Should've been a damn marriage counselor."

With a quiet chuckle he turned and went back inside.

34

At that hour the quiet of the bus station was tomblike. The few people making use of the long wooden benches that occupied most of the floor space were either lounging lifelessly or stretched out asleep. The room was cavernous, musty with age, and shabby, and the shabbiness was accentuated by the gloomy light from inadequate fixtures suspended far above in the high ceiling. The cigar-and-candy counter was not yet open for business. Toward the back of the room a thin bespectacled young man sat in a small island of light from a shaded bulb above the ticket counter and bent his head low over some kind of paperwork.

Meg walked across the room toward him, and as she approached the young man looked up, swept his eyes swiftly up and down her body, flashed a toothy grin, and said, "Hey, hey hey! Glad to see we're gettin' a little higher-class clientele around here!"

"Excuse me—" Meg began.

"Wait a second," the clerk said quickly. "What's a five-letter word for a small South American mammal?"

Meg smiled weakly. "I'm sorry, I never was very good at things like that."

The young man pushed his crossword puzzle aside. His grin grew wider.

"Okay. Sell you a ticket, then? Goin' to the big town today?"

"No, thanks. I was just wondering—"

"Bus'll be here in a few minutes. Leaves at six twenty-five. Your golden opportunity to get out o' this creepy burg and go seek your fortune in the sinful city." He gave her an elaborate leer. "Bet you wouldn't have any trouble finding it, either."

"No, thanks," Meg said again, and shook her head. "All I want to find right now is a phone booth. Could you direct me?"

The clerk jerked his head to the left. "Go around the end of the counter. You'll see it in the far corner."

"Thank you."

"Why, it's a pleasure, honey," he said cheerily. "And you can have *my* number anytime."

He leaned far forward over the counter top to watch her as she walked away.

Bart answered the phone immediately after the first ring. She could hear the tension in his voice when he blurted, "Hello?"

Then the long-distance operator gave her clipped mechanical spiel: "I have a collect call for anyone at that number from Mrs. Meg Hannah, in Diamond Bay. Will you accept—"

"Jesus Christ! Yes, Operator, hell, yes!" Bart fairly leaped at her down the miles of electronic circuitry. "Put her on, put her on!"

"Hello, Bart?"

"Oh, God . . . *Meg!* Meg, what are you . . . what are you *doin'* to me?! Oh, thank God, thank God you called!"

"Bart, I'm sorry. I feel terrible, I really—"

"Oh, Christ, Meg—where the hell *are* you? Jesus Christ . . ."

"I'm in Diamond Bay."

"Oh, yeah, yeah, the operator said that. For God's sake, Meg, what the hell are you doin' in Diamond Bay?! What *happened?!* Did you go plumb out o' your mind, or what?!"

"I guess we both did, Bart."

"Yeah, yeah, Jesus Christ, you're right, baby. Seems like my whole life's been turned into one great big nightmare. It's been pure hell, Meg, you don't *know*—I been sittin' here by the phone ever since yesterday morning, just prayin' you'd come to your senses and call. I haven't told a soul you were gone, not even Herb and Rita. The only time I been out o' the house was to make a quick trip up to the Emmons cabin again, to see if maybe you went back there. I knew if I could only *talk* to you and tell you how I feel, everything would be all right. 'Cause, Meg, I swear to Christ, baby, I've had my eyes opened. I'm a new man. You punished me, and you were right, God knows. I deserved to suffer, and I *have* suffered—"

"I never meant to *punish* you, Bart. That wasn't the idea at all, and I'm sorry—"

"Ah, no, honey, don't you say you're sorry. That's for *me* to say, and I'll be sayin' it for a long time. You just say you forgive me, and tell me where you are so I can come get you and bring you home, where you belong."

"Well, Bart, it's not quite that simple—"

"I swear, baby, I'm a changed man. Believe me, I'm turning over a new leaf, starting today. You won't even know me."

"But I have to tell you, Bart, I'm changed, too. And when I say I'm sorry, I don't mean I'm sorry for what I did. I'm only sorry for the way I did it. We need to sit down and have a serious talk, Bart, because things are all different—"

"Oh, sure, baby, sure. Listen, you don't need to worry about a thing. Whatever you want, baby, you're gonna have it. By the way, they towed your truck down off the mountain yesterday, and I had 'em take it right straight to Martin's Garage in Caxton. I'm gonna have it fixed up like new for ya. Even a new paint job. How 'bout that?"

"That's nice, Bart. But listen—"

"And guess what else. You know how you've been askin' for a dishwasher? Well, I just decided I'm gonna order one, right away. No more dishpan hands for Mrs. Bart Hannah, no sirree!"

"Bart, please. Those aren't the things I want to talk about."

"Oh, I know, honey. You got all kinds o' deep philosophical problems on your mind. That's all right, we'll discuss anything you want, for as long as you want. I just thought I'd let you know you're not gonna have any further cause for complaints, 'cause from now on it's your happiness that's uppermost in my mind. I swear to God, I really mean that."

"Bart, may I just tell you something, please?"

"Just tell me where you are. We can talk when I get there."

She sighed. "I'll be at a little cafe called Oley's Sea Shanty. It's right at the end of Mission Street, next to the harbor."

"Oley's Sea Shanty. End o' Mission Street. Okay, I got it. I'll be there in an hour and a quarter. Just sit tight."

"Wait, Bart, listen to me a minute. Before you make the trip, there's something you've got to know. I want to do what I have to do in a civilized way, not by running away and all that—but in the long run it amounts to the same thing."

251

She hesitated and gripped the phone with both hands. "Bart, I really don't think we can go on being married to each other."

He was stunned into momentary silence. "Meg, you don't mean that."

"I'm afraid I do."

"No, you don't. I don't believe you. You're just suffering from some kind o' crazy guilt complex, or sump'm. But it's all so *unnecessary*, baby. Hell, you had yourself a little fling—so what? That's not the end o' the world. It happens to the best o' people."

"Bart, for heaven's sake—"

"Sweetheart, I don't hold it against you, d'ya hear me? I don't hold it against you at all—in fact, I've got a brand-new kind o' respect for you. Frankly, I didn't know you had it in you. And from now on, baby, I'm treatin' you like royalty. Just give me a week. I'll have you so spoiled you'll be purrin' like a kitten, so help me."

"Bart—oh, Bart, why can't I ever *talk* to you?!"

"I told you, we can talk all you want when I get there. Oley's Sea Shanty, end o' Mission Street. Right?"

"Yes, but Bart, you've got to *understand* this—the thing I want most of all right now is to help Lonnie Hayward. I'm dedicating myself to that, because all of a sudden he's become the most important person in the world—"

"Meg, don't say that."

"I have to, I want to be honest with you—"

"You haven't heard any news reports, have you?"

"Yes, I have. I know Lonnie's in jail. All the more reason I'm determined to—"

"That's stale news."

Stale news. She turned the words over in her mind. "What does that mean, Bart?"

Unexpectedly he laughed—a tight, forced laugh, unrelated to amusement. "I swear to Christ, Meg, this has got to be the weirdest damn case them poor boobs in the sheriff's office ever had to contend with! You wouldn't believe it—what it amounts to is, it's all over and done with. Case closed. You don't have to worry about it anymore, you can forget about it completely. Now, ain't that a relief?"

"I don't . . . I don't understand, Bart."

"Well—lemme just tell you the funny part. Last night Betty Emmons showed up."

From her sitting position in the phone booth Meg was on her feet instantly. "What?!"

"Didn't exactly *show* up. Called home. Saw a story in the newspaper and was wonderin' what all the fuss was about. Can you beat that?"

"My *God*, Bart! Where had she *been?!*"

"Visitin' some friends in Santa Cruz, she says. Shacked up with another one of her many ex-lovers, if you ask *me*."

"Oh, Bart, how can she possibly explain—"

"She admitted she'd left Frisco on Saturday and gone back to Mayfield. She claimed she'd gone for a walk with Hayward, he'd made advances, she'd fought him off and run back to the house and locked herself in. Then she called this guy—whoever he is— in Santa Cruz, and asked him to come get her. Dumbfounded to hear she was thought of as missin'. Of course she hadn't known Hayward was gonna lam out and old man Emmons was gonna come home unexpectedly and start jumpin' to con- clusions."

Meg was squirming, struggling without success to contain her excitement. "Oh, Bart, Bart! That's wonderful! She's lying about Lonnie, but who cares?! The important thing is, he's not really in very much trouble, after all—oh, that *is* good news! I just *knew* everything would turn out all right. Lonnie wouldn't do anything bad—that poor guy's been so terribly misunderstood by everybody, it's just ridiculous—"

"Hold it, Meg."

Something cold and hard in Bart's voice stopped her.

"Lemme tell you sump'm. You're gonna give up thinkin' about Hayward, you hear me? You're gonna put him out o' your mind for good. He's part o' your past now."

She felt a burning sensation in her cheeks. Impatiently she pushed her hair back and took a deep breath.

"Bart, I will not stand for you telling me what I will do and won't do. I'm all through with that—"

"You haven't heard all the news yet, Meg. There's more."

The silence on the line seemed jarringly abrupt.

"More . . . ?"

"Listen, baby." Bart's voice carried a sudden urgency. "You

253

just sit tight at Oley's, you hear, and I'll gun my motor like crazy and be there in an hour flat. Then on the way home I'll tell you all the rest—"

"No. Tell me now."

"Not on the phone."

"Yes. On the phone."

"Not on the phone, Meg. You won't like it."

The burning in her cheeks was growing mysteriously and creeping upward to her eyes and forehead.

"Bart—tell me everything. And tell me *now.*"

He heaved a long sigh. "All right. You asked for it. I said this was a weird case, didn't I? And yesterday it all came clear why. It's because that Hayward was a complete nut. Just pure and simple cuckoo is the only way to describe him."

One little word leaped at Meg, burned itself into her mind like a white-hot iron. *Was.*

"Yesterday afternoon—this is *before* they'd heard from the Emmons dame, understand—Hayward sort o' came apart, started babblin' to the sheriffs about how he thought he'd *killed* her. He said he couldn't remember exactly what happened, but he could see her in his mind's eye, lyin' in the dry wash out behind the Emmons place, with her head bashed in. I got all this from Carl, y'see. He was there."

Meg stood rigid. She gripped the phone so hard her fingers ached.

I've got to get myself ready, she thought wildly. I mustn't let myself be surprised. I hate surprises.

"Naturally the sheriffs pressed him for details. They'd been all over that wash, several times, and hadn't found a thing. Hayward said he'd lead 'em to the place. So they took him out there."

Meg was trembling. She clutched at her forehead, trying to retain control.

I know what's coming, she told herself. I won't be surprised.

She found it curiously difficult to pay close attention to what Bart was saying.

"Well, he led 'em on a wild-goose chase, way the hell back up in the brush, a mile or more from the house. Acted like he didn't know for sure what he was doin' or where he was goin'. Then all of a sudden, he just—he tried to make a break. He ran

254

for it. What *for*, for Christ sake—nobody can figure that out."

Meg felt as if she were suffocating, as if her lungs were paralyzed and incapable of drawing breath. Her legs were dangerously weak. She put a hand on the side of the phone booth to steady herself and sat down.

"Meg? Are you listenin'?"

She was staring at an obscene verse scrawled on the wall. Her eyes moved uncomprehendingly over the words, again and again. She managed a feeble whisper. "Go on, Bart."

"Sergeant Mulray—you remember Sergeant Mulray? No, you prob'bly don't. He was that big dumb-lookin' deputy who was with us up at the cabin."

The wait was agonizing. *Go on, Bart. Hurry, please. Get it over with.*

"Well, I got news for ya, Mulray might be dumb, but he can sure as hell handle an emergency, all right, all right."

Good old Sergeant Mulray. Oh, God help me.

"He shouted 'Halt!' three times, just like it says in the book you should. Then he went down on his knee and fired once. Well—I'll spare you the gory details. But Mulray's one hell of a fine shot. Y'see, Meg, that's why I said the case is closed, and that's why I said you've got to put that guy out o' your mind, right now. Just forget about the whole thing, okay? That's all there is left to do."

Meg's eyes were shut tight. She swayed gently back and forth. Somehow her breath had returned.

Well, there it is. And I wasn't surprised.

She felt suddenly calm, but the calm was tremulous and uneasy, as if covering some screaming madness that would break the surface at any moment and rend the air.

I must say it out loud, so I can see how it sounds. How it feels.

"He's dead," she said in a firm voice.

"That's right. Stone cold in the morgue. I understand they're tryin' to get in touch with his mother—she lives back East someplace." Bart sighed again. "Hey, look, honey, I know this is tough on you. That's why I didn't want to tell you right off, like that. I know you got yourself involved with that guy some way and . . . But I said it before, and I'm sayin' it again—I'm holdin' nothin' against you, absolutely nothin'. He who lives in a glass house, as they say, and God knows I'm not without sin—"

255

"He's dead." She said it again, in a faint whisper. "Lonnie's dead."

"Look at it this way, Meg. We're both gonna come out o' this better people. I'll forgive you and you'll forgive me, and we'll wipe our slates clean and start all over again, fresh, what d'ya say? Just like we were newly married. Oh, I'm gonna treat you so *nice*, baby, 'cause you're my sweet little mouse, and for the first time in my life I *appreciate* you. Now, what I was thinkin'—we both need a vacation, that's for damn sure. So I thought we'd take a week off and run over to Vegas, live it up a little, see some shows. Sort of a second honeymoon—"

Something caused him to stop—a sudden clattering noise, then silence, an unexplainable emptiness on the telephone line.

"Meg? Are you there, baby? What's the matter?!"

The silence was terrible, deafening in his ear. His voice rose in swift panic.

"Meg! Sweetheart, answer me! *Meg! Answer me!!*"

The clerk from the ticket counter flung open the glass door of the phone booth and stared down at the young woman with a look of alarm that was rapidly turning to fright. He leaned down and studied her face, and the wild eyes, stricken with some unfathomable pain, caused him to shudder. He ignored the phone, swinging freely on its cord near the floor, and the thin squawk of a man's voice rattling the earpiece.

"Hey, lady, are you all right?"

Frantically he looked around the nearly deserted station, seeking in vain for some source of quick aid. Then he turned back to the woman, slapped her sharply on the cheek, and croaked, "Say something, lady! Speak to me!"

She put out a hand and grasped him by the shoulder, and pulled herself up toward him. He grasped her awkwardly by the elbows, trying to help, but not sure what she wanted to do. Her burning eyes locked on him as she struggled to her feet.

"I'm all right," she whispered. "Thank you. I'm all right."

35

At Oley's the two most regular of the regular customers sat at the counter and worked at the destruction of large plates of ham and eggs, and complained loudly about the fact that the hot cakes weren't ready.

"You gents don't like the service here, take your business elsewhere," Oley said flippantly.

"Like where?" demanded Al. "To the Golden Horn down the street, where it costs a buck and a half to look at the menu? Where, if you wanna buy a meal, you take out a loan and make monthly payments?"

Oley shrugged. "Look—Oley ain't good, but he's cheap. That's why you're stuck with me, just like I'm stuck with you. So feed your faces and quit your bitchin'."

Mack finished his eggs and shoved his plate toward Oley. "Come on, Oley, get them hot cakes cookin'."

Oley got the hot cakes cooking, got them served, and poured more coffee. Then he sat down on his little stool behind the counter. At that moment a dark figure went past the front window on a bicycle, and something slammed against the door.

"Ah!" Oley said. "Mornin' paper's here." He went to get it.

"Good thing we got our grub served, Mack," Al said. "Once Oley gets his face buried in that newspaper, forget it. That's all, folks."

Oley settled himself again on his stool and turned rapidly through the paper, as if looking for something. Then he stopped and, true to form, buried his face between the pages.

"Think what it would be like if he could *read*," Mack said.

After a little while Al called out, "Hey, Oley, tell us the news. How'd the stock market treat you today?"

"Don't get 'im all confused, Al," Mack said. "He thinks stock market is a place where you buy cattle."

Al tried again. "What country's havin' a revolution today, Oley?"

"Aw, he don't pay no attention to that *international* crap," Mack said. "Just the important stuff, like sex, and murder."

"Who got raped lately, Oley?" Al yelled. "Who got caught in bed with somebody else's wi—"

Oley lowered the paper abruptly and stared at his two customers. His bushy brows quivered. His face was ferocious.

"Shut up," he said quietly.

Al's jaw went slack. He looked at Mack and then back at Oley.

"Uh, sure, Oley. Jeez—did somethin' get you upset?"

"No." Oley closed the paper and rolled it up tight, and slapped it sharply into his palm. "Just shut up, that's all."

Al exchanged another look with Mack. "Sure. Okay, Oley."

They ate in silence, while Oley leaned on the counter top and gazed stony-faced straight ahead, out the front window.

In a few minutes he got up and came out from behind the counter. "'Scuse me," he said brusquely. He went to the door. "You guys need anything, just get it yourself," he called over his shoulder, and went out.

Mack grunted. "Holy Christ! What the hell got into *him?!*"

Al had twisted in his seat, staring after Oley. He punched his companion on the arm.

"Hey, Mack, looka there! It's that cute little number that was in here last night. Jeez—you s'pose ol' Oley's got somethin' *goin'* with her?"

Mack turned to look. "Be damned!" he breathed. "Just goes to show you what happens when an old coot like Oley starts foolin' around with women. Ruins his disposition."

Oley watched her as she crossed the street and came toward him, and saw by the way she moved, even before he could see her face clearly, that she carried the burden of grief. When she came closer and he saw the empty bleakness in her eyes, he moved quickly forward to meet her.

"Hello, little lady," he said gently.

258

"Mr. Oley . . ." she began, and stopped. Her voice was weak, her gaze vague and wandering.

"You got the news, I guess," he said.

She looked at him blankly and said nothing.

"Is your husband comin' to get you?"

"My husband . . ." Her mind seemed to be groping in a fog. She put a hand to her face and absently touched her cheeks with her fingertips. "Yes, my husband. I expect he'll be here soon."

She swayed slightly. Oley reached out and grasped her by the elbow.

"Come on inside and sit down, and tell me about it."

She stood still and gazed at him as if she hadn't heard. "Mr. Oley, you've been so kind to me. I don't know how I could ever thank you enough."

He tugged at her arm. "Thank me inside. There's no sense in standin' out here."

"No." She held back. "I have to go now, Mr. Oley."

"But what about your husband? Ain't you goin' to wait for him?"

She frowned, as if troubled by a confusion of conflicting thoughts. "When he comes, tell him I'm sorry. Just . . . terribly sorry, about everything."

He wouldn't let go of her arm. "Listen, you better come in awhile. You're all upset."

"I have to go." She disengaged herself from his grasp.

"Go where?"

"Away. Far away."

"Someplace where you got friends?"

She shook her head.

"You got any money?"

"A little. Enough for a while."

"That don't sound good. How about I advance you a little loan?"

"No, thanks. I'll be fine. You've done enough for me already."

"Hey—" He fixed her with a stern frown. "You ain't about to hitchhike again, are you? Promise me no more hitchhikin'."

"I promise."

"Well, then, how you goin' to travel? You goin' to take a bus?"

He looked sheepish when she didn't answer immediately.

"I got to stop bein' so nosy," he said. "None o' my business, anyway. But for some fool reason you make me feel sort of . . . fatherly, or somethin'. I don't know what it is. Maybe you remind me a little of my daughter."

"She's lucky to have you for a father."

He flashed a quick smile. "Well, don't worry, I won't give you away. I'll tell 'em you took a steamer to China."

She made a valiant effort to return his smile. "I keep wanting to say thank you, Mr. Oley. Over and over again, thank you."

Oley's expression turned solemn as he gazed at her from under his bushy brows. "I know what happened," he said quietly. "It's in the paper. You want to see the story?"

It seemed to him she flinched a little, but her gaze held on him steadily.

"No. Just tell me what it says, if you don't mind. Just . . . quickly."

Oley opened the paper. "Well, the headline says: 'Kidnapping Suspect Slain in Escape Attempt.' "

She put out her hand and touched him on the arm. "That's enough," she whispered.

Oley folded the paper and stuffed it under his arm. "I'm sorry, little lady."

She extended her hand to him. "I've really got to go now, Mr. Oley. For the umpteenth time—thanks."

He took her hand and held it. "But what do I tell your husband when he comes? Besides you're sorry, which he'll think is a lousy message."

"Tell him . . ." Her chin lifted slightly. Her eyes were bright and her voice firm and level. "Tell him I've gone to follow the seabirds."

Oley nodded. "Okay. He'll think that's a lousy message, too, but—okay."

She leaned forward and kissed him on the cheek. Then she removed her hand from his and took a step back.

"Goodbye, Mr. Oley."

"You're crazy, you know that?"

She smiled. "That's not the worst thing you can say about somebody."

"Will you come and see me again? Someday?"

"Yes. Someday I will."

He gave her a jaunty little salute. "Well, then, goodbye, little lady. And, as seafarin' men are not in the habit o' sayin'—smooth sailin' to you."

She smiled again, and turned and walked away from him, across Mission Street and up Boardwalk, the way she had come. She did not look back.

Oley watched her until she was out of sight. Then he walked very slowly back to the entrance to the cafe. He paused there and carefully wiped his eyes with his fingers before going in.

36

At the corner of Boardwalk and Chestnut Street Meg stopped and looked toward the bus depot, a block away. Now a great silver bus was parked at the curb in front of the station, its massive rectangular bulk occupying almost half the width of the narrow street. The motor was running, spouting a steamy exhaust from underneath. The driver was sauntering on the sidewalk, puffing on a cigarette.

Meg glanced at her watch. Six-twenty. She looked toward the harbor. Though the streets of the town still lay in shadows, there was an early-morning sunglow playing on the sea out beyond the breakwater, creating a soft luminous shimmer. The fog of the night had vanished without a trace.

It's going to be a nice day, Meg thought. A pretty, pleasant day for millions and millions of people who don't know what's happened, and wouldn't care, anyway.

Her eyes moved down along the iron railing on the breakwater, then searched among the boats riding at anchor near the far end, and found the *Nellie D.* From that distance it appeared as nothing more than an insignificant bit of flotsam on the oily water.

Poor little ship. Your master is not coming. He is not coming ever, and you and I are left to find our separate ways alone.

One or two other vessels were moving out of the harbor, gliding past the *Nellie D.*, rocking her in their wakes with taunting carelessness, and she tossed and pulled and struggled to go with them.

Look at her, Meg thought. Straining at her anchor chain. Restless as a colt, yearning to get out of the corral and go chasing after the wind.

Do you believe in dreams, little ship? I hope so, because that is all we have now, you and I. Dreams. Dreams and shadows. Her gaze lay on the *Nellie D.* for a brief moment longer. *Goodbye, little ship. And, as seafaring men are not in the habit of saying—smooth sailing to you.*

Then she lifted her eyes to the distance where the bay was lost and the ocean began, where the wide ocean spread to infinity and formed a curving horizon of bright blue haze along the sunlit edge of the world.

Dreams and shadows.

She was remembering a gentle voice, softly touched with melancholy, near her ear:

How sweet is love itself possessed . . .

Memory is fickle. How does it go?

. . . When but love's shadows are so rich in joy.

Yes. She closed her eyes for a moment. My love is a shadow now.

Far out there a bird was flying. A large bird, splendid in solitude. Its great heavy wings beat ponderously, carrying it outward toward a destination unknown, for a purpose that was locked and hidden in the mindless instincts of eons. She watched it as it slanted relentlessly away from the land, growing smaller and smaller.

I never told you I love you, Lonnie. You asked me to tell you, and I didn't. I couldn't—somehow there wasn't time. I'm sorry. I'm telling you now. I love you. I hope you can hear me.

The bird was gone, swallowed in distance.

She looked back up Chestnut Street to where the huge bus sat throbbing in front of the station. In the lighted sign window above the windshield, big white block letters proclaimed its destination—a large city, hundreds of miles away. A great, glittering, teeming city, pulsing with sound and energy, the repository of human desires and visions, of ambition and yearning and

263